CHOCOLATE CHIP CITY

BE STEADWELL

2025

Bywater Books

Copyright © 2025 Be Steadwell

All rights reserved. No part of this book may be reproduced, stored in a retrieval system, or transmitted in any form or by any means, without prior permission in writing from the publisher.

Print ISBN: 978-1-61294-315-2

Bywater Books First Edition: June 2025

Printed in the United States of America on acid-free paper.

Cover design by ggggrimes

Bywater Books
PO Box 3671
Ann Arbor MI 48106-3671

www.bywaterbooks.com

This is a work of fiction. Names, characters, places, and incidents are the product of the author's imagination or are used fictitiously. Any resemblance to actual events, locales, or persons, living or dead, is fictionalized.

For my sisters

1. THE SISTERS

Once upon a time
somewhere far, far uptown
tucked behind a veil of white oak leaves in the thick DC summer heat
three Black women were at peace.

The pool glittered. Sunlight cut through the treetops and a breeze whispered at smooth slabs of concrete. Lush spheres of hydrangeas lined the walls of a glass-sided mansion. Their laughter peppered the air. Their toes drew lazy circles. At the far edge of this secluded estate, three sisters lay in the grassy lap of the garden.

The Jones sisters looked out of place. Like feral mermaids at the edge of an infinity pool. But there they were. On a blanket in the grass, Jasmine, Ella and Layla lay on their bellies. A bowl of cherries, a bag of chips, a jar of shea butter, a dozen books and three sweating bottles of cold water. Jasmine sat up. She opened a worn copy of *The Baking Bible*. Limbs splayed and boyish, she leaned into the book. Her loose white tank top and basketball shorts were seasoned with white flour. She squinted at it and laughed. She raised her eyebrows and nodded as if she were having a conversation with the book. She ran her fingers over the words, imagining how the soufflé would feel on her tongue. Goat cheese and smoked thyme melting into nothing.

She turned the page and cupped the nape of her neck with her palm.

Ella sat up and pulled her hair back into a swinging ponytail. Her hair was long and done. Conditioned, flat-ironed, a shining black waterfall. She tightened the strings of her bikini, and her belly folded over in a soft curve. Her lips naturally curled up into a smile. She looked nice. Like a sweet, Southern girl who might call you sweetheart if you acted right. She reached into the jar of shea butter. She warmed it in her hands and massaged it into her forearms and shoulders, each inch of her body glowing as her hands touched the skin.

Layla rolled onto her back and tipped her chin up to the sunlight. Her skin was adorned with silver rings and studs, gleaming like stars across the midnight sky. She lifted her phone up to the clouds, squinting through sunlight as she swiped at the screen. Long, fat braids danced down her back, glints of yellow beads catching the sunlight as she shook her head. She scrolled through photos from the protest, stopping to study a picture of herself. Protest signs blurred in motion around her. Her fist in the air, her eyes closed. She looked like she was praying.

Anyone who knows DC (for real) knows that summer in this city is insufferably hot and humid. Stay inside, don't move, don't eat, don't even think kind-of-hot. But *this* summer was exceptional. If you wanted to spend a minute outside, you had to be in somebody's pool. So, the Jones sisters decided to "borrow" their "neighbors'" pool. A For Sale sign went up in May and the five-million-dollar mansion sat empty all summer. The Realtor (a friend of a friend of their mother's) gave showings by appointment. A team of landscapers and maintenance workers visited every other Wednesday. The estate was pruned and manicured and the pool was clean. So, every Saturday Jasmine, Ella and Layla walked to the rich, rich part of town to swim and float in a fantasy. They affectionately referred to the mansion as their "summer cottage."

Layla tossed her phone into the grass and sighed. She looked at her older sisters basking in the sun. "Let's get naked," she said.

"Yep," Ella replied, pulling at the strings of her bikini.

"Breaking and entering . . . *and skinny-dipping*. Sounds like us," Jasmine said as she dog-eared a page in her book. She pulled her shirt off and threw it into an azalea bush. Layla stood and tossed her bikini top to the ground.

Jasmine slowly climbed to her feet. She stretched up toward the sun.

The three sisters stood butt ass naked at the edge of the pool. Jasmine danced to a song in her head. "Rock the boat, rock the boat, rock the boat, work it in the middle." Jasmine sang as she looked over to Layla. Layla nodded her head and joined in, attempting to beatbox.

Ella jumped in with a melody. "Work the middle, work the middle, work the middle." Ella closed her eyes and danced. This was her song. Aaliyah always made her feel sexy. She moved her hips as she sang along.

They yell-sang a slow jam, drunk with joy. Ella body-rolled, Jasmine did an underwater running man. Layla was twerking in the pool, letting her tiny ass hit the crest of the water. Waves crashed around them. Their laughter moved the air around them. The density of everything changed. The sky above reached down to pull them closer. With each breath in and out, they made space. All the anxious thoughts about fat, and hair, and being invisible, and being strong, and too sexy, and not sexy enough—all the ties that held them back from joy melted away. For the sisters, gravity was only a suggestion. A rule whispered by a weighted, simple world. Slowly, they rose above the water. Each inhale lifted them up and up. Their shadows danced on the waves. Three shades of melanin gold dripping with cold beads of light. Their breasts, calves, arms, the curves of fat that jiggled, Ella's stretch marks like bolts of lightning, Jasmine's wide back, Layla's long limbs dancing above the water. It was like remembering. For one blissful moment they remembered that God made them, and everything was exactly where it should be. With the ground far beneath them, they held each other's beauty up to the light, holding their own beauty until everything glowed, warm in the sun. This was the secret of the three sisters: they had power. On their own they knew how to conjure and heal and see beyond this world. But together they knew how to fly. The Jones sisters levitated. And then. All their buttery harmony and laughter was cut by the sound of a man's voice.

"Hello?"

The sound bounced against the mansion's concrete walls. With three small splashes, the sisters slipped from the air back into the water. The music in their minds vanished. The three sisters froze, mouths agape, their heads peeking up above the water line. Ella ineffectively attempted to look respectable, using her hands to cover her nipples and crotch. Layla and Jasmine looked up at the young man standing in the glass doorway of the mansion.

He was in his thirties. Dressed in summer slacks and a fitted button down. Deep brown skin, strong jawline, close-cut beard, and a sharp fade. Young, Black and handsome. He looked down at the grass, his hand at his brow—embarrassed to be there. "Oh. I am so, so sorry. I just . . . I-I-I—"

Jasmine walked swiftly out of the pool. She gathered her sisters' clothing as she spoke in her *I am the eldest sibling, I'm in charge* voice. "We were just leaving. We're well acquainted with the realtor, so we were basically . . . watching it. The house. Until it was sold. We figured the property could use some . . . watching."

"And some love! An empty house could always use some love." Ella interjected, giggling. Jasmine threw a look at Ella.

Layla—still waist-high and naked in the pool—didn't budge. "I'm sorry, *who* are you again?" She put her hands on her hips. "The pool guy? The gardener?"

The young man kept his gaze low, chuckling. "Well no. Actually. We just bought the house... last month?" He said softly, as if he were apologizing for it. Ella gasped. Jasmine and Layla exchanged a glance. "But you're more than welcome to come here. Anytime! I mean it. You don't even have to ask." Gaining confidence, the young man began to talk a mile a minute.

"I love having visitors, and meeting neighbors, and I agree, a house could always use some love, especially an empty house. Do y'all live around here?"

He lifted his gaze to Ella, now mostly dressed, tying the strings of her bikini top, her sarong draped over her head like the Virgin Mary. Ella looked up at him.

"We're in the neighborhood," Layla replied flatly.

"This is gonna sound weird. It looked like you guys were floating just now. How did you do that?"

"No," Jasmine replied, staring the young man down. Layla and Ella exchanged a glance.

"Um. Okay . . . Well. My name is David Scott," he said, staring at Ella. "I've seen you before . . . I think?" David smiled, tilting his head.

"I don't think so," Ella said. She hopped on one foot, pulling at the sling of her sandal.

"No, I'm sure," David said, grinning.

Ella giggled. Layla narrowed her eyes at Ella.

"Did I see you at Tone? The gym?" David asked.

"Oh yea. I work there." Ella smiled.

"I thought so," David said, crossing his arms. He smiled again. Ella looked away, blushing.

Layla and Jasmine stared at her, then back at David, baffled by this oddly timed flirtation.

"Well. How about we let you settle in," Jasmine said, as she herded her sisters to the side gate. "We're just down the street, so. If you ever need some neighborly things. You know, flour or butter or . . ."

"Sugar?" Ella called out. David laughed.

"Ella!" Layla hissed.

"Hey. It was really nice meeting y'all! I—didn't get your names?" David walked to the end of the deck as the sisters scurried away.

"That's because we didn't tell you our names," Layla called out with a smile on her face.

"Nice meeting you too." Jasmine saluted David as she opened the garden gate for her sisters.

"Hey! Me and my sister are having a housewarming party this Friday. Around seven? Y'all should come!" His voice was boyish and hopeful.

"We'll be there!" Ella shouted.

"Oh, and I'm Ella! And these are my sisters Jasmine and La—"

"Ella!" Jasmine and Layla whined in unison, covering Ella's mouth as they jogged away. David watched them disappear down the road.

2. MAMA RO

Rosaline Jones made music as she walked. Little brass bells and bangles adorned her wrists and ankles. Short gray locs sprayed out from her white head wrap. Her floor-length indigo dress was so thin it hung in the air for a moment after she'd gone. She danced barefoot in the kitchen. Ro's home was littered with color and light. Vases of wildflowers and pots of tropical houseplants perched cheerfully on every counter. Oversized red picture frames featured black-and-white prints of her chubby-cheeked baby girls. The Black Lives Matter and Trans Pride flags draped down from the ceiling. When the wind blew, you could hear the music of wooden wind chimes hanging on the bottle tree out front. Every corner of the house held an artifact of Mama Ro's life as a Black feminist, teacher and mother.

Growing up, Rosaline was a wild, long-legged fairy child in 1960s Durham. What the old Southern folks would call *spirited*. She ran barefoot down dirt paths, climbed trees, rode her bike down to Twin Lakes Park, and floated in the water for hours. She made mud pies adorned with shiny yellow buttercups and clover. She was ten years old when her parents moved to DC and, at the time, she truly believed she would hate that city forever. She couldn't run barefoot anywhere. She couldn't make art out of mud or stay out at night and look at the stars. Not like she did before. It felt like her mother expected her to grow up that summer. And no matter how hard she pushed back, the wall of city life and adolescence hit her all at once. She couldn't remember when things changed. But things did change. It took Rosaline a thousand quiet moments to fall in love with DC. A beautiful boy kissed her in the old library bathroom stall. The day she saw Betye Saar's *Black Girl's Window* at The National Gallery of Art. She tore up all of her mother's magazines that night. Eating blue crabs on newspaper with all that Old Bay. Her cousin Anne taught her how to use the curling iron. Sweet Honey in the Rock at the Black Rep Theater. Rosaline walked home singing freedom songs and spirituals. Smoking weed in Rock Creek, lying down and watching autumn leaves fall around her. Still that wild fairy girl from the South—but DC made her something new. She decided all on her own from her first day at Howard when people asked for her name. "My name is Ro," she said. Not that soft flower her mother imagined her to be. She was an artist.

At Howard, Ro made collage installations like Saar and Joseph Cornell. She made art with Black women's faces in the center of every piece. Her installations grew larger and larger. In her 20s, Ro's work was celebrated. She was high on all of it. Changing the way Black people made and looked at art. Challenging the structure of it all. For a while she made good, institutional money. The accolades, the ego-stroking, and glamorous wild artist life took her all over the world. Until it didn't. When the Black art fad began to die out in the mid '80s, Ro got a teaching gig in DC. She always intended on going back to making art full-time. But more and more, teaching began to consume her thoughts. She didn't want to make art. She wanted to teach a room full of kids about Romare Bearden and see what they made. She wanted to take a dozen teenagers to see Faith Ringgold for the first time. You're angsty? You hate your father? Your girl broke your heart? Use it. Make something. Cry and paint and call yourself an artist. What happens when you sculpt your people, your heart, your struggle into color and texture? She watched them change before her eyes. Instead of making art, Ro made artists.

Ro spent the last twenty-three years of her life teaching at DC's most elite private high school, The Beechwood Academy. Coaxing wealthy white teenagers beyond the confines of their gilded bubbles. Mostly, she loved those kids. She had a thousand beautiful memories. She held space for the few Black and brown faces in her classroom. She changed the hearts and lives of a dozen of DC's most privileged children. A small fraction of them even used their privilege for good. It was Ro's form of subversive activism. Ro cherished her memories of the connections made. And of course, she had bad memories too. In her twenty-three years at The Beechwood Academy, four pimple-ridden children had called her a bitch. One rosy-cheeked student preceded the B word with the N word. *You're just a nigger bitch.* The thirteen-year-old white boy turned hot and red around the ears as he said it. As if he were equally terrified and thrilled to utilize the sharpest weapon he owned. Ro praised every ancestor and God in her pantheon for giving her the strength not to slap the little munchkin into next semester. She praised God for the strength to not slap a lot of people. The gaggle of students in the room who chuckled when the boy said it. The students who fell silent with fear. The parents. The school director who insisted on "dealing with the issue discreetly."

She spent over twenty years fighting fragile, privileged white folks' ignorance with patience and art. She worked her way up from part-time art teacher to director of the Beechwood art department. She taught the children of two sitting presidents. She moved her family from a one-bedroom on Ninth Street to a bungalow uptown. She negotiated three full scholarships for her daughters. She held her tongue when her colleagues, superiors, students and their parents regarded her with thinly veiled condescension. Then, she spent the past year fighting breast cancer. Consumed with worry, her three daughters moved back into their mother's home. Then, they watched their mother fall apart. Then, they watched her build herself back up again. As soon as her doctor cautiously gave her permission to go back to work, she decided she wasn't going back. Now she was living her best life. Sipping gin, making bad art, dabbling in tarot and transforming into the priestess she always dreamt she'd be.

Mama Ro kissed each one of her daughters as they poured into her kitchen.

"Do we have green tea?" Layla asked as she opened a pair of cabinets.

Ella gazed wistfully out the window at the bottles on the bottle tree. Swinging slowly.

Jasmine pointed. "It's above the stove, that one." Jasmine examined her mother's attire. "Well good afternoon, Miss Cleo."

Mama Ro laughed, giving Jasmine's cheek a playful smack and a kiss.

Layla chimed in as she slammed the kettle onto the stove, "Psssht. You really wanna throw shade looking like a dusty wannabe baller? You better let mama live."

"Girls." Ro's stern voice cut through the sisters' playful chatter.

Jasmine looked down at her undershirt and basketball shorts. "It's not dust. It's flour. And I look cute in this!" Jasmine tugged on Ella's shirt. "Ella, tell her! The vegan soul food girl flirted with me in this outfit."

Ella looked up and shrugged. "It's true."

"Girls!" Ro said, louder this time.

Layla rolled her eyes. "Dolores? She flirts with everyone. She flirted with *Mom* last time we went there."

Mama Ro waved her arms, and her wide wizard sleeves accentuated her movements dramatically. "Girls. I need you to sit down. Now."

"Mom?" Ella looked at her mother with concern.

"Now," Ro said.

Layla turned slowly. Jasmine looked to Ella.

The three sisters slid into the chairs around the kitchen table. They were all suddenly children, looking at each other, wondering what they might be in trouble for. Mama Ro approached the table, her hands clasped together. "Last night," She breathed in, allowing silence to hang in the air. "I had a vision."

The three sisters shared a collective sigh of relief. Ella rolled her eyes and looked out the window. Layla laughed, "Jesus, Mom."

Jasmine held her mother's hand. "Ok, so no one's dead or dying? This isn't another cancer talk?"

Mama Ro pulled away, annoyed. "No. No one is dead or dying."

"We're all dying. Technically," Ella said, studying her nails.

"Ella!" Ro and Jasmine said, glaring at the middle child.

"Okay, Mom. What's up?" Jasmine asked, squeezing her mother's hand.

"Last night. I had a vision, and spirit is telling me that it's important to—" Ro crossed her arms, waiting for her daughters to stop giggling. The three sisters held their laughter and painted their faces with the appropriate solemnity for the moment. Ro had a lot of visions. She'd always had an eerie ability to *see* things before they happened. And as her daughters grew up, she realized she'd passed along gifts to her three daughters as well. The four women all had magic, but they spent most of their lives focused on getting by. Ro never taught her daughters to harness their power. She didn't know how to harness her own. So those other worldly things would always come up with giggles, some sign of apprehension. It was daunting to acknowledge the energy beneath the surface of things. But when she retired, Ro bought a big box of incense, an armful of tapered candles, and a library of witchy books. Now, she took these visions seriously and expected her daughters to do the same.

Jasmine's voice was soft. "Okay, Mom. Tell us what you saw."

Mama Ro ceremoniously looked at each daughter. She closed her eyes and inhaled deeply. Then, she lifted a stick of incense from some hidden pocket in her dress. She lit a match and waited for the flame to catch. Incense smoke bloomed in the air. When she handed the burning stick to Layla, a line of smoke curled into a column of sunlight. Mama Ro pulled a chair out and sat at the table. She took in a deep breath then closed her eyes. Her head tilted back slightly, as if she were falling into a deep sleep. She paused there for a moment.

"The dream came to me in layers of shadows. Silhouettes. They were difficult to make out, but some things were clear. I saw a kingdom. I just walked through it; no one could see me. I sort of floated through. And I watched everything. The kingdom was like the ones in all the fairytales. The royalty, the gentry and the peasants. Extremes. There was a castle on the hill, of course. And there was a king. A beautiful man with immense power. His presence felt . . . ominous."

"Wooo . . ." Layla sang. Layla and Jasmine exchanged exaggerated, wide-eyed looks. Mama Ro ignored her daughters.

"The king carried shadows with him. They sort of clung to him. Like a smell. Or a sad memory."

She opened her eyes for a moment, taking another long, deep breath. Leaves brushed the kitchen window as a breeze stirred up. The wind chimes and glass bottles danced. The air in the kitchen suddenly felt cool. Jasmine's bare arms prickled with goosebumps.

Again, Mama Ro tipped her head back. "The king had two sons. Two princes. The princes held both light and dark in their spirits but they didn't carry shadows like their father. They were young. And one was full of bright, warm light. The other had a silver, more hushed glow."

She began to smile as she spoke. "I'm not sure I can explain how it felt. I just saw them and I knew. I could feel their energy.

Their potential. The princes have the power to change everything. But they can't see it yet."

Ella turned to look at Mama Ro. Her eyes searching. Mama Ro continued, she turned her gaze to Ella, pointing her finger. "Before I woke up, I saw one prince hand in hand with you."

Ella sat back. Then Mama Ro looked to Jasmine. "And the other prince. He was hand in hand with you, Jasmine."

Layla stood, one hand on her hip, waving the incense stick in the air. "So. Do *I* get a prince?"

Mama Ro pointed to Layla. "And I saw you, Layla. Planting a seed in a big, empty garden."

Layla squinted, unsure whether to be disappointed or excited at this strange prospect. Mama Ro held her hands up with finality. "And that is all I saw."

She clapped her hands. "Did you girls eat dinner yet?"

"Back up, Mama; come again?" Ella said, tilting her head to the side.

"A seed? I'm planting a seed?" Layla asked, squinting her eyes at Ro.

Jasmine stood, staring at Mama Ro. "So in your vision . . . I was straight? You know I'm really, really gay, right? Did you forget that?"

"Well, I don't usually dream in fairytales, but here we are. Maybe we don't have to take it so literally?" Mama Ro replied, shrugging.

"But . . . you know I'm really, *really* gay, right?" Jasmine repeated her words slowly.

"Of course I know that, Jasmine," Mama Ro replied. "Everybody knows. You never let us forget how gay you are, honey."

"I just want to make sure you're not developing dementia," Jasmine said. "Because prince or not, I'm not desperate enough to marry a man—"

"I can't tell you what it means, honey," Mama Ro said,

patting the top of Jasmine's head.

"Well, I'll take him. I'm just over here gardening in mama's vision," Layla said, folding her arms.

Ella walked to the window and settled into the window seat. She watched the leaves on the trees flutter in the summer breeze. She took a breath. Ella felt something change in that moment. A flicker of energy. She stood.

As Layla and Jasmine talked over one another, Ella riffled through the books and newspapers on the kitchen table. The kettle whistled. Layla yell-talked as she poured herself a cup of tea. Mama Ro watched Ella pull something from the pile.

"This came in the mail today." Ella whispered as she pointed to a thin magazine.

The four women met back at the table as Ella gently handed a magazine to Jasmine.

The sisters hovered over her, staring down. The cover photo featured a dapper sixty-something salt and pepper Black man in a fine suit. He smiled confidently, sitting back on a slate gray leather couch. His deep brown skin stood out against the glowing white opulence of a luxury apartment lobby.

Jasmine read the cover heading: *"Development King: Malcolm Scott, Rebuilding Chocolate City."*

The four women paused.

"Malcolm Scott?" Layla began.

"The king," Ella whispered.

Jasmine thought for a moment, then looked to Ella. "What was that guy's name? The one who just saw us naked?"

"Naked?!" Ro snapped.

"Shh Mama!" Layla hissed.

"What was his name?" Jasmine asked again.

Ella looked at Jasmine. "His name was David. David Scott..."

Mama Ro sat back in her chair and smiled.

3. JASMINE

The T Spot.

Espress	3/shot
Latte	5
Coffee	3
teas: red, black, white, green	4
treats: croissant, pain au chocolat, Danish, shortbread	4

When the cafe was empty and quiet, Jasmine spent her time thinking about sex. And the cafe was often empty and quiet. She had a collage of moments playing on loop in her mind. She would lean against the metal counter, mindlessly wiping the same shining spot with a dish rag. She daydreamed about the last girl she slept with, Jess. It was more fling than relationship. Casual. When they met, Jasmine had already given up on love. But Jess was fun. And if she couldn't have love—or five to ten beers—she could at least have fun. Fun or, more specifically, sex, was all Jess and Jasmine really had in common. In any other context, they seemed to vaguely dislike each other, but the sex was quite good. And different. Jess wanted to fuck constantly. They were both toppy and they fucked like puppies playing. Rolling around and tearing at each other's clothes. Masculine and boyish, each with a bit of softness. Jess could fuck hard and loved when Jasmine fucked her hard. She had a way of saying the most inappropriate things when Jasmine was right at the edge of her orgasm. She would command Jasmine to choke her. Call her daddy. "Spit in my mouth," Jess whispered aggressively into Jasmine's ear. That sort of thing had never turned her on before. It wasn't supposed to. She was used to having sensitive, quietly cinematic lesbian sex. But with Jess, Jasmine's spine turned liquid. She felt like a teenaged boy, confused and bewildered at how she could be so turned on by the mention of sexual violence. Who am I? She would briefly think to herself. But instead of being a sensitive, quiet lesbian, or stopping to have a heartfelt check-in, she would breathe faster, cover Jess's mouth and come hard. Yeah. Jess was not her soulmate, but the sex was really good.

Eventually the mutual dislike became too much for even the best sex to bandage. They decided to part ways months ago, but the memory of Jess still plagued Jasmine in these daydreamy moments. That strange, aggressive fucking and coming and coming and coming . . .

"Are you okay?" A short woman with long curly hair waved meekly behind the counter. Jasmine snapped out of her daydream and took the young woman in. Curvy, brown skin and beautiful. A short glass of sweet tea in a sundress.

"Hi. Yes. Sorry. What can I get you?" Jasmine asked, stepping quickly to the register.

"Can I have two small lattes aaand . . . what's the best pastry? I wanted to get something for my friend. I mean . . . what would you order?" The woman smiled as she spoke. She leaned down and peered into the glass case.

"What kind of pastry does your friend like?" Jasmine asked.

"I'm not sure. But I know she used to live in Europe. So she probably knows her shit."

Jasmine cocked her head. She smiled and gazed down into the display case. Jasmine knew her shit. She made the pastries herself. She was proud of them, boastful. Cooking was Jasmine's magic. Some days she could feel it; she could put her energy into a cup of tea, or her grief could push its way into the dough as she kneaded. Her food could change the curve of your spine and make you walk taller. The way good love can bring you closer to God—her food could do that to people. It was hard to control, but Jasmine knew that when she made things, she was a kind of healer. She didn't think about it too hard, but she knew something was there.

Still, she didn't rely on her natural talent. She was also a scientist, a meticulous student. She spent two years perfecting her croissant recipe. She studied shortbread for another six months, developing a slightly different variation on her recipe for each season—accounting for the changes in climate and humidity. She obsessively produced the highest possible quality of coffee, teas and pastries because she believed that this navy blue-clad city desperately needed quality. Government workers in suits. Lobbyists. Diplomats. A mecca of cultural conservatives. The folks who colored inside the lines. All the money and power and a deeply troubling lack of taste. The T Spot was the last cafe in DC with in-house baked goods. Jasmine's cafe stood out. But after eight years in business, Jasmine learned the sad truth about DC. This city didn't want something that stood out. Nobody cared about quality because Starbucks was easy, familiar and everywhere. Why, why, why she opened a cafe in a city full of bad coffee-drinking, stale pastry-eating cavemen was more of a mystery to her every day. She shook off this sudden wave of darkness. She pointed into the glass case, smiling proudly at her works of art.

"The cheese Danish. That's my favorite," Jasmine said, smiling. "Just the right amount of sweet."

"Okay then! One cheese Danish. Please." The woman smiled sweetly. She was kind. *Why don't I date girls like that?* Jasmine thought to herself as she rang the woman up.

"Can I have a name for your order?" Jasmine asked as she handed the woman her change.

"Marie." She smiled and walked to the table by the window. Jasmine made designs in both lattes. A gift she now only bestowed on customers who treated her like a human being. Two white, foamy flowers opened up as she tilted the cup. As Marie carried the coffee to her table, the cafe door opened slowly.

Something changed. The air in the room turned thick and warm and everything was slow. Heavy. The music playing in the cafe faded into a deep hum, the sound of underwater. A woman in all black walked into the cafe. Tall. Tight jeans, fitted T-shirt. Big, dark eyes swam across the span of the room. Long locs fell down her shoulders in thick ropes. Her face looked ancient, like an old portrait. Cheekbones high and sharp, jawline sharper. Cut from the smoothest stone. She looked hard and soft all at once. The way the hardest marble could look like flesh. Her skin was deep, dark brown with a cool, silver glow. She was a vampire, Jasmine thought. She had to be. Impossibly beautiful, poised, skilled. Like she had three hundred years to master her walk, the way she stood. Her eyes skimmed past Jasmine, settling on Marie at the front table. Jasmine felt like she should lean forward. She felt the need to be seen by this creature. The desire to be taken in by her eyes. To be stared at. And somehow also she hoped the woman wouldn't see her. She wanted to disappear. The vampire took Marie's hand, hugged her softly, then sat.

Jasmine stared. Her mouth may have been open. She was stuck. Staring at this . . . person. This perfect being. This is why she didn't date nice girls like Marie, those smiling angels in sundresses. She couldn't date angels because she craved vampires. Women who looked like mean, perfect, immortal gay boys. This mastery of masculinity that no man could dream of achieving. This woman was the definition of her type. There was nothing more gorgeous than this. Jasmine stared.

The vampire turned her head, instinctively feeling Jasmine's gaze. Jasmine's body stuttered. She looked for something to do. She reached for knobs on the espresso machine, then the dish rag; she picked up a spatula, but her brain was too overwhelmed to even pretend to use it. Then—having no plan—she turned her back and slid down to the floor. Her face tightened in horror, immediately realizing how strange that probably looked. Am I HIDING? Who the fuck am I? What a fucking goofball! She gritted her teeth. Jasmine. Get it together. Breathe. Jasmine willed herself to be normal. To be calm. This was her cafe. She was a human being and a beautiful woman (vampire or not) would not make her heart explode in her chest. She meditated for a moment. Breathe. She crawled to the espresso machine and slowly floated back up, pretending to clean it as she forced her breath to slow down.

She rose to the counter and fiddled with a jar of loose tea. She pulled one of the tiny glass teapots from the shelf. I look very busy and very calm. I look normal, Jasmine thought as she scooped a spoonful of dried chamomile, then poured a stream of hot water into the pot. She kept her back to the window and gazed at tea leaves swimming in hot swirling water. And I am not weird, she thought to herself as she poured the tea. I am not weird. She nodded to herself. She gave herself a thumbs up. She continued nodding until she noticed something in the distance. Marie was waving her hand across the cafe. Jasmine looked around. Is she summoning me? Is she saying hi?

"Excuse me! Are you the owner?" Marie called out.

"I am," Jasmine replied.

"Can I ask you something?" Marie said, waving Jasmine over.

Jasmine sighed. She should have said no. No, she was not the owner. She should have sat on the floor for the rest of the day. She set her cup of tea down, rounded the counter and approached Marie and her date. When Jasmine arrived at the table, the vampire pulled out her phone and stared down at it. Rude.

"Where do you get your coffee beans? I'm not an expert or anything, just curious," Marie asked.

"Oh. Well, you're drinking a Columbian blend. But this coffee is a little different because of the roasting method. Most chain roasters burn their coffee beans. The origin of the coffee beans is important, but the roaster can actually be just as important. We use a local roaster, which offers us more choice when it comes to flavor development. So it's more about the how than the where . . . basically . . ." Jasmine's voice trailed off. She realized she'd gone too far into coffee science mode.

"Well! Whatever it is, you're doing something right. This is the best coffee I've had in a long time. I just really wanted to tell you that," Marie said, beaming. Jasmine exhaled.

"Oh wow. Well thank you. The quality is really important to me," Jasmine replied, grinning. Her smile fell when she looked at the other end of the table. The coffee and Danish sat untouched. The hot vampire masc person hadn't even tried it—any of it. Jasmine stared at the vampire, who stared down at her phone.

"Can I get y'all something else?" Jasmine asked.

"Oh, I'll probably drink both of our coffees," Marie said, patting the table politely. "She's not going to have any."

"I can make you a different drink if this isn't your preference. Pour-over?" Jasmine offered, waiting for the vampire to look up from her phone.

"I'm particular about my coffee." The woman's voice emerged. Low, calm, disinterested.

"So am I," Jasmine replied, folding her arms.

The woman's eyes flicked up to Jasmine, then back down to her phone. "I'm good. But thank you."

Jasmine's smile didn't reach her eyes. She turned to Marie. "Well. I'll be right over there if you need anything else. I hope to see you again, Marie."

Jasmine turned on her heel. Fucking asshole. Fucking masc vampire tall fine mean ass, who cares about what you think about coffee anyway. Jasmine exhaled and shook her head. Good riddance. Tall, cute boys were always mean. They knew they could be. Fucking pretty boy privilege is what it is, she thought. That type never went for her anyway. They went for girls like Marie. Those perfect femmes with long hair and heels and sundresses. Jasmine felt like a football player whenever she wore a dress.

Jasmine poured a cup of coffee beans into the industrial grinder and flipped the switch. This was her loud, not-so-subtle way of managing her annoyance. She ground beans for what felt like ten minutes before Marie and her rude date left the cafe.

Jasmine chuckled to herself as she crossed the cafe to bus the dishes. When she looked down at the table, there they were. The latte with its wilting flower and a perfect Danish sitting abandoned on its plate. Not one bite. Not one sip. Jasmine slumped into the chair. She didn't used to be this sensitive. Why did she feel so deeply wounded? Her cafe was already failing. She already felt rejected by the entire city. What difference did one little pretty boy make? Jasmine lifted the Danish, took two oversized bites and chewed slowly as she gazed out the window.

4. LAYLA

The door of the microwave creaked open. Layla scrubbed its yellowing walls with a sponge. The microwave always smelled like soup. The entire office smelled like soup. It was a cloying, artificial, chickeny smell. This is what disappointment smells like, Layla thought to herself. Week-old Campbell's soup steam. The hot, misty yellow veil pulled over the beginnings of her so-called career. Layla scrubbed the microwave aggressively and wondered how she got here.

She went to Wesleyan on a partial scholarship. She was an outcast in high school, but college life suited her perfectly. She charmed the entire theater department. She wrote a paper on the disservice of race-blind casting, while challenging gender-specific casting. As a freshman, she managed to land the role of Othello, which stunned the gaggle of young theater boys competing for the role. She fell in love with Black studies and became a double major. She challenged her teachers and inspired her peers. She led protests on campus and founded the radical student group, BFB (Black Feminist Brilliance, also known as Black Feminist Bitches depending on who asked). In her second year, BFB's protests encouraged (or rather, forced) the administration to add a gender pronoun option to all school registration forms. In her third year, the group shamed the school's president into renovating the Black Heritage House. Small victories, but in this tiny ecosystem they meant something. Layla made tangible change. She was the only one of her sisters to get a bachelor's degree, and she did it her way. She finished Wesleyan with honors and a handful of glowing recommendations from her favorite professors. It was only reasonable to assume that graduation would mark a beginning for her.

But here she was. Scrubbing the inside of a microwave in a dark, chicken-scented office. In spite of her scholarship, Layla graduated with $90,000 in high-interest, private student loan debt. She applied for thirty jobs. Twenty-nine of them never called back. Rise DC wasn't at the top of her list, but when they offered her a position, she took the job. The pay was shit, but the work was good. Rise DC was one of the few nonprofits advocating for affordable housing in the city. It was an uphill battle. Gentrification spread like wildfire across the city. Most Black and low-income folks scattered to PG County, Baltimore and Virginia. Some jumped ship completely and moved to Atlanta. About ten years ago, the historically Black "Chocolate City" became what Layla called a Chocolate Chip City. If you were a native still living in DC, people called you a unicorn. A Black unicorn was the rarest variety. By the time Layla was born, the Jones family had already moved uptown and were nearly middle class. Layla was too young to witness the changes firsthand. But she could feel it like the pain of a phantom limb. Her mother called it ancestral memory. It was as if she felt the weight of everything Black folks had lost in DC.

Finally satisfied with the state of the microwave, Layla heated up her vegetable pad see ew. With a mouthful of noodles, she pulled a chair to her desk. She googled Malcolm Scott. She couldn't find much. She glanced at the Washingtonian cover article she'd already seen at her mother's house. The King of Real Estate. She skimmed a New York Times piece about Black developers. Malcolm at a gala grinning casually next to Michelle Obama. Malcolm standing at the foot of a gleaming new high-rise in Baltimore. Layla gathered a few basic facts. He's a self-made millionaire. He's from DC. He's the CEO of an investment firm. He had already developed apartment complexes in Brooklyn, two high-rises in Baltimore, and he was getting ready to break ground in DC. Most of her research revealed glowing praise. Which made sense. Who doesn't love a Black man who made it? He looked like a hero. And now it appeared that Malcolm was giving back to his hometown— "Rebuilding Chocolate City." Another millionaire developer in DC. What could go wrong, Layla thought.

Layla shoveled another pile of noodles into her mouth as her boss, Carmen, walked in. Rise DC's Executive Director Carmen was a Black-Dominican superwoman in a blue wrap dress and Gucci pumps. She was gorgeous, brilliant, and a little bit intimidating. Layla had opinions about the fact that her boss could afford Gucci while she could barely make a living wage. But she had no illusions about the nonprofit world. Everybody was a hustler. And Carmen's wildly expensive taste aside, she was a brilliant fundraiser. Layla once watched Carmen charm $10,000 in donations from some tech guy in line for beer at a Wizards game. Carmen was not perfect, but Layla knew she had a lot to learn from her.

Carmen smiled at the sight of Layla. "Hey Layla. Whatcha working on?"

"I'm looking into this developer..." Layla said, covering her half-full mouth. "Malcolm Scott?"

Carmen scoffed. "Funny you should mention him." She pulled a chair up to Layla's desk. "Remember that block they demolished on U Street?"

"Yeah! I just saw that the other day." Layla swallowed dramatically.

"Well. It looks like that's a Malcolm Scott development."

"Shit. The whole block?" Layla looked back at the photograph of Malcolm.

"Yep. He's rich, powerful, cozy with the mayor and half the city council. And he's Robin Hood, apparently. He claims to work for the people." Carmen held her hands up in air quotes. "But his other two properties were high-end luxury. Same old bullshit. They call it mixed income and then end up with 2 percent affordable units." Carmen shrugged.

Layla set her fork down. "Okay. So this guy isn't offering anything different?"

Carmen shook her head. "Same shit. And calling it progress. And of course, no one bats an eye. Maybe it's more satisfying to watch a gorgeous Black man do it."

"Huh," Layla said. She stared at the array of photographs. Malcolm Scott. A wolf in the finest wool suit. Her blood pumped with adrenaline. This is it. She knew she couldn't save the whole city, but maybe she could save this one block. Maybe she could save the city from Malcolm Scott.

5. ELLA

TONE was DC's brand-new high-end gym with all the perks. It was brand new, mysteriously lit, and expensive. TONE had locations in big cities across the country. There were already several in Manhattan, Brooklyn, LA, Seattle and now DC. The gym had all the best instructors, body workers and a culture of shameless excess. The marketing for TONE implied that somewhere between your Peloton ride, pedicure, freshly pressed green juice and your deep tissue massage, you could find God. And who wouldn't? It was a modern cathedral for the wealthy. It cost an arm and a leg to be a member, but for the few who could afford it, TONE was heaven.

TONE was not heaven for Ella. It was work. Of course, she had to get used to the "you're so brave" or "you go girl" comments from bird-like white women. She was mistaken for the maid on a few occasions. And as a member of the staff, she could never really relax there. But she enjoyed the perks. She made good, steady money. Some days she even felt comfortable there. Today, the staff locker room was quiet. She sat on the bench and stared down at her phone. She stood up. She paced. Don't google David Scott, don't google David Scott. She clicked her nails against her cell phone case. Make yourself busy. Find something else to do. Look up techniques in Thai massage. Find a recipe for a mango margarita. Send a text to that guy from Tinder who wears weirdly short pants. Run a mile on the treadmill. Meditate. Light something on fire! Just don't. Google. The rich boy. Don't Google the rich, nice, and gorgeous boy that maybe you're meant to fall in love with?! Don't google David Scott. Don't google David Scott. Don't—

Ella sighed. Well, why not? It's not stalking, she thought to herself. It's more like . . . research. She typed away. David Scott. David+Scott+DC. David+Scott+DC+Black. David+Scott+DC+Black+son of Malcolm Scott+real estate. And there he was.

David Sterling Scott. Sterling. Jesus. She shook her head and swiped through his Instagram gallery. He had a thin social media presence. This kind of rich folk was classy enough to be rich in private. But she found a few scraps here and there. David was apparently the pretty face of The Scott Group Community Relations arm. It was probably a fluff job, but it looked like he did some good work—and he looked good doing it. Ella stared at a picture on her phone. A wide shot of David on a sailboat. Jesus. A sailboat? She rolled her eyes, then ran her finger along the ripple of his abs. The cut of his arm muscles. He looked like he could pick her up. She swiped to the next picture. A photo of David dancing with a little girl in a glowing white hospital room. The caption read: "Scott Group donated $15K to Children's Hospital Oncology. And I got to dance with Jamie! Best day ever." Ella rolled her eyes. Wow. This is subtle, she thought. But she couldn't stop looking at the photo. The child's frail body was swimming in her hospital gown. No doubt she had the most painful, fatal kind of cancer. They probably picked the sickest-looking kid for the publicity. Fucking typical. Ella wanted to believe that it was all an act. She wanted to suck her teeth and scroll past the photograph, but she just kept looking at this little girl. Her eyes were tired but her hands were in the air, imitating David's dance move. Both of them grinning. This little frail child actually looked happy. And David looked like a goddamned hero.

Ella scrolled down to a photograph of David on the red carpet for some indie film. He wore a slim-fitting suit. His eyes squinted into the camera's flash. The D-list actress on his arm was pretty. In that very conventional way skinny girls can be pretty. Ella recognized her from . . . something. A clothing ad? Or an old sit-com maybe? She looked too serious. Simple. But she was very pretty. Probably his model/actress girlfriend. Ella resisted the urge to google her too. Instead, she pushed a button on her phone and watched it power down. It's fine, she thought. She accepted the fact that she was amazing and gorgeous. But she didn't date boys like that. Boys like that didn't see fat girls. They were usually too dumb or too insecure. Or they simply couldn't handle a woman with opinions. Ella folded her arms. She decided that when it came down to it, he really wasn't good enough for her. That was that.

Ella slammed her locker closed and walked to the bathroom mirror. She pulled her hair back into a silky ponytail. Her black employee T-shirt pinched tight at the seams. The staff didn't offer XL tees. She stared at herself in the mirror. She put her hands on her hips and sighed at her reflection. She was too smart to care about this shit. But she did. Ella had to be stubbornly self-assured. Confidence was always defiance. Loving her body always felt like a fight with the world. But it was either fight or die. Every magazine, every movie, commercial, even her skinny sisters' bodies were reminders that she was different. So, she wore the loudest colors and the shortest skirts. She painted her nails pink and wore the dress dripping with sequins. Wide-eyed women approached her with praise. They'd say, "Wow. You are so beautiful! You really inspire me!" Ella would smile and nod. She knew what they were thinking. "Wow. All this time I've been skinny and insecure. But look at you. If you can be this fat, and this confident, I could be confident too!"

But she wasn't always the confident fat girl. She was ten

when she realized she wasn't one of the pretty girls. She couldn't buy clothes in the Juniors section anymore. Her breasts were puffy, protruding softly against her cotton T-shirts. The other girls in her class were still mostly flat as bean-poles. Her mother gave her extra attention. Standing with her in the mirror, telling her in soft, sweet tones that she was just growing faster than the other girls. Jasmine gave Ella her sports bras. She told Ella that Black girls sometimes have different shapes than white girls. And that's okay. People kept telling her it was okay She was okay. And the more they insisted, the more she felt like something was wrong.

When she was eleven, Ella had a crush on Isaiah. She'd write his name in her notebook, then scratch it out aggressively so no one would know. Her notebooks were full of black scratch clouds and black holes. Isaiah was the cutest boy in her class. He had curly hair and a gap in his front teeth. Isaiah was Black and Japanese. He was a sixth-grade rockstar. All the white boys followed him around like groupies. He'd already kissed two of the most popular girls in the class.

Growing up in her mostly white elementary school in the late '90s, the rules of the sixth grade were set by the white, MTV-watching preteen majority. They were confusing at first. But Ella learned quickly. You could be Black and a boy. But not too Black. If you were really Black, you could be funny. And good at sports. But not cute. It was better if you were mixed with something—like Isaiah. They might think you were dumb and they might assume you were good at basketball. But the kids would like you. The girls would want to go out with you. The boys wanted to dance and be like you. If you were an Asian boy, nobody thought you were cool. Some Asian girls were cool, but only if they didn't look too Asian. If you were Latino (which the kids still called Spanish or Mexican) you could be cool but only if you didn't have an accent. Accents were not cool. Those light-skinned Spanish girls like J-Lo were cool. But if you weren't like

J-Lo, you were too different. Being different was not cool. If you were a Black girl, it was a lose-lose. They thought you were dumb and nobody wanted to go out with you. The boys didn't ask you to dance even if they were Black too. The girls didn't want to be like you. If you were a Black girl in a white school in the sixth grade, you were mostly invisible.

Ella's childhood felt like a bad dream. She could only remember the hard days. She remembered how Isaiah giggled as he approached her desk. Her eyes peeking shyly over the top of her book. Isaiah's pretty almond eyes glittering. Ella squinted at him, already suspicious. He'd never talked to her before—something was off. He managed to stop giggling. He stood up straight, almost formal. He stepped toward her.

"Hey Ella, will you go to the fall dance with me?" he asked.

Ella's heart stopped. Isaiah was talking to her. Isaiah knew her name. But she saw the gaggle of pimpled white boys hiding behind a brick pillar in the distance. She wasn't stupid. He was trying to make a joke out of her. She knew it was a lie. But she remembered squeezing her eyes closed and blowing out the candles on her eleventh birthday cake. She wished for this. She was kind to everyone. She did all her homework early. She helped take care of her little sister. Wouldn't it be fair? For her to have the power to make a cute boy like her? She pushed her glimmer of hope somewhere far and deep into her heart.

"No," Ella said. She lifted her book up, blocking Isaiah from her view.

"Your loss, Miss Piggy!" Isaiah yelled. Everyone in the room turned to watch. He giggled as he skipped back to his posse. The boys' laughter seemed to carry through the entire classroom. Ella held her book still. She pretended she didn't hear him. She turned the page. She pretended to read for the remaining twenty minutes of school.

The bell rang. She walked with Layla to the bus stop to meet Jasmine. She held Layla's hand as they climbed the steps of the bus. She rode the bus home with her sisters, listening to Jasmine rant about the GSA at Beechwood. She nodded and chatted with her sisters. When the three sisters got home, Jasmine and Layla wandered into the kitchen. Ella ran up the stairs, and shut the door to the bathroom. She turned the shower on. Hot beams of water hit the tiles. The room filled up with steam. She took off all her clothes, got in the shower and wept. She scrubbed her body and cried and cried.

Inner child Ella. Still crying in that bathroom in her mind. Ella laughed at herself in the TONE locker room mirror. That was so long ago. I know better now. And yet this fifteen-year-old memory still stuck like a splinter in her brain. She scrambled around in her purse, pulling out a black and gold tube. She leaned close to the mirror and painted her lips ruby red. She flirted with her reflection, lifting the soft inside of her wrist to her lips. She tilted her head and kissed the thin blue veins. The kiss was slow and deep. She kissed herself like a lover would. She kissed each of her hands. She kissed up and down her arms, peppering skin with lipstick. Now she kissed herself like a doting auntie. Sappy sweet kisses on every inch of skin she could reach. She laughed at herself in the mirror, covered in lip prints. She pulled her cell phone from her bag and took a picture of her reflection. She gazed at the photograph and grinned. She couldn't make a boy fall for her. But she could fall in love with herself. Over and over. Ella pulled a pack of makeup wipes from her bag. Then, one by one, she wiped each print from her skin.

Ella walked through the locker room into the splendid, black-tiled spa room. She was one of the best massage therapists at TONE, though she wasn't a favorite. Some of her colleagues offered "extras." She didn't judge them; it just wasn't her style. Rich people thought they could buy everything. She felt a thrilling satisfaction, being the one thing they couldn't buy. "Just to be clear, I am not on the menu," she said to one balding white man who left four $100 bills on the table before the massage began. After a long and awkward massage, she tried to hand the bills back to him, but he was so horrified he refused them. Ella had no problems setting boundaries and saying no. She learned this lesson early. And this made her job manageable.

Ella stood at the threshold of her massage room. She removed the intake binder from the door and skimmed it. No allergies. No scent preferences. No injuries. Deep tissue. Pretty standard. Ella squinted at a note handwritten at the bottom of the intake form.

I wasn't sure how else to get in touch with you. I hope this is ok. :)

Ella frowned. Who wrote this? The client? Maybe it was booked over the phone. She looked down at her watch, then knocked gently on the door.

"Hello there. Are you ready?" She asked in a soft tone.

"Um yes," a man's voice responded.

"We can start with you face down. Just tell me when you're all set," Ella whispered.

"Okay, I'm good," the man replied, his voice muffled.

Ella entered slowly and carefully. Soothing flute and rain sounds drifted gently from the speakers. A man lay face down on the table, his back a deep chestnut brown, wide and roped with muscle. Ella raised a brow. Her clients were mostly women, white and over forty.

"I'm Ella," she said in a whisper. "If anything feels uncomfortable or painful, just let me know."

"Um. Okay." The man nodded enthusiastically into the face cradle.

"Would you like me to turn on the heated blanket?" she asked.

"Yes. Please. Thank you!" the man whispered.

Ella clicked the switch on the end of the table. She turned to the altar of glass bottles at the head of the room. She poured a pool of oils in her hand. Lavender and bergamot. She turned back to the head of the massage table, took a breath, then held her hands over the man's back for a moment. She set her intentions: to transfer healing, light and calm to this man. She did this for all her clients, but she gave Black clients a special treatment. She prayed over his body. She prayed for his protection from police, from the fear of the world, from grief and anger. The muscles of his back expanded and contracted slowly with each breath. When her hands gently met the smooth skin of the man's neck, he flinched. Was he anxious? She breathed in deeply as she warmed his muscles. Her strength and precision would calm him. She felt him melting under her touch. The tangled mass of muscles pushing back again and again—then slowly softening, relenting to her hands. Ella found a stubborn knot at the base of his neck. She worked it, pulling the fibers down slowly. Her thumbs slid down the length of his neck to the base of his shoulder blade.

Ella smiled. She loved being good at her job.

"Um. I don't want to interrupt but I meant to say hi before . . . before the massage started?"

The man's voice was muffled. Small and vulnerable.

"No need," Ella replied flatly, wondering what the man was getting at.

"Did you see the note? Ella?"

Ella's hands froze when she heard the man whisper her name. He shifted in the face cradle.

"Yes?" She replied, hesitant.

"I really just wanted to see you. That's why I came here." The man's voice sounded nervous. Ella felt her heartbeat in her ears.

"I don't. I don't do . . . release massage. I mean. If that's what you're looking for, I can recommend another . . ."

"Release massage?" The man repeated the phrase. Ella sighed. What the fuck was up with this guy?

"I don't fuck my clients," Ella blurted impatiently.

"Oh no no no!" The man shook his head frantically in the

cradle. He put his hands up. He was suddenly rambling, talking a mile a minute at the floor.

"I don't want that! I didn't, I would never have expected . . . That's not. Oh God no. I just wanted to. Meet you? I-I-I've seen you here before. I work out here and I've seen you working out here and I met you and your sisters and I thought this was a good idea. But it was a bad idea. This is where you work. It's wrong. I was wrong. I'm-I'm so sorry." The man dropped his hands on the table, deflated.

Ella turned and stepped forward, recognizing something familiar in his voice. The young man slowly lifted himself up and turned to her. She squinted her eyes at him. Even in the dim lighting, she knew his face. "David?"

David Scott smiled, astonished. "You remember me?"

6. THE PARTY

The sisters all dressed in black. Since they'd moved back into their childhood home, they'd revived their collective get-ready routine. Layla blasted vapid pop music from her room. The sisters walked the upstairs hallway like runway models, cheering and catcalling one another. Jasmine's outfit was thick thigh femmeboy punk. Too old to try too hard these days, but not old enough to give up entirely. Ella's all-black was a '50s pinup, and Layla's was a kind of goth high fashion. Jasmine did the makeup. She smudged her sisters' eyelids with thick swaths of black shadow. A pop of fairy dust silver at the corners of their eyes. Ella gave her sisters a spritz of geranium rosewater.

As they walked slowly up the winding road, their heartbeats collectively quickened. Anxiety prickled at their fingertips. They each held the seed of a secret, too small and new to share. Ella didn't mention her moment with David. Him appearing shirtless and anonymous at her job. The way they talked for an hour in the soft darkness of the massage room. The way they laughed about how strange it was. He laughed like a kid. Not childish, exactly. But free. Unafraid to lie back in the bed of his joy. She didn't want to leave that room. Against all her better judgment, Ella liked the boy. She knew it was a bad idea. Maybe it was nothing. Maybe it was something. Maybe her excitement frightened her too much to put it into words. Ella decided she would say nothing.

And Layla said nothing about her plan to protest Malcolm Scott's new development. She was calculating the odds in her head. How hard would it be to challenge a Black developer? How much good could this protest really do? How much good could any protest do? Gentrification in this city felt so inevitable, so accepted. Luxury condos obliterated blocks of buildings and whoever lived there before seemed to evaporate into thin air. Every day she'd drive by a shining new building and forget what was there before. She could see the ghosts but couldn't remember their names. And people just went on. They bought quinoa and kale at the new Whole Foods and custom-made bicycles at that new bike shop, and they didn't think about what memories they were stepping on to get there. They didn't care. But she couldn't stop caring. To her, gentrification felt like building on burial grounds. It felt like an assault. And she needed to fight back.

The sisters entered the threshold of Rock Creek Park. In this green cathedral of leaves and soft shadow, the air was cooler. The flirtatious ballads of cardinals and robins trickled through the leaves. Jasmine looked up at the trees and sky, praying for calm. She thought about the woman in the cafe. Somehow, this stranger, this vampire had completely invaded her thoughts. Jasmine had absolutely no desire to know this person. She didn't actually have any real respect for the vampire. But physically—that was another story. For some reason, an image of the mystery woman would flash into Jasmine's mind when she was about to come. She felt the vampire on her skin, in her breathlessness. It reminded her of the way porn was gross the minute after your orgasm. She would finish and think: what the fuck was that? She was probably just very horny and very bored. And regardless of how emotionally bankrupt this person was, physically she was perfect.

Jasmine was restless. She shook out her hands, bouncing and humming, looking for some distraction.

"Let's take a photo!" Jasmine sang, holding her phone up in exclamation.

"Ooh yes," Layla chimed in.

"Aren't we late already?" Ella asked, tapping at her phone.

"Come on, boo. It's a Black housewarming; there's no such thing as late," Jasmine said, swatting at the air.

"Maybe it's not Black. Maybe he has a white wife and a bunch of white friends..." Layla said, pondering.

"He definitely doesn't have a white wife," Ella said. Layla cut a glance at her.

"How would you know?" Layla prodded.

"I wouldn't. I don't," Ella said, folding her arms.

"Ella. He's a filthy rich Black man. It's very, very likely this man is ebony to some lady's ivory. Maybe an older wiiiser woman, you feel me?" Layla said.

"I didn't get that vibe," Ella said, shrugging.

"Shit. I'd fuck an old white lady if I could live in that house," Layla said, pulling her fingers through the holes of lace on her dress.

"Mmmhmm. I bet you would," Ella snickered.

Layla punched at the air as Ella ducked behind a tree. Jasmine ignored her bickering sisters, already curating the photoshoot. She found a rock in the dirt and set her phone on it, tilting it up to the road.

"Jazz, that low angle will not do us any favors," Layla said.

"Baby sister, hush. This shit right here is about to be art." Jasmine gestured with her arms as she set the timer.

"Okay so what's the look? Are we cheezing? Are we serious? Are we cute?" Jasmine said, running to stand with her sisters.

"Yes, can we decide? Cuz I'm always smiling and y'all are up to some light-skinnt eye squinting model shit," Layla said.

"Let's be silly?" Jasmine asked.

"Let's be serious," Layla said.

"But also sexy," Ella chimed in.

The phone beeped a warning at them.

"Yep. Serious, sexy, silly. Alladat," Layla said as she settled into her pose.

The trees shushed around them.

Layla planted both hands on her hips. Tall, dark, and apathetic in her black lace dress, and red hightop chucks. In the middle, Ella perched in thick wedge sandals, a paper-thin silk tank top, and a fitted black pencil skirt, everything hugging and dripping from her curves. Her hands on her knees in a 1950s pinup pose, blessing the camera with a tasteful peek of cleavage and a pursed lip kiss. And Jasmine took a knee, boyish and goofy in her loose black jeans, a hole-ridden T-shirt, and punky black boots. She lifted a too-cool peace sign in the air, her head cocked to the side. Three Black witches posed in the woods as the trees and the wind and Spirit whispered their praise.

The three sisters stood in the shadow of the mansion, dwarfed by the oversized wooden door. Chatter and music pulsed gently from inside. Jasmine ran her fingers along the art-deco designs burned into the panels of wood.

"Am I insane? Or is this a sexy door?" Jasmine whispered.

"No, you're right. That's a sexy ass door," Layla said.

"I want to make out with this door," Jasmine said, moving closer.

"Jasmine. Please don't fuck the rich guy's door." Layla laughed.

"Let's be rich," Jasmine said.

"Nah. We're too nice to be rich. People with this much money always step on somebody's back to get it," Layla said as she pressed her cheek to the door.

"Could we just be a little bit rich?" Jasmine pouted, still caressing the door.

"Shhhh!" Ella nervously swatted Jasmine away and pushed the doorbell.

The three sisters stared nervously at one another, waiting.

When an elder Black woman in a gauzy white dress opened the door, her smile turned stale.

"Hello . . .?" Her voice curled up into a question at the end. Her silver fro bounced as she cocked her head to the side.

"Hi! We're here for David," Ella said grinning.

"Oh I'm sorry. I wasn't sure because of—well—please, come in!" She extended her hand and stepped to the side.

The sisters inched their way into the room. Dampened horns and lazy soul beats pulsed and swam through the air. The house looked even bigger on the inside. High ceilings with raw metal beams cut through the space. Enamel-glossed concrete floors that looked like placid lake water. The hard edges of the industrial structure were softened with finely detailed Persian rugs and velvet couches. A wall of glass windows featured the breathtaking view of a thousand trees, an oversaturated sea of undulating green. And there was white. So much white. The house was full of elegant Black folks, all dressed in clean, sterile, blinding shades of white. White sweaters. White linens. White silks. Mother of pearl necklaces. Cowry shells. Clean cotton white.

The sisters, all in their witchy black attire, huddled together, frozen.

"Fuuuuuck. It's a white party," Jasmine whispered as her head darted around.

"Do people still throw white parties?" Layla giggled.

"Apparently," Jasmine said.

Ella traced the line of her bangs, nervously searching the room. "A white party. One teensy, beensy detail he forgot to mention." Ella muttered.

Layla basked in all the strange looks cast their way. She laughed. "Dress codes are a little young, don't you think? Shit, I probably would have worn black either way. Oooh snacks!"

As Layla sprinted toward the snack table, David emerged from the crowd in a cream-colored linen set. He was waving and yelling excitedly at Ella. "Ella! You made it!"

David scooped Ella into a bear hug. When he noticed Jasmine, his eyes lit up with joy. "Get in here, sis!" David said as he motioned for Jasmine to join in the group hug. She awkwardly obliged for a moment, then leaned away.

David took Jasmine's hand. "Jasmine! I'm David! We already met—technically—but it's nice to meet you again! Ella couldn't stop talking about you."

Jasmine looked at Ella, more confused by the second. David went on, his hands gesturing excitedly as he spoke. "Oh and I can't wait to visit your cafe! I love anything, everything sweets, and bakeries, I mean I'm not really picky, if it has sugar in it, I'll probably love it. I'm obsessed with Oreos. And I really like those donuts they have at the grocery store. The chocolate ones? So I'm clearly not a foodie. But I really love the real thing too. Ella told me you're the best baker in the city."

Jasmine folded her arms. "Well. That's. Generous. Ella, when did you manage to tell him such great things about me?" Jasmine asked, staring wide-eyed at Ella.

David smiled. "Really. It's so good to meet you again, Jasmine. And you're both wearing clothes this time!" He laughed heartily.

Ella ignored Jasmine's not-so-subtle tugs and pinches. "The wrong clothes, it seems," Ella said, looking around the room. "David. You didn't tell us this was a white party." Ella whispered the word white like a curse.

David suddenly noticed their black attire. He waved his hand in the air.

"Oh, that's nothing! You both look so pretty! The white party housewarming thing is just a snobby tradition. Something about ancestors and new beginnings, all that. I promise, no one is offended."

"Will the ancestors be offended?" Jasmine asked dryly.

"Shit. If the ancestors are pressed about our clothes, they're not invited to the party," David said.

Ella giggled. Jasmine frowned. David took Ella's hand. "Jasmine, do you mind if I borrow Ella for a bit?" he asked.

"Actually I—" Jasmine reached desperately for Ella's hand as it drifted away. David pulled Ella into the sea of white. Jasmine folded, then unfolded her arms. Her mind raced with questions. How did David suddenly know so much about them? When would they have met? She hated when her little sisters kept secrets. She put her hands in her pockets, struck suddenly by the familiar feeling that even in a room full of beautiful people, she was alone. She slowly wandered to the edge of the room, studying the art on the walls, looking for any excuse not to talk to strangers.

Meanwhile, Layla was camped out at the snack table. After she tasted the cookies, the mini turkey burger, the beet salad, she scrutinized a platter of tiny puff pastries. From the corner of her eye, she noticed a young, bespectacled white man in a trendy button-up watching her. Layla looked warily up at him as he leaned and pointed across the table.

"You have to try the feta lamb tartlets. They're really good," he said, grinning. Layla's eyes shot up at him, instantly questioning his motives. He was smiling too hard. She didn't smile back. He was the only white guy in the room and he seemed desperate to make a friend. Layla rolled her eyes, perpetually annoyed by white strangers' projections. *All the privilege in the world but y'all can't handle ten minutes on the margin*, she wanted to say, but didn't.

Layla stuffed two tartlets into her mouth and chewed, her cheeks cartoonishly full.

"It's good, right?" He asked, nodding. Layla chewed.

"It's. There's something sweet in there too. Fig. I think?" He asked, now nervously chuckling. Layla chewed.

"So how do you know the Scotts?" he asked.

Layla stared wide-eyed, waiting for him to run out of polite questions.

"I work for Mr. Scott . . . Are you a friend of Zora's?"

When Layla said nothing, he studied her expression. Probably wondering if she was crazy. He pretended to look at his phone as he slowly wandered away. She waved as he disappeared. Maybe she was too hard on him. He was right, the tarts were quite good.

Layla chewed her lamb tart as she scanned the room. She recognized a city council member from a meeting she'd been to recently. Shirley . . . something. Shirleysomething looked like a sweet old cookie-baking grandma but was actually a fucking shark in local politics. Across the room, Layla spotted Derek Vance, a hotshot news anchor for CNN. Vance was her mother's hero. One of the first Black lead anchors in the country. She remembered watching him on TV as a kid. He looked so majestic in person, like royalty. This really was like visiting the royal court of Black DC.

Layla was reaching for another tartlet when she saw him. Malcolm Scott. The handsome sixty-something Black man her mother had dreamt about. The king. His oxford button-down shirt and white slacks fit him perfectly. Everything bespoke. A Panama hat snug on his head. His short black hair gilded with flecks of silver. He leaned casually against the stone mantel, chatting with an older couple who looked more like disciples than friends. Layla pretended to wander across the room toward the sound of Malcolm's voice.

"You'll never guess . . . but I'll give you a hint. It's something you'll find in every kitchen, but you've never cooked a dish with it."

The woman giggled girlishly. The man by her side nodded his head mechanically, barely present. The woman touched Malcolm's shoulder as she spoke. "Well, what is it, Malcolm? Dish soap?" Malcolm's booming laughter carried across the room. He was everything his glossy magazine cover promised he'd be.

"Good god, Dianne, no! You think I'm trying to poison you? I'm creative but I'm not that creative."

Layla's heart raced. She felt like a spy. She stepped into the circle. "So, what are we guessing?" she asked. Dianne looked disappointed by Layla's interruption.

"We're guessing the secret ingredient of Malcolm's world-famous chili," the man said dully.

Dianne teased Malcolm with a grin. "He promised to give me the recipe if I guess it."

"Can I play?" Layla asked casually.

"Of course!" Malcolm responded. "But you should know—it's not dish soap."

"So what kind of chili is it?" Layla asked playfully.

"Texas chili," Malcolm said. "My folks are from Houston, originally." He tipped his head to Dianne. She rolled her eyes girlishly.

Layla drew out her words. "Well. My sister makes a good chili; I'm remembering some really strange ingredients in that one."

Malcolm smiled.

"Is it chocolate?" Layla asked.

"Ah! Very, very good guess. It's not chocolate. But I've met a Southerner or two who messed around with some cocoa powder." Malcolm smiled as he spoke. Layla rifled through her brain for that Houston chili recipe Jasmine used to make.

"Oh! I remember! Is it coffee?" Layla asked.

"Coffee! You're absolutely right." Malcolm shook his head, laughing.

"Well. How about that," Dianne said, folding her arms. "Are you in the culinary industry?"

Layla held her hands up humbly. "No, no. Not in the culinary industry. But my sister Jasmine is. I just reap the benefits," Layla said, smiling.

Malcolm was still shaking his head. "Dianne, John. I'd like

you to meet my long-lost daughter whose name is . . ."

Daughter. That word made Layla feel something. Just for a moment. According to her mother, their father had disappeared with a new woman just after she was born. He was somewhere in North Carolina. Maybe he had a new family too. She didn't know. She didn't really care. She didn't know him enough to miss him. And she never felt the need for a father figure, but something about Malcolm saying the word daughter made her feel exposed.

"I'm Layla," she said. Malcolm shook Layla's hand.

"Great to meet you, Layla. I'm Malcolm. So how do you know my kids?" Malcolm asked.

"I'm a friend of David's," Layla lied.

"David's? Well, I'm glad to know he has good taste in friends these days."

Layla noted the veiled critique.

"Actually," she chirped, "I was really excited to meet you. I'm interested in property development and I thought maybe sometime I could pick your brain?"

Malcolm's eyes widened with joy. "Ah HA! Do I have a young real estate tycoon on my hands?"

Layla smiled and clasped her hands together like a toddler. "I wouldn't go that far. For now I'm just curious."

"Well, I'd love to talk property development with you. My kids and I call it PDs. Most of my work is in New York and Baltimore, but I'm actually working on a new project here in DC," Malcolm said.

Layla tipped her head innocently. "Really?"

Jasmine wandered into a wide, empty corridor. The walls were lined with large black-and-white prints encased in oversized glass frames. The photographs were lit by crisp, glowing circles of light. It looked like a gallery. Jasmine considered the stark contrast of this wide space to the cluttered homemade museum her mother had constructed at home. She noticed a familiar image at the end of the hall. The photograph featured a Black woman standing at the end of a kitchen table, opposite the camera. Jasmine quietly approached the photograph and stared. The woman stared back at her with a confident smirk. "Shit," Jasmine whispered. A Carrie Mae Weems print? How rich are these people? Jasmine thought to herself. The print was smaller than she imagined it would be. But it felt big somehow. The woman looked like she had a secret. Jasmine didn't know what the secret was but she knew that face. She knew that feeling. A woman's knowing look. A memory. Something flickered in her peripheral vision. Jasmine's eyes wandered past the photograph to the top of a wide set of stairs.

And there she was, the vampire. The woman from the cafe. Descending each step with slow and measured skill. That same razor-sharp jawline, those same full lips. Her ancient cheekbones. Her glowing skin looked rich against her white cotton tunic. The hem of the garment danced at her knees. The fabric was so thin Jasmine could see the white tank top beneath it. Her slacks were tight enough to see the strength in her calves. The vampire's long locs were swept up into a wild bun, strays bouncing with each step down. Her eyes held that same glaze of boredom. She looked out at the people in the room as if she'd done it a thousand times before. As if nothing would surprise her.

Jasmine wondered if she'd finally lost her mind. Was she imagining this? Something like sleep-walking pulled her closer as she watched this woman descend. When the vampire reached the bottom step, a look of recognition brightened her expression. She nodded at David, cutting his way through the room. Jasmine snapped back to reality, realizing too late that she'd walked nearly all the way to the foot of the stairs.

"Zora!" David called out as he rushed across the room with Ella at his side.

"This is who I wanted you to meet. Ella, this is my sister

Zora," David said.

And even Ella, the straightest woman in the world, was visibly taken aback by the vampire's androgynous beauty as they shook hands.

David turned his head. "Ohh! Hey Jasmine!" he called out.

Jasmine froze as everyone turned to look at her. She closed her eyes, exhaled, then approached the trio, smiling politely.

"Haaaay," Jasmine said, pretending to be casual.

David looked at Ella. "Now my sister can meet your sister!"

Jasmine looked at the vampire, who stared blankly back at her.

"Jasmine, this is my sister-slash-housemate, Zora. Zora, this is Jasmine, Ella's sister!" David was endlessly tickled by this situation. Ella eyed Jasmine with a nudge nudge look.

Here they are, Jasmine thought. David and Zora, the two princes from her mother's vision.

"Nice to meet you," Zora said coolly as she held her hand out. Jasmine took it. They shook like business associates.

"Actually, we've already met—" Jasmine began. The music in the room seemed louder.

"What's that?" Zora asked.

"Nice to meet you," Jasmine replied. Zora's gaze quickly flitted to the far corner of the room.

"Ella, I have one more person for you to meet and then you have to see the music room. Zo, don't disappear," David said, pointing at Zora. Ella waggled her eyebrows at Jasmine as they skipped away. Zora and Jasmine stood awkwardly alone together.

The silence between them lasted for what felt like an eternity.

"I've seen you before, actually," Jasmine offered. She started sweating under her arms.

"Oh yeah?" Zora replied distractedly.

"You came into my cafe the other day. The T Spot?" Jasmine searched Zora's eyes for a feeling.

"Oh. You work there?" Zora asked, her eyes wandering

across the room.

"It's my cafe. I own it."

Zora turned. She took Jasmine in. "That's right. Yes. You were talking with Marie about the coffee." Zora nodded.

"Yeah," Jasmine replied. She nodded and turned to look for whatever Zora seemed to be staring at. She hated when people couldn't maintain eye contact.

Zora said nothing.

"I guess it didn't go well?" Jasmine said. She folded her arms as they stood side by side, looking at nothing together.

"What didn't go well?" Zora asked.

"Your date. It was . . . short?" Jasmine said casually.

Zora turned to consider Jasmine for the first time.

And there it was. Jasmine had said just enough to shake Zora out of the daydream she seemed so consumed by. She nearly smiled.

"It was as long as I needed it to be. The date," Zora replied.

"What? Ten minutes?" Jasmine said.

"Well. I met her. We talked and I knew it wasn't a good fit. You know?" Zora said as she took Jasmine in.

"I see. I met her too. And she seemed lovely," Jasmine replied, smiling. Was she flirting?

"I agree. She was lovely. Also, she wasn't for me," Zora said.

Jasmine fumed. That poor girl probably cried her eyes out over that ten-minute date. But of course. Someone as gorgeous as Zora could have her pick. Jasmine exhaled aggressively.

"Right. You didn't try the food either. I noticed."

Now Zora looked amused. She folded her arms and smiled as she spoke. "Also, not for me," she shrugged.

"So, you're basically judging something you never tried. Right?" Jasmine's voice sounded a bit angrier than she intended it to be. This is definitely not flirting, she thought.

"What's that?" Zora asked.

"I mean, you can't judge something you haven't actually

tried. You should give things a chance."

Zora's eyes widened slightly. "I should give things a chance . . ."

"Yes," Jasmine said. She thought for a moment. Zora's eyes took Jasmine in again. Feeling disarmed, Jasmine folded her arms.

"I don't know. I doubt a ten-minute date is long enough to give someone a chance. You know? And you didn't even try the food. What are you, gluten-free or something?"

"No," Zora said flatly.

Jasmine's mind drifted for a moment. She'd forgotten her point.

"Am I missing something?" Zora asked. She spoke slowly, drawing out the length of her words.

"I don't know you. I'm just saying. You should try things, you know? You should try things."

Zora stared at Jasmine. ". . . Right," Zora replied.

Jasmine turned on her heel and squinted her eyes shut as she walked swiftly away. You should try things. YOU SHOULD TRY THINGS? What in the gay hell was she talking about? She wanted to disappear. As she pushed past the horde of beautiful Black folks, her mind landed squarely at the truth. She had no respect for this pretty boy, this Zora person. She hated everything about her. Yes. She was fine. Yes, she was physically attractive, practically perfect. But she wasn't a nice person. She didn't care about or even notice Jasmine's presence. Jasmine didn't chase people who didn't notice her. And yet. She cared what Zora thought. Why did she care so much what this person thought of her? Jasmine walked faster, the words YOU SHOULD TRY THINGS burning into her brain.

Jasmine crashed into someone dancing. A hoard of people were drunkenly electric sliding and howl-singing to Frankie Beverly and Maze. The music was suddenly too loud and chaotic and everything smelled like vodka and everything annoyed her. Jasmine looked desperately around the room for an ally. As the only other blasphemous partygoers in black, her sisters were easy to spot. Layla was cackling at an older man's jokes. Ella was grinning at the bar, watching David shake a cocktail with ridiculous enthusiasm. Where the fuck am I? Jasmine thought. She hurried to the glass door and slipped away from the noise.

In an instant, the hush of the trees pulled her back into her body. She sighed into the heavy summer air. The sky was purple with the last milky stroke of sunlight. She walked down the deck stairs and stood by the pool, staring for a moment at the flickering mirror of trees and sky on the water. She lay down in the grass and looked up at the branches swaying. Sparrows fluttered and chirped in the bushes. The forest sang her a soft lullaby as the sky melted into blue. "Hey, God," Jasmine whispered into the night. A couple years in recovery and Jasmine still didn't really know how to pray. Her concept of God was flexible. Sometimes God felt like an iron-fisted supervisor. Sometimes God was a song that made her cry. A delicious orgasm. Tater tots. Grief. For Jasmine, God took a thousand shapes every day. But most often, Jasmine saw God in the trees. She closed her eyes, her ears drinking in the ocean hush of breeze in the leaves. Just then, the screen door opened, releasing a flutter of music and laughter. She heard soft footsteps in the grass.

"Hey," Layla said, her face appearing in the sky. "You okay?" She asked as she sat at Jasmine's side.

"Yeah," Jasmine said, closing her eyes.

"Fucking rich people," Layla said. She lay down and looked up at the sky.

"Fucking rich people," Jasmine repeated softly.

The porch light cut on as the screen door opened. David and Zora laughed as they walked out onto the deck. Layla and Jasmine huddled together, looking upside-down at the two figures.

"Oh shit." Jasmine sat up.

"Shhh!" Layla hissed as she pulled Jasmine down into the

slope of the lawn.

"Let's go," Jasmine whispered.

"Hold on," Layla whispered back.

Jasmine and Layla listened from the shadows of the lawn.

"I like her a lot. Don't you like her?" David paced the deck excitedly as Zora casually leaned back against the rail.

"You like everyone," Zora said, as she studied her watch.

"This is different." David raised his index finger solemnly.

"How is this different?" Zora replied.

"She's smart. But in a different way. I feel like she's deeper, you know?"

Zora sighed. "Okay. She's smart and deep. You want me to help you pick out a ring?"

David pulled at a deck chair. "I'm serious."

Zora slapped David on the back. "She's very cute. But we just got here. Let's take it slow. OK?"

"OK." David slumped. Then he sat up, suddenly excited again.

"What about Jasmine? Did you like her? Ella said she's gay!"

Zora sighed. "You can't set me up with every gay girl you meet. Especially not your new girlfriend's sister—"

"But she's cool! I thought you'd really like her!"

Zora shrugged. "She's a little strange."

Jasmine felt Layla's hand squeezing hers.

"What does that mean?" David scoffed.

Zora walked to the edge of the deck and looked out into the night. "I don't know David. The women in DC are a bit underwhelming, you know? Don't you find this town a bit boring?"

David wrapped an arm around Zora's shoulder. "Oh Zora. Zora, Zora, Zora. My sister, my sister. When we're in Brooklyn, you want Atlanta. When we're in Brazil, you wanna go to LA. When we're eating sushi in Tokyo, you want tapas in Barcelona. You feel me?"

"What is that supposed to mean?" Zora scoffed.

"The grass is greener, bruv. Nothing is good enough for you. And everyone, shit—every thing underwhelms you."

"So?" Zora looked at her watch.

"What do you want? You want a girl to overwhelm you?" David asked.

"Let's get you some water," Zora said, pulling the sliding door open and holding her little brother as they walked back in.

"You're too good for everybody. Shit, if I wasn't your brother, I definitely wouldn't make the cut. I'd underwhelm your ass too—" David's voice faded as he closed the sliding glass door.

Jasmine and Layla lay in silence for a moment.

"Well, that's fun. You ready to go?" Jasmine asked.

"You are not boring," Layla whispered fiercely.

Jasmine smiled, her eyes watching the trees lean with the wind. "Aw, honey. Thank you. I know."

7. ELLA

Meet me at the bridge tonight.

Ella and David stood on the dirt path along the canal. Ella's long summer dress fluttered at her ankles. She rested her hands on the stone wall. Since before she could remember, Ella could touch a stone, a wooden table; she could touch a person and she would hear things. It was only a matter of listening. The memories sounded like chords. Melodies that came from instruments she'd never heard before. The memories sang songs with no words. Just melody, energy and space—a subconscious score. She didn't understand what the sounds meant, and she didn't understand what she was supposed to do with this knowing. Her sisters knew what to do with theirs. Layla used her magic for activism. Jasmine used hers for cooking. For Ella, magic was harder to channel into action. She enjoyed singing but she wasn't a musician. She didn't have any way to translate the sounds into something people could hear. Ella only knew she had to choose when to listen.

As a child she heard too much. The memories would overwhelm her. Some memories were none of her business. She learned to tune out the memories in her client's muscles. She didn't listen to the concrete walls of office buildings. She didn't listen when she touched money. Some memories were too painful. And the wound songs were always louder than the other memories. Pain could sound like screaming. The sound was hot and pulsing, an infection collecting blood at the surface. She could hear love too, but only if she listened closely. Those sounds were more quiet. Love wasn't screaming hot and loud like a wound. To Ella, love memories sounded like a hushed wind. Like the sound of someone's breath in a deep sleep. Or the sound of freshwater trickling through rounded stones.

Georgetown wasn't her favorite place. Of all the neighborhoods in DC, this was perhaps the richest, whitest, and most conservative. White people here donned boat shoes and polo tees unironically. In Georgetown, they didn't have the sense to mask their filthy rich aesthetic with that bo-ho quirk, like the liberals in Takoma Park. The people in Georgetown were summers in Nantucket, waspy rich. But the neighborhood was old world beautiful. Cobblestone streets and brick homes with freshly painted shutters. To Ella, the stones felt like portals. They held memories. Love, wounds and ancestral gossip. Ella was careful not to read too deeply. Two hundred years ago, Georgetown was a port for slaves. Those memories soaked into the old structures too. She brushed her fingertips along the stone wall. She felt the crumbling surface of the rock and the soft, green tufts of moss. Her fingertips vibrated. She heard a quiet memory in the mossy stone. The chord sounded like one hundred summers ago. When Georgetown was a Black neighborhood, the shadow of this bridge harbored a secret young love. It sounded like a breathy hum. Meet me at the bridge tonight. The sweetness of a first kiss. There was something sad in the music, too. Something that kept the young lovers apart.

Ella pushed into the stone, closed her eyes and lost herself in the melody.

"Are you okay?" David asked softly. His hand hovered in the air above her hand.

"Yes. I'm sorry . . . I just love these old bridges," she said.

She smiled and skipped along the dirt path, shaking the melody from her mind.

Ella didn't tell her sisters about the date. She had the feeling that Layla and Jasmine would find something to roll their eyes at. Lunch on the water with the prince. A stroll along the canal? A picnic with the pretty rich boy? How quaint. How very cute, they'd say. Layla was too busy saving the world to take boys seriously. And Jasmine was deeply wary of most cis guys, especially when they were courting her sisters. To be fair, she was right to be. Most men Ella dated weren't much to write home about. They were mostly handsome and kind, but not extraordinary. This felt different. David felt different.

The sweet, tart aroma of barbeque seeped from the brown paper bag in David's arms. He grinned at her. Men had tried to impress her before, but this was the first time she truly wanted to reciprocate. She wanted to impress him too. She bought a new dress and wore her hair down. She shaved her legs! That morning, Ella sat naked on the floor of her bedroom, her two hands pressed to her heart. She whispered a prayer to the ancestors:

> *Spirit. Protect my heart. Give me the strength to honor you. And if it's right for us, let me spend some sweet time with this sweet boy.*
> *If it isn't right. Please. Protect my heart.*
> *Protect my beautiful garden of wildflower self-love.*
> *And please. Don't let this boy shake me.*
> *Don't let him shake me.*

David smiled at Ella, his hand outstretched, reaching for her. She stared at it for a moment before she rested her hand in his. He led her up a set of stone steps. At the top, they found themselves on a landing of grass and wide granite adorned with colorful graffiti tags. Ella stepped toward the edge of the drop-off, looking out at the expanse of the Potomac River, Virginia dwarfed in the distance.

"Wow," she gasped.

"Right?" David smiled, watching Ella take it all in.

Ella pulled a blanket across the grass. David laid out the food: a selection of ribs, wings, mac and cheese, summer salad and fried brussels sprouts.

"Can I make you a plate?" David asked.

"Yes."

Ella took a breath. She stared out at the wide ribbon of water.

"I'm starving," she said.

"Me too," David said as he handed her a plate heavy with food. Ella smiled politely.

"David, this is enough food for a small village."

"So what?" he said, scooping a half pound of mac and cheese onto the plate.

"Honey. I know I'm thick, but I can't eat all this."

"You probably should," David replied as he plopped an extra rib onto her plate.

"Okay ..."

"I'm serious," David continued. "I've seen you at the gym. Out here running 10K on a treadmill. You gotta keep your strength up."

Ella squinted. "Do you have a food fetish I should know about?" Ella asked, eyeing the plate cautiously.

"I don't. But I have a feeling I'm going to love watching you eat," David said grinning.

Ella rolled her eyes. "Don't be weird."

David threw his hands up. "Not weird. Just excited to share food with you," he said.

"Whatever. And just so you know, stalking women at the gym is generally frowned upon," Ella said, daintily waving a hot sauce packet.

"Good thing I'm so cute," David said, waggling his eyebrows.

Ella ignored him, her teeth now sinking into the tender flesh of a perfectly cooked rib, the sweet, tangy sauce sticking to her lips. David watched her as he bit into a fried chicken wing. They simultaneously sighed. "Mmmmmh."

Ella watched David as he fell back in laughter. Ella laughed too. His joy was contagious, effusive. She felt boyish with him.

"Did you always live in DC?" Ella asked, a barbeque smudge staining the corner of her mouth.

"Mostly," David replied. "We grew up here. Then I went to Morehouse. Tried to do the art thing in Atlanta for a while. Pretty much failed miserably at that. I tried and failed a whole rack of things and eventually I moved to New York to work for my dad. Then Zora and I moved back to DC for Dad's expansion."

The joyful lilt of his voice fell slightly.

"What kind of art? And what kind of failure?" Ella asked.

"I tried a little bit of everything. But music production was always my favorite. I actually had a little mini hit collab with this R&B folk singer in Atlanta. It was really cool. Got some props and shout-outs from a couple fancy blogs."

"You called it R&B folk?"

"Yeah, it sounds weird, but it's actually really beautiful, unique stuff. Kind of like mixing bluegrass strings with 808s. The singer has this really smooth soulful voice."

"I'd like to hear it," Ella said.

"Yeah, I'll play it for you some time," David said, grinning.

"That doesn't sound like failure to me," Ella said.

"Yeah. But I basically never made enough money. And Dad kept offering me this job," David said. He looked down and pulled at a tuft of grass.

Ella nodded.

"I still do it on the side, though. The music. I know it's not serious, but I really love it."

David drummed his hands on his knees. "Did you always live here?" he asked.

"Yeah." She smiled meekly. "I grew up here and I went to Howard."

"YOU KNOW!" David recited the HU call with cartoon vigor.

Ella laughed. "I didn't finish though. I decided to go to school for massage therapy instead."

Condensing the events of her life into a few sentences made it sound so small. "I thought about moving, but I kept putting it off. And then Mom got sick. We all felt like we had to move back home to help her. She's better now. But I don't know. Everyone I love is here. Seems hard to leave now." She looked out at the water.

"They're lucky to have you." David smiled.

Ella picked up a rib, then placed it back on her plate.

David stared. "Hey," he said, looking back at her.

"Hey."

"I . . . want to kiss you," he said, staring at the jewel of sauce in the corner of Ella's mouth.

Ella grinned, licking her fingers.

David leaned in. He smiled. "I know I'm supposed to wait until I tell you my life story and you tell me yours. But—"

Ella felt the heat in her cheeks.

"Right now, I'm so jealous of that barbecue sauce on your upper lip." David smiled playfully. Ella wiped her mouth, blushing. "Wow, David. So, is this your hustle? You buy a girl some food and tell her you're jealous of the mambo sauce on her lips?"

David fell back with laughter. "Mambo sauce, alfredo sauce, barbeque. It works every time," he said.

"Wow David, you're a fucking genius!" Ella said, shaking her head.

"Hey, give me some credit!" He laughed. "I could have done

the old you've got something on your lips, here let me get it thing."

"David. You are silly."

"Ella. Do you like silly?"

Ella sighed. She looked down, lifted a sauce-drenched rib to her mouth, and smeared it across her face. David exploded with laughter. Ella puckered like a fish: her lips, cheeks and chin smudged with a glossy streak of barbeque sauce. "Oh no," she said in a breathy vixen voice.

"Do I have something on my face?" She fluttered her lashes and flashed a toothy, saucy smile.

She crawled to David and pressed her face against his. When his hand met the nape of her neck, Ella listened to the sound of David's song. She listened from a distance, from a door in her mind. Just to hear the tone of him. She couldn't remember ever hearing a song like his. It sounded like an upright bass and low, low voices—if the melodies were made of smoke, thick blankets, and warm water. They laughed as they shared a sticky, sweet barbecue kiss.

8. LAYLA

Layla stepped from the subway escalator and strutted down U Street. Hot neon light pulsed around her. The smell of fried everything hung in the air, music poured out of the bookshelf buildings, cars honked, people flooded the streets. As she walked, she took note of the shops with new names. The brick storefronts with new coats of paint. U Street on a Saturday night was a messy metropolitan buffet, offering up paper plates of hot jumbo pizza slices, fresh donuts, tacos, half-smokes, and a few dozen swanky bars full of drunken optimists. Layla hated these people. Every last one. She knew exactly who they were. They all moved here a year ago. They all worked on the Hill. They all belonged to the carefree club of white kids swimming in connections and generational wealth. Mommy and daddy paid rent for their place in NOMA or COHI or some other newly colonized and abbreviated neighborhood. They loved running along the Potomac as the sun rises and taking photos of the cherry blossoms blooming. They loved wearing red at the Nats games. They never went east of the river because SOUTHEAST IS DANGEROUS. And they all loved, loved, loved U Street. This ten-block corridor afforded them the space to feel safe and a little bit dangerous all at once. Just the right amount of city.

Layla put a little stomp into her walk. Her hair was picked

out, wide and supple. Her very own black cloud. She wore a plain black tee, cutoff shorts, and red Chuck Taylors. She walked stubbornly in the middle of the sidewalk, offering drunken passersby one of two choices. Option one: move the fuck around her. Option two: collide. She secretly savored those collisions. A twenty-something GW kid wobbling in her heels. A boisterous middle-aged businessman doused in cologne. She could knock anyone off their course. Most people were too self-absorbed to see her. But when they stumbled, confused and spinning to the curb, they had the privilege of watching her walk away, unfazed. It was her small indulgence. These people were colonizers. Getting shoulder-checked was a small price to pay for her hometown.

Ordinarily, Layla avoided U Street. She avoided this neighborhood altogether. To Layla, U Street was one Starbucks away from becoming a tourist trap and she'd sooner visit the White House. But she couldn't let it go. This place had history. Growing up, Mama Ro taught her daughters the Black histories of the world, starting with DC. She'd talk at them every car ride home. Jasmine and Ella would roll their eyes and sigh, exhausted from a full day of being the agreeable, above average students they had to be. But Layla listened, soaking in all the history she could. As a kid, she heard whispering spirits speaking to her in those history lessons.

As Layla walked down U Street, she remembered fragments of her mother's stories. She stopped at the corner and looked at the expanse of row houses and concrete. The whole street turned into vapor. The white kids, the neon and all the clattering sounds of that night became a river of light and shifting time. Layla could see it. Ro's voice narrated a vision of DC one hundred years ago. There was always joy. You just have to remember it. Close your eyes and dream it up, Mama Ro would say.

> *"It was 1921. They called it Black Broadway, the bloom of DC's Black arts movement. The sister of the*

Harlem Renaissance. DC had the Saturday Nighter salon parties for the deep, artsy types. You would step into a living room filled to the brim with breath, voices, weeping trumpet melodies, poetry and cigarette smoke. A pair of women holding hands somewhere in the hazy darkness. A young man standing in the center of that crowded room, describing his father's hands. Somebody fell in love. Somebody cried. We gave voice to our yearning here. Black Broadway was the exception to the rule. Three hundred Black-owned businesses blooming on and around U Street. Black folks came from New York, Philly, North Carolina, Richmond and Boston just to walk this street in their shiniest shoes. At the 12th Street Y, Black folks organized protests, movements, and celebrations. Ellington played at the Caverns. U Street had it all. Our restaurants, churches, the movie theater where we could sit anywhere we wanted. The butcher. The Whitelaw Hotel, Duffy's Tavern. Tiny, brown-skinned ballerinas learning to pirouette at Hammond Dance Studio. You could Charleston at The Hollywood. Buy your sweetheart an armful of pink carnations at Lee's Flower Shop. Black people made money here and we had a Black-owned bank for it too. Young men sliding down the street in tailored suits and hats cocked back. Ladies in long fur coats with shining pressed curls."

Mama Ro dreamed it all up for them in vivid detail. Layla felt like she could see the orchestras, the cars with gleaming lacquer, the nightclub dancers with wide smiles and feathered costumes.

Layla loved her mother's way of teaching. Mama Ro taught her more than she could get at Wesleyan or Beechwood or any other fancy PWI. She taught with poetry and balance. She pushed back against the propaganda of Black folks painted as an endlessly suffering people. The pornography of Black tragedy that even some Black folks seemed to enjoy. Black folks frozen in the stream of the water hose. "We have to dream up the good. Teach ourselves how to find the joy in our history. There was always joy. That's why we're still here." Mama Ro said a lot of things that went right over Layla's head at the time.

In spite of Ro's sage advice, Layla always focused on the pain. All the shining shoes, horn sections, and moon glow were eclipsed by that pain. When Ro described the sad chapters of Black history, Layla felt her throat pinch tight with anger. Some part of her loved that feeling. It made her want to tear things down. Anger felt productive. Ro's voice lost its music when she told that part of the story. The poetry, the dreams turned into shadow.

> *"It was the 1960s. White flight increased with promises of integration. DC was still violently segregated and a whole lot of us were still suffering. The civil rights movement must have felt like a hard-earned glimmer of hope, what looked like the beginning of a change in this country. But all that change and movement hit that brick wall in 1968. King was murdered and an army of heartbroken people set the city on fire. Black people with nothing but their grief. And grief soldered its armor into anger. The first window shattered at 14th and U. History books call them riots. Three days of searing, screaming pain. Three days of glass breaking and fires burning. How do you mourn the loss of hope? The death of a messiah. Black business owners put "soul brother" signs in their windows, hoping the crowds would spare them. But it would take more than a sign to save*

them from the years to come. Then began the decades-long season of white flight from the city. The '70s and '80s brought the crack epidemic. The war on drugs put a third of DC's Black fathers and brothers into jail. Ro's generation watched Black people turn into zombies, zombies turned into corpses. At the end of the '80s, the construction on the U Street subway tore the whole street up so bad it looked like a war zone. And by the time the sparkling U Street metro doors slid open in '91, only three of the original three hundred Black-owned businesses remained. Ben's Chili Bowl, Industrial Bank, and Lee's Flower Shop."

A car horn blared. Layla opened her eyes, snapped back into her body. She stood in the window at Lee's Flower Shop. She looked out past the orchids, watching strangers barrel down the street. She wondered what the street looked like back then.

Laya walked out of Lee's with a bouquet of purple irises. She held the flowers close as she walked down the block and descended a set of dimly lit stairs. She ducked into the dark room, packed wall-to-wall with young Black folks. The music was loud. A ten-piece band crowded a small stage. Red stage lights beamed down on the drummer, congas, keys, synth, guitar, bass, and a gaggle of dudes on vocals. The crowd on the dance floor stepped and shuffled as the band attempted a go-go cover of Badu's "Window Seat." As soon as Layla's sneakers hit the sticky floor, she was dancing, flowers held high in the air. She sang along. She looked up at Sean, the bass player. A rasta beat-poet-looking dude with waist-long locs. Sean nodded at Layla when he caught her eye. She waved and stuck her tongue out at him. She closed her eyes and drifted back into the song. Layla danced until sweat ran down her neck and arms.

The beat was a time machine. She danced into the dream of her youth. She was her 14-year-old self at the high-school go-

go. The hard hit from the drum set. The flirtatious syncopated percussion. The yelling. The harmony. The room full of young Black kids from all over the city. She had her first kiss on the dance floor. A lanky boy named Justin with a sly smile. His lips were sweet and Big Red cinnamon spiced. The scraps of paper with scribbled numbers. Peeling off her puffy jacket, revealing a strappy tank top and too tight Parasuco knock-off jeans. She and her friends danced in a circle. Guys walked up to her and awkwardly, wordlessly tried to grind up on her. She developed a code with her girl Monica to signal if the guy was cute or busted. She'd dance with boys, but more than anything she loved closing her eyes and dancing, spinning, stepping by herself. This was her coming of age. She found West Africa in NW DC. Shadows of Blackness on the blonde wooden floors of a private school basketball court. A dark, sweaty gym full of legacy.

The drummer teased the cymbals as the song ended. Layla returned to her older, more jaded, twenty-three-year-old self. She cradled her flowers, clapping and whistling for more. The front man thanked the crowd as the band filed off stage. It felt too early to go home. But Layla knew why they ended the show. This old music venue was at the mercy of DC's new noise violation codes.

Fucking colonizers.

Layla and Sean walked together down U Street.

"These are for you." She handed him the flowers, now slightly wilted.

Sean held his hand on his heart dramatically. "For me?" he asked.

"Yes, for you," Layla replied, dully.

"Why Miss Layla Jones. If I didn't know you better, I'd think you were trying to win me back." Sean grinned, cutting a look over to Layla.

"Well, good thing you know me better." Layla gave him a no-nonsense look. She hooked her arm in his.

"You know I'll always be a little bit in love with you, Layla," Sean said, grinning.

"See, this is why we never worked. You are too damn emo my guy!" Layla said, shaking her head.

"And you aren't emo enough. As I recall."

"I'm emotional about work. Which feels a bit more productive than crushing on boys," Layla replied.

"Boys. That's your problem. Messing with these boys when you really need a man," Sean teased, shaking his head.

"I need a man like I need white friends. Hard pass."

"Damn, Layla."

"But I do need a favor," she continued.

"Of course you do," Sean said, nodding.

"I need the band to play an event for me."

"You gonna pay us in flowers?" Sean asked.

"No," Layla replied, annoyed. "I can do it on a small budget. But there's about a hundred of y'all, so I don't see how anybody could make any money in the first place..."

Sean interrupted her. "You can't, I repeat, you CAN NOT skimp on a go-go band, Layla. Trust me, we've all tried. You take one thing out, it's just wrong."

"Come on. Y'all can't take one thing out?"

"Nope." Sean shook his head.

"Not even the hype man who just dances and yell echoes everything y'all say?" she asked, exasperated.

"Not even Jameel," Sean responded, laughing.

"Well, tell me what y'all charge, and I'll make it happen. Okay?" Layla resigned.

"What's the venue?" Sean asked.

The couple approached a chainlink fence bordering a construction site. Layla stopped. She threaded her fingers into the fence and gazed out at the black abyss beyond it. A giant hole. Someone had torn down an entire block of U Street and carved a deep black hole into the earth.

"It'll be here," Layla said, keeping her eyes fixed on the texture of the dirt.

"Here?" Sean repeated in disbelief.

"The developers are having an official breaking-ground ceremony in four months. And I'd like to crash their party." Layla smiled.

"You want to crash their groundbreaking with a go-go?" Sean asked.

"Something like that. Honestly, I have no idea why. I just feel like we'll need y'all there at the protest." Layla said. She felt Sean's eyes on her. She looked at him, waiting.

"What?" she asked, annoyed again.

"Shit. You gonna change the world, Layla."

Layla rolled her eyes.

"I don't know what you're planning," Sean continued, all riled up. "I don't know what it's gonna look like, but I got a feeling . . . you gonna change the whole goddamn world."

"Well, I'm definitely gonna try." Layla sighed.

"We'll be there. Even Jameel," Sean replied softly.

He pulled her to his side and squeezed her playfully. They stared out at the darkness together. Layla imagined what it could be. She dreamt in silence for a moment.

"Do you remember what this block used to be?" she asked, weakly.

"I don't," Sean replied.

"Me neither."

9. JASMINE

The first cup of coffee was her favorite part of the day. The way the cream hit the surface of that black abyss. The swirling galaxy. That sharp, bitter scent in the air. The heat on her lips. The first cup always felt like hope.

And then she thought about Zora. Blah, blah, blah. Hot. Physically perfect. Blah, blah. ZORA. The actual literal embodiment of my fantasies. But she's mean and rude and she actually hates me and I'm fated to be obsessed with and annoyed by her face until the end of time. What a fucking snob. Gorgeous, selfish, spoiled snob. Underwhelming. Boring. Who cares? Blah blah blah. She didn't know shit about shit. She didn't know what she was missing.

Jasmine's gaze wandered. She looked up to the clock. 7:19 a.m. Marble was late. Again. Probably out being young and dumb and having wild, queer, college orgies. Good for them. Jasmine met Marble two years ago when she hosted a baking workshop for the Howard queer club. Marble was a naturally brilliant baker, and they became quick friends, despite their nearly ten-year age difference. Marble helped Jasmine with social media and manning the store. Jasmine liked to think they kept her young.

A tiny bell jingled as the door opened.

"Morning, morning, morning!" Marble sang as they walked into the cafe, their silky kimono fluttering. Marble always either looked like a queer priest from the future or the love child of Grace Jones and Jimi Hendrix. Marble also had a shaved head and when they worked together at the cafe, it looked like it was part of a very queer staff dress code.

Marble skipped to Jasmine and kissed her on the cheek. "Sorry I'm late!"

Jasmine rolled her eyes. "How did your workshop go? What was it again? Spanking for beginners?" Jasmine asked dully, as if that was a perfectly ordinary sentence.

"Spanking and the senses, actually. More of a 200-level course. And it was lovely. The workshop ran till 1 a.m. And the party ran till three so . . ." Marble gave Jasmine a wink.

"Jesus. Did you sleep?" Jasmine asked, shaking her head.

"No. But I meditated for an hour so I should be good. And I brought you a gift!" Marble was singing again, fishing something from their satchel.

"You meditated for an hour? Wow. The life of a twenty-something. If I did that, I would probably have a minor stroke." Jasmine sighed, shaking her head.

"You're not that old," Marble said.

"Who said anything about old?" Jasmine snapped.

Marble ignored Jasmine's attitude and handed her a soft knot of black rope. Jasmine held it up, frowning.

"This seems like a two-person gift," Jasmine said.

"It's an affirmation," Marble replied, lifting a pastry from the display case and taking a ravenous bite.

"What am I supposed to do with this? Tie myself up?" Jasmine asked.

"You're going to imagine who you'd like to tie up. Or who you'd like to be tied up by," Marble said, their mouth full of Danish.

"Great," Jasmine said flatly.

"Then . . . maybe you'll get laid." Marble cut their eyes to the wall.

"Hey, Marble?" Jasmine flashed a plastic smile.

"Yes, Jazz."

"Next time bring me a vibrator. Not a fucking affirmation," Jasmine said, imitating Marble's sing-song voice.

"You're welcome." Marble stepped into their work apron and sang their way to the storefront.

"So how was the housewarming?" Marble called out as they pulled a chair down from the table top.

Jasmine looked down at her beige cup of coffee. Too much cream. "It was fine," Jasmine blurted.

"Details?"

Jasmine sighed impatiently. "Pretty much what you'd expect. Rich Black people being rich. Fancy house. Fancy outfits. All that." Jasmine straightened a large painting behind the counter and stared up at it.

Marble skipped to the storefront. They turned the closed sign over, unlocking the door and glancing out to the street.

"And the prophecy? Did Mama Ro's vision come true yet?" Marble asked, turning back to Jasmine.

"Well . . ." Jasmine began.

Marble leaned in. "What? What happened?"

"Well. Mama wasn't wrong. Exactly. There are definitely two princes. And one of them happens to be a very handsome, very gay woman."

Marble squealed with joy. "Oh my god, oh my god!" Marble took Jasmine's hands and jumped up and down.

"No, no, no!" Jasmine interjected, shaking her head. "She is very handsome and also very rude and also she has absolutely no interest in me. So that's that."

"Are you sure?" Marble asked.

"I'm sure. It was actually humiliating. I talked. A lot. I tried to flirt? And ended up just being weird." Jasmine's smile turned an endearing shade of goofy. Marble smiled warmly. "But Ella and her prince seem like the perfect heterosexual match. And he really, really likes her. So mom was half right."

"Good for Ella," Marble said sincerely.

The tiny bell jingled.

Jasmine's throat was suddenly dry. She had to be seeing things. Was this a dream? David stepped into the cafe, grinning and waving. Zora followed behind him, having donned a slim-cut lavender button-up with a band collar and an ash gray suit. The strength in her arms pulled at the seams of her jacket. It fit her perfectly. Everything fit her perfectly. Jasmine's whole body contracted. She looked up at the clock, then at Marble, then David, then Zora. She couldn't imagine how and why they would show up to her cafe at 7:30 in the morning. And she couldn't think of a single word to say. Hello? Good morning? What are you crazy kids doing up so early? She thought and thought and said nothing. Marble watched the pair, staring at Zora.

"Jasmine!" David said, grinning boyishly. Zora smiled weakly as they approached the counter. "Hey!" David nearly shouted.

"Hey," Zora whispered.

"Heeeeey," Jasmine said coolly.

"Hiiii?" Marble interjected, their eyes darting from Jasmine to the two strangers, and back again.

"Um. David and Zora, this is Marble. Marble, this is David and Zora. We just met at their housewarming yesterday?" Jasmine smiled; eyes wide. Marble nodded with exaggerated enthusiasm.

"Aaaah. It's very nice to meet you both!" Marble cooed; their eyes fixed on Zora. Zora is definitely Marble's type, Jasmine thought. Zora is probably everyone's type.

"Can I help you with anything?" Jasmine asked, looking straight at David, avoiding Zora's eyes.

"Well, we were headed to a meeting with the board and I

heard you have the best pastries in the city," David said, peeking into the display case.

"And the best coffee," Marble interjected.

"There we go! And the best coffee! So we figured we'd come get some to go! If that's alright with you?" David flashed his winning smile.

"Of course." Jasmine smiled graciously. "What can I get you?"

"I'd like a coffee and a Danish. Zora?" David nudged Zora. She stared blankly at the menu.

"A latte and a croissant. Please?" Zora said, looking at Jasmine.

Jasmine busied herself with the register. "No problem. To go?" She asked.

"Yes, please." David smiled.

As Jasmine prepared the coffee, David and Zora explored the cafe. Admiring (or judging) the decor. Jasmine felt oddly self-conscious by the way Zora's eyes followed every line in the space. The T Spot was a clean and quirky space with a black, white, and yellow theme. The floors had classic black-and-white diamond tiles. The walls glowed with white and lemon cream yellow stripes. All the paintings were oversized images of ink blot tests. The paintings were abstract, but they all vaguely resembled vulvas. It was supposed to be cute. Funny, but elegant. Queer enough to make straight people a little uncomfortable, but not enough to keep them from spending money there. It was her style. She was proud of what she had made. But when Zora and David pointed up at one large painting, she winced. She looked down into the hot cup of espresso and considered making a design with the milk. She poured the milk into a swirling lotus flower, opening up as she tilted the cup. She stared down at the white foam flower for a moment, then took a spoon and scrambled the flower into beige foam. Marble watched Jasmine with a look of concern.

"Um. You okay, Jazz?" Marble asked.

"Yes. I'm fine." Jasmine nodded vigorously.

"Want me to ... bring them the coffee?" Marble asked.

"Yes, I would like that. Thank you," Jasmine replied, still nodding.

Marble handed David and Zora their cups. Jasmine attempted a smile, still confused about the purpose of the visit. Did Ella tell David what Zora said? Was this a pity visit to make up for that? Was this Zora's very weak way of attempting to apologize for insulting her? Or did David force Zora to come? All prospects seemed equally horrifying. Jasmine smiled through her paranoia.

"Thanks for stopping by. Come back soon," Jasmine said in monotone.

"We will! Thanks!" David grinned and waved as he turned to go. Zora didn't move. She stood at the counter. Her expression remained serious and distracted. She looked up at Jasmine and for the first time that morning, their eyes met. Jasmine held her breath.

"Thank you," Zora mouthed, then turned to leave. The bell rang and they were gone.

10. CHRCH

Amber ribbons of light cut through stained glass. Liquid flute melodies washed the vaulted walls of an old church. Coconut-oiled and shea-buttered hands floated up in the air. Mama Ro stood at the foot of the altar, breathing deeply. The loose cotton of her T-shirt stuck to her skin. Ro gazed up, watching her hands swim and turn like wisps of smoke. She bent her knees, and the worn wooden floor creaked beneath her. As she moved, the people followed. She smiled and they smiled. She laughed a wild, crazed laugh and the people echoed in an explosion of joy and sound. She tipped her head back and shot her hands up in the air with a high note that grazed the cathedral ceiling and gently soared back down to a thunderous low note. The people in the church followed, a sudden blossom of notes bending up and down. This was chrch. Not "c-h-u-r-c-h", rather—chrch without the "u," a Black feminist spiritual space. When Ro was in her twenties, she and her girlfriends invented this weekly tradition.

Ro remembered her grandmother's North Carolinian Baptist church with fondness. Of course, she clocked the hints of misogyny. The homophobia. The fear. But she loved the music. The smell of cakes and coffee and booming waves of voices singing together. That love kept her looking for God. As a grown woman, Ro encountered a rebranded kind of fear in her peers'

Afrocentric Christianity. These were the original Hoteps. The sons of Panthers who still called women "queens" and "sis." They put djembes and kente cloth on the altar. They sang Kwanzaa songs and mounted paintings of Black Jesus. They changed a lot about church but some things didn't change. For example, the music director was still very gay and still very deep in the closet. Some traditions just wouldn't break.

So, Ro looked for God elsewhere. She studied astrology. She wore only shades of blue for Yemeya. She read hooks, Parker, Angelou and listened to Makeba. She prayed alone in the candlelit corner of her studio apartment. All the Black intellectuals and artists in DC quietly searched for spirit. The lesbians and too-loud women. They all knew they were witches and priests. They had their spell books, stars and candles, but something was missing. Nobody worshiped together anymore. Their power and prayer was isolated. So, one Sunday afternoon, half a dozen Black women brought their tarot cards, crystals and star charts into a room and emerged with an idea.

chrch. A collective ritual, led by the flock. In terms of creed, chrch was not defined as any one thing in particular. It was about the people. It was built upon the practice of a rotating ministry. Every week the minister would change, and the minister could be anyone in the chrch. They could be an elder or a four-year-old. And they could lead the congregation in any way they pleased. They could bring popcorn and their favorite movie. They could play "Kind of Blue" on repeat or read Baldwin for an hour. chrch was about being close to Spirit and finding God in each other. It was their attempt to take the trauma and the patriarchy out of religion. Ro knew her people needed this. She could see it in how fast the word spread. The group grew larger and larger: congregations filling up living rooms, then basements, then parks and sanctuaries. People shared their rituals. They expressed grief. They danced and prayed. They shared hot coffee and cake. They sang songs with thick, churning waves of harmony. They made God big and wide. And then after five years of collective magic, chrch lost its congregation. Some folks wanted to find a brick and mortar. Some folks wanted rules. Others wanted men in leadership roles. Some didn't. But Ro believed that chrch had simply run its course. It healed a lot of folks and then they all moved on. People had work, kids, errands to run. The friendships and traditions faded away as the women grew up. By the time Ro was pregnant with Jasmine, everyone was just too busy to show up anymore. "Black women sometimes get too busy to keep saving the world," Ro would say.

Thirty years later, Ro's doctor told her she was dying, and the thought of dying made her yearn to live harder. She knew her calling was to hold the community. She found her power there. As facilitator. Sculptor of the container. She had her doting, worrying daughters. She had teaching. But she wanted more. She needed to do something with whatever life she had left. So she called every college, shelter, community center, and public school. She sought out the women who had open, empty arms. She sought out the women who had wounds and no one to tend to them. She called on Jasmine's queer communities. She met people who Jasmine called non-binary and genderqueer. She learned how to ask about pronouns. She built an army of Black women and queer folks who needed something. A hand to hold. A listening ear. An hour dancing in an old church on a Saturday morning. Nearly two months after receiving her cancer diagnosis, Ro gathered a booming congregation and made a whole new chrch movement in DC.

Ro opened her arms up to the sky and laughed from the bottom of her belly. The congregation laughed with her. Ro spotted her mischievous daughters in the back of the sanctuary, attempting to blend in.

The three sisters glowed together.

Ella laughed up at the ceiling. She felt that fizzy sheen of joy. She dreamt of David. Moments came back to her in warm waves.

She brushed her brow bashfully, then smiled into her hands.

And Layla leaned into a catlike stretch as she dreamt about her protest. She was building a production in her mind. She reconstructed the old photos of DC's Black Broadway. She envisioned a celebration. A choir of voices chanting and singing. She saw herself surrounded by protestors and wild, raw power. She imagined what her movement could be.

And Jasmine thought about sex. She shook her head. Horny in chrch. Again. Even in a feminist church, it felt like she was breaking a rule ... which of course made it even hotter. The congregation followed Ro as she tried her hand at some modern dance moves. Jasmine stumbled along, tripping a bit on herself. She glanced over at a boyish person on the other side of the room. Kinda cute, she thought, squinting. A little bandana with twists peaking out. Any diversion from her recent obsession with Zora was a blessing. The boy was shorter than she preferred, but also quite handsome. Snack sized. In her experience, what the shorties lack in height, they usually make up for in zeal. Napoleon complexes could be hot. Jasmine stared, moving slower. She dreamt of a world where queer AFAB folks cruised their crushes like gay men. She could simply stare this boy down and meet up in the bathroom. No names exchanged. Just efficient, emotionless sex. She imagined pulling on those twists and pushing the boy's face into her. Letting them fuck her with a thick, long tongue. The boy stared back at her. Jasmine looked away for a moment. She melted the fantasy into her dancing. Her hands lingered too long on her body. I could do it, she thought. I could totally have casual sex at feminist chrch. It would be fitting! It would be an adventure. It's probably what God wants for me. She nodded to herself.

When Jasmine looked back up, her eyes caught the razor glare of a femme in zebra-print sweatpants on a neighboring yoga mat. The boy suddenly looked away. The zebra-print femme watched Jasmine. Jasmine shot her eyes to the opposite side of the church. A territorial femme girlfriend. Fucking typical, she thought.

"Nobody wants your short-ass boifriend anyway," she muttered under her breath.

"And here it comes . . ." Layla said, gesturing toward their mother.

Ro gracefully leaned down to the boom box at her feet.

"Doin' the what?" Jasmine playfully sang.

"Doin' the butt!" Ella and Layla sang back with a practiced off-color harmony.

"I said doin' the whaaaat?" Jasmine repeated.

"Doin' the butt!" Ella and Layla sang louder.

The sisters muffled their laughter, catching the eye of one disapproving auntie.

A drum beat erupted into the room. A horn section of exclamation. EU's DC classic Da' Butt smacked every brick on every wall and echoed back. The women screamed with excitement. Jasmine covered her face, pointing at Ro's animated body rolls. Layla danced across the room to her mother and shimmied in a circle of sixty-year-old women. Ella giggled and the room lit up with movement. Everyone loved the Saturdays when Ro was minister. She always, ALWAYS played Da' Butt. Her joy was embarrassingly corny but it was also undeniably contagious.

"Every time!" Jasmine shouted.

"Shit. If it ain't broke." Ella shrugged.

Jasmine watched Ella sink into a slow twerk.

"Okay, okay!" Jasmine said, nodding to the beat.

Ella peeled her T-shirt off and waved it in the air like a flag. Her belly and breasts bounced as she played in the beat, Harlem shaking her shoulders.

"Ella!" Jasmine screamed. Seeing this, another woman shrieked with joy, pulled her T-shirt off and threw it across the room. Another followed suit and soon the whole room was full of shirtless people laughing, giggling and dancing.

Jasmine's mouth fell open. "Are you high?" Jasmine asked mid two-step.

Ella threw her shirt, hitting Jasmine square in the face.

"Nope," Ella said, grinning.

Jasmine stared at her sister. "Oh God. Are you in love or something?" Jasmine asked. She stopped to put a hand on her hip.

"Girl no," Ella said. She continued dancing.

"Are you fucking the prince? Is that it?" Jasmine asked warily.

"I. Am. A lady," Ella replied, clutching her imaginary pearls.

"You didn't answer me," Jasmine said.

"No. I am not fucking the prince," Ella said as she did a spin. "But. He does want me to come have dinner with his dad . . . ?"

"He wants you to meet Dad and y'all didn't fuck yet?" Jasmine asked, her arms folded now.

Ella shrugged.

"Damn," Jasmine said.

The sisters watched as the chrch congregation formed a circle. Ro set the example by dancing as silly, goofy wild as she possibly could. And the congregation followed her lead. They all danced and laughed with wide mouth, all-the-front-teeth smiles. They twerked and jumped and two-stepped. There were elders who looked like eight-year-olds. There were youngsters trying their very best to look grown. They all played in the beat, their joy pulsing from the center of the room.

Ella danced over to Jasmine and took her hand. Jasmine relented and danced with her.

"Will you come?" Ella asked as she twirled Jasmine.

"Nope," Jasmine said as she did the cabbage patch.

"Please?" Ella pleaded.

"Nope."

Ella stopped dancing. "David asked me to ask you. He really likes you," Ella said in her sweetest little sister voice.

"He likes everyone," Jasmine said, as she attempted to moonwalk.

Ella smoothed the back of her hair with an open palm. She chewed at her bottom lip.

Jasmine two-stepped closer.

"I don't want to go alone," Ella whispered.

"Why?"

"I like him. A lot," Ella said.

"And he likes you back; what does that have to do with me?" Jasmine asked, searching Ella's eyes.

"I don't know," Ella whispered.

"He would be a fucking idiot not to love you. Ella come on. You're a fucking bad bitch."

"Jasmine."

"You are," Jasmine snapped.

"But it's dinner with his dad! He seems so . . . intimidating. I want to be impressive, you know?"

Jasmine shook her head. "I said it already. You ARE a bad bitch. If his rich daddy isn't impressed by you, he can fuck off."

Ella thought for a moment. "I just want to be comfortable. You're the best part of me. You and Layla," Ella said with a weak smile. ". . . and I can NOT bring Layla." Ella nodded in Layla's direction across the room. She was twerking shirtless with somebody's grandmother.

Ella took Jasmine's hand. "Jasmine. Please."

As if summoned, Layla skipped across the room toward her older sisters. The three sisters danced wildly in their circle.

"OKAY I'll go," Jasmine sighed.

"Yes!" Ella squealed as she jumped up and down.

"Go where?" Layla asked, panting.

"To the rich boy's daddy's house for dinner," Jasmine said through a smirk.

Layla lifted an eyebrow.

"What?" Ella asked.

"Nothing!" Layla replied, her hands rising defensively up in the air.

"You made a face," Ella said, her hands on her hips.

"No I didn't," Layla replied.

"Your eyebrows did that thing," Ella said, pointing to Layla's face.

Jasmine stepped between her sisters. She wiggled into a goofy dance in her attempt at peacemaking.

"Okay, baby sisters. Here's what's up. Layla, you and I will support Ella to the best of our ability in her love affair with the handsome prince." Jasmine stared at Layla as she spoke. She then shifted her gaze to Ella.

"And Ella, you will give Layla the gift of not having to come to this dinner. AND. I will agree to come, but only under one condition!"

"Anything! Anything," Ella pleaded.

Jasmine's face was stone serious, her hands held together gravely. "I'm not coming if the other prince is there. Okay? No Zora."

Ella pulled Jasmine into a bear hug and nodded into her shoulder. "NO. ZORA."

11. MALCOLM

From the street, Malcolm Scott's house almost looked small. It was nestled into a hill on the Gold Coast of 16th Street. Jasmine did not tell Ella that she googled the address. She did not tell Ella that the house was estimated to be worth six million dollars. David beamed and waved at them from the doorway. As they crossed the threshold, they found themselves transported into another world. Jasmine cursed under her breath. Ella said nothing. The sisters took it all in. They walked around calmly as if they were not overwhelmed by the impossibly high ceilings or the new, sparkling appliances. Slender vases full of fleshy green orchids. Hand-crafted wooden dining chairs and forty-foot narrow windows looking out at the sunset. Jasmine kept her hands in her pockets. The sisters had seen fancy houses. The Beechwood Prep parents were all pretty wealthy, but this was next level. This is what rich-rich looks like, she thought. What movie stars' houses must look like. Understated and clean. The absence of things was what really made the place look rich. A wealth of empty space. It made you feel like you could breathe better. You could do anything you wanted in here. You could drive a car in this living room. You could roller skate! You could install a ninety-foot Christmas tree. Rich people would never actually do any of these things. But how good must it feel to know they could.

David gave them a brief tour. He waved his arms around, pointing out a few sentimental trinkets, his favorite artworks and features of the house. Jasmine tuned his voice out. She felt her jaw ache with envy. She didn't want to want all this. But she did. Who wouldn't? No loans. No coming up with the rent. No wondering if your mother would die because her healthcare was shit. The Scotts had the privilege to do everything because they chose to. Not because they had to. The freedom to cartwheel in your kitchen even if you never actually did.

"Ladies!" Malcolm emerged from behind the kitchen island.

"Hellooo!" Ella and Jasmine said sweetly, synchronized in their awkwardness.

"I'm guessing you're Ella, and you're Jasmine?"

"Yep!" Jasmine faked a smile as she replied. No, the very gay-looking one with the bald fade is not your son's girlfriend, she thought to herself.

"Such a pleasure to meet you. I'm Malcolm! But feel free to call me David's dad. Ha!"

Malcolm wrapped Ella up in a bear hug, then Jasmine. He bubbled over with joy. Jasmine recognized the roots of David's boyish energy.

"I'm so glad you both could make it!" Malcolm grinned. The sisters followed as he headed back to the kitchen. He bounced cheerily in a pair of worn jeans and a black T-shirt.

"I'm afraid my cooking is awful," Malcolm went on. "But I make a great summer salad and I've ordered some fantastic Jamaican food from Spice." Malcolm uncorked a bottle of red and tilted the glass as he poured.

"Your home is really gorgeous!" Ella gushed.

Malcolm grinned. "Ah, well I can't take too much credit. The design was all Zora."

Jasmine nearly flinched at the mention of Zora's name. She rolled her eyes. Begrudgingly, she had to admit it: Zora had good taste. Really good taste.

"Can we help?" Jasmine asked.

"Absolutely not. Please! Make yourselves at home!" Malcolm handed each sister a glass of red wine.

Ella took Jasmine's wine glass and discreetly handed it to David. David nodded. Malcolm took note of this.

"I'm sorry, Jasmine, I didn't even ask. Would you prefer white? Or a cocktail? I make a famously dangerous mojito . . ."

"Oh, no I'm okay," Jasmine began. She felt the weight of Ella's gaze.

"I think I also have an IPA. And somewhere in here there's a beautiful rosé—" Malcolm went on as he opened and rummaged through the oversized fridge.

"I'm sober. Actually," Jasmine said.

She watched David and Ella nodding in vigorous harmony. Malcolm emerged from the fridge.

"Well, that's very—very admirable," Malcolm said with a slow nod.

Jasmine smiled. "Thank you." She nodded back.

Malcolm glanced back into the fridge. "I'm sure I have something that—hmm . . ."

"Oh. Water is fine," Jasmine offered.

"Water," Malcolm repeated.

"Yep. I love water. I know people don't love water, but it's really like my favorite drink. Other than coffee. And it's probably too late for a latte."

Ella frowned. Jasmine squinted at Ella.

"What?" Jasmine whispered.

"I'm sure we have something more exciting to offer you than—" Malcolm went on, rifling through the fridge's depths.

"Ok, Dad. I'll take care of Jasmine's drink. Why don't y'all go ahead and sit down?" David gave his dad a shoulder pat.

"Alright, well," Malcolm said, reluctantly letting go of the refrigerator door.

Ella and Jasmine smiled stiffly as Malcolm led them to

the dining room.

When they sat down to eat, the table was glowing. A quiet bossa nova tune hummed from the kitchen. Curry and turmeric yellows, the deep reds of wine, tomatoes, oxtail, and a bright green summer salad shimmering with strawberries, corn, and goat cheese.

Malcolm raised a glass. The party followed his lead.

"To summer in DC. And to new friends." He flashed a wide smile at Ella.

"New friends," David echoed.

The sisters relaxed into the evening. Even Jasmine's shoulders unclenched as they ate. Malcolm was charming. In spite of his immense wealth, it appeared that he was not snobby. He was kind. He possessed all the endearing, goofy dad qualities Jasmine and Ella imagined a dad should have. Like the dads in the movies. Or the dads they met at their friend's houses in high school. Jasmine was pleased that he'd ordered out. She didn't call herself an expert by any means, but she did have strong opinions when it came to cooking. The Jamaican food was perfect. Jasmine managed to eat only one beef patty when she really wanted to eat four and slide the rest into her backpack. The salad was lovely, the vinaigrette light with a hint of sweetness. And David doted on Ella with graceful subtlety. Jasmine noticed the lovebirds holding hands under the table. If it were any other straight couple in the world, she would have sucked her teeth at this. A deep eye roll at the cliché. But Ella was so full of joy around him that Jasmine couldn't feel anything less than happy for her sister.

"I'd love to visit your café some time," Malcolm said, pointing at Jasmine.

"I'd love to have you." Jasmine pointed back.

"We're a big coffee-drinking family," David said, smiling at Ella.

"You know what. I'll have Justin grab coffee for the office

next week. I'll make sure he calls a day ahead so you're not swamped?" Malcolm grinned into his wine glass as he took a sip.

"Oh. That's so generous! Thank you," Jasmine grinned.

"So, was Layla busy tonight?" Malcolm changed the subject.

Ella and Jasmine exchanged a look. "Our sister . . . Layla?" Ella asked.

"Yes! I had the pleasure of meeting her at the housewarming. We must have talked a whole hour about real estate. I don't want to get ahead of myself, but I think I might have a protégé on my hands," Malcolm raised an eyebrow at David.

Ella looked at Jasmine and frowned.

"Well, she is. Very passionate. About real estate . . ." Jasmine said, watching Ella. Neither of them knew what kind of lie they were supposed to tell on Layla's behalf.

Malcolm nodded in agreement. "It's a challenge to find someone excited to chat about this stuff. Most Black folks have an aversion to talking about high-end development. Makes them uneasy." Malcolm poured himself another splash of red wine. He stood to offer some to David and Ella. They both refused.

"Why is that?" Jasmine asked, innocently.

"Well. Most people have no perspective for the economic angle. The investment required to develop in a city these days— it's necessarily high risk." Malcolm spoke with the precision of a well-practiced lawyer. He's delivered this speech before, Jasmine thought.

"High risk requires high yield." He gestured with his hands. "As much as we'd all like to live in a world with equal distribution of wealth, we just don't. And as long as we don't, well. The world keeps turning." Malcolm shrugged.

David sighed. Ella looked at her plate, praying for a new topic. And Jasmine fumed.

David placed his hand on the table. "Dad has problems with the G word," David said, glancing at Jasmine.

"Gentrification isn't necessarily a dirty word. But these

days the perception is such that—well, the perception is always negative," Malcolm said warily.

"Well, my perception is that it displaces Black and low-income communities. Especially luxury development. Is there another way to . . . perceive that?" Jasmine pretended it was a question. Her polite young lady act was fading away.

"You're absolutely right. And of course it's not fair," Malcolm said, nodding. "But that's why we're so passionate about the community outreach work we do. We can't level the playing field, but we can use our resources to give back as much as possible."

David shifted nervously in his seat.

"So gentrification is okay as long as you're making a profit and giving back? As much as possible?" Jasmine asked.

Ella cleared her throat.

Malcolm appeared unfazed. He sipped at his wine glass then sat back in his chair. "I love your passion, Jasmine. I would honestly expect no less from friends of David's. But I hope you'll consider this. When white people are wealthy, successful in their business, what does the world expect from them? How does the world perceive them? A rich white man is ordinary. He may be celebrated. He may be condemned. But ultimately, we expect nothing of him. If he gives to charity, he's a hero." Malcolm paused. "When a Black man becomes wealthy as a result of his successful business, the world expects him to correct the system? Reverse the effects of colonization, close the racial wealth gap, and lift every Black community out of poverty? Even if I had the ability to make a dent in all that, why exactly would that be my responsibility?" Malcolm's voice remained calm, but his smile faded slightly. "Gentrification is a product of capitalism. Not Malcolm Scott." Malcolm smiled. It was a good speech. He was older, wiser and richer than anyone at the table and nothing could shake his confidence.

Jasmine didn't fake a smile for him. She couldn't manage the polite gesture. She looked past him at the front door, imagining what Layla would say if she were sitting at the table. Imagining what she'd say if Ella's joy didn't hang in the balance. As Jasmine got lost in her hypothetical counterargument, a melodic tone hummed from the foyer as the front door opened.

Jasmine's wide-eyed expression was stuck for a moment as she watched Zora casually slip into the house. ZORA. Of course she's here, Jasmine thought to herself. Here's Zora, at the dinner party she was explicitly not invited to. There's Zora in her cafe on a date. Zora in her cafe at seven in the morning. Zora in her thoughts all fucking day. Because she's everywhere now, apparently. Zora sauntered into the dining room. Jasmine pushed her chair back as she stood up. Zora entered the room, expressionless.

Jasmine's eyes wandered up to Zora's locs, pulled into a bun atop her head. She wore fitted slacks and a button-down tee with cuffs that pinched at her arms. Zora's shirt was black with thin white lines, tucked neatly into her waistband. Jasmine glanced at Zora's belt. Her eyes drifted and caught on the pull of the seam. Don't stare, Jasmine thought to herself. Even in this just-left-the-office, metrosexual men's wear, Jasmine could trace every line of Zora's body. The strength in her abs, her biceps, her thighs. Jasmine was lost in this thought for a moment.

"OH hey!" David called out.

"Hey," Zora said as she stared at Jasmine.

"Hey," Jasmine responded in an uncharacteristically high voice.

Jasmine looked around. She realized she was the only one at the table standing up. She hurriedly sat back down.

"Zozo!" Malcolm lit up and reached out to hold Zora's hand. "I thought you were out of town this weekend?" He looked at her with confusion.

"I'm not sure why . . ." Zora said, as she glanced at David. David studied his food.

"Then come eat with us!" Malcolm continued.

Jasmine's heart skipped. She wanted so badly for Zora to stay. She also wanted Zora to leave immediately, so she could breathe and sit and talk like a normal person again.

"I can't stay," Zora said, as she handed Malcolm a folder. "Just making a delivery. Good to see you, Ella. Jasmine." Zora stared at Jasmine again. Jasmine was sweating.

"Not even a drink?" Malcolm smiled sweetly up at his daughter.

Zora looked at her watch.

Tssss. Rude, Jasmine thought. And what kind of watch was that anyway? A desperately masculine, leather-strapped, oversized thing. Jasmine hated it.

"Um. Alright," Zora said.

"Great! Malcolm's famous mo-ji-to?" Malcolm asked as he danced out of the room.

"Sure," Zora called back, as she sat across from Jasmine. She stared at the table. Jasmine felt the tension thicken with every second of silence. Zora pointed at the table suddenly.

"Let me help you clear." Zora leaned across the table to retrieve the wooden salad bowl. Jasmine closed her eyes. What was that scent? Cedar? The scent of Zora lingered. She could taste it.

"Oh please, Zora! You didn't even eat! Let us do it!" Ella chirped, as she collected the plates and utensils.

"Just sit down and stop being weird." David punched Zora's arm playfully, then gathered up the serving bowls.

By the time Jasmine reached for a plate, they were all gone. David and Ella shuffled into the kitchen. Ella looked back, catching Jasmine's wide-eyed expression. Ella mouthed SORRY as the couple walked away. Plates clattered in the distance. Malcolm seemed to have begun an impromptu mojito tutorial. Ella was oohing and wowing throughout the lesson to Malcolm's delight.

Jasmine sighed. Alone with Zora. Again. She would

definitely curse Ella out for leaving her like this. Zora stared at her. Jasmine's heart beat hard in her throat.

"How was dinner?" Zora asked.

"It was nice," Jasmine snapped.

"Good," Zora replied, nodding.

"How is . . . your weekend?" Jasmine asked.

"It's been okay," Zora began. "I had a lot of work for the firm. So not ideal. But I'm glad it's done," Zora said, her hands clasped together.

"What kind of work do you do?" Jasmine asked.

"Real estate law, mostly. For my dad's development group," Zora replied.

"Ah," Jasmine nodded.

"Yeah. It's not exactly thrilling. Editing contracts all day. But I'm good at it." She shrugged.

Jasmine tilted her head.

"Do you like it?" Jasmine asked.

"Well, it's work. I don't mind it. But—" Zora shrugged again. Her posture fell slightly. "I don't love it. To be honest."

"So. What do you love?" Jasmine asked.

Zora blinked. "What do you mean?"

Jasmine leaned forward. "Well, it's the DC cliche to ask what you do. Right? Whenever you meet anybody at a party or something, that's always the first question. What do you do. Like your job defines you," Jasmine continued.

"Doesn't it? In part, at least?" Zora asked.

"Well. Maybe for some folks."

"Right," Zora nodded.

"I like to ask people what they love. What do you love?"

Zora considered this. Jasmine watched Zora's eyes change. Her gaze fell. What was that look?

"I . . . I don't know," she said, thinking.

"You don't know?" Jasmine asked.

Zora closed her eyes. "No one ever asked me that before."

Zora blinked.

"Oh," Jasmine replied.

"I don't know," Zora said again.

"What else do you do? Besides work?" Jasmine offered.

"Well. I travel. I love food. I like to study design, architecture sometimes. But that's less about doing. More enjoying things other people do. Sort of frivolous I guess."

"It's not frivolous if you love it," Jasmine replied.

They sat in silence for a moment.

Zora shifted her weight. "What do you love?" she asked.

"I'm lucky. I actually do what I love," Jasmine replied. "I love baking. I love creating space for people to eat and feel comfy." Jasmine breathed into herself.

Zora nodded.

"You have a talent for it. Your cafe is beautiful," Zora replied. Her face remained expressionless.

"Oh. Thank you," Jasmine said, touched. She smiled in spite of herself.

"Is the business doing well?" Zora asked.

Jasmine's smile remained, but her bubble of joy deflated.

"It's fine," Jasmine lied. She took a breath. She could wax poetic all day about making work out of your passion. But what happens to the passion when the work fails? When business is bad. When you put your magic into the world and nobody wants it. When people don't care. She still didn't have an answer to that question. Jasmine searched for a pleasing conclusion to this topic.

"It's hard work." She rolled her shoulders back.

"Honestly, I'm better at baking than business," she said with a sharp laugh, now praying for the emotionless relief of small talk. Jasmine's fake smile grew wider as she fidgeted with a hole in her jeans. Zora stared at her blankly.

"Why do you do that?" Zora asked.

"Do what?" Jasmine asked, suddenly impatient.

"Why do you smile when you don't want to smile?"

Jasmine nearly scoffed. Her smile fell. "That's a good question. Maybe I was attempting to be polite?"

Zora considered this.

Jasmine went on. "But if you'd rather I not, just let me know. I don't want to underwhelm you." Jasmine smiled sincerely now. "You know how the girls here in DC can be so underwhelming? So boring?" Jasmine said, gesturing wildly with her arms.

Zora raised an eyebrow. "Ah."

"But you're absolutely right," Jasmine went on. "Why would I smile at you when I don't want to? I could just look at you and make a thousand assumptions about how and why you're not good enough for me. Is that what you do?"

Zora sat back in her chair, folding her arms. She squinted her eyes slightly, staring at Jasmine. Jasmine couldn't read her face.

"You heard me that night," Zora said, speaking gently now. Her voice was buttery. Low and smooth, melting into the air.

"Yes." The word barely left Jasmine's mouth.

Zora closed her eyes again. Her head tilted down. "I shouldn't have said that."

Jasmine said nothing.

"I was wrong. You're not underwhelming. That wasn't—I was wrong." Zora tripped on her words, losing grip of her composure for the first time.

"You . . ." Zora shook her head as she spoke. "You are . . ."

Zora squinted again. "Jasmine, you are . . ."

Jasmine flinched as Ella, David, and Malcolm cut the moment with raucous cheers and chatter, dancing back into the dining room with drinks.

"I made you a NO-jito," Malcolm announced to Jasmine proudly. Jasmine nodded.

"Basically, just mint, sugar and limeade." David laughed.

"Thank you. Wow. This is lovely." Jasmine took the glass into her hand. She felt Zora's eyes on her. When she returned the gaze, Zora didn't flinch. She stared. Jasmine looked away again.

Zora stood with finality. "I wish I could stay. But I have to go."

"Oh, come on, Zozo! Stay!" David whined.

"What about the mojito?" Malcolm sighed.

"Next time."

Zora smiled cordially at Ella. "So good seeing you again, Ella. David. Love you, Dad." Zora kissed her father on the head. Jasmine's chest throbbed at this expression of tenderness she'd assumed Zora incapable of. She held her breath when Zora's eyes met hers.

"Jasmine."

"Zora."

Zora nodded to her and smiled. And Jasmine knew in that moment—she was lost to this woman. Lost in that smile. Zora was already beautiful. Terrifyingly so. Mean and gorgeous and rude. But her smile. This was a shade of beauty Jasmine couldn't bear. A warmth Zora never once showed in her presence. No. No. No. Don't fall in love with a snobby prince. She is cruel and out of your league and just STOP IT. Jasmine told herself she didn't care. She wouldn't. She smiled and nodded at David's jokes. She sipped her drink. She didn't notice Zora turn to leave. She didn't watch Zora walk down the hall to the front door. She didn't stare at Zora's ass as she walked. She didn't wish Zora would turn and come back. And Jasmine felt absolutely, positively nothing when the door slammed closed.

12. LAYLA

The Rise DC office thrummed with music and energy. Layla's shift ended at five, but she decided to stay late. She needed a strong proposal for the action, and so far nothing clicked. Carmen offered to stay late too. She said she wanted to help Layla brainstorm and offer feedback, though Layla had the suspicion that Carmen had doubts about Layla's skills. Either way, Layla welcomed the help. She was stumped. So she quietly asked for the ancestors to join them. She played her favorite Ellington record on the office speaker, a solo piano concert somewhere in Paris in the '80s. No orchestra. No bells and whistles. Just melodies like rainy days dripping with nostalgia. She turned it up, and the whole office was fuzzy with the blanket of an old recording. She burned Palo Santo and danced the smoke through the office. Layla and Carmen paced loops around the white board. Lines, scribbles, photographs, and maps littered the wall like the ramblings of a conspiracy theorist. Carmen sipped at a mug of cold coffee. Layla bounced restlessly, pausing for a moment with the fragment of a thought.

"What if we..." she began, looking up at the board. "No, no, no, no." She went on pacing, shaking her head.

Layla had to write her proposal by Wednesday. This would be the biggest action she'd planned since her start at Rise DC. The biggest protest she'd planned in her life. The assignment lit a fire in her. She hadn't cared this much about anything since college. She glanced down at her notebook, a finger grazing the collection of hastily scrawled notes. The list of her favorite protest movements. She focused on one cluster of notes: the 1980s.

- AIDS Coalition to Unleash Power (Act Up) curates a flood of bodies on Wall Street. Die-in on the stone steps of government buildings.
- Hundreds of people lie down on the pavement to represent the thousands dying daily of AIDS. Death. Visual. Urgent. Protestors become it, literally embody it. And the world can see.

Layla had only learned about the Act Up movement in college. Her elite DC high school somehow managed to leave the AIDS epidemic out of their world and US history lessons. The history baffled her. She remembered visiting the AIDS quilt on the mall with Ro when she was a kid. She remembered looking across the expanse. Attempting to feel the weight of it all. How could the government allow so many people to die in silence? Of course, she knew the US government was capable of overlooking the deaths of Black and poor folks, but wealthy white men? She couldn't imagine the stigma of queerness being so powerful that it overruled the privilege of whiteness and class. Layla skipped through her notes down to the Black Lives Matter movement. She had marched with them a dozen times. She had felt hot tears streaming down her face in the sea of protestors. Marching with BLM, Layla felt the conflicting mixture of grief and pride. Screaming, singing, "Who keep us safe? We keep us safe!" She would march in the streets every day if she could. Just to do something with her sadness. It was her only way to mourn and honor all the lives stolen. There was beauty in all that grief. Layla sat back in her chair and gazed up at the off-white ceiling tiles. Her body stiff, her mind in a cloud, she took a deep breath. She prayed for her power to come tonight. Layla prayed for an action that grew from its predecessors and bloomed into something different. Layla. Think.

She knew this was her calling. Layla's magic was in building community. She was born to create spaces for people to see each other, to collect. She may have been a shitty friend. And most of her romantic relationships were . . . brief. But it wasn't out of self-centeredness. She just couldn't stop working. She couldn't stop organizing. She could never do enough. For Layla, every taste of change felt like touching God. DC needed the Black community to claim it. Shit. Brooklyn, Oakland, Atlanta, London—the whole fucking world needed the Black community to claim it. It shouldn't be our jobs but nobody was going to hand it to us. But the way she saw it, Black folks were responsible for both the cultural and capital wealth in this world. If nobody was going to give us reparations, we have to take them. Layla's brain danced circles around her. What am I doing? Why am I doing this? What the fuck difference will it make? She felt like the director of the world's oldest play. The drama of dissent: the people versus the power. And since this play had been staged so many times, she had to find a way to reinvent it for this moment. What kind of protest does DC need right now? She lit a stick of incense and closed her eyes. The warm, earthy scent transported her. Ellington's keys swelled and trickled softly. Layla imagined Ro in that old church sanctuary. The queer folks and old folks and her crazy mamma, dancing topless in the morning light.

"It could be a block party . . ." Layla heard herself say aloud. "A celebration . . ." she continued. Her thoughts erupted out of order as she approached the white board. She pulled a photograph down and stared at it. A black-and-white shot of Crystal Caverns in 1922. Six Black women posing in beaded costumes. Dancers sporting golden heels, shining fringe, and ornate headpieces. Each woman tilted her head up and smiled proudly.

Carmen watched Layla, waiting.

"Ellington, the music, the food, the outfits, the businesses, the pride," Layla went on, pushing her hands over the stacks of paper on her desk.

"Say more," Carmen coaxed.

"A celebration of DC's Black Broadway," Layla said as she walked to the whiteboard. "I'll invite the whole city to the party. I can write a piece about Black Broadway. Like a booklet? But also, it's an invitation. It'll have little facts about the Black history of U Street. The good stuff. The beauty, the music, everything," Layla said, pulling picture after picture from the board. "Start with joy. The economic growth, the culture, the community. All that pride and love. THEN we end with the bad stuff. The gentrification—the new Scott building. Like a party and a protest, all in one."

Layla handed Carmen the pictures. Carmen tilted her head, looking concerned. "I'm not sure joy is the best way to get people out there."

"I know it's different, but I think we need different," Layla said, folding her arms.

Carmen exhaled, scanning the photographs with her eyes. "We know the most effective movements are motivated by people getting fucking pissed. Desperation. A breaking point. Don't you think it would be more powerful to distribute facts about homelessness, displacement . . ."

"We know tragedy works. I get that. Every protest I've been to was about grief. But what if we can show people what we had? Most people don't even know the Black history of this city. They can't imagine what we could have here. What we've already had here!"

Layla was buzzing now. She ran back to the map and held her finger along the line of U Street.

"We start here. We walk with a choir, singing, chanting. Gather marchers. Maybe we're all wearing something. Black? Or gold? I don't know yet. But we'd congregate here—" Layla's finger traveled across the map to the star labeled Scott Development. Layla remembered Sean, the band. That's the feeling she had. That's why she asked Sean about his band! "And we stop here. There's a go-go band, there's food. There's a stage for folks to talk about the history of DC and our demands for the future." Layla was panting. She could see it all. She had the vision. She had no idea how to get there, but she knew exactly where she wanted to go.

Carmen folded her arms.

"It sounds beautiful. But it's a leap. And there's a lot missing. This is a nuanced concept. How do we market? How do we get the word out? How much will it cost? We need to identify our tangible goals and demands," Carmen said.

"It's possible. I'm telling you. I can do it," Layla said. "I know I can."

Carmen held her gaze, then looked at the whiteboard.

"What would you need?" she asked cautiously. Layla paced, thinking to herself. She stopped and pointed at Carmen.

"I can do the invitations, social media, door to door. I got that. But I need a journalist to do a piece the week before. Do you know anyone at the local news station? Or The Post?" Layla asked as if she was in a hurry.

"I can try to cash in a favor. But they don't usually report on this kind of thing."

"I'll call them. At least once a day. Start pushing the story. And I'll call the mayor's office. Maybe we can get a statement from her." Layla raced to her notepad, jotting everything down.

"What else?" Carmen asked.

"The budget . . . ?" Layla winced.

"You won't get much." Carmen shook her head. "But we'll

see what we can do." She smiled as she looked down at the old photographs.

"A DC Block Party," Carmen mused.

"A Black Broadway Block party?" Layla replied hesitantly.

Carmen shook her head.

"Too much alliteration?" Layla asked.

"Focus on the event. Pick the name later."

"Got it." Layla nodded.

"Layla, if this works, it's going to be something."

"And if it doesn't, at least it'll be a good party," Layla said, grinning.

13. ZORA

Zora watched the steam rise from the ironing board. She sprayed the fabric with a mist of bergamot water, and the iron sighed. Zora lifted the shirt and studied it. The morning sunlight shone through the fabric. She slid her shirt on, relishing the feeling of warm cotton on her skin. The scent of citrus and earth. The crisp white cotton against her skin. She lifted and tied her locs into a low knot. She took a breath. She thought about work. The list of tasks she needed to accomplish in the day. Which contracts were due this week. Which suppliers she needed to call. Make time to go to the gym. Make time to go abroad. How she would have her coffee this morning.

Then she thought of Jasmine. The black smoke around her eyes. Her penetrating stare. Zora sat on her crisply made bed. She leaned forward, clasping her hands together. Who was this girl? From the minute they met, Jasmine had been rude. She was willful, and strange. Zora hadn't noticed much about her before. At the housewarming, she just seemed insecure. Unsure of herself, and a bit needy. Boyish, but not enough masculine confidence to really pull it off. Cute—but a bit forgettable, honestly. In the moment, she really did believe what she said. Jasmine wasn't striking at first. But that second time at the cafe, something felt entirely different. She had some kind of magnetism in that room. It radiated from her. That morning,

Zora could barely look Jasmine in the eye. She was powerful. Her makeup was messy. Her hair looked soft and fuzzy. The cafe smelled like bread and coffee and melted butter and Jasmine was at home there. She had an attitude, but there was still a pulse emanating from her. The way she pulled at the silver knobs of the espresso machine. Her apron pulled tight above her waist. Her hands on her hips. And the coffee. And the croissant. How did it taste like Paris? Zora wanted to see her again. To tell her how much she loved the croissant—that she couldn't wait to come back to the bakery—but at the dinner party, Jasmine was just rude. Zora wasn't sure if Jasmine liked her or hated her. Was she rude because she was hurt, or was she just pissed off because she thought Zora was a snob? Or both?

Most people thought she was a snob. But how would they define the word? Someone who has exquisite taste and accepts no less? Or someone who looks down on anything that doesn't measure up to that level of taste? She wanted so much to transcend the limitations of her own judgment, but she simply couldn't. Zora had been everywhere and seen everything. She tried the most delicious food and looked out at the most breathtaking vistas. She'd seen all the wonders of the new and old worlds. Zora spent a year of undergrad in the culinary center of the universe. She was at home in Paris. She ate the finest foods and drank the finest wines. She could order her coffee and croissant in perfect French. She ate the freshest, flakiest pastries, and she was convinced that nothing could compare. And mostly she was right. How good could it be when you've had the best? Being this well-traveled really is a doubleedged sword, Zora thought to herself. To have tried the best of nearly everything. It meant that consuming anything mediocre felt unbearable. And she couldn't hide it. She wouldn't. Zora recalled the time she tried a Starbucks croissant. How deeply it offended her senses. It tasted like old bread and cake and crackers all at once. It was too soft and somehow simultaneously stale. It wasn't a croissant.

It wasn't bread. It was an assault on her sense of taste. And if that opinion made her a snob, well then, she was a snob.

But her snobbery only extended into certain areas of life. It didn't mean she only dined at the finest restaurants. She could eat a burger and fries at a diner if she felt so moved. She could read trashy magazines and watch brain-numbing reality TV shows. Not all of the women she dated went to fancy colleges. Some of them didn't go to college at all! Not all of the women she slept with looked like models. She dated plenty of girls who were more charming than physically stunning. Occasionally, she was very open minded. But it's true, she was particular most of the time. Picky, perhaps. She'd lived in DC, Paris, and New York and at this point, nothing moved her. Everything and everyone looked dull. To Zora, this wasn't pride. To her, pride implied a sense of self-importance. Believing you were better than everyone else. She never saw herself that way. She was just a Black girl who grew up with a lot of money and a wealth of opportunities. She had class privilege, but she didn't think she was better than anyone. She wasn't snobby. She was particular. And she wasn't interested in apologizing for it.

When Zora moved back to DC, she felt the urge to find a hook-up buddy. If this sleepy city was going to be her new home base, she needed someone to pass the time with. In hindsight, she realized the tipsy late-night swiping was probably a poor choice. But she was restless, and all the women she'd casually dated were too many zip codes away. Left, left, left, she swiped. How are there suddenly so many white lesbians in DC? Zora thought to herself. She often wished there was a way to filter out the white girls. She swiped left for a good fifteen minutes before a photo caught her attention. Marie. She had a pretty smile in her first photo. Wearing glasses. At work. Cute. She looked smart. She looked like she had a job. And in the next photo, Marie was not at work. Marie was on the beach. In a bikini. Her ass was consuming the thinnest slice of spandex. Her skin dusted with fine grains of sand like sugar on an old-fashioned donut. There she was. On her knees with clear blue water glittering in the distance. Melanin glowing in the sunlight. God damn. Marie knew what she was doing. Zora's clit grew hard and pulsed against her briefs. So. She swiped right.

"IT'S A MATCH!"

The phone lit up.

What are you waiting for? Send Marie a message!

Zora sent a message. Quick and to the point.

"Hey. I'm Zora. Can I take you out tomorrow?"

"♥♥♥ I'd love to! Your profile says you love espresso. Coffee? I know a cute Black-owned spot downtown. What time works for you?"

Zora absentmindedly responded, then proceeded to stare at Marie's thick curves on the beach and efficiently made herself come.

And when the next day arrived, Zora was already annoyed. Marie had gotten to the cafe fifteen minutes early.

"Just ordered you a latte! ♥"

Zora felt rushed.

"I hope your on the way! ☺"

Zora was walking from her parking spot when Marie's text buzzed in her hand. Your? I hope your on the way? Zora looked at the screen, then itched at her scalp. Not knowing the difference between YOUR and YOU'RE probably meant nothing. It probably meant less than nothing. Marie could still be brilliant. She could still be great in bed. She could be a great cook! It meant nothing. Less than nothing. And yet. Zora couldn't stop thinking about it. She greeted Marie with a hug and a tight smile. It means nothing, Zora told herself. Hope your on the way. You're profile said you like pastries. Your so cute! You're grammar sucks. Zora couldn't keep it out of her thoughts. Zora stared down at the coffee Marie had so generously bought her. Why am I here? Zora wanted to fuck.

That's all. She wanted to fuck Marie from behind and watch her ass bounce back. She wanted to make Marie's legs shake. Zora wanted to fuck an anonymous, beautiful woman and leave. And she knew she wasn't a monster for wanting casual sex. But she felt like a monster for wanting it with the fucking girl next door. This girl wanted to date and hold hands as they skipped into friend's birthday parties and weddings and family barbecues and on and on. This girl wanted to be adored and cherished, and she deserved all of it. But Zora couldn't be the one to give it to her. She couldn't give that to anyone.

"What do you love?"

Again, Jasmine appeared in Zora's thoughts. Her eyes were disarmingly serious. Jasmine's question made Zora's brain stop for what felt like a whole minute. As if it were the simplest question that no one had ever asked her. She felt silly even thinking about it. Stupid. She was always wealthy and spoiled! She had everything! Sure, she missed out on some things. Her mom was an alcoholic, and her dad was basically a single parent for a decade of their lives. But they all worked through it eventually. When the dust settled, she ended up with two parents who loved her fiercely. She had an optimistic little brother who thought the world of her. The best education money could buy. Trips abroad. Beautiful lovers all over the world. A great, high-paying job at her father's investment firm and the law degree to back it up. But how much of it did she actually love? How much of it did she choose? She'd waved off her dreams of architecture for real estate law. In her mind, she could have both. She could have the job that made sense and leave the rest for vacation. Visit Gaudi in Barcelona. Buy the house of her dreams rather than designing one. It was practical.

Zora looked around the room and felt satisfied. Everything was clean and in its place. She couldn't ask for more. She wanted for nothing. But Jasmine. She wanted Jasmine. She didn't completely understand why. Jasmine was more abrasive than any woman she'd ever found herself attracted to. And less feminine. Maybe it was the thought of something different. Maybe she was just confused. Zora stood, tucked in her shirt, and sauntered down the stairs. She found David fiddling with the espresso machine. She walked into the kitchen, shaking the thought of Jasmine away. David slid a steaming cup across the island to Zora. She lifted the cup and took a sip.

"Mmm. Too sweet," Zora said, wincing at the coffee.

"You're welcome, and good morning to you too!" David said in his impossibly cheerful voice.

"Good morning," Zora said, looking at her watch. David took the cup from her hands.

"I'll make you another. But I'm not sure it'll hit the spot . . ." David said as he tiptoed to Zora mischievously.

"You know, the T Spot?" David giggled.

"Huh?" Zora knitted her brow.

"You know what I'm talking about. Jasmine's cafe . . . the T Spot?" David waggled his eyebrows at her. Zora looked at her watch again.

"Oh. Right," she said.

David peeked at Zora from the corner of his eye as he steamed the milk. Zora pretended to read something on her phone.

"You wanna go to the cafe today?" David asked, grinning.

"I have some contracts to finish. I think if we leave in the next five—"

"I mean if my coffee isn't good enough, we could stop by . . . the T Spot . . ." David shrugged casually.

"Not today," Zora said, shaking her head.

"You wanna stop in for lunch?" David asked, batting his lashes.

"I'll meet you in the car," Zora said, rolling her eyes.

The art-deco iron fence retracted as Zora slid into the driver side of her matte black Tesla Model X. What do you love? Zora thought to herself. She loved her Tesla. She loved how sleek it was. She loved that it didn't look like any other car. This was her Batmobile. Materialistic? Maybe. But she knew she deserved it. David popped into the car, handing her a mug. Zora took a sip and pretended not to hate it. They pulled off onto the road.

"I can't believe we have the hots for two sisters!" David said as he rolled the window down.

"The hots?" Zora scoffed.

"If we all got married, like what would our kids be? Siblings-in-law? I mean that would be cool, right?" David fiddled with the dashboard touchscreen.

"Jesus," Zora replied.

"I don't think I ever saw you so weird over a girl before." David clicked at his phone, cueing up one of the newest mumble rap party anthems. Zora sighed.

"I'm not weird. I'm just . . ." Zora gazed out at the road. She looked for the right word.

"Pressed? Sprung?" David guessed with an overly serious face.

"Annoyed," Zora replied.

David shook his head.

"Sis. You have a crush on this girl. Can you not fucking see that? What did she say to you that night? You've been all day dreamy ever since."

"Day dreamy?" Zora furrowed her brow. She wasn't sure if she should take that as a compliment or an insult. She wasn't the dreamy type.

"You're crushing," David said, decisively.

Zora thought for a moment.

"I'm intrigued," Zora replied.

David stared at Zora. "Well. I've never seen you this intrigued before." He danced in his seat and sang at her in a schoolyard sing-song voice. "Zora and Jasmine sitting in a tree. I-n-t-r-i-g-u-e-d!" David attempted to make the letters fit. He laughed.

In spite of herself and all her effort to maintain her stoic gaze, Zora's face broke into a smile.

14. JASMINE

Business at the T Spot was slow. Again. Jasmine spent the morning frantically rearranging and dusting the teapot shelves. She was out of breath, scrubbing and wiping with obsessive vigor. Maybe if she reorganized the tea pots, everything would be okay Maybe if she cleaned and cleaned all day, people would finally actually come in and fucking buy something. Marble pretended to wipe down the toaster, watching Jasmine cautiously from afar. By now, Marble could anticipate Jasmine's anxiety. Dusting, organizing, and pacing were a few of her tells. Marble watched Jasmine delicately place the last ornate teapot up on its sparkling shelf. She stared up at it.

"I think I should knead some dough," Jasmine said suddenly.

"Are you okay?" Marble asked.

"I'm fine," Jasmine snapped.

"Good," Marble said, nodding slowly.

"I mean we could use a bit more business. Obviously," Jasmine said, taking a moment to look around the empty cafe.

"Maybe we could host some more Howard events. Or I could work on social media?" Marble offered.

Jasmine stared up at the teapot. "Sure."

She put her hands on her hips. "It's just. It's not what I thought it would be ..." Jasmine said, trailing off. Marble waited for her to finish. "You want people to come. But, you know.

You want them to want to come. Right? I mean everything is homemade here. It's fresh. The coffee is good. The pastries are good, right?"

"So good," Marble said.

"I'm not crazy, right?"

"It's the best. Like. Actually," Marble replied, nodding.

"So shouldn't they just—come? On their own? Shouldn't they just know it's good?"

"I don't think that's how capitalism works," Marble said, shrugging.

"Right," Jasmine replied. She reached up to the shelf, slightly adjusting the placement of the teapot.

"Did you ever think about moving the shop? Downtown is kinda dead," Marble went on.

Sure. Do you have the deposit and rent for another year's lease? Do you have money for a second renovation? Jasmine didn't say it.

"We'll figure it out," Jasmine said, staring up at the teapots.

Marble scrubbed the toaster. "So. Have you thought any more about Zora?" Marble asked casually.

Jasmine chuckled. "No," she said, turning to look at Marble.

"... OK," Marble replied.

"I mean, I saw her this weekend. She was a prick. Again. It's her personality I guess? But. She's still so fucking hot. So. It's annoying. You know?" Jasmine said.

"Yep. The fine ones are always jerks. They get away with everything," Marble said, rolling their eyes.

"Right?" Jasmine folded her arms.

"So don't let her," Marble replied.

"Don't let her what?" Jasmine turned to Marble.

"Don't let her get away with it," Marble said, wiping their hands on a dishrag.

"Right," Jasmine replied. She looked back up at the teapot. Marble clapped their hands excitedly.

"Okay! It's dough-kneading time! Right?" Marble nearly yelled as Jasmine snapped back into reality.

"Right. Okay. You're right. I'll be in the back. If you need me."

Jasmine stood at the steel-plated counter, elbow deep in dough. She breathed heavily, her arm muscles flexing into the movement. She dusted the counter with flour. As she slammed the dough down, white clouds shot up into the air. She paused to stare down at the fleshy mass. The past two years, she'd made over a thousand loaves of bread, but this part still left her in awe. Each new batch of dough was like her first child. She felt godly. She marveled at the elasticity. She lifted it up to her nose and inhaled. Her senses filled with the sweetness of the yeast blooming. Her mind wandered to Zora. The way she smiled at the dinner party. The way Zora looked at her. Jasmine couldn't stop wondering what Zora was about to say. Wondering what Zora thought of her. You are . . . You ARE . . . You are the love of my life? You are a very cool person? You are weird but kind of hot? Is that what she would have said? And why did she leave right when it felt like they were finally connecting?

Jasmine was lost in the dream of that night. She melted into the dough, savoring every detail in her memory. The deep tone of Zora's voice. The way her slacks fit tight on her thighs. The way she smelled. What would it feel like? To touch her. To be touched by her.

Jasmine couldn't deny it. She wanted to feel Zora. She felt her body weaken as the heels of her hands moved deeper into the dough. She rocked closer to the counter's edge, her hips pushing against the cold steel.

"Hello?"

Jasmine jumped at the sound of a voice. She inhaled sharply and looked up to see a figure in the kitchen doorway. Zora. The vampire. The perfect, mean, gorgeous human stood in her bakery kitchen.

In real life.

"Zora?"

Jasmine held her hands in the dough. Zora shifted her weight and shoved her hands into her pockets. Jasmine looked down the hall. She felt her heart racing.

"How did you . . . you shouldn't be back here."

"I just wanted to talk," Zora said, staring down at the dough.

Jasmine looked up at Zora, her skin prickling with confusion. Zora pulled her hands from her pockets, her arms stiff and formal at her sides.

"You were right. I should have tried it," Zora said, looking down apologetically at the dough. After a long moment, she looked up at Jasmine.

"The first time I came here . . . I didn't know you. Honestly, I just assumed everything would be mediocre. A lot of the food in DC is mediocre. I don't take a lot of chances. But you were right. I should have tried it. I should try a lot of things. I've been . . ." Zora's eyes wandered up and across the pans on the top shelf. "I've been close-minded," she finished.

A scoff escaped Jasmine's mouth. Zora looked down. Jasmine cleared her throat.

"It's fine, honestly." She dusted her hands off and turned to face Zora. Zora was still studying the kitchen tools and machines with her eyes.

"It's just where I'm coming from. I spent a year in Paris and fell in love with the cuisine there. So I'm a bit particular about the things I try when . . . ugh. Sorry, that's not really the point. What I mean to say is—"

"Wow. A year in Paris. Must be nice," Jasmine said, putting her doughy, floured hands on her hips. Jasmine had been to Paris too. She'd poured over French recipe books for years. She spent one week there and felt like a tourist. It rained every day and her French was awful. Every cafe she went to was overpriced. Every Parisian she attempted to speak to looked at her with disdain. She felt completely isolated. She wondered how good Zora's French was. She wondered how many Parisian women Zora had kissed that year?

Zora cleared her throat. "I've had a lot of really good food. That's what I mean. And I didn't expect it."

"What. You didn't expect me to be good at my job?" Jasmine cocked her head.

"No. I just . . . that croissant," Zora continued. Her eyes seemed to be asking, pleading for something. "It's the best one I've had in a long time. One of the best I've ever had." Zora looked hopeful for a moment.

Jasmine swallowed her impulse to smile. "That's very generous. Really. But I have to finish this so maybe we could talk another time and I'd—"

Zora stepped closer.

"I feel . . . drawn to you," Zora said softly. Jasmine searched Zora's eyes. Her heart sprinted in her chest.

"What?" Jasmine whispered.

Zora took a breath. "What you said at my dad's house. No one ever asked me that before."

Zora waited. She seemed horrified by Jasmine's silence.

"I got that sense." Jasmine replied.

"I don't know what it means, but I feel drawn to you. I felt like I had to come here."

Jasmine's arms dropped to her sides.

"I don't get it."

"Why not?" Zora said. She was still.

"Zora. Pretty much everything you've said and done since we met . . . you've made me feel like you really, really don't like me."

"I think I do."

"Why do you think that?" Jasmine scoffed.

"I like you because you challenge me." Zora interrupted. Her eyes pinned Jasmine's in their gaze.

"That sounds like it's more about you than me."

"Do you think—do you think about me?" Zora whispered.

Jasmine folded her arms.

"Of course, you're fucking gorgeous and I mean what person in the world could see you and not have . . . feelings. But, Zora. You're not just close-minded. You're judgmental," Jasmine said, firmly.

"I know," Zora replied.

Jasmine exhaled. "You're a fucking snob."

"I know." Zora waited.

"And honestly. I don't want to have these feelings. But I do," Jasmine said. She looked up at Zora.

"Can I kiss you?" Zora whispered.

"Oh." The word fell out of Jasmine's mouth.

"We kind of hate each other and we kind of like each other and we're both confused so now maybe we should just kiss?" Jasmine said.

"Maybe we should," Zora replied.

Jasmine felt the heat of sweat under her apron. Her whole body was buzzing. Her heart beat faster and faster in her throat. In her mind, she was jumping into a freezing cold lake. She was clawing up and through pitch-black water for air. She was nervous, annoyed, confused, terrified. But at the bottom of that cold body of ice water, she found herself. She felt exhilarated. She tore at the surface of it, breathless. Full of life.

"Fuck it," Jasmine whispered.

They walked into each other. Their lips met. Kissing gently, then firmly, Zora's tongue pushing into Jasmine's mouth. She shuddered as Zora's tongue moved slowly along the inside of her lips. They were both breathless. Zora's hands guided Jasmine's hips into her. Flour wafted like fairy dust around their shoulders and feet. Jasmine ran her hands up Zora's belly. Finding her nipples, hard and pushing against the thin cotton of her shirt. They rushed with the urgency of two teenagers. They were grown enough to know what to do, but they couldn't pretend they had the patience to wait for it. They forgot how to slow down. How to savor. No. This wasn't about slowness. This moment was a lit match. Zora's hips pushed Jasmine's ass into the cold of the steel counter. Jasmine took Zora's earlobe between her lips as Zora moaned. Jasmine's sticky hands pulled at Zora's locs, leaving a trail of flour in their wake. Jasmine pushed back as Zora rocked into her. Zora held Jasmine's hips in her hands and lifted her onto the counter. Jasmine gasped as Zora moaned into her neck. Jasmine pulled Zora into her.

Marble's operatic voice sang from down the hall.

"JAAAAAASMINE!"

Jasmine's heart dropped.

Marble's voice grew closer and louder.

"We need dark roast for a pickup; is there more in the back or do we need to make an order?"

Jasmine pulled away from Zora, searching her eyes. Zora mirrored her dumbfounded stare.

Marble stopped at the kitchen door. Jasmine jumped down from the counter. Zora brushed a trace of flour from her shirt. They both turned to Marble.

Marble took a small step backward, an open-mouthed grin spreading across their face.

"Oh. Hey kids . . ." Marble said. They leaned against the doorway and crossed their arms like a suspicious parent.

"Hey Marble, you remember Zora. Zora, Marble." Jasmine moved her ball of dough an inch to the left, busying herself.

"Hey," Zora waved robotically.

". . . I didn't see you come in . . ." Marble tilted their head.

"Yeah," Zora said, nodding.

Everyone waited for something.

"Well, thank you," Zora said, turning to Jasmine suddenly. She looked down at the ball of dough. "For the recipe. I've never . . . made bread before." Zora stared wide eyed at Jasmine.

"Oh sure!" Jasmine responded. She looked up at Marble, waiting for them to leave.

"Please! Don't let me interrupt! I was just looking for the dark roast . . ." Marble frowned cartoonishly.

Jasmine looked back at Zora.

"It's cool. We were just—" Jasmine nodded. Zora nodded.

"Well, let me know how it goes? The recipe?" Jasmine said, smiling.

"I will." Zora nodded enthusiastically as she walked to the door. Marble stepped aside as Zora crossed the threshold. Zora looked back at Jasmine, flashing a bashful smile.

Jasmine's face filled with heat.

"Bye Jasmine," Zora said. She turned to go.

Marble looked down the hall, watching Zora disappear. They slowly turned back to Jasmine.

Jasmine rolled her eyes and turned back to the counter. She pushed her hands into the dough.

Marble sauntered over to Jasmine's side.

"That must have been a really, really good recipe." Marble watched Jasmine blush.

"Yeah. It was," Jasmine said, staring at the dough.

"Did you . . . want to wash your hands? Before . . ."

"Shut up, Marble," Jasmine said, smiling through her words.

15. JASMINE

The church basement floors were lined with red carpet. The air smelled of stale coffee and Pine-Sol. The ambiance was less than pleasant, but to Jasmine this place was sacred. Because this terrible coffee, this fluorescent light, this place had saved her life. First it was the breakup. Her partner left her for someone better and the moment she realized Dia wasn't coming back, she decided to hate herself. Every day she'd wake up in searing pain. Sweating, nauseated, and swearing she'd never do it again. And every night she'd drink until she couldn't walk straight. Then came Ro's cancer diagnosis. Moving back home. Holding herself together just enough to show up for her mother and her sisters, then shutting the door to her room and falling apart. She made herself a martyr. She drank at work. She woke up next to people she didn't know. She stopped eating. She stopped calling friends. She stopped calling her sisters. Two years ago, Jasmine walked into this sad room in a church basement because drinking herself to death wasn't working fast enough.

And today, Jasmine walked into this sad room in a church basement with A CRUSH. She felt the memory of Zora on her lips. Jasmine could barely catch her breath. ZORA had just KISSED HER. She wasn't insane. She wasn't losing her mind. She liked a girl and the girl liked her back. Jasmine floated to the snack table, still wrapped up in the swirling dream of that kiss. She nodded and grinned at everyone in the room. Some familiar faces, some new. Mostly white men upwards of fifty and a few white women. Jasmine spotted another Black woman in the corner. Any time she saw Black folks in the rooms, she made sure to befriend them. AA wasn't supposed to be about race, in theory. But finding other Black folks in recovery reminded her she belonged here.

Jasmine turned to pour herself a cup of terrible coffee. No sugar. No powdered creamer. She hated the stuff with a passion, but she liked having something to do. She focused on the warm cup in her hands and settled into the folding chair next to the other Black woman. Her eyes were closed.

"Hi," Jasmine whispered.

The woman didn't open her eyes, but the corners of her mouth curled up into a smile.

"Hello," she whispered.

Jasmine stared. She waited for the woman to open her eyes. Or extend a hand. Or something. Instead, the woman just sat there. Maybe she's high, Jasmine thought. Not everybody who came to AA was ready for recovery. But she didn't really look high. Jasmine couldn't stop looking. Who was this woman? She could have been sixty-something. Nice clothes. No shakes. She looked calm. Content. She had a look like those statues of a young Buddha. In spite of her gray curls, she looked youthful. Blissfully serene, like she was drifting somewhere above and beyond this world. She seemed out of place. It occurred to Jasmine that she'd never seen a Black woman look so calm in public. Of course, she'd seen Black women meditating before. Sure, she'd seen Black women relax someplace safe, but not out in the world. Much less in a room full of strangers. Black women had to be on guard just to exist in the world.

"How's your day?" the woman whispered. Her eyes remained closed. Jasmine hesitated.

"It was okay . . ." She suddenly felt the need to say more.

"It was really good actually. I'm having a lot of feelings about a person. Like romantic feelings. And I know this person feels things too. I'm excited. And scared?" Jasmine took a breath. The woman's smile widened. She nodded slightly.

"Sounds like a good day to share," she whispered.

"Yeah. Well, this one is a popcorn meeting. So, I guess I'll share. If someone picks me." Jasmine shrugged.

The woman said nothing. Jasmine felt uncomfortable. But also intrigued. Was this woman tuning her out? Or meditating? Right now? In the middle of small talk? Could people do that?

Jasmine turned to the front of the room. She wasn't sure how to feel. This woman was either crazy or magical. Or both?

"HEY YOU BEAUTIFUL DRUNKS, YOU! SHUT YOUR YAPPERS SO WE CAN START, WON'T CHA!?" The secretary shouted above the chatter in the room.

He was a wacky fifty-something white guy in a Hawaiian shirt. He smiled at folks in the room as he read the meeting script melodically. "We'll begin this meeting with a moment of silence for those still sick and suffering in and out of recovery, followed by the serenity prayer."

Jasmine closed her eyes and took a breath. She was not thinking about those still sick and suffering in and out of recovery. She was thinking about that kiss. She was thinking about Zora's tongue pushing her lips open. She was thinking about sucking Zora's earlobe into her mouth.

"God. Grant us the serenity to accept the things we cannot change. The courage to change the things we can. And the wisdom to know the difference." The monotone prayer hummed in the background of Jasmine's thoughts. The whole meeting melted into a fuzzy white noise as Jasmine imagined Zora. Jasmine touched her own skin and wished her hands were Zora's—grazing her wrist, her shoulder, her lips. Jasmine blinked slowly. She shook her head. Damn. Thinking about sex. In church. Again. She closed her eyes. Her head tilted to the side. She grinned. When she opened her eyes, the wacky man in the Hawaiian shirt was pointing directly at her with a hopeful, expectant look.

"Would you like to share, Jasmine?" he asked politely.

Of course she gets picked first in a popcorn meeting. She shot up in her seat, her posture becoming unnaturally rigid.

"Oh. Yes. Sure. Okay. Hey, I'm Jasmine, I'm an alcoholic," Jasmine stuttered.

"Hi, Jasmine," The room hummed in a monotone response.

"So. Today feels weird. I'm happy. Really, really happy. And that's weird? It shouldn't be. But it is. And whenever I'm happy, I think about what brought me here. The last time I loved someone. I just remember waking up wishing I didn't. Back then, my relationship was my higher power. So when I woke up and she was gone, I had nothing. So I drank. I think part of me wanted to get so close to death that she had to come back. Like I had this fucked-up fantasy that I'd be in the hospital and she'd come and I would look so pathetic and frail and her heart would just burst open with love and she'd have to take me back." Jasmine laughed. "Seems like a flawed plan when I think about it now. Even if she did come to that hospital room and see me all broken and bloody, even if she did take me back, I would still be me. A lying, manipulative, deeply insecure, selfish alcoholic who had no idea how to love her. Or how to love myself."

Jasmine crossed her arms then uncrossed them. Unsure of where to go from there. She took a breath.

"I'm glad it all happened, honestly. Cuz it brought me here. And sobriety is so fucking cool."

Jasmine's eyes flitted to the meditating woman by her side. Her eyes were open now, staring up at Jasmine. They were dark and magnetic.

"Okay so. Anyway. I kissed someone today," Jasmine said, blushing.

The room erupted with oohs and bursts of applause. Jasmine laughed.

"I don't know what this means. Maybe nothing. Probably nothing. I've dated here and there. Slept around. You know. But I haven't really been in love since then."

Jasmine sighed. "And I think I'm scared."

Her words dissolved into a whisper. Her throat pinched with emotion. She looked back to the meditating woman whose eyes were closed again.

"Thank you for letting me share," Jasmine said weakly.

"Thank you for sharing." The words echoed softly around the room.

Jasmine couldn't figure out why she said any of that. She wasn't in love with Zora. She wasn't in danger of having her heart broken. They kissed once. Jasmine attempted to listen to the shares as she replayed the moment in her mind. Her hands. Her lips. Her tongue. The weight of Zora's body pushing against her.

Jasmine listened to the low hum of people in the meeting telling their stories. The lilting energetic rise when the room filled up with laughter. The newcomer crying in the corner. The old-timers nodding with conviction. The meditating woman kept her eyes closed for the whole meeting, breathing deeply, smiling now and then. Was she listening? Jasmine thought to herself.

Jasmine's phone buzzed in her pocket. She fumbled with it, attempting to turn it off. She glanced at the text from Ella.

> Ella: You and Zora KIIIIIIIISSSSSSSSSED???!!!!

Jasmine sighed.

> Jasmine: Wow. News travels fast?

Ella: Zora asked David to ask me to ask you for your number. Can I give it to him to give to her? Also. How did you kiss and not get her number????????????

Jesus, Jasmine thought. Why does this feel like middle school?

Jasmine: Long story. Yes, give him my number. To give to her . . .

Jasmine turned her phone off.
"Thank you to all who have shared, and all who have done service for this meeting. Special thanks to Miss Angie who brought homemade cookies. They're absolutely delicious, Angie. Now if y'all will stand with me, we have a nice way of closing this meeting. Today, we're closing with the third-step prayer."

The crowd hummed with chatter and shuffled their way into a circle, lining the walls of the room. Jasmine stood near the snack table. She linked hands with the two middle-aged white men. She closed her eyes. The voices overlapped low and soft in one final monotone prayer.

"God, I offer myself to Thee—to build with me and to do with me as Thou wilt. Relieve me of the bondage of self, that I may better do Thy will. Take away my difficulties, that victory over them may bear witness to those I would help. Of Thy Power, Thy Love, and Thy Way of life. May I do thy will always. Amen. KEEP COMING BACK, IT WORKS IF YOU WORK IT SO WORK IT CUZ YOU'RE WORTH IT!" They all waved each other's hands like children and cheered as they ended the prayer.

Jasmine smiled, then looked up. Her eyes scanned the circle of faces, searching the room for the meditating woman. Where could she have gone? Jasmine decided to wait a while. She had to meet this woman. But ten minutes, then fifteen minutes went by, and Jasmine couldn't find her face in the crowd. As the last few fellows stacked their folding chairs in the corner, Jasmine walked to the door and turned to search the room again. The meditating woman was gone.

16. THE JONES HOUSE

If you ever forgot DC was south of the Mason-Dixon line, August would step in to remind you. Every year, summer came and knocked the hustle right out of the city. The midday summer heat turned everything molasses slow. The air hazy and thick. Politicians and lobbyists all vanished into thin air and materialized somewhere in New England.

"God DAMN it's hot." Jasmine wiped her brow as she handed a pair of tongs to Ro.

"Jazz honey, don't forget the bug spray too," Ro called out as Jasmine jogged back to the kitchen door.

You could smell the grill from down the street. Small flames licked at the bright and browned rainbow of vegetables. Ro danced to Marvin Gaye in a cloud of grill smoke. She wore a tank top and a well-loved apron with a cartoon whisk and loopy cursive letters reading "I take whisks." Marble leaned boyishly in and watched Ro grilling. They wore what looked like a 1920s newsie costume. Despite the fact that Marble was probably less than half Ro's age, they grinned like an old man admiring a pretty young thing. Ro pointed with her tongs at the grill.

"Grass-fed beef burgers, bean burgers, chicken thighs, bell peppers, peaches, pineapple, zucchini, bacon, and . . . broccoli."

"Wow," Marble replied, leaning closer to get a better look at the spread. "Tall order!"

"Well, my daughters are spoiled and neurotic. Who knows what food-related political cause or diet they're into these days. I figured I'd just grill everything and we'll be fine."

"They're very lucky to have you, Ro. Remind me, what's Ro short for?" Marble asked, grinning wider.

Jasmine kicked the back door open, her arms full of bowls and utensils.

"Ey Marble!" Jasmine called out. "You wanna stop flirting with my mother and help us set the table?"

Marble shook their head and gave Ro a "kids these days" look. Ro shook her head and deftly flipped a sizzling burger with her spatula. Layla and Ella emerged from the back door carrying drinks.

The five of them sat down at the old picnic bench in Ro's backyard. The table held enough food for an army. Watermelon, arugula salad, lavender lemonade, heirloom tomatoes, avocado, chilled bottles of white wine, and Ro's plate of grilled everything. Ro, Marble and the sisters joined hands. Following Ro's lead, they all closed their eyes.

"Ancestors, goddess, universe, mother earth," Ro said as her head tipped up to the sun, her eyes closed. "We thank you for the fruit of your bounty. We thank you for the love and family we have here and beyond this table." Ro squeezed Marble's hand. Marble stared at her, amazed. Jasmine kicked Marble under the table. Ro continued.

"Let us pray for our Ella and her sweet, sweet romance with the young prince, David. May he treat her like the princess she is."

"I know that's right!" Marble interjected.

"Mom." Jasmine peeked one eye open.

"Love is the magic we create, is it not?" Ro continued.

Jasmine sighed.

"Hey ma? Is this the kind of prayer where you tell everybody's business? Because I'd love to skip some of the—"

"And spirit won't you pleeeease bless my daughter Jasmine,"

Ro interrupted Jasmine, her voice growing louder.

"Bless her with patience. Humility. And the courage to give romance a try and accept her feelings for the other prince, Zora."

Layla opened her eyes and shot a glare at Jasmine.

"What?" Layla snapped.

Jasmine sighed.

"Shhhh!" Marble hissed.

"Bless Marble for their charming, sweet energy."

Marble bowed their head and nodded.

"And bless Layla. Give her strength and focus in her incredibly brave upcoming activist endeavor."

Ella turned to Layla. "What endeavor?"

Layla kept her eyes on Ro, thinking.

"Layla?" Ella whispered.

Layla stood and placed a hand on her heart.

"And spirit, bless our sweet mother for this incredibly beautiful meal and for all this love and generosity, ASHE, AMEN, woop, woop!"

"Here, here," Marble said, staring at Ro.

"Ashe," Ro whispered, nearly hiding a mischievous smile.

They all squeezed hands.

Layla passed the salad bowl to Marble. "Love the outfit, Marble. That Harlem Renaissance realness is in style huh? Very cool," Layla said, grinning.

Marble grinned back. "Why, thank you Layla."

"For some reason I thought you only wore kimonos. Way to mix it up." Layla nodded.

"Aw honey. My wardrobe is actually quite rich. But don't you worry, love. I'm sure you'll catch up when you're older," Marble said, batting their lashes.

Layla scoffed, rolling her eyes. "I'm a year older than you, Marble."

"I know, right?" Marble said.

Ro smiled at Layla. "Layla, honey. Did you tell your sisters about your event?"

Layla clenched her jaw. "No. I didn't."

"Don't you think it might be relevant?" Ro asked casually.

Layla sighed. The bowls and plates made their way around the table. Distracted, Jasmine served herself a helping of grilled vegetables.

Layla shifted in her seat. "I'm directing an action for Rise. It's my first one as lead . . . so. It's a big deal."

"That's great, Layla!" Jasmine said, grinning with a mouth full of pineapple.

"Wow. That's cool. What's it for?" Ella asked.

"I wanted to focus on joy. So it's a kind of celebration of Black Broadway and U Street. Basically . . . it's a party with a DC Black history theme."

Layla served herself a bean burger.

"That's so cool, Layla!" Jasmine said.

"What's Black Broadway?" Marble asked.

Ro turned to Marble. "Sweet child. I need to give you a history lesson."

"I would absolutely love that," Marble responded.

"Marble's from Georgia, Mom. And even DC natives don't know about Black Broadway," Jasmine said.

Ella glared at Layla, suspicious. "So, Rise DC is paying you to throw a party?"

"Well, it's also a protest," Layla said.

"What are you protesting?" Ella pried.

Layla took a bite of grilled peach. She chewed as she spoke. "Gentrification."

Ella stared at Layla.

"Ella. Stop reading me," Layla whispered.

"I'm not reading you, Layla. You're just a shitty liar," Ella whispered back.

Marble frowned.

Ro cleared her throat. "Layla, honey?"

Layla went on. "We're protesting the new U Street development."

Jasmine looked up. Marble froze.

"The Scott development. You're protesting the Scott Development." Ella didn't ask.

"Yes," Layla swallowed.

"Of course," Ella said, nodding.

"What?" Layla snapped.

"Did someone assign this . . . action to you?" Ella asked.

"No," Layla replied flatly.

"So you chose to target the Scott Development. Out of all the new developments in the city you decided to protest that one?" Ella asked.

"I did," Layla replied.

"Fucking typical, Layla. I know you. I know you're gonna turn this into a war," Ella said.

"It's already a fucking war," Layla scoffed.

Ella looked at Jasmine, then back at Layla.

"Malcolm Scott thinks you're his protegee. Did you know that?" Ella said. "He thinks you're passionate about high-end real estate."

"I am passionate. Passionate about tearing it the fuck down," Layla said, laughing.

"You lied to him."

"I didn't lie to him. I met with him once and asked him about the building and he believed what he wanted," Layla said, massaging her temples.

"You met with him?" Jasmine asked.

"These are people's lives, Layla," Ella said.

"I'm sorry if my activism is getting in the way of your fucking fairytale," Layla said.

"It's not about me, Layla. They're good people," Ella said.

"You know you sound like a white person right now," Layla scoffed.

"Jesus, grow up," Ella said, rolling her eyes.

"I'm sure there were plenty of slave owners and overseers who were nice, church-going good people. But good people do things that put other good people at risk, you know? How good can people be if they keep other good people in chains?" Layla asked, a condescending smile pinching at her face.

"Oh, here we go. You got an expensive degree in Black Studies, so every conversation must be all about slavery. Layla, it's more nuanced than that and you know it."

"Right, right, well everything actually is connected to slavery. Are you saying slavery is nuanced? Do you think displacing low income and Black communities is nuanced. Ella, what do you think happens when you—"

"My darlings," Ro interjected.

"I think we need to pause. Take a moment to breathe together. Burn some sage, perhaps—" Ro said, her voice soft and soothing.

"We can't fix everything with sage, Mom," Layla said.

Ella stood. "I'm sorry, Mom. I can't do this." She turned and walked toward the house.

"Ella, honey!" Ro called out, following Ella into the house.

Layla, Marble and Jasmine stared down at their plates.

Marble turned to Jasmine, their eyes wide.

"Well. Maybe this was not the best day to come to the Jones house for dinner. I'm sorry, Marble," Jasmine sighed.

"Oh please! No apologies necessary!" Marble replied. "I'm having a lovely time. And if you don't mind me saying—your mother is absolutely . . . exquisite."

Jasmine shook her head. "Yeah, about that. Marble, I knew you were a flirt but for some reason I did not expect you to hit on my mother. I'm not sure if I'm impressed or disturbed." She took a generous bite of her burger, then glanced at Layla.

"You okay?" Jasmine asked.

"So Mom was right? You started something with Zora?"

Marble and Jasmine exchanged a glance.

Layla nodded her head. "So. Was anybody gonna tell me?"

Jasmine sighed. "We kissed. Once. And I have no idea what it means. It probably won't happen again."

Marble sipped their wine, raising a doubtful eyebrow.

"Well, I'm happy for you." Layla offered a weak smile. "But you should know. I'm not gonna pull any punches."

Layla stood.

"You shouldn't. It's your job. I get it," Jasmine said.

Layla stood there for a moment. "It's the right thing to do."

"Well . . . it's complicated. Ella hasn't been this happy with a guy in a long time. Maybe ever."

"If it's real between them, nothing else should matter," Layla said.

"I think she just wants you to acknowledge—"

"I get it," Layla interrupted Jasmine, her hand in the air.

Jasmine snapped her head to Layla. "Layla, don't take your shit out on me. I'm trying to help." Jasmine's tone grew stern.

"Yeah. Thanks for your help. I'm gonna go. Good seeing you, Marble," Layla said as she walked away.

Marble and Jasmine watched as Layla disappeared into the house.

"Okay!" Marble said, clapping their hands together definitively.

"I have to say it . . . I fucking love your family."

17. LAYLA

Layla was a blur. A Black girl on a single-speed bike racing through the crowds in downtown DC. She decided to get off the Metro early. Give herself some time to ride the bike a while and calm her nerves. She was nervous. Some days she walked with a confidence so fiery she knew she would change the whole world tomorrow. But on days like today, she wasn't sure. Of anything. This protest might be a complete waste of time. It might be an embarrassment. What if nobody cared? What if nobody showed up? Take M Street to West Virginia Ave. Bike through the monuments. Past the White House, the Capitol, Lincoln, Jefferson. Straight across the edge of the city to get to a homeless shelter in Trinidad. She had a feeling. When she got to the shelter, when she met Brianna, she had a feeling something would click. The protest would make sense. Her obsession. Her need to make all this happen would somehow feel justified.

    Layla gazed up at the Washington Monument as she biked down the curved path. Layla biked past federal courthouses and colossal sculptures celebrating presidents and war heroes. Her black cloud of hair bounced and brushed at her shoulders. She passed throngs of tourists in FBI hats and American flag T-shirts. Young runners in red Nats baseball caps. Manicured lawns and art museums grander than cathedrals. The glittering Potomac River. She passed renovated row-houses and restaurants with gleaming glass windows. Layla rarely visited The National Mall. She mostly came for the protests, sometimes for art exhibitions. Whenever she visited, she couldn't stop thinking about the hypocrisy of it all. This display of patriotism and wealth. The thousands of American flags blowing in the wind. The pageantry of pride and war and that familiar, deep-fried American superiority complex. The greatest country in the world.

Layla biked faster and faster. She stood up on the pedals, panting, attempting to outrun her thoughts. Slaves built this country. Not metaphorically. Literally. Brick by brick. The government owned slaves. Slaves carried every block of marble and sandstone. They don't put that shit in the movies. Hollywood films point to easy targets. The gluttonous redfaced white men kicking back in their pastoral Southern plantations. It's simple, isolated. But Layla knew it went deeper than that. The US government bought and leased slaves to build these monuments. Slaves built the Capitol, the White House. In her senior year, Layla learned about it in a Black studies course at her very expensive, very white liberal arts college, which now felt ridiculous to her. But where else would she have learned it? Those little details didn't usually come up in American history classes.

Layla wondered what it would have felt like to be enslaved by the US government. Who did you answer to? Where would you sleep? Did the people who built these monuments have calluses and sores that scraped and bled into the sandstone? Did they have families somewhere? Were they allowed to have families? She biked past giant white columns and stairs gleaming like veneers in a toothy grin. She turned down North Capitol Street and biked as fast as she could, her breath turning hot and labored. The summer air rushed past her. It took her only six minutes to bike from the White House to the hood.

Layla locked her bike to the bus stop pole. She looked up

at the neon sign reading Colony Liquor. Subtle. She looked around as she caught her breath. A middle-class dark-skinned Black girl in the hood. She felt comfortable here, but a part of her wondered if people could look at her and tell she didn't belong. But she cared about the people here. Maybe caring meant she belonged. Loving the parts of the city that everyone else wanted to forget. The politicians, the rich folk, white folk, even some rich Black folks wished this whole section of DC would disappear. And since killing poor Black people is mostly frowned upon these days, they picked the second-best option: abandonment. Abandon the schools and parks and hospitals. Put a liquor store on every block. Raise the cost of living. Poison the air, surveil, police, incarcerate. And wait for the poor Black people to disappear.

Layla looked down at her cell phone. She opened her to-do list. Call The Post (again). Call the mayor's office (again). Call MPDC for permits (again). Layla exhaled. She didn't mind harassing the mayor, but calling and paying the cops for a demonstration permit felt like a special kind of torture. Layla stepped over a stack of smashed pizza boxes on the corner. She walked down the street, searching for the numbers on the buildings. The middle-class, dark-skinned Black girl is lost in the hood. No. She wasn't lost. She was focused. There was only one thing that separated her from this reality. It was not her go-getter attitude. It wasn't her brilliant mind. It wasn't her bootstraps. Nope. What separated Layla from poverty was her mother's proximity to whiteness. Nothing more.

Her heart beat against her chest. She was beginning to doubt herself. She knew that Ella really, really liked David. She'd never really liked a guy this much before. And now apparently Jasmine had something going with the other Scott kid? This was all more complicated and messier than she wanted it to be. What if she went after another development? A corporation, something big and anonymous. Did it need to be the Scotts? They were the only Black developers in the city. It would have been so much easier if they were white. Malcolm Scott wasn't evil. She knew the problem was bigger than him. He had become too human. But Layla knew this was the right thing to do. There was power on U Street. Layla could feel it. She felt it when she studied the history. Spirit was leading her here. And the Scott family was only one family. How many families had lost their homes when he decided to build his property? When someone demolishes an entire city block, what memories are left? That black hole used to be someone's life.

Layla glanced up from her phone, squinting at the weathered sign. Sanctuary: Resources for Families and Children. Maybe this was a bit beyond her job description. But this was Layla. She was thorough to a fault. She knew there was a bigger story. Layla dug up the names and numbers of some of the original families living on that U Street block. She was only able to reach eight of the residents. Of those eight, only three agreed to speak with her. She decided to visit one of the younger former residents and talk in person. Brianna and her son were staying at Sanctuary, one of the city's two homeless shelters specifically catering to families. Layla entered the building. It smelled like an elementary school auditorium. Like tuna sandwiches and bleach. She looked through the yellowing plexiglass partition at the movement of figures in the distance. The security guard poked at the contents of Layla's bag with a baton, then slid it back to her.

Layla walked through the metal detector into what appeared to be the living room. It was as cozy as a living room could be if it were set up in an office building. All the furniture was new, modern and covered in plastic. Brianna and her son sat together on the couch. The boy appeared to be around eight.

"Brianna?" Layla asked gently.

"Hi," Brianna replied, standing as Layla approached. Layla rested a hand on her heart.

"Layla."

They both hesitated. Brianna held her hand out.

"Can we hug? I'm a hugger . . ." Layla regretted saying it as soon as the words left her mouth. Layla was not a hugger. But she wanted so badly to make Brianna feel comfortable. It seemed like the kind of thing a person would say.

"Oh. OK, sure," Brianna replied, a hint of suspicion in her voice.

They embraced stiffly. Layla smiled at Brianna then looked down at the boy. He was holding a chunky tablet, transfixed.

"Hey there. I'm Layla."

"I'm Jayden," he mumbled, his eyes stuck on the tablet screen.

"Jay," Brianna whispered sharply. Jayden squirmed and sat up.

"Sorry. What's your name?" Jayden asked half-heartedly.

"Layla. It's nice to meet you, Jayden."

"Hello, Miss Layla," he said, his eyes darting back down to the screen.

Layla smiled.

Brianna sat on the low couch. She wore a simple, fitted T-shirt and dark jeans. She looked about Layla's age. Layla blinked, taken aback for a moment. Brianna was striking. Her hair was pulled up into a bun of box braids. She stared at Layla with big, almond-shaped eyes. Layla attempted to suppress the calculating side of her brain, but she couldn't help it. Brianna was the perfect poster child for this action. She was an innocent, doeeyed, beautiful young mother and because of this new development, she was homeless. Layla hated herself for thinking this way. But this was how it worked. She needed a person people could relate to. Someone to speak firsthand about why this was all so wrong. Facts and figures just made people shake their heads and say "gentrification, what a shame." "This city has changed so fast." Layla needed to make people cry. She needed to make people do something. As if reading her mind, Brianna didn't waste any time.

"I don't want to be in the paper," Brianna blurted out as soon as Layla settled into her seat.

"Oh. Okay . . ." Layla replied.

"I mean I don't want people to know I'm here." Brianna looked around.

"Well, I'm not a reporter. And no matter what happens, your boundaries are important to me. I won't ask you to do anything you're not comfortable with. Okay?"

"Yeah, okay," Brianna softened slightly.

"Can I tell you more about what I do?"

"Yeah, sure," Brianna replied.

"So, Rise DC is a nonprofit that advocates for affordable housing. Our work takes a lot of different shapes. We organize actions and protests, we work to uphold restrictions for developers, and we advocate for people in the city who need affordable housing."

Brianna nodded. Layla smiled as she spoke. The pride in her work was beginning to show.

"I came because I wanted to hear your story. I'll be honest, Brianna, I think your story is important and I think people should hear it. And I believe you deserve to be heard. But it only works on your terms. There are a lot of options. You can tell you story anonymously or—"

"I'm not homeless," Brianna said, glancing out the barred window in the distance.

Layla instinctively opened her mouth, but said nothing.

"I was staying at my cousin's place. But I don't like the way he treats Jayden. He's too rough." Brianna looked down at Jayden.

"I have a Section 8 voucher, but I haven't found a good place that'll take it. Anyway. I'm just here until I make enough to buy a car and go down to North Carolina. That's where my mom's sister lives," Brianna said.

Layla nodded. "Of course. I won't use that word . . . if you want. Or we don't have to talk about that. If you don't want to. Do you feel comfortable talking about the house on U?"

Brianna sighed. "That was my grandparents' place. They left it to my mom. So I grew up there. My mom passed when I was seventeen, and she left the house in my brother's name."

Brianna shook her head. "By the time they were buying up the block, the bank pretty much owned the house."

Layla shifted forward in her seat.

"I didn't really know how any of this works. Like how it was our house and all of a sudden it wasn't and now it's just gone. But I know a little bit more now. I think they had a reverse mortgage and so . . . It wasn't. We couldn't afford to keep the house." Brianna's eyes sparkled with tears. She looked back to the window.

"Are you still in touch with your brother?" Layla asked gently.

"He's in PG now. But I haven't seen him since we moved out. I don't know. Maybe we could never afford that house. I just feel like—it was important to my mom. We could have done something different."

Layla nodded. Probably not, she thought. When a big developer wanted a block in this city, they always got it. But Brianna should have been compensated. Or had some choice at least.

"I'm sorry, Brianna." Layla closed her eyes.

"It's not your fault," Brianna replied, shrugging.

"I have to be honest—you could really make a difference. If you spoke to a journalist about your experience. Otherwise, you can't—"

"I already told you I'm not doing that." Brianna's voice turned cold. Layla stiffened.

"I understand. I just want you to know it could give you some options. It might help your situation, and it could make a difference for other families who are—who have been displaced by developers in DC. That's what I'm working on with this event. I'm trying to expose the—"

Brianna stood. She pulled the tablet from Jayden's hands.

"Thank you for coming today, Miss Layla. I can't help you. I'm sorry you wasted your time coming here." Brianna pulled Jayden from the couch. Layla stood.

"Wait, Brianna. I just wanted to tell you what options you'd have if you told your story."

Brianna shook her head. "You don't want to help me. You want me to help you. I told you I don't want people to know I'm here. I don't want people to know what happened to us. I already said that." Brianna's voice grew louder. The security guard turned his head. Layla sat down and stared blankly at the wall as Brianna packed Jayden's tablet into a small backpack. How could she let this happen? Jayden stared at Layla. He looked up at his mother, then back down at Layla.

"Are you gonna cry?" he asked Layla. She hadn't realized her eyes were welling up.

"No," Layla replied.

"Mommy. That lady is gonna cry," Jayden said, giggling.

"Jay, don't say that," Brianna said. She hesitated and looked down at Layla.

"Are you okay?" Brianna asked blankly.

"Yes," Layla said. "Thank you for meeting me, Brianna. You're absolutely right. I wanted to get something from you. And I should have listened to what you said you wanted. I'm really sorry."

Brianna folded her arms. "It's fine."

"No, it's not. I was wrong. I'm so sorry." Layla stood and turned to go. She didn't cry. She didn't beg for sympathy. That's white woman shit. This wasn't about her. Jesus. Why did it feel like her eyes were burning with tears? She turned and rushed through the door. The security guard pretended to stare at his phone.

Layla nearly sprinted to her bike. Jesus. Fuck. She completely fucked up. She came here to use Brianna for her story. Thinking about how beautiful she was. How Brianna would look in the paper. Fuck. Layla hated herself for this. How could she have gotten so lost in her own tunnel vision? Her hands shook as she attempted to unlock her bike. And the tears came, running hot down her cheeks. Her heart pulsing in her throat. Save the world. No matter who you hurt in the process. She was just like her mother.

"Hey, wait." Layla heard a voice in the distance.

She looked up and saw Brianna jogging down the street.

Layla wiped her face before she turned to Brianna. They stood face to face for a moment. Brianna exhaled. Layla met her gaze. A police siren blared as a cop car raced past them. They stared at one another.

"Look . . . I don't want to talk to journalists. But I didn't have to say all that."

"No. You were right. You want to protect your privacy. Brianna, there's absolutely nothing wrong with that," Layla said, shaking her head.

"Yeah. But it's not a good example for Jay. He said I made you cry." Brianna smiled slightly.

Layla folded her arms, her eyes welling up again. "Well. I'm definitely not crying. So. You can tell him that."

Brianna nodded, her face softening with pity. "You seem like you care a lot about what you do."

Layla nodded. "A little bit."

"So if I don't want to talk to a journalist about this, what could I do? I mean is there any way for your organization to help us?"

"Yes," Layla said.

"OK," Brianna replied hesitantly.

Layla frowned. "Are you sure? You want to keep talking?"

"I want to keep talking," Brianna said, nodding.

"Okay. Okay!" Layla beamed, her eyes shining. Now she really felt like she would cry. She took a breath.

"If it feels good for you. I think we should make this list."

"A list," Brianna echoed.

"We can write down all your short-term needs. The practical things. Housing, moving down south, job stuff. Rise is connected with some community organizations that might be able to help."

"OK, I can do that. I want to do that," Brianna said.

"And if you feel comfortable. On your own, you can make a second list. Write down all the things you dream about. What you would love your life to look like. I know it sounds silly, but it helps us get an idea of how to build your life with things you really want in mind. Maybe even Jayden can make a dream list too?" Layla didn't have enough hope left to smile. She watched Brianna take it all in, nodding slowly.

"My dreams," Brianna repeated, chuckling. She nodded. "That sounds nice."

18. JASMINE AND ZORA

Jasmine.

Jasmine walked through the haze of smoke and cologne. The room swelled with the bass drum of a trap beat and a cascade of silken Sarah Vaughan samples. Oversized purple neon letters spelled L-O-R-D-E across the wide brick wall. Tight corners of the club spilled over with cool light and bodies in motion. Tall glasses clinked with ice and pink fizzy liquid. Fine-ass queer eye candy everywhere you looked. Well-oiled brown skin and frayed denim edges. Long braids cascaded down arched backs. Locs swung. Thick silver chains glittered. Closed eyes and heads tipping back with laughter. Pigmented color shone like abstract art across eyelids, cheeks and brows. Baby's breath laced through luscious clouds of curls. The club's walls were peppered with portraits of Audre Lorde and tropical photographs of Grenada. Her words glowed against the brick walls in purple neon. "Women are powerful and dangerous."

Jasmine had some reservations about meeting Zora here. DC had one of the largest Black queer communities in the world. And yet, the girlies still made it feel incredibly small. Incestuous. If you were going to Lorde, you had to accept the fact that you'd run into an ex, or three. And if you went to Lorde with someone, you also had to accept the fact that they would run into an ex, or three. Jasmine figured it was somewhat safe since she hadn't really dated in the past five years and Zora hadn't lived here since high school. Jasmine squinted into the crowd and prayed for a room full of gay strangers. So far, her prayers had been answered.

Zora.

Zora sat at the other end of the bar. She watched the dance floor, drinking in the colors and textures of the scene. She grew up in DC, but she had done most of her adulting and partying elsewhere. Brooklyn, Atlanta, Paris, LA, London. She assumed DC was too sleepy and small-town for a good night out. Apparently, she was wrong. The room was packed with gorgeous Black and brown folks. Femmes, androgynous folk, bois, boys and girls. Gorgeous and fashionable. And they all seemed to stare Zora down as they walked by. Zora's eyes fell. She had to be painfully obvious to most people. Her appearance seemed to read as an invitation for aggressive flirting. Being masculine and fine meant that people wanted her. And they didn't hide it. She knew her looks had that effect on people. But it meant nothing to her. Her bone structure had nothing to do with her character and being approached by a stranger was mostly a turn-off. These people didn't know shit about her. They just assumed things and she knew she would disappoint them. She wasn't nice. Or charming. Or fun. She wouldn't flash them a grin and flirt with them so everybody could get a little ego boost. She wasn't what they wanted. So she did her best to avoid the confusion all together. She stared coolly at the ice in her drink, hoping that would be enough to stave off flirtatious strangers. What would it look like if Jasmine appeared while she was talking to another woman? It would look like flirting. Not a good move for a first date. Was this a date? Zora wondered.

Jasmine.

Jasmine danced through the room. She wore her favorite shirt. A long, translucent black piece made with the thinnest sheer. It was wide at her shoulders and tight down at her thighs, hugging her curves. She wore a white sports bra and white jean shorts under the shadow of the black sheer. Jasmine wore punky dramatic makeup with thick black smoke accentuating the corners of her eyes and fading to a shimmering silver-green at the bridge of her nose. Her heavy black boots gave her five-foot-six an extra inch and a dash of big dick energy. She strutted into the dark room, walking halftime with the beat. She glanced around. She tipped her head down, palming the freshly cut skin fade on the back of her neck. Her barber gave her the perfect fade with a straight-razor-cut part. This was one of those good days. She didn't try on one hundred outfits. She didn't huff at the mirror when her makeup didn't look right. She was calm and confident. She looked good, and she knew it.

Jasmine spotted Zora at the end of the bar. Zora wore tight black jeans, her legs long and muscular, stretching out from the bar stool to the floor. One leg crossed over the other. Very cool. Black hightop Jordans and a white band-collar shirt made of something impossibly thin. Her whole outfit looked simple and expensive. Effortless. Jasmine wasn't the only one who noticed Zora. Everyone within a twenty-foot radius was pretending not to stare. Fucking sharks, Jasmine thought. Another reason why she didn't go to Lorde anymore. The exes, and the sharks. Jasmine swatted her dark thoughts away. Fuck it. She looked hot. And tonight she was going home with the finest young thing in the room. That was that. As Jasmine made her way across the bar to Zora, a sudden squeal of sound erupted from the dance floor.

"ZORA!" A woman in a silky olive romper and impossibly high heels danced over to Zora. Her long curly hair bounced as she pulled Zora into a long embrace. A very, very long embrace. It was long enough to make Jasmine stop, wait, and wonder if she should turn around and leave.

"Aubrey?" Zora smiled.

"Oh my God, Zo! What are you doing here?" Aubrey asked as she tilted her head to the side.

"David and I got a place uptown. I moved back a couple weeks ago," Zora said.

"Aw! Baby brother David! I miss you both so much!" Aubrey squealed.

"Yeah, he told me he saw you the other day. How are you? How's BET?"

"Oh my god. It's so great! So much is happening! I'm technically an executive now. Can you believe it?" Aubrey danced as she spoke.

"I can," Zora replied. "You were never really the middle-management type."

Aubrey beamed as she moved in closer to Zora. "You're so sweet. Blah Blah. Enough about me. How are you? Whose heart are you breaking these days?" Aubrey asked, giggling.

"Heyyyy," Jasmine said, stepping hesitantly toward Zora and Aubrey.

Zora flinched. Aubrey whipped her head around.

"Sorry to interrupt? I'm Jasmine." Jasmine looked at Aubrey, a blank smile on her face.

Zora straightened herself and stood. "Hey!" Zora opened her arms. Jasmine cautiously moved in for an embrace. She closed her eyes for a moment and breathed Zora in. As they pulled away from one another, Aubrey looked stunned.

"Jasmine, this is Aubrey. We went to high school together and—"

"Zora was my first love," Aubrey finished Zora's sentence with a giggle. "No, I'm kidding," Aubrey went on, delighted by her own joke. "We dated a thousand years ago in high school and basically haven't spoken since. Right, Zo?"

Aubrey gave Zora a nudge. Zora looked uncomfortable.

"And Aubrey, this is Jasmine."

Zora and Jasmine exchanged a look.

"My date. We're on our first date. Actually." Zora smiled at Jasmine, then looked away. Jasmine tilted her head. They never really said what this was.

Aubrey's smile turned stiff at the sound of this. "Wow!" Her voice jumped an octave up. She nodded too enthusiastically. "Zora, lucky, lucky you. She's goooorrrrgeous."

Jasmine's face twitched. "Oh no. I'm the lucky one," Jasmine said. "Not only do I get to go on a date with Zora Scott . . ."

She paused for dramatic effect.

"I also get to go on a date with her beautiful ex-girlfriend from high school! It's a two-for-one deal, y'all!"

Jasmine laughed, waiting for everyone to join in. Aubrey, who seemed like a pro when it came to fake laughter, managed only a plastic smile. Zora smiled at Jasmine. Aubrey lifted her dainty cocktail glass.

"Well, I'll drink to that! I wouldn't kick either of you out of bed," Aubrey said.

"Ha!" Zora added.

"I'm sorry, remind me of your name again?" Aubrey patted Jasmine's forearm.

"Jasmine," she said, smiling.

"Jasmine!" Aubrey chirped and went on, looking only at Zora. "Jasmine doesn't seem like your type, Zo. I mean what an upgrade! I'm so glad you're done with all those boring, prissy femmes. I mean borrrring," Aubrey said, pointing to herself.

Zora looked at Aubrey, eyes widening.

Jasmine grinned. "What? Aubrey. Girl stop. You're stunning," Jasmine said. She felt Zora's hand on her hip. Zora leaned into Jasmine's neck.

"How do I get rid of her?" Zora whispered into Jasmine's ear.

"Don't ask me, she's your first love!" Jasmine whispered back.

"I'm sorry." Zora's whisper was so close, her lips touched Jasmine's neck.

Jasmine felt like a stream of cold water was trickling down her spine. Her back straightened. She leaned back, bringing her lips to Zora's ear.

"You owe me," Jasmine whispered. Her lips hovered there. She wanted to put Zora's earlobe in her mouth again. But she didn't. Meanwhile, Aubrey pretended to notice something on the other side of the room. She looked up with a hopeful expression.

"Well. I insist on buying you both a round of drinks," Aubrey said. "I've completely ruined your date and it's the least I could do." Aubrey patted Jasmine's forearm again.

You could leave, Jasmine wanted to say.

"Um. Sure." Jasmine looked at Zora.

"No. I'll buy the drinks. I insist." Zora stepped to the bar, then looked at Jasmine pleadingly.

"What would you like, Jasmine?" Zora asked as she flagged down the bartender.

I'd like for your thirsty ex to leave, Jasmine didn't say.

"I'll have a club soda with pineapple and lime," Jasmine replied. She looked at Aubrey, attempting to normalize the situation by ignoring it.

Zora stared at Jasmine.

"You don't drink?" Aubrey asked.

"I don't," Jasmine shook her head definitively.

"Good for you!" Aubrey said, her eyes wide with amazement.

"Aubrey?" Zora interrupted.

"Oh! I'll have a Manhattan."

"And a Walker soda please," Zora said as the bartender nodded.

"So what is Zora's usual type, Aubrey?" Jasmine asked.

Zora stared at Jasmine, horrified.

"Oh yes! The tea!" Aubrey cooed. "Well, of course she'll only date intelligent women. Brilliant, thoughtful, educated. The talented tenth." Aubrey began, watching Zora squirm.

"But from what I've seen on social media, they're also very feminine and very gorgeous. I mean no exceptions. So basically IG models with advanced degrees." Aubrey giggled.

Zora gritted her teeth.

"Jasmine," Zora began. "Maybe we should head out soon. I want to catch the previews . . ." Zora nodded wide-eyed at Jasmine.

"Riiight. The previews," Jasmine replied.

"Oh. Y'all are going to see a movie?" Aubrey asked.

"Yeah."

"Yep."

Zora and Jasmine nodded and stared at each other.

"Oh cute. What are you seeing?" Aubrey asked, folding her arms.

"Oh," Zora stared at Jasmine.

"We're gonna see the new—" Jasmine began.

"It's yeah the new um—" Zora pretended to remember the name of the film they weren't going to see.

"Yeah. The new horror film about the, you know?" Jasmine went on.

"Yes. That one," Zora nodded.

"EYYYYOOOOJAAAAAAZ!" Shouting pierced through the beats and chatter in the room.

A short, boyish woman in a loud Versace-via-Migos-style shirt emerged from the crowd, covered in glitter and sweat. Jess bounced over to Jasmine. She dribbled an invisible basketball, shot and held her hand high in the air for an imaginary three pointer. Jasmine winced. Zora and Aubrey watched Jess with equal parts amusement and confusion as Jess dribbled up to the group. Jess looked like she could be the front man in a R&B boy band.

"Hi Jess," Jasmine said, defeated.

"Hi sweetheart," Jess replied, her golden locs dancing around her hazel eyes.

Those eyes. People used to ask her if they were contacts. Strangers would stop her on the street and tell her they were the most beautiful eyes they'd ever seen. But Jess's famous hazel eyes creeped Jasmine out. They always reminded her of the light-eyed Black villains from movies she'd watched growing up. There was always a cheating man or an evil light-eyed woman with finger waves plotting against the hero of the story. Reverse colorist, maybe. But it stuck with her. Beautiful, creepy-eyed Jess was Jasmine's last lover. And the last person she wanted to see tonight.

Jess smiled as she danced over to Jasmine and held her in a tight embrace.

"Mmmmh. Ass still fat, I see," Jess said in a hushed tone.

"Just like your ego," Jasmine whispered.

As they pulled apart, she nodded politely to Zora and Aubrey.

"Hey, kids!" Jess said with a friendly wave and a winning smile.

"Um. This is Jessica—" Jasmine began.

"—her mistress," Jess interrupted. "Oh no, I'm sorry. Ex mistress." Jess giggled as she shook Zora's hand. She winked as she shook Aubrey's.

"No. No. We are not ex anythings. Jess, will you kindly please go back to the fucking hobbit hill you danced out of," Jasmine whispered aggressively.

"Well, look at that. A double date," Zora said, smirking.

"What's that?" Jess asked, regarding Zora.

Zora smiled, folding her arms. "It seems Jasmine and I have both run into exes on our first date. It's almost like a prank. Or a nightmare. Ha," Zora said, cutting a smile at Jasmine.

"Well, I think it's a brilliant idea," Aubrey said, now leaning flirtatiously in toward Jess.

"I mean your date's ex is the perfect companion on a first date. An ex will give you all the information you really need, right?" Aubrey said, smiling at Zora.

"Right! The good stuff, the not-so-good stuff . . ." Jess chimed in.

"Oh! Fears? Special skills?" Aubrey giggled.

"Favorite foods, pet peeves, attachment styles, character flaws . . ." Jess listed items on her fingers.

"Life goals? Dreams . . ." Aubrey added, now counting on her fingers as well.

"Favorite positions, role-play scenarios, strap sizes . . ." Jess went on, her counting fingers now making a suggestive shape.

"Okay!" Jasmine interrupted. "Y'all are hilarious. But uh. Uh. How about we workshop this idea on another day?"

"Well, I think this is a flawless plan," Jess said to Aubrey.

"I completely agree," Aubrey replied.

Jasmine felt Zora's hand on her hip again. Zora pulled Jasmine up against her body. Zora's lips hovered next to Jasmine's ear.

"Looks like we're even," Zora whispered coolly.

Jasmine's ear tickled. Her body felt warm with this gesture of intimacy.

"It was great running into you both, but I think that's the end of this touching moment," Jasmine said, her smile tightening.

"Well. That's just fine cuz I'm ready to dance!" Jess said, suddenly restless.

"I'm in," Aubrey said.

"And we should head to that movie," Zora lied.

"Right," Jasmine cut in, pointing at Zora.

"OK. We're leaving now. Let's do a raincheck on the ex double-date plans," Zora said definitively.

"Mmhmm," Jess said, crossing her arms.

"A likely story," Aubrey added.

"It was great seeing you, Aubrey, and meeting you, Jess,"

Zora said as she cordially hugged the two exes. Jasmine followed suit.

"Good luck on your date," Aubrey said.

"Call me when you're single again," Jess called out as she and Aubrey laughed their way to the dance floor. Zora rolled her eyes and flagged down the bartender.

"Wow," Jasmine said, watching their exes dance flirtatiously.

"I think my ex likes your ex," Jasmine said.

Zora turned to look. "Good for them."

The thumping bassline faded into the distance as Zora and Jasmine walked in silence down the street. Jasmine smiled at her feet as she walked. Something about this night felt worn in. Like they'd walked down Rhode Island Avenue a dozen times before. It almost felt like she could remember pieces of this moment. The soft summer breeze. The trees glowing gold in the streetlight. Zora's hand around her waist in the bar. Familiar.

Zora.

"This is me," Zora said as a parked car's lights suddenly emerged from the darkness.

"This?" Jasmine pointed to the car.

"Yeah," Zora said. She opened the passenger door, waiting for Jasmine to step into the car.

Jasmine nodded. "You didn't want to go full Musk and spring for the cybertruck?"

"Actually, my cybertruck is being shipped as we speak," Zora said sarcastically.

"Are you serious?" Jasmine said.

"No."

"Thank God," Jasmine said, wiping imaginary sweat from her brow.

"I don't love Elon Musk, but . . . I love my car." Zora shrugged.

Zora nervously adjusted the climate controls. Growing up, she was always a bit nervous about people seeing any evidence of her wealth. The younger version of her drove a Prius. Something preowned. She didn't wear the new Jordans she got from her dad for Christmas. She'd wait months before bringing a girl home. She learned early on, expensive things could intimidate people. But she was nearly forty. She didn't have the energy to care what people thought anymore. Still, she felt herself fidgeting with worry over what Jasmine might think.

"Hey," Jasmine said as she clicked in her seatbelt.

"Hey," Zora replied.

"What do the Germans call a Tesla?" Jasmine asked, staring at Zora.

"Um. I don't know. What?" Zora replied.

"A VOLTS-wagon," Jasmine said, staring deadpan at Zora.

"Wow," Zora replied.

Jasmine attempted to hold in a snicker.

"You liked it. I can tell you liked it." Jasmine said, grinning.

"She's a master of the culinary arts and she got dad jokes too?" Zora said as she pulled out into the road.

Zora looked briefly over at Jasmine, still cracking up at her own joke. Zora couldn't help laughing with her. She exhaled and relaxed back into the vegan leather seats.

"So what do you feel like?" Zora asked as she turned on to Georgia Avenue.

"Hmm. I'm not super hungry. Maybe fries?" Jasmine studied the intricate details of the car.

"Sure. Anything you know that's open this late?" Zora asked.

"Do you even eat fast food? Isn't it too lowbrow for you?" Jasmine teased.

Zora sighed. "No. It's not."

"Well, I'm sure our humble city's french fries couldn't possibly measure up to Parisian French fries."

"Alright. Alright. I get it. I'm snobby. Haha," Zora said, nodding. "You're quite the comedian today, huh?"

"Sorry, I couldn't resist," Jasmine said, grinning.

"So when you're done clowning me, where would you like to go?"

"HoChi, maybe," Jasmine replied.

"Ho-Chi?" Zora repeated.

"Howard China? It's the takeout spot next to campus," Jasmine said, staring at Zora. "Oh, Zora—you know where Howard is right?" Jasmine went on, looking concerned.

"Yes, Jasmine. I've never heard of HoChi. But I know where Howard is. I did grow up here and I actually am a Black person," Zora said, rolling her eyes.

"Right," Jasmine replied, frowning and nodding.

"Oh, and there's Ben's Next Door," Zora added.

Jasmine scrunched her nose a bit. "Um. I think HoChi is closer. And I'm not a huge fan of bars."

". . . says the person who asked me to meet her at a gay bar?"

"That was a very, very poor decision on my part. I thought we would dance." Jasmine sighed, watching Zora study the road.

Jasmine turned her head toward the passenger-side window.

"And you don't drink," Zora didn't ask.

"And I don't drink," Jasmine said. "But I mean I can still have fun at a bar."

"Do you mind if I ask? Why you don't drink?" Zora asked softly.

"I'm in AA. And no, I don't mind talking about it," Jasmine said.

Zora nodded.

"I've been sober for two years. I was sad . . . and very self-centered when I drank. My life is just. It's better now. It's more full. That's the abridged version of the story," Jasmine said.

The lights of the city flashed by.

"My mom's in AA," Zora said.

Jasmine looked at Zora.

"She's been in the rooms for twenty years. It saved her life."

"That's amazing," Jasmine replied.

"I used to go to meetings with her. I still go to her anniversaries. I'm really proud of her." Zora smiled.

Of course, for Zora it wasn't that simple. Her mother's recovery couldn't heal everything. She wouldn't recover those fragments of childhood. The birthdays her mother missed. The signs she learned to read as a child. When Mom's words run together, she can't hear you anymore. The shouting matches with her father. The nannies he hired in an attempt to replace the one person he could never replace. The years she spent calling her mother by her first name. She was too young at the time to understand addiction. She was practically a baby. David was younger. In Zora's eyes, David had the blessing of understanding less and missing more. Her mother was sober for years before Zora felt safe enough to let her in again.

Zora stopped at a red light. Jasmine's eyes found Zora's. The light turned green and Zora looked back out at the road. She breathed into the hum and soft rocking of the car.

"It's on the right up ahead," Jasmine said, pointing.

Zora pulled up to HoChi, a hole-in-the-wall takeout spot nestled into the corner. Zora and Jasmine walked in to find it packed with Black college kids. The one table in the place was littered with takeout boxes full of fried chicken and french fries, open and steaming. The kids around the table were loud, most of them clearly drunk. One group of girls danced to a song playing low on a cell phone speaker. Zora observed the scene. Jasmine leaned up to the window with authority.

"Fries with ketchup and mambo sauce on the side please," Jasmine smiled and yell-talked at the elder Asian man behind the thick plexiglass partition. She watched Zora.

"Yes, I know what mambo sauce is, and yes I've had it before," Zora said.

"I didn't say anything," Jasmine responded, both hands raised in the air.

Zora reached for her wallet, but Jasmine slid a crumpled

bill through the window before she got to it. Zora couldn't remember the last time one of her dates offered to pay.

Zora and Jasmine walked out into the night. They wandered back toward the car, taking their time.

"Where should we go?" Jasmine asked. She opened the box to admire the nest of perfectly golden crinkle fries and sauces.

"You know that hill on Thirteenth?" Zora asked.

"By Cardozo?"

"Yeah," Zora replied.

"I love that hill," said Jasmine, smiling. "I used to bike down that hill to get to work."

"Let's go," Zora said.

"Are you sure you want to drive?" Jasmine frowned, looking down at the takeout container.

"Yeah. It's too far to walk," Zora replied.

"Your precious car is going to smell like hot fries for a week," Jasmine said.

"Great," Zora said, opening Jasmine's door for her. Jasmine climbed into her seat.

"It'll remind me of you," Zora said. She closed the door, jogged around the car and jumped into the driver's seat. She found Jasmine grinning and shaking her head.

"What?" Zora asked.

"Nothing," Jasmine replied, her mouth full of steaming french fries.

Zora and Jasmine sat on the stone wall on Thirteenth Street. They ate slowly and looked out at the lights of downtown DC. They swung their legs like children. Zora pulled out her phone and looked down at it for a moment. Her rich brown skin glowed silver by phone light. Jasmine reached for another fry and watched the red and white car lights dance up and down the hill.

Jasmine tilted her head back and gazed up at the black, purple sky freckled with stars. Tonight felt clearer than the usual

DC summer night. Almost like spring. Zora watched Jasmine as she closed her eyes and shook her head.

"I thought you were such an asshole when we met," Jasmine said, chuckling to herself.

"Yeah. I know," Zora replied flatly.

"I mean I still think that. To be honest."

"Nice." Zora nodded.

"I mean you seemed like you were just this rich snob. But you're really not what I expected."

Zora folded her arms. Jasmine tilted her head and looked back up at the stars.

"Maybe you're kind of . . . deep," she said to the sky.

"Deep?" Zora repeated.

Jasmine sighed. "Whatever."

"Okay. Deep. Sure. I mean it's not the most poetic compliment I've ever received, but it's a big step up from asshole so—"

"Yeah. Fine. That's fine. No more compliments for you," Jasmine said, grinning.

Zora sighed.

"So. You said this was a date," Jasmine said hesitantly.

"I did."

"Did you mean it? Is this a date?"

Zora tilted her head. "Do you want this to be a date, Jasmine?"

"I asked you first."

Zora took a breath. "Honestly, I'm not looking for a relationship. But I feel drawn to you. I want to explore that. Does that feel good to you?"

"Yeah. I get it," Jasmine said, looking out at the city lights.

Zora looked down at her phone.

Jasmine tilted her head back and searched for a constellation in the sky.

"OK, I got one. Why do bakers always marry their siblings?"

Zora asked, looking down at her phone.

"Good lord. Did you just look up dad jokes on your phone? In front of me?" Jasmine asked, giggling.

"Maybe," Zora said, hiding her phone conspicuously behind her back.

"Very smooth. Okay, I don't know. Sounds gross. Why do bakers marry their siblings?" Jasmine asked.

"Because they're all in bread," Zora said dully with a straight face.

"Eeew," Jasmine said, shaking her head and smiling.

"Oh come on. It's perfect. Spicy and topical," Zora pleaded.

"Topical!" Jasmine tipped her head back, laughing.

Zora looked out at the horizon.

Jasmine watched her.

"Would you like to kiss? I mean, can I kiss you? Right now?" Jasmine asked. Zora's face lit up with a bewildered smile.

"What is it?" Jasmine asked.

"Sorry . . . I guess I'm used to making the first move," Zora replied.

"Well, you wanna try something different?" Jasmine said.

"You really want to kiss me after I made in incest joke?"

"I really do," Jasmine said.

"You want that to be part of our story?" Zora said, leaning closer.

"Not really but I kind of couldn't wait any longer—so."

"All right then," Zora said, grinning.

Jasmine leaned over the half-empty takeout box and kissed Zora. They both closed their eyes and leaned into the kiss. Their smiles pulled tight with laughter.

19. ELLA

"She wears these Fendi yoga pants every time. A different color for every day. So I looked them up yesterday. And David. Look. Look at this shit. Five hundred dollars. For yoga pants!" Ella said, gesturing wildly with her phone.

"Wait, wait. Which client? The one who moans or the bad tipper?" David whispered.

"Bad tipper. Of course."

"Well, you can't blame her. She spent all your tips on yoga pants," David replied.

"Rich people are wild."

"Well, I think we're in the wrong business," David said.

"I mean are they diamond-studded? Laced with gold leaf?" Ella chuckled.

"Should I get you some for your birthday?" David grinned and waggled his eyebrows.

"If you bought me five-hundred-dollar yoga pants, I would never speak to you again. I like you a lot, so please don't," Ella said.

Ella and David sat in the lobby of TONE, both rosy-cheeked and dewy. The pulse of poppy dancehall vibrated through the walls. They each sipped from tall glasses of freshly pressed green juice. This had become a ritual. David and Ella met in the gym every night. David stole glances at Ella running on the treadmill. He made faces at her from the stationary bike. And Ella watched him too. While she was stretching, David would join a gaggle of bros in the lifting section. He was much too silly to make friends with the power lifters. Even at a distance, she could tell he was making bad jokes. He danced when he finished a set of curls. He snorted when he laughed.

As part of the gym staff, Ella was allowed to work out at TONE, but socializing with club members was frowned upon. So they'd stare at each other from across the room and imagine what they'd do when they got back to David's place. Ella sipped at her juice, dreaming of the last time she and David slept together. Her cheeks burned hot with the memory of that night. They were like athletes in bed. Ella had to close her eyes when she came. Pulling back just enough to feel his skin, to float above him without listening to his memories. She couldn't allow herself to let go. If she did, she might not like what she saw. She might see too much. And Ella knew how to hold her power at a distance with boys. She knew how young straight men thought, and she knew most of them didn't deserve her. Shit. Most straight men didn't deserve a home-cooked meal. But she enjoyed having a bit of harmless fun with them here and there. Her plans for David were no different. Have fun. Don't listen to his memories. Keep your distance. That was the plan. But something had changed over the past few weeks. Somehow, as if by osmosis, David's spirit materialized next to hers. She never activated her gift around him, but his memories could just appear in her mind. It felt like a misting rain that slowly turned into a body of water. Beautiful, sweet and sometimes somber memories flooded into her mind. His inner child was always making noise when they were together. Ella could hear a little baby David laughing when he laughed. She found herself wanting to know that child. She wanted to understand what made him smile. What made him cry.

Ella looked down at her bag as David sipped his juice. She

pulled her bag up to the table.

"I brought you something," she said casually. "It's not a gift," she added.

"Oh? Okay..." David smiled. Confused, but happy.

"It's been lying around the house forever and I thought you'd like to have it?"

Ella watched David peer into the duffel bag, discovering the small instrument in what looked like a soft case. He gently lifted the ukulele from its case as if it were a newborn. He stared down at it with reverence. He said nothing. Ella shifted in her seat.

David shook his head. "Ella. It's beautiful. But I can't accept this. I'm sure your family would miss it."

Ella sighed. "OK. Actually, it wasn't lying around the house. I don't know why I said that. I bought it for you. I know you already have a dozen instruments. But I thought maybe something new would inspire you? I don't know." Ella shrugged.

"Ella. This means so much to me," David said quietly. When he lifted his head, his eyes were sparkling with tears. Ella choked back her laughter.

"David? I—" Ella tried to speak. She stopped herself. David was looking back down at the instrument, running his fingers along the designs burned into the wood. Ella touched his shoulder gently. "David, are you okay?" She whispered. She looked around the cafe, praying none of her supervisors were nearby.

"Nobody ever wanted me to... I mean," David said, sniffling. A stream of tears ran down his face. He took in a sharp breath. "I bought my first guitar when I was eighteen. And since then, I've bought myself keyboards, drum sets, pianos, and a hundred random instruments. I bought them for myself, you know?"

Ella leaned in to hear David's voice, emerging in a deep and wavering whisper.

"I was the artsy kid, but nobody really wanted me to be, you know? I mean Zora wanted me to be happy. She did her best to show up. But my dad. I could tell he wanted me to grow out of it."

"I know," Ella whispered.

David looked up at Ella. His cheeks were wet and shining.

"Well, I'm glad you're the artsy kid."

David fell into her, his head heavy on her shoulder. He wept quietly in her arms.

"Aw honey," Ella said, her voice sugared with concern. David looked up at her. His face was puffy with tears but to Ella, he'd never looked more beautiful. This was too good, Ella thought. It couldn't be this simple.

"I got you a gift too. I got it the day after our first date. But I was scared it was too soon. Or too creepy. I don't know. I was waiting for something."

"Hmm. Yeah, I get that," Ella said.

"It's at the house. You wanna go home?"

Ella nodded.

"Let's go."

20. JASMINE AND ZORA

Jasmine

Zora ascended her front steps with perfect posture. Her back straight as an arrow, she held the door open with such formality it made Jasmine blush.

"After you."

Zora was the handsome gentleman from one of those Victorian-era romance novels. Rich and confident in shining boots and velvet coats. Regal and smoldering. And Jasmine was nervous. Her palms were sweating again. Her armpits were sweating again. She was flustered. She wasn't sure how to receive it. She wondered if she should be demure and shy like the ladies in those novels. Was she supposed to giggle and grin behind a lacy handkerchief? That wasn't really her style. But that gentlemanly confidence wasn't her style either. She could make the best pastry you ever ate in your life. But she had no game. Just muted anxiety. Or passionate intellectual rants. Or inelegant conviction. Nothing much in between. Perhaps she could match Zora's knightliness with her own. Why not? Their fantasy could be anything they wanted it to be. They could both be princes, hailing from neighboring countries at war. They could slip away to have forbidden hot gay sex and later unite their nations in peace. Or she could be the brave knight returning home from battle, receiving the medal of valor from her prince. Kneeling to be knighted. Maybe she was the peasant stable boy who fucked the prince after his riding lessons. Jasmine got lost in her fairytales for a moment. She inhaled Zora's smoky scent as she crossed the threshold.

And there she was again, in Zora's palatial home. Silver moonlight shone through the window. Outside, the trees stood still and quiet. The concrete floors looked wet in the dark. Thin lines of soft light glowed, illuminating sharp corners, white dishes neatly organized in frosted glass cabinets, sculptural couches, and the wide stairs leading up. Those stairs. Jasmine's eyes sauntered slowly up the stairs to the dark corridor in the distance. That's where she'd seen Zora for the second time. She remembered Zora descending those stairs, looking impossibly gorgeous and bored. She'd decided then that Zora was nothing more than a very spoiled rich boy. But the more time Jasmine spent with Zora, the more she realized it wasn't that simple. Zora was honest. And yes, she was a fucking snob. But now, instead of imposition, it was a challenge. Zora was hard to impress. And that made Jasmine want to impress her even more.

Jasmine's gaze wandered around the large room. Zora pulled at the tie in her hair, letting her locs cascade down to her shoulders. She sauntered toward the kitchen, turning back to Jasmine.

"You want something to drink? I have some juice ... or tea?" She opened the fridge and her face lit up with white light. She surveyed the fridge's contents.

Jasmine sighed. "No, I'm good. Thanks." She pushed her hips into the island counter, her palms pressing down on the cold black marble.

Zora closed the fridge. She walked to the island and stood opposite Jasmine.

"Do you want to watch a movie?" Zora asked. Her eyes wandered down Jasmine's body, resting at her hands on the counter.

Jasmine smiled. "No."

Zora looked up, pretending to think. "Do you want to . . . play a board game?" She asked, grinning.

Jasmine looked up at the ceiling, pretending to consider this option. "Hmmmm. No." Jasmine said, pointedly shaking her head once.

"Ah." Zora's smile curled into something mischievous. She leaned into the island and wet her lips with her tongue. "Do you want to go upstairs?"

"Yeah. I do," Jasmine said, nodding as Zora laughed. Jasmine hadn't planned on being so rigorously honest. But the words sort of fell out of her mouth. Zora appeared to be amused.

"So just cut to the chase, huh?" Zora asked. Jasmine took a breath.

"Zora. I really want to kiss you again. And maybe get into your bed? And kiss you some more in your bed. That's honestly all I want right now. But it's your call. If you want to play Scrabble, I'm down. If you want to have tea, let's do it. It's your world." Jasmine shrugged.

"Come on." Zora nodded her head toward the stairs and walked past Jasmine. Her fingertips trailed behind her. Grinning, Jasmine took her hand.

Zora's room was all slate gray and lined with books. Every object sat up with perfect posture. Narrow and expectant, like it was begging to be pushed, to be made crooked. It was the kind of neat that made Jasmine want to mess it all up. Thin lines of light illuminated the narrow bookshelves. Jasmine reached up to touch the books with her fingertips. She skimmed the titles of law school and architecture textbooks, a collection of scholarly tomes that looked weighted and soul-numbing. Jasmine's eyes wandered up and caught on a selection of novels by Black authors. She nodded approvingly at Zora's collections of Baldwin, Adichie, Morrison, and her namesake (Jasmine assumed) Zora Neale Hurston. She wondered how many books

Zora had actually read. Really, really read.

Zora

Zora watched as Jasmine studied her room, wondering what Jasmine might think. She wondered if Jasmine would approve of her books. She had so many textbooks. She'd probably never open them again, but she was proud that she'd read them once. Those books were reminders of all her hard work. Zora wondered what Jasmine's favorite books were. She imagined that Jasmine probably read Butler or Emezi, or something very sad and drenched in allegory.

Zora stood by the door and watched Jasmine turn in the middle of the room, following the lights and shelves with her eyes. Zora told herself she wasn't nervous. She told herself she didn't care what Jasmine thought about her room. Who cares? It's just a room. But it wasn't just a room. Zora obsessed over paint samples and feng shui. She loved the beauty of a well-designed space. And this room was more her style than anywhere she'd ever lived. She wanted Jasmine to see it. Zora watched Jasmine's movement. She traced the lines of her body. She studied the curves of Jasmine's ass and thighs in her tight shorts, the hint of her soft skin whispered through the dark shadow of the fabric. Jasmine's hands caressed a row of books. Zora felt the urge to grab her wrist hard—and kiss it softly. She wanted to lift Jasmine's ass onto the bookshelf and open her legs. Instead, she stood still by the door and waited.

Jasmine wandered to the far end of the room where a large frame hung on the wall. A black-and-white copy of a blueprint. The words and letters in the frame looked like they were written with a needle, scrawled beneath spindly angles and perfectly straight lines. The ghost of a structure obsessively detailed with angular precision.

"Is this Fallingwater?" Jasmine asked.

Zora's face lit up. "Yes! How did you know?"

"My mom was an art teacher for twenty-five years. So I know a little bit about a lot of things. Mostly not very useful things, actually," Jasmine said, looking back up at the print.

"Frank Lloyd Wright is my favorite architect. I mean. He's everyone's favorite I guess. But I really do love his work."

"It's beautiful," Jasmine said.

"And the way he worked it into the landscape? It's so brilliant. I didn't go to school for architecture. But I've always liked it." In her excitement, Zora was suddenly wordier than usual.

"What does school have to do with anything?" Jasmine's words lifted with a nonchalant chuckle.

"Well—" Zora began.

"Have you seen it?" Jasmine asked, looking back at the print.

"Seen what?"

"The house? Have you gone to see Fallingwater?"

"Actually . . . I haven't." Zora folded her arms.

"No? It's pretty close, I think."

"Really?" Zora replied.

"Zora! You've gone everywhere else in the world, I'm surprised you haven't seen it!"

"It just didn't occur to me," Zora said.

"Well, I guess a small town in Pennsylvania doesn't compare to Paris. Probably not glamorous enough for you, huh?" Jasmine said, giggling. Zora's smile deflated.

"Oh. Zora. I'm kidding."

Zora unfolded her arms and stared up at the print. "You still think I'm pretentious."

"Ha!" Jasmine threw her head back in laughter. Zora scowled.

"So what? Maybe you're too fancy to visit some random corner of Pennsylvania or you're too busy visiting Europe. Whatever! Your life is fucking awesome!" Jasmine said, gesturing wildly with her hands.

Zora stared at the print.

Jasmine sighed. "And you are pretentious. But you're open-minded too, right?"

"Right." Zora shrugged.

"Then we should go. Pack up the fanciest cheese board you got, and drive to Pennsylvania to see your favorite architecture."

"Sure," Zora replied, nodding. She stepped closer to Jasmine and they looked up at the print together.

Jasmine

"So. Wait. Where do you sleep?" Jasmine asked.

Zora's hand gestured toward the end of the room. She pulled a metal handle and a thick steel panel slid open, revealing a wide bedroom. Of course, Jasmine thought, Zora was so rich that even her bedroom had bedrooms. When Jasmine turned the corner, she nearly gasped. A line of white light glowed around the base of the oversized, crisply made bed. Beyond the gray suede headboard, there appeared to be a shimmering floor-to-ceiling wall covered completely in hammered silver. A silver accent wall.

"Woooo," Jasmine uttered, looking up. She walked to the wall as if it were pulling her. Her hand hovered an inch from the metal.

It was breathtaking. An elegant yet industrial halo of metal around the altar of Zora's bed. Everything in the silver reflection undulated like a dream, like a slow rippling body of water.

"Tell me the story." Jasmine turned to look at Zora.

"About the wall?" Zora asked, grinning.

"Yes. About this gorgeous portal of a wall!" Jasmine walked to Zora's side. They stared up at the wall together.

"There's not much to tell," Zora said.

"Zora please. I'm sure it wasn't easy to line an entire wall of your bedroom with silver. There's gotta be a story." Jasmine stared at Zora, waiting.

"Well, I really like this DC architect."

"Another beloved architect. I'm noticing a theme—" Jasmine interjected. Zora continued.

"So his signature is copper and steel siding. He uses copper on the outside of his houses and incorporates the metal into the interior design. It's not really functional. It's kind of like a signature. Anyway. I thought it would be cool to duplicate his technique. So I basically stole it," Zora said.

"I mean that's how art works, right? Good artists borrow, great artists steal. And so on," Jasmine said, touching the wall with cautious fingertips.

"Art?" Zora scoffed.

"Yes, Zora," Jasmine replied.

Jasmine watched Zora. Her rich brown skin glowed in the silvery light. When their eyes met, Jasmine resisted the urge to look away. This felt more intimate than kissing, more intimate than sex. For the first time, Jasmine noticed the nuances of color in Zora's eyes. They looked like glossed wood. Every angle revealed a new splinter of dark earth tones. Zora stared back at Jasmine fearlessly.

"I don't know," Jasmine said, shaking her head. She looked back up at the silver wall.

"Maybe the lawyer stuff is who you are. And that's the end of the story. But Zora, this is magic. Your room, your house? You created all this," Jasmine said.

"Yeah, but—"

"Well, call it whatever you want, boo. I think you're an artist," Jasmine said.

Zora shook her head.

"More specifically, I think you might be a closeted architect," Jasmine said, looking at Zora with an exaggerated expression of concern.

Zora's head fell back in laughter. Jasmine watched Zora shimmering with joy.

Zora.

"Come here," Jasmine said softly. She took Zora's hand and pushed her to face the steel wall. Zora's lips hovered inches from its radiating coolness. Jasmine stood behind her and parted the stream of locs down her back, breathing in her scent. Zora's face glowed silver. Jasmine touched her lips to the back of Zora's neck. Zora felt the urge to take back control. To push back. But this felt good. Her body rocked. She looked up at the wall as Jasmine's fingertips traced the nape of her neck, her shoulder, her forearm. Zora's breath quickened. Jasmine held Zora's hand up and pressed it high against the wall. Zora exhaled as she felt the cold metal against her palm. Jasmine pulled Zora's earlobe in her mouth and stroked it with her tongue until Zora's skin prickled with goosebumps. Jasmine's hands wandered down to the hem of Zora's waistband. Fingers pushing gently below her bellybutton. Zora exhaled again. This time, a quiet, low hum escaped her lips. Zora was open-minded, but none of her previous lovers ever touched her from behind like this. Especially not against a wall. This loss of control felt unfamiliar. And good. And too much. Zora's body shifted to turn and Jasmine paused.

"Do you want me to stop?" Jasmine whispered into Zora's ear. Zora's heart pounded. She took a breath.

"No," Zora said.

"Can I unbutton your jeans?" Jasmine whispered breathlessly.

Zora pushed her ass against Jasmine. She bowed her head.

"Yes. Do it," Zora said, her breath catching as Jasmine tore the buttons of her jeans open. Jasmine's hands gently traced Zora's underwear. Almost touching the place where Zora's lips met. Zora's clit throbbed an inch away, aching to feel Jasmine's fingers move lower. Instead, her hand traveled back up to the hem of Zora's shirt.

"Fucking tease," Zora hissed, shaking her head.

Jasmine said nothing. She ran her tongue along Zora's spine. Their bodies moved together and against each other. The pushing, pulling and lifting the weight of their wanting. Their heads tilted down in reverence, in prayer. They both prayed for more and more, to taste and touch and feel each other closer. Jasmine pinned Zora's hand to the wall. Zora's nipples grew hard between Jasmine's fingertips. Jasmine moaned as she traced cursive lines back down to Zora's underwear. Zora bucked back at Jasmine. And Jasmine held her still, fingers working down below Zora's clit. Wetness soaked through Zora's underwear. Zora buckled at the knees for a moment, feeling herself getting wetter as Jasmine pushed her fingertips against the slippery cotton.

Fuck! Zora thought. She was losing control. She was losing. Lost. No. Maybe she didn't have to lose control. Maybe she could give it away. Maybe she knew exactly where her power was. But she wanted Jasmine to have it.

Zora's breath quickened. A sound was stuck somewhere at the base of her throat. She slammed her hand against the wall. Their bodies pushed and pulled closer to the cool metal surface. Their forms undulated and distorted in the reflection. Jasmine tried to go slower, to graze the edge of it until they were both close, but she didn't have the patience for an artful crescendo. She couldn't wait a second longer. She tore Zora's pants down below her ass and stood behind her, savoring the last moment of almost.

"Can I touch your clit?" She whispered in Zora's ear.

"Yesss," Zora hissed impatiently, and Jasmine slid her fingers slowly across slick folds of lips, pushing softly on her clit and Zora let go. There was nothing more for her to do. It felt too good to pretend to resist. Zora's breath bloomed foggy clouds on the cold silver wall. Her nipples perched, exposed and hard. Her bare ass pushed back against Jasmine.

"I wanna be inside you." Jasmine breathed into Zora's neck.

"Do it," Zora snapped.

Jasmine reaching behind Zora pushed two fingers inside as her other hand slid along Zora's clit.

"Fuuuuuck." Zora shook her head again. She couldn't come now. She didn't want to come now. Jasmine felt Zora clenching. She changed her stroke, pulling out slow and pushing back inside, hard. Zora couldn't keep it.

"Shiiiit," Zora whispered.

Now Jasmine's breath quickened. As Zora clenched tighter, she went faster, deeper. Jasmine's weight pushed Zora against the wall and as her stiff nipples touched the cold metal, a frozen electric shiver ran through Zora's veins. The orgasm tore at her throat. Her lips pressed against the silver as she moaned through the waves of pleasure. Jasmine held her up against the wall. Zora felt herself collapsing and rising to stand and collapsing again. As her muscles dissolved into stuttering aftershocks, Jasmine released her grip. She watched as Zora turned and slid to the floor. Jasmine slid down at her side. Zora's eyes were barely open. She used her hands to search for Jasmine's body.

"Oh," Zora whispered between labored breaths. Zora's eyes blinked open.

"Oh?" Jasmine giggled.

"You . . ." Zora sighed, leaning sleepily into Jasmine. Her tongue spread Jasmine's lips and pushed into her mouth.

Through the haze and exhaustion, Zora could feel the weight of Jasmine's come. She was close. Zora needed to touch her. To make Jasmine feel as good as she felt. She wanted to taste Jasmine. To smell her. Jasmine pulled her shirt off as Zora crawled forward, pushing Jasmine to the floor. She unbuttoned Jasmine's shorts and pulled them off impatiently. Jasmine's briefs clung to her. Zora grazed the crease of Jasmine's lips with her middle finger. Her underwear was soaked through, even more than Zora's had been.

Zora pulled at Jasmine's underwear. She stretched it tightly to the side and let it softly snap back to Jasmine's swelling lips. Jasmine whined and pushed her hips up to Zora. Zora giggled. She watched Jasmine's wetness drip from her like a clear dollop of honey, rolling slowly down to her ass. Zora leaned down to Jasmine.

"You want me to fuck you?"

"Yes." Jasmine tilted her head back.

Zora ran her finger down Jasmine's lips, gently stroking her clit and lingering down. She lifted her glazed fingers to taste. Jasmine pushed her hips up. Zora's fingertips rested at the edge, almost inside. Jasmine whined impatiently.

Zora leaned in again. "You want me to fuck you?"

"Yes."

Zora's fingers took an inch, feeling Jasmine pulsing tighter.

"Say it. Tell me to fuck you," Zora whispered. Jasmine pulled a fistful of Zora's locs.

"Fuck me."

Zora pushed her fingers into Jasmine. Jasmine fell back, rolling on the floor as her back arched into the movement.

Jasmine moaned as her hand slid down to her clit.

Zora fucked her hard and fast, moving her hips as she pushed into Jasmine. She was almost jealous, spiteful as she watched Jasmine touch herself. She wanted to have it all. Jasmine wrapped her legs around Zora's back. She opened her eyes and held Zora's gaze.

"I'm gonna come," Jasmine said between gasps of breath.

"Then come," Zora said, her voice low and determined.

"It's too soooooon," Jasmine whimpered.

"So what?" Zora whispered.

Jasmine

Jasmine looked up into Zora's eyes. They both held each other there for a moment. Open. Jasmine held her breath. Closed her eyes tight. No. Don't go there. Her mind flashed to moments with Dia. Searing memory of how Dia used to fuck her. No. Jasmine could feel the dizzying motion of being drunk. Her car turning over. Her sister's faces in the hospital. Her mother's long locs in her hands. Dia turning to leave for the last time. Her failure. Her regrets. The moments when she didn't want to live. She felt all the deepest pain she knew.

"Hey—" Jasmine heard Zora's voice in the dark. Jasmine opened her eyes. Zora looked down at her, searching.

"Come back," Zora whispered.

"Okay," Jasmine whispered, nodding.

And then all she could feel was Zora inside her. All she could feel was her body pulsing against Zora's fingertips. Zora pushed faster and faster into Jasmine. Jasmine raised her hips, moaning and grinding. Zora couldn't catch her breath. She leaned in, pushed deeper, faster and harder and then—Jasmine was gone. Quiet, still.

Coming felt like time stopping. Like diving into a crashing wave. They could feel the storm of current, they could hear the low hum of the ocean. Jasmine let it all wash over her. Zora felt Jasmine convulsing again, and again. Time bent into one long, breathless moment. They both closed their eyes and felt their bodies lifting into the air. And they crossed over together. They turned into water and soil and sunlight. Their ancient ancestors blushed and snapped and threw their heads back with laughter. They mixed the colors of their magic together and made a green-blue that no one had ever made. Jasmine gasped herself back to life and they drifted, spinning like petals back to earth. And the earth received them anew. Silver-skinned and shining.

When they returned to consciousness, their minds were too

small to know how far they'd gone together. But when Zora lifted Jasmine's tired body into her bed, when their slow blinking eyes met, they remembered something. Just for a moment, Zora and Jasmine could remember the color they made. That green blue. It was all over them. Zora and Jasmine smiled at this otherworldly light. They fell asleep in each other's arms and that green blue melted into their dreams.

21. THE SCOTTS

Jasmine opened her eyes slowly. The morning light bloomed around her in creamy shades of white and summer green. Trees in the sunlight. The blankets thick and airy around her like peaks of whipped cream. Her whole body felt weighted under the blankets. The spell of sex and a full night's sleep settled in her muscles. She licked her lips and tasted the rich scent. Zora. She arched her back and exhaled at the memory of last night.

Zora was already awake. She was still, observing. She watched Jasmine's shoulder rise and fall with her long, steady breaths. Her eyes rested on the soft skin behind Jasmine's ear where her hair faded into peach fuzz. Zora felt the urge to kiss her right there. What should I say, she thought. Something sweet? I'm glad you're here? Last night was . . . hot? Remember when you fucked me against the wall? Remember when I fucked you on the floor? Do you know you make sounds when you sleep? Last night you snored like a baby bear and it was cute. I want you to stay. Zora thought and thought and then said nothing.

Jasmine turned. At the sight of Zora, she covered her face with her hands.

Zora grinned.

"Hey."

"Hey," Jasmine whispered. She pulled the covers up to her

chin and smiled.

Jasmine blinked, squinting into the light. Zora leaned in and their lips met slowly. As she pulled away, she held Jasmine's gaze. Then she closed her eyes. Maybe they could just read each other's minds now. Maybe a kiss could say everything she wouldn't.

Jasmine's breath caught in her throat. There was something about that kiss. Zora's hand on her cheek. The taste of sweetness and cream. Zora's rich brown skin in the glow of morning light. The way she looked at Jasmine and closed her eyes, still smiling. The weight of Zora's hand on her hip. Her chest was suddenly heaving, her throat pinched with a feeling. She pulled the blankets over her head as tears ran down her cheeks. Jasmine pushed her face against the sheets. A sudden flood of emotions washed over her. Oh no. This was one of the side effects of sobriety. A kind of IBS for emotions. She couldn't tell if her heart was this magical, complex spiritual muscle or if it was dumb as a rock. Maybe she had the heart of a toddler. Maybe she could fall apart at the blink of an eye and that was just who she was now. No beer or wine or shots of whiskey to drown the feelings. It was the wrong place and the wrong time, but she felt like a broken dam. She cried for the love she'd lost, the people she'd hurt. She cried because she truly believed she didn't deserve to be loved. Not after everything she did. She cried because she yearned for a future with Zora. That weight on her hip. That feeling like home. Jasmine rubbed and dried her face under the covers and emerged looking cheery and slightly pink around the eyes. Zora gave her a look of confusion.

"Well, Zora. I'm really glad we had a date. I think you're hot. And wonderful," Jasmine said, grinning.

"Thank you. I think you're hot. And strange," Zora said, laughing. "I mean. In the best way."

"Hot and strange. I'll take it," Jasmine said, sniffling and nodding enthusiastically.

"Are you—are you crying?" Zora leaned in to study Jasmine's

face. Jasmine slid back under the covers.

"Oh. No. It's allergies. Do you have a cat?" Jasmine yell-talked underneath the comforter.

"We don't."

"So weird!" Jasmine said as she squirmed to the edge of the bed and reached down, feeling the floor in search of her underwear.

Zora followed Jasmine's lead and slid out of her side of the bed. She watched Jasmine dress.

"Do you have time for breakfast?" Zora asked, opening a drawer.

"Oh my god. I wish," Jasmine said, sincerely. "But on Saturdays me and Ella ride together to my mom's church thing. It's a lot. But it's fun. It's like Black elder feminist church? Well, no, it's more than that. It's all ages. And basically, everyone in the church gets to be a minister for a day. It's a very cool concept, actually. Kind of like AA, very democratic. Though everyone shouldn't necessarily be a minister. One week, we just watched The Color Purple and then we had to respond to it through modern dance. I mean I love TCP, but it was . . . very weird."

"Cool," Zora replied. She wrestled a black T-shirt over her head. She pulled and swung her locs out from the neck of the shirt. Jasmine stared. Zora's brown skin looked like it was misted with coconut oil. Even her bare feet looked sexy. Long and elegant against the honey brown hardwood floor. Zora jumped into a fresh pair of black briefs. Jasmine looked away.

Zora watched Jasmine lace up her boots. Why did this feel like an insult? Zora thought. She never asked people to stay for breakfast. She wanted to snap back to that rational, cool side of her. The version of Zora who had casual sex and was slightly disappointed by everyone. A persistently faint distaste was much more comfortable than wanting someone like this. Jasmine was tying her laces up and she had feelings. These feelings were uncomfortable, to say the least. It's fine, Zora thought to herself.

She has to go. It's fine. You wanted to get laid. You wanted something casual. That's what this is. This is what you wanted.

"Can I get you a Lyft?" Zora asked as she opened the bedroom door for Jasmine.

"Oh no, that's really sweet. But I'm good," Jasmine replied, hurrying through the doorway.

As Zora and Jasmine descended the stairs, the sound of music and clanking echoed from the kitchen. Jasmine looked up at Zora.

"Is someone here?" Jasmine whispered.

Zora frowned. "David, probably. You know we're housemates, right?"

"Right . . ." Jasmine replied hesitantly. She pulled down on her black sheer shirt.

"Don't worry. He knows about you. And—" Zora began, the sound of a woman's voice interrupting her thought.

"Is there a girl here?" Jasmine asked.

When Zora and Jasmine entered the kitchen, they were met with a cannon of screams and laughter. In a flurry of excitement, David and Ella ran to their sisters. Ella hugged Jasmine and looked at her, wide-eyed and giddy. Jasmine shook her head. David greeted Zora like she just beat the buzzer and hit the winning three-point shot. He jumped and danced. He hugged her and quickly lifted her in the air for a spin. Everyone talked at once. David and Ella spoke in gossipy voices, asking about the date, who kissed who, when and where is the next date? Zora attempted to settle her brother down with monotone non-answers. Jasmine rolled her eyes and answered all of Ella's questions with additional questions. Unsatisfied with Zora's deadpan energy, David bounced over to Jasmine, pulling at her hand like a small child.

"Jasmine please, please, help us make breakfast! Ella will not stop raving about your famous crepes. I made her pancakes yesterday and I did my best. They were from scratch and they—

well they were more like cupcakes than pancakes—" David talked as if he were telling a hilarious joke.

"They were like four inches high, but they were actually really good," Ella interrupted, nodding at Jasmine.

"Well they were aaaiight, but they weren't as good as your famous crepes, that's what I heard," David went on.

"They were good, Jasmine. And he claims he's terrible in the kitchen, so I was shocked," Ella said.

Jasmine was confused. She knew Ella had been sneaking around with David for the past few weeks. She knew they were talking. But this was something different. It sounded like Ella and David had been dating for years.

"Well, Jasmine was just leaving," Zora said coolly.

"Well, I thought . . ." Jasmine began. "I thought we were going to chrch together?" Jasmine cocked her head toward Ella.

Ella smiled. "Oh come on, big sis. We always go. We can skip one day," she replied without hesitation. She looked mischievous like a teenager scheming to skip class.

Zora folded her arms, then glanced at her watch. Jasmine squinted her eyes at Zora, suddenly annoyed. The looking-at-her-watch thing. What is that about? Jasmine thought. Does that mean "hurry up I have more important shit to do"? Or does it mean "I feel vulnerable and scared and I need something to do to make me look important and nonchalant"? Jasmine huffed.

"Please stay! We're already so late anyway!" Ella said.

Ella and David looked at her like pleading puppies.

Jasmine sighed. "Okay, I'll stay."

David and Ella squealed and high-fived each other.

Jasmine watched as Zora unfolded her arms.

"Do you have a crepe pan?" Jasmine asked.

"Yes," Zora replied. She pointed up at the chandelier of shining pans hanging from the ceiling. She pulled down a wide disk of iron with a thick wooden handle. She handed the pan to Jasmine. Jasmine lifted an eyebrow. Of course. The prince's fancy castle has all the fancy kitchen toys to match. Zora had spent a year in Paris, after all.

"That should work," Zora said, her face now austere and unreadable.

"Yeah. Thanks," Jasmine said. She smiled at Zora weakly.

David and Ella skittered together around the kitchen. Jasmine called out the ingredients and tools she needed and the lovebirds flew about, collecting and preparing each item like a pair of giggling sous chefs. Zora watched Jasmine work from across the island, blank-faced. Jasmine felt Zora's gaze searing into her. Why was Zora acting so cold? Didn't they just have life-altering sex? Maybe it's because she'd been too vulnerable. Maybe it's because she just cried in Zora's bed and told her it was allergies when it was very obviously not allergies? Jasmine kept her head down. She moved quickly, expertly. She hummed to herself, whisking a bowl of milky liquid. David and Ella chirped around her, but Jasmine was alone with the batter.

Zora looked down at her watch, then back up at Jasmine. She knew Jasmine wanted to leave. That was clear. She didn't take it personally. But really? Church? She couldn't make an exception this one time? Zora had made an exception. She rarely brought women home, she never asked them to breakfast–and when she did, they never said no. She almost felt . . . used. No. No. She didn't feel used. Just annoyed. Zora looked up at Jasmine as she cracked an egg. She was so proficient in the kitchen. So confident. It was like watching a good dancer. Or a sculptor. Zora softened a bit. It almost made her forget about that tiny splinter in her ego.

David made everyone espresso. Ella carefully instructed him on how to make Jasmine's cup.

David settled next to Ella, sipping his coffee and giggling with her. Zora rounded the corner of the island with her coffee. She stood at Jasmine's side.

"Can I help?" Zora asked. Jasmine smiled, keeping her eye

on the pan.

"Anything you might put on your crepes? Since you're the honorary Parisian and all." Jasmine hovered her palm over the pan.

"Honorary Parisian. Yeah. Okay," Zora muttered. She opened the fridge and pulled out a handful of items. Jasmine poured the mixture onto the pan, tilting and coating it with a thin layer of batter. Zora worked by Jasmine's side. She poured a small carton of heavy cream into the stand mixer. Doing her best to stay out of Jasmine's way, she collected glass bottles from the cabinet. She slid a small saucepan onto the stove, adding a splash of orange juice and a pinch of sugar before turning the burner on. Jasmine pretended not to scrutinize Zora's every move. She was particular in the kitchen, and for that reason she preferred to cook alone. Jasmine noticed the long, narrow jar in Zora's hand. Zora carefully lifted a shriveled black twig from the jar. She caught Jasmine staring.

"Vanilla beans," Zora said, holding the jar up delicately.

Jasmine nodded. Casual.

Zora leaned down with a small, sharp knife and cut one careful line along the narrow bean. She used a spoon to scrape the black paste into the cream.

Jasmine tore her gaze away. She shook the fine skin of the crepe from the pan's edges and flipped it. Perfect. Light golden brown and peppered with tiny bubbles, its edges barely crisped by the heat. Jasmine slid the crepe from the pan to the plate and the stand mixer hummed as it beat the splashing cream. Zora leaned down again, now cutting strawberries and tossing them into the steaming saucepan.

David and Ella scurried outside with plates and utensils, setting the dining table on the deck. Jasmine slid the last crepe onto the plate. She sighed, satisfied. Eight paper-thin crepes, perfectly cooked. She looked at the stove. The saucepan steamed with the scent of strawberries, saturating the air. Jasmine looked over to Zora as she shook the cloud of whipped cream into a small silver bowl. Zora looked up at Jasmine.

"Go ahead, I'll meet you out there," Zora said. Jasmine nodded and carried her coffee and the plate of perfect crepes to the deck. She found Ella and David sitting at the table. A pink-purple burst of hydrangeas from the yard sat cheerfully in the center of the spread. A carafe of orange juice and long white plates sat on a vibrant kente tablecloth. Jasmine set down the crepes and coffee and sat across from the lovebirds.

"Woo!" Ella gushed over the crepes.

"Wow! Iron chef Jasmine out here! It's a quickfire challenge and you win!" David said laughing.

"Oh, David." Ella giggled, covering his mouth with her palm.

"You are not on the chopping block," David mumbled through Ella's hand.

"No, no. You're much cuter when you don't talk," Ella said, giggling.

Jasmine noticed a thin silver chain sparkling around Ella's neck. The chain disappeared into her shirt. Jasmine pointed to the chain. "Is that new?"

Ella blushed. She looked at David, then back at Jasmine. She lifted a tiny pendant at the end of the chain. Jasmine leaned across the table to study it. It was the world's smallest hand mirror decorated with small beads and curling silver accents.

"Wow." Jasmine admired the piece.

"It's from David," Ella said. She looked proudly at him, then bashfully away.

"And she got me a ukulele," David said, grinning.

"I usually don't wear necklaces, but I really like this one," Ella went on.

"So what's the occasion? Your five-minute anniversary?" Jasmine chuckled at her own joke.

Ella's face tightened.

David stared at her, waiting for a translation.

"Jazz," Ella said, giving her sister a look.

"Sorry! I'm just messing with y'all. Big sister type shit," Jasmine said.

"I wanted her to have a reminder of how beautiful she is. Even if she never needs it," David said earnestly, staring at Ella.

Jasmine resisted the deepest urge to roll her eyes. Corny corn corn. This was a cloying, saccharine sweet that she had no palate for. Especially when it came to straight folks. David sounded like a damn Hallmark card. But it was also Ella. Her little sister. This beautiful, sweet, simple boy loved on her even harder than she loved on herself. And that was saying something. Ella deserved this kind of love.

"That's—that's really fucking cute," Jasmine said, shaking her head.

Ella folded her arms and nodded.

Jasmine sipped her coffee.

Zora emerged from the house with a bowl of whipped cream, dusted with something finely grated. Nutmeg? Jasmine thought. In her other hand, Zora held a small glass bowl of thick red sauce with a sprig of mint on top. Where in the hell did she get fresh mint? Jasmine sat quietly as her thoughts raced around her brain.

"Wow!" Ella said. Her eyebrows raised as she looked at Jasmine.

"Oh yeah. Unlike me, Zora is a great cook. Mitch LANE star quality. Five Mitch LANE stars FOR YOU!" David said joyfully.

"Michelin," Zora and Jasmine interrupted in French-accented unison.

Ella and David stared at each other. Zora massaged her sharp jaw, a grin peeking through her attempt at indifference. Jasmine looked at Zora and chuckled.

Ella raised an eyebrow.

"Wow, Jasmine. You found someone as pretentious about food as you. Bravo."

"Well goddamn! Mish-LEH . . . my apologies to the boujee police," David said, grinning.

"So what is this?" Ella asked Zora, pointing to the red sauce.

"Strawberry compote," Zora said.

"Aaaah! Strawberry compote," Ella said, looking at Jasmine again. Jasmine sipped her coffee. Zora sat by Jasmine's side and they each dressed their crepes. Jasmine slid her bite of crepe through the cloud of whipped cream and the thick red sauce. She closed her eyes. David and Ella's chatter faded to muffled humming. She smiled as she chewed, the flavors flirting with her senses. The compote was just sweet enough. A pinch of salt, the acid and natural sweetness from the juice and the tart cut of the strawberries and lemon pierced through, bright and sharp. The whipped cream was just thick enough. A blink away from butter. And what was that flavor in the cream? Something aromatic, ancient and round. Cardamom. It was cardamom. Jasmine could cry. It was the perfect bite. When she opened her eyes, David and Zora were conspiring across the table. Ella was smiling and slowly nodding at her. Ella knew exactly what Jasmine was thinking. It was over. She could obsess over the past. She could bake four hundred cakes. She could be slutty and kiss a dozen other girls. And she would probably try all of these things, just to see if they worked. But nothing in the world would keep her from falling for Zora.

22. LAYLA AND RO

Ro and Layla careened down the Virginia backroad in the old family Subaru. Ro's erratic driving and the lurching sounds from the old car made Layla's shoulders tense up.

"Did you hear from your sisters?" Ro asked.

"They're not coming," Layla replied quickly.

Ro nodded. "So. Have you talked to Ella yet?"

"No."

Ro turned the car onto an old dirt road, and Layla winced at the car's squealing.

"Layla," Ro began. "I'm not gonna lecture you. I know you're grown. But. Putting your work above your family isn't really a healthy choice. You know? It's not a good look." Ro smiled as she spoke.

"A good look?" Layla cut her eyes to her mother.

"I'm serious."

"That's rich coming from you." Layla chuckled.

"What does that mean?"

Layla picked at her nails. "Nothing. I get it. I'll talk to Ella. If she ever comes home again." Layla ducked as a cluster of leafy shoots swatted at the car. Ro stared at the road. Work above family. Layla thought of how often her mom chose to prioritize her work over her daughters. Precancer, it was the school. And now, it was chrch. Everyone in the community called her a saint.

And she was. She saved people's lives every day. But she missed a lot at home when she was out saving the world. And Layla was just like her.

"Here we are!" Ro announced excitedly. Layla sat up in her seat as the river appeared in the distance, a band of sparkling water flickering through the trees.

"Finally. Hey ma, maybe you should let me drive back," Layla muttered.

"Oh Layla. Relax. You're too wound up." Ro pinched her daughter's cheek. Layla recoiled.

"I'm very relaxed," Layla said with a rigid smile.

"What about sex? Do you have any new boos?" Ro asked.

"New boos? Mom. No. Jesus," Layla replied, sliding down in her seat.

"What about Sean? He was so sweet with you."

Layla sighed. "I don't really have time to date, Mom. I'm pretty sure I'm happier when I'm single."

"You're twenty-two, Layla. When I was your age, I probably had a dozen gorgeous artsy boyfriends."

"I bet you did," Layla muttered.

"Do you think maybe you're gay?" Ro ventured.

"Mom, I don't need to have sex or date to be happy."

"Oh Layla. We all need sex. If you get sucked up in all this work, you might lose your people. Or yourself," Ro replied.

"What about you, Mom? Any new boos for you lately? Any new boos in the past thirty years?"

Ro straightened in her seat. "Well, I'm old. It's different. And I find ways to ... get what I need," Ro replied, shrugging.

"OK, I think that's more than enough information about that, thank you so, so much." Layla gave her mother a thumbs up.

"I just don't want you to be lonely. You're always so wrapped up in the next project. I want you to remember to live. You know?"

Layla sighed. "It's the right thing to do, Mom."

Ro looked at her daughter. "I know, honey. You know I'm proud of you."

Layla nodded. "I got us a feature in *The Post*."

"As in *The Washington Post?*" Ro asked, wide-eyed.

"I called them. Every day."

"Layla! That's incredible! Oh honey, congratulations." Ro squeezed Layla's hand giddily. "So what's the story about?"

"From what I know, I think it's supposed to be different perspectives on gentrification in DC. I don't think I'll be in it, but they asked for an interview. They want to talk about Rise and the protest party. I think it'll really help to get people there. Maybe donations." Layla tried to temper her excitement.

"Oh, it'll definitely help! What about the woman you met at the shelter? Will she be in it?" Ro asked.

"Brianna? No. Probably not. She's really private about what she's going through. Which makes sense." Layla thought back to the last time she talked with Brianna. They were getting closer. She said she was willing to come to the protest. She sounded exhausted, but hopeful.

"Is Brianna coming today?" Ro asked.

"I told her about it. But I doubt she'll come. Whenever I try to describe chrch to people, it sounds very culty and creepy. Plus, she has a lot on her plate."

Ro nodded. "We'll say her name in the prayer today. OK?"

"That would be nice," Layla said.

Layla took her mother's hand. She really was some kind of saint. Not perfect. But still, godly. She wasn't always home for dinner. Maybe she spent too much time saving strangers. But she really meant it. She really loved people. In moments like this, Layla remembered why she wanted to be like her mother. The old Subaru squealed as Ro pulled into a dusty parking lot. When Layla opened her car door, she could hear the rush of the river in the distance.

Black and brown folks quietly gathered at the river's edge. The wind pushed through the trees like a deep sigh. Layla turned to feel the warm air brush against her cheek. Ro riffled through her oversized tote bag. She hummed as she lined the hood of the car with sunflowers, candles, wooden bowls, and bundles of incense sticks. Across the expanse of the beach, the congregation stepped through the trees wearing thinly draped fabrics of yellow, white and gold. Neat pairs of shoes dotted the pebble beach. All around them, a procession of people slowly walked into the quiet current of the Potomac River. Ro wore a long white sundress with yellow bursts of ink splashed across the skirt. She carried a small wooden bowl full of honey and blew a kiss to Layla as she linked arms with a silver-haired woman and helped her into the water. Ro's skirt fanned out around her like flower petals. The silver-haired woman held tightly to Ro's arm as they walked slowly to a quiet cove sheltered by rocks and roots. Ro helped the woman find a seat on the warm, smooth face of a boulder. The woman watched the water gently dance around her. She grinned wide and silly, like a little girl.

Layla walked slowly into the river. The rhythm of her breath turned staccato as the cold water rose up the warmth of her ankles and calves. The current pulled and rushed past her, playing at her skirt. She held a tall yellow candle in one hand and a stick of incense in the other. The wind sucked at the flame. Smoke whipped out from the burning ember. Yellow rose petals, marigolds, and crumbles of tobacco swam past her on the rushing face of the water. Layla breathed in the sweet smell of wet leaves, soil and incense. She heard humming in the distance. Solymar, an Afro-Cuban woman in her fifties, sang as she walked through the trees to the water. Her song held a sweeping sorrow and a hint of hope in its lilting high notes. It wasn't a melody Layla knew, but it felt ancient and familiar the way a spiritual feels ancient and familiar. Layla joined in, humming with Solymar. And one by one, people walked into the water and thickened the melody with harmonies and soft improvisations. The river sang with them. Layla watched the smoke rushing from the stick of incense. She closed her eyes and listened to the water and the singing. She hadn't really prayed in years. She used to speak to the ancestors, and she believed they listened. She believed she could hear them speak. But when she came back to DC, their voices fell silent. It felt like everything around her was dying. She had moved back home because her mother had cancer. Now, it was two years later. Her mother survived, but in DC the cancer was spreading. It was everywhere. She wanted to pray for freedom. But what did freedom even look like for Black folks these days? What did freedom look like for her? She closed her eyes. Took a breath. She imagined Brianna and Jayden and she prayed for them. She didn't know what she was praying for, or who she was praying to, but she prayed anyway.

Solymar sang words to the melody now. The humming quieted as she lifted her face to the sun, singing up and out into the air.

> "Oshun, oshun
> water soft and sweet
> Oshun, oshun
> carry my love to me.
> Oshun, oshun
> water soft and sweet
> Oshun, oshun
> set my spirit free."

The congregation quieted to a hush as they listened. Then one by one, they joined her. Singing the words, swaying in the pull and laughter of the water. Layla noticed a flutter of movement up-stream. Ro's skirt floated around her as she walked back to the river's edge. Ro was walking to meet a stranger standing on the beach, looking out at the ritual. A woman? Layla squinted.

She didn't recognize the woman from this far. She watched Ro embrace the woman. Layla closed her eyes and continued singing. She leaned against the push of the water and felt the wind whisper through her hair. She felt something. Like floating. She felt high. A power glowing in the gold flecks of sunlight in the water.

> *"Oshun, oshun*
> *water soft and sweet*
> *Oshun, oshun*
> *set my spirit free."*

Layla opened her eyes and found her mother next to her. They stood side by side, singing and rocking with the current.

"She's here," Ro whispered as she took the candle from Layla's hand.

"Who's here?" Layla asked.

"Brianna," Ro said, looking at Layla with her knowing smile.

Layla turned her head to the beach. It was her.

Ro tugged the thick stem of a sunflower from her hair and handed it to Layla.

Layla held the flower in her palm. She watched the reflection of bright yellow petals against the dark green water. Ro touched Layla's shoulder, then walked slowly back to the silver-haired woman on the rock.

Layla walked toward the beach. She found Brianna looking out at the river with an expression she couldn't read. Was she confused? Or afraid? Layla wasn't sure. Brianna wore jeans and a black T-shirt. Layla hadn't told her what colors to wear because she was sure Brianna wouldn't come.

"Brianna. Hey," Layla said. Her voice was calm. "I'm glad you came."

"Thanks for inviting me," Brianna replied, still studying the scene.

"We're giving offerings to the river. It's—I know it might seem strange. But it's just our way to connect to nature?" Layla posed it as a question, hoping it didn't sound crazy. She turned to look out at the water. All the people dressed in white and yellow, singing into the river. Brianna watched and said nothing.

"Do you want to ... make an offering?" Layla whispered.

Brianna said nothing. She stared out at the women in the river.

Not knowing what to do, Layla handed her the sunflower. Brianna's face lit up with an innocent smile. She looked down at the flower, then back out to the water. Layla considered explaining the ritual to her. Telling her the stories of Oshun and the Orisha and where these traditions came from. But she couldn't decide where to begin. The voices singing and the sound of the water rushing down-stream explained more than Layla could put into words.

Brianna moved suddenly, as if something pulled her. Layla turned to watch as Brianna stepped out of her flip-flops and walked into the river. She didn't hesitate or brace against the cold. She just walked and walked into the water. Layla held her breath, watching from the beach. Brianna's hands floated out at her sides. The wind pulled at the air. The water darkened the denim at her thighs and Brianna kept walking. And walking. In the distance, Ro turned to watch. She glanced at Brianna then looked back at Layla on the shore. As Brianna reached the deepest part of the river, the water lapped at her waist. She held the sunflower just above the water. As the wind picked up, Solymar sang louder, then splashed her hands in the water and let it fly up into the air like pearls of sunlight. And the congregation joined her. The wild energy of excitement grew with the sound of the whipping wind.

And when Brianna sang, everyone turned to watch her. Their voices hushed again; their eyes wide with wonder. Who was this young woman singing with them in the river? Brianna's voice carried across the water. She tipped her head back to catch the sunlight, breathing deep between melodies. The river was changing her. It brought her closer to herself. Her voice was a prayer for all the pain she'd numbed to survive, the desires she wouldn't allow herself to admit. Layla heard God and Oshun and Xango in Brianna's voice. It was clear and sharp like cold water. She sang the song like she'd known it for years.

When her voice fell silent, Layla walked back into the water and stood at her side. Brianna held the sunflower in both palms and lowered it into the water. She held it there for a moment, then let it go. Brianna and Layla watched it float downstream and disappear.

23. RO

Ro sat barefoot in the garden. She cradled a handful of small white seeds and carefully pushed her index finger into the black soil. Silver locs falling into her eyes, blue green tufts of lavender sprung up around her. Ro's garden was too much. Like a painting with too many colors. Things that didn't go together. There were fragrant climbing jasmine vines, bursting purple peonies, freckled stargazer lilies, pink hydrangeas, peppers, tomatoes, a black mulberry tree, kale, collards and a scattered bunch of herbs. In the middle of this wild assortment of plants, a thick copper half circle curved six feet high from the dirt. Weathered and green, it looked like a half moon rising from the ground. A stone sculpture of a woman sat cross legged at the center of the altar. She looked like a bald, curvy combination of Buddha, Mother Earth and Yemaya. Ro called her altar goddess Blackberry—the name of an old friend who had sculpted her years ago. Since she retired, Ro sat with Blackberry everyday. She adorned the altar with lit candles, vases full of flowers, laminated pictures, fruits, and plates of food.

When Ro bought the house, the backyard was a sad patch of yellowing grass, and she'd spent the past fifteen years transforming it. Every year, she dreamt up a new project for the garden. One year it was all about heirloom tomatoes. All winter, she read books about raised beds and how to harvest your own vegetables. By August you could find a basket of orange-red, misshapen orbs in every corner of the kitchen. She brought boxes of tomatoes to the Beechwood summer school, and a dozen calculus students skipped class to paint tomato-themed still-life paintings. She made pesto, tomato salads, pizzas and pasta sauces until everyone was sick of them.

The next year it was all about tulips. An ancestor had visited her in a dream and told her to plant one hundred bulbs. She worried about the colonial implication of the traditionally Dutch flowers, but she planted one hundred and fifty bulbs, just to be sure. Do what the spirit say do, etc. And it was worth it. The tulips were gorgeous. They were everywhere. Ruby reds, black purples, and white frilly petals with streaks of pink. She planted tulips for two years after that but the tradition ended abruptly as Ro grew tired of trying to fend off the neighborhood deer. Three years ago, Ro made a big production about the herb garden. Herbs were easy because the bugs didn't care for the taste. The mint was so wild and invasive it spread everywhere. Ro had to cut it back every week. Jasmine would come to harvest arms full of rosemary, thyme and dill for the cafe.

Then came the cancer years. When the chemo started to take a toll, the Jones sisters switched off helping in Ro's garden. Ella learned to make tinctures, juices and teas for nausea and fatigue. Jasmine organized, pruned and raked. And Layla bought and planted every seed she could get her hands on.

Ro pushed her hands into the dirt. She felt a strange kind of nostalgia for the cancer years. Of course, she didn't miss the feeling of her body attacking itself from the inside, or the feeling of being slowly poisoned to death by doctors. But she missed the way her daughters all gathered around her. That despair made room for such delicate grace. They took care of her and they took better care of each other. Ro's illness meant that they had to be a family RIGHT NOW. They had to love with urgency because they were running out of time. It was terrifying and also beautiful. But then prayers were answered. Ro got better. And the collective sigh of relief melted right back into apathy. All the time in the world. And now the Jones sisters were so consumed with their own lives, Ro had trouble getting them all together for anything. Ella was falling in love. Layla was trying to save the world. One sister's desire stepped on the toes of the other's. And Jasmine was falling in love too, but that didn't help the fact that her cafe was failing. She wouldn't talk much about it, but Ro could tell. She wondered if she should interfere. She wondered how she could help. Ro looked up at Blackberry, the altar goddess and smiled weakly.

Looks like this is it. I worked my whole life to give these spoiled little babies everything I never had. And how about that? They're all just as fucked up as me.

Ro sighed and perched up on her knees. She tore at the weeds on the edges of the flowerbed. Her head swarmed with buzzing worries. *Should I have kept their father around? Would that have made a difference? Maybe I should have found some filthy rich man to marry so I could stay at home and do nothing but read books with my girls and grow dahlias. I never had the time to grow dahlias. I could have married Jeffery from undergrad. He's a doctor or something now. Probably rich. But goddamn, he was boring as a box of rocks. Am I a shitty person? Am I a shitty mom?* Ro scoffed at her own anxious train of thought. *No, no, no. My mom was a shitty mom. And those girls didn't need a man to raise them. Especially not a man who wanted to be somewhere else. I did okay,* Ro thought. *They're going to be okay* But still, she worried. Even now that the girls were grown, why did everything still feel so hard?

Ro ripped at the weeds angrily, sweat beading her brow. Layla graduated with a student loan interest rate that horrified her. Ro had cosigned the loan absent-mindedly. She assumed that Layla was brilliant and tenacious and she'd be just fine. But she wasn't fine. In spite of her intelligence and tenacity, she had no job prospects. She was essentially paying a mortgage and she had no house to show for it. Eventually she landed a job at Rise, but what kind of career would she build there? Where could she go? Do you get promoted as an activist? Do you get health insurance? She was too smart to sit in a dark office all day. She could be a leader. She could do so much more than I did, Ro thought to herself as she pushed seeds into the dirt, now with an urgency she hadn't felt before.

Meanwhile, Ella was floating. She never aspired to be book smart, though she could have been. She'd started up with dreams of being a healer, offering services to communities of color and teaching wellness. But she learned quickly that the communities she wanted to serve couldn't afford something as extravagant as bodywork. Ella had to pivot. She found work at the fancy gym and she seemed satisfied to be a masseuse to rich white folks, but Ro sensed that she wasn't. She wanted to be a healer. She wanted to use her gift for people who really needed it.

And Jasmine, her eldest was—Ro wasn't sure how Jasmine was. The breakup with Dia didn't seem so bad. She was drinking more. She just seemed like she was grieving. But there was so much more pain than they could see. Ro didn't know Jasmine ever had real problems with drinking. She drank a lot. All the women in their family drank a lot. Ro got the call when she was still working at Beechwood. Layla's voice. Ro knew right away she was on the verge of tears and Layla never cried.

"Mom, she's Okay. Jasmine ran her car off the road. She's Okay. We're at the Hospital Center."

Her eldest daughter ran her car off the road. How could she have missed it? The weeks after the accident, Ro, Ella and Layla went everywhere with Jasmine. Outpatient rehab. Meetings. Into the cafe to keep it going. Jasmine immediately fell in love with AA. She even became a bit fanatical about it. But the cafe was doing worse and Ro still worried about Jasmine. She worried about her daughters constantly.

Ro made this house into a parallel universe. A Black Feminist fortress where they were safe. They could cry here. They could regain their strength and go back into the world stronger. In this house, the world could be fair. Ro used to stand with her daughters one by one in front of the mirror. She'd whisper affirmations to them. "Your skin is beautiful. Your thighs are beautiful. Your toes are beautiful. Your tummy is beautiful. Your lips, your nose, your hair, your eyes." She'd whisper each phrase so sincerely and the girls would try to squirm away. Too young to understand the armor Ro was crafting for them. She raised her Black daughters like Cinderellas of the world. Like ugly ducklings. She warned them. They would be rejected, psychologically spat at and feared. She told them that most of the world, especially white folks, would be ignorant. But they were the heroes of the story. They were the true royalty. The princesses in the fairy tale. Now, many years later, Ro realized there was a problem with that story. It was a fallacy. It implies fairness. Morality. A happy ending. Cinderella's hard work pays off. Her good deeds and good character eventually get her what she wants. Acceptance. Love. Wealth. And the ugly duckling is revealed to be more beautiful than all the ducks. She was a swan all along and now everyone can see they were wrong.

But this is not how the world works for Black girls. No matter how beautiful and brilliant her daughters turned out to be, the world would offer no admission of guilt. Every privileged, ignorant person in the world would not simply wake up one day having learned the moral of the story. And as Black women (brilliant, educated, accomplished or not), they would bear the weight of all that ignorance. All of their lives would be like this. Praying, fighting, and looking for the few places where they could let their guard down. It was a relentless practice. So Ro learned, for herself and for her daughters, how to build sanctuary. To find families of Black folks, people of color, hardcore allies and surround yourself with that love. That was the happy ending she could give to her daughters. But it wouldn't be that simple.

Ro knew she was dying. From her first diagnosis, she knew she would win the first fight and forfeit the second. This time, the cancer would take her life. So she prayed every day for a year. She prayed for light. Her daughters needed light. Not a happy ending, necessarily. Just a big spot of sunlight to show them the world is not all bad. There is still love. Ro built this altar to connect her daughters with the ancestors. It was her portal to the other side. She sang and whispered to the ancestors some mornings for hours. She heard them singing back in the wind through the leaves, in the stuttering movement of a hummingbird, in the summer thunderstorms. They were listening and sitting in the garden with her.

A month ago, Ro spent the whole day stewing oxtails. The recipe called for eight hours, the meat cooking so slow it would melt on your tongue. That day, the whole house smelled of thyme, slow-cooking oxtails, and onions. She thickened the dark juice with a pinch of flour and poured the rich umber gravy over whipped potatoes. The flecks of softened carrots and garlic slid down the sides of the plate. She made a whole placesetting at the altar. She laid the plate out on a bed of freshly cut lavender, sage and echinacea flowers. Then she placed one of Jasmine's fancy cake stand covers over the plate. The glass fogged up; then beads of condensation collected at the top like jewels. Ro left the plate out all night, and when the sun rose in the morning, she dug a deep hole in the wet soil and buried the meal. That night Ro's vision came to her in a dream.

Her vision arrived in a swirling series of shadow puppets. A backlit, smoky collection of cut silhouettes and shapes. She saw her daughters, the princes, and the kingdom. She felt her spirit glowing through her skin. Ella and Jasmine would fall in love. Layla would hold the city in her arms. Their family would expand. But of course, nothing is free. Ro knew the ancestors loved a good lesson in balance, and this time was no different.

Ro laughed when she connected the dots. Her daughters would have to fight for their gifts. They would have to disagree. They would fight each other. Ro was mostly amused by this twist. She wagged her finger at the altar and laughed. Her mother would have said something Christian, like "if you want to make God laugh, tell him about your plans." Ro pushed the last seed into the dirt as Jasmine emerged from the back door and looked out at her.

"Hi, honey," Ro spoke, looking up at her daughter. "Will you bring me the hose?" she called out as she patted down the soil. Jasmine leaned down to turn the faucet cap, and the sound of water rushed through the hose. The sweet smell of copper and DC tap water reminded her of childhood. Dancing in the sprinkler with her sisters. Jasmine walked the hose to Ro. Ro sprinkled the soil until puddles formed.

"Cilantro," Ro said.

"Good," Jasmine replied, nodding.

"You need some herbs for the cafe?" Ro asked, as she watered the neighboring clusters of plants and flowers.

"I could use some rosemary," Jasmine said. "The shortbread sold out already."

"That's great, honey," Ro said, pointing to the picnic bench in the clearing. Jasmine walked to the table and found three bundles of neatly bunched rosemary.

"Thanks, Mom." She smiled, touched by the gesture. It felt good to be known this well.

"How are you?" Ro asked as she stood and wiped her hands at her sides.

Jasmine noticed a peony with a plump, blooming bud. She held it gently in her palm. She thought of Zora. Since last night, she felt like she'd scrubbed her whole body with sugar. Her skin felt new. Sensitive. Like every nerve on her forearm reached out to feel the breeze and sunlight.

"I'm good," Jasmine said, smiling.

"Good," Ro said.

"How are you?" Jasmine squeezed her mother's shoulder and searched her eyes. Ro recognized this look. Like Jasmine could sense the sickness in her eyes if she looked hard enough.

"I'm great. Actually, I'm going to a movie with Marble today," Ro said as she walked the hose back to the flowerbed.

"Okay... are you sure that's a good idea?" Jasmine shook her head and followed her mother.

Ro leaned back slightly to look past Jasmine. "I love it when my daughters act like they gave birth to me. How sweet and strange," Ro said to the altar. Jasmine had learned to ignore her mother's spiritual eccentricities. She'd been talking to Blackberry for months now.

Jasmine folded her arms and sighed.

"I'm not going to tell you what to do. I'm glad you're making friends..." Jasmine said stubbornly.

"Why, thank you," Ro said as she watered a bunch of lilies.

"... friends who are younger than me. And very gay. Friends who maybe have a crush on you," Jasmine went on.

"You're so generous, honey." Ro smiled at the lilies.

"So. Are you gay now?" Jasmine asked, raising her eyebrows.

"I'm not gay. As far as I know. But you're absolutely first on my coming out list if anything changes." Ro chuckled.

"Okay, Mom."

"How's AA?" Ro asked.

Jasmine rolled her eyes. "It's fine. I'm going to a meeting tonight."

"Good," Ro replied.

"Do you want to come with me? To my meeting?" Jasmine asked weakly.

"I have plans, honey. But we'll go another time. Okay?"

Jasmine pinched a lavender bud between her fingers.

"What about the cafe?" Ro kept her eyes on the lavender.

Jasmine folded her arms. "It's fine."

"Did you decide to renew the lease?" Ro asked. Jasmine attempted to catch her mother's eyes, but Ro continued to water the flowers as if they were discussing something casual—like the weather, or what to eat for lunch. Not the death rattle of Jasmine's dreams.

"I don't know," Jasmine said dully as she pinched another lavender bud between her fingers. She rolled the flattened tiny petals in her palm.

"Did you ever think about one of the bakeries downtown? Firehook or Breadfurst?"

"Mom." Jasmine rubbed her temples.

"You were so happy at that place in Old Town. What was it called?"

"I was an apprentice there. You think I should go from being a cafe owner to an apprentice?" Jasmine felt her face getting hot.

Ro looked up from her flowers. "You know I don't want that for you. I'm just reminding you that there are options. It won't be the end of the world if this one doesn't work out. There's time."

"Cool," Jasmine said, nodding.

"Jasmine."

"So I guess I'll start sending out applications?"

"Jasmine, honey—"

"Since you're demoting me, I should definitely keep my options open. I could be the world's oldest busboy." Jasmine scoffed.

"Now wait a minute; there's no shame in bussing tables." Ro gestured sternly with a pair of gardening shears in hand. "If you were undocumented, you might not have the choice to—"

"Jesus, Mom, just fucking stop," Jasmine said, her hands raised in the air.

"I'm trying to help," Ro said softly. Jasmine sighed.

"I get it. Thank you. For now, I'm okay So let's talk about something else, yeah?"

Ro shrugged and snipped the end of a peony.

"How's Zora?" Ro asked.

Jasmine folded her arms. "Oh. She's good."

"I'm glad you're making friends too." Ro looked up at Jasmine and smiled.

The screen door slammed open and they both turned to see Ella peeking her head out.

"Y'all want ginger shots?" Ella called out.

"Yeah," Ro and Jasmine yelled in unison as they walked to the door.

The kitchen smelled sharp and fresh like ginger and springtime. Ella bounced around the kitchen to something boppy playing from her phone. She danced two dark green shots to Jasmine and Ro.

"Honey, what's in this?" Ro looked warily at the shot.

"Ginger. Spinach. Apple. Some other stuff. It's reeeally good, I promise." She nodded quickly, apparently high on endorphins and green juice.

"Mmmm." Jasmine nodded.

The three women sipped at their tiny shots of juice. At the sound of the front door, they all sat up straighter.

Layla entered the kitchen slowly, her eyes darting to Ella.

"Layla!" Ro reached out to Layla, wrapping her up in an embrace.

"Hey Lay," Jasmine smiled.

Ella sipped her shot silently.

"Oh that's really fucking mature, Ella. The silent treatment, how clever," Layla said, throwing her bag on the table.

"I'll talk to you when you decide to show me some respect, Layla. I think that's a pretty reasonable boundary. But you're the mature one apparently, so you let me know." Ella slammed the juicer down onto the counter.

"Stop," Ro said, clasping her hands together.

"Well, I don't have a lot of respect for you at the moment, Ella."

"Stop it—" Ro snapped.

"Mom—" Ella sighed in Ro's direction.

"Sit. Down," Ro whispered, pointing at the kitchen table. It was time for a lecture. Their mother may have retired from teaching, but she still had lessons for her daughters. They knew better than to talk back. Jasmine, Ella and Layla quietly took their seats at the table. Ro pressed her palms together and stared at her daughters.

"You are powerful women. You hear me? You are POWERFUL," Ro said, pointing and closing her eyes as if she felt a sermon coming on.

"We know that, Mom," Layla replied, rolling her eyes.

"You know that? Oh really? So how powerful do you think a leader is all by herself? How powerful is a priestess with no community? Awo? Mambo? Y'all are so beautiful and magical you can go off on your own and conjure up all the things you want? Is that right?"

Her daughters stared at her quietly. They understood that this was not a call-and-response kind of moment.

"No. You can't. This is simple math, my children. Your power is greater when you are together. Jobs will come and go, ọmọ. Boys and boyish folks will come and go. You WILL NOT bicker and pick at each other like this in my house."

"Boyish folks?" Jasmine snickered to herself.

"What would you do if I died tomorrow?" Ro asked casually.

"Mom!" The three sisters scolded her simultaneously.

Ro stood at the kitchen table, pointing ominously at her daughters. "As long as the three of you are in my house, you need to at least pretend to love each other."

"She's the one with the issue," Layla mumbled.

"ZZZZTTTT!" Ro snapped at the air. "I don't want to hear it." She cut her glare to Layla.

"Now. Ella. Make your sister a ginger shot." Ro smiled sweetly and sat at the kitchen table. Jasmine's eyes widened. Ella poured a shot and handed it to Layla.

"Thank you," Layla said to Ella.

"Sure," Ella replied dully.

The four women sat at the kitchen table and sipped their shots silently.

24. JASMINE

Jasmine rang the doorbell. She couldn't stop thinking about Zora. She closed her eyes and swam into the memory. She could feel Zora inside her. Zora's hungry, slow strokes. Lips pushing softly against her skin. The muscle of her tongue. Jasmine released a whispered moan as the door swung open. She snapped back to herself and smiled as Anika greeted her with a lengthy hug. Anika was one of her first AA friends and the host of the weekly DC women of color meeting. Anika was a fifty-something Indian anthropology professor and self-proclaimed art collector. Her Capitol Hill row-house was peppered with West African art. Masks, baskets and wooden bowls that screamed: I HAVE BEEN TO AFRICA AND I AM CULTURED! Anika would rant at length about the ceremonial purpose of one thing or another over tea and ginger beer. She was a sweetheart, but Jasmine felt her enthusiasm bordered on objectification. Non-Black folks obsessed with Africa made her feel a bit unsettled. Shit, even Black Americans obsessed with African art made her feel unsettled. She felt a possessive impulse to steal all the artifacts, sprint up the coast of Ghana, and throw them in the ocean.

Jasmine handed Anika a basket of pecan sandies.

"Cookies," she said, smiling politely.

"Have I told you that your food is my favorite part of this

meeting?" Anika asked, her hand over her heart.

"It's my pleasure." Jasmine grinned back.

Anika lifted the cloth to admire the cookies as she stepped into the house. Jasmine followed, hearing the familiar sounds of the Northern Ugandan folk music Anika played every week.

The living room was packed with women.

"The cookie fairy is here!" Anika sang as she lifted the basket in the air.

The women all lilted their voices sweetly as she entered.

"Jasmine!"

Jasmine waved. She hugged some old friends and introduced herself to some unfamiliar faces. It wasn't perfect, but the group was incredible. There were women from all over the world in this room. Asmara, London, Bahia, Manila. Librarians, diplomat's daughters, politicians, musicians. People you'd never expect to have such dark stories. Washington women with sharp wit and big, sincere smiles. Jasmine loved those smiles. She'd learned quickly that this was the secret of AA. There was joy here. Not just the sad stories and tears. There was loud, milky laughter and sweetness. More than anywhere she'd been. Because people who pulled themselves through addiction knew how precious life was. Jasmine curled up in the window seat and watched the room from a distance.

"Ladies, ladies!" Anika waved her arms like a conductor at the center of the room.

"Get your snacks and drinks and we'll start the meeting up in five."

The women cheered. Jasmine giggled.

"Oh and everyone! This . . . is Leslie! She's new to the meeting so everyone make sure to say hi!" Leslie, an elegant Black woman in a flowing green dress, materialized at Jasmine's side. Her curly fro framed her angular face in a silver halo. She smiled deeply. Jasmine looked up at Leslie as she took a seat on the other side of the window seat. Jasmine sat up. She felt like a groupie spotting her favorite celebrity. THE MEDITATING WOMAN. There she was. That calm, smiling, glowy woman she'd seen at the meeting some weeks back. Jasmine had thought of the woman again and again over the past few days. Who was she? What was her secret? Jasmine leaned forward. Leslie looked the same. She closed her eyes for a long time and when she opened them, she looked so calm. Like she was sitting on a quiet beach.

"Oh my God, it's you," Jasmine said.

Leslie turned towards her.

"Hi," Jasmine whispered.

"Hello." Leslie smiled.

"I think I saw you at the noon meeting. In Silver Spring?"

"That's a good one," Leslie said, sitting back onto the stack of colorful pillows.

"Yeah," Jasmine said, nodding, starry-eyed. She went on. "Okay so, I'm not a person who talks about energy or whatever. I'm really not that guy but I have to say I love your energy."

"That's sweet of you!" Leslie said.

"I'm Jasmine."

"Leslie."

They shook hands.

"So are you a yoga teacher or a therapist or something?" Jasmine asked.

"Ah. No. I'm just about at the opposite end of the spectrum. Wealth management." Leslie whispered the words wealth management with feigned solemnity.

"Woah. Okay," Jasmine replied, wide-eyed.

"So how are you this . . . calm? Do you meditate? Like constantly?" Jasmine asked.

Leslie laughed. "Sort of."

Jasmine folded her arms and leaned in. "Sort of?"

Leslie laughed. "Well. It's actually pretty simple. When I close my eyes, I try to thank Spirit for something new. Like a mobile gratitude list. Did you ever smoke weed, or . . . take other substances?" Leslie asked with a wink.

"Oh, I did many drugs. In excess. Clearly," Jasmine replied.

"Well. Whenever I can, I close my eyes and breathe in, kind of like you would if you had a J or whatever. And I think about that one thing on my gratitude list. And then exhale. Gratitude, breathwork, and meditation all in one. It's a tool my therapist gave me a few years ago. And now it's just a habit."

"Wow," Jasmine said, nodding.

"Sometimes it gives people the creeps, actually."

"Not me," Jasmine said.

"I'm glad."

"Can you give me an example?" Jasmine leaned in again.

"An example?" Leslie tilted her head.

"Of what's on your list?"

"It's usually about breath. Being grateful for breath and life. Or it's my family, my sobriety, sometimes about dessert." Leslie closed her eyes as if she could feel the goodness of everything she described.

Jasmine took this in. She closed her eyes and tried it. Dreaming up her mobile gratitude list. Coffee. Sobriety. Cookies. Zora's lips. Zora's hands. She opened her eyes and felt the room softening around her. Jasmine looked up at Leslie.

"Do you think—" Jasmine began, then stopped. Leslie tilted her head.

"Do you think we could have coffee one day?" she asked.

"I'd love to," Leslie said.

"You're so cool," Jasmine whispered.

"You think I'm cool?!" Leslie exclaimed. She leaned back into a burst of laughter. Her serenity felt contagious. She rested her head in her hand.

"Can you write that down and sign it so I can show it to my kids?"

"Absolutely," Jasmine said, laughing.

25. JASMINE AND MARBLE

Jasmine carried a hulking thirty-pound bag of flour over her shoulder. She whistled. She wasn't a whistler. But today she whistled. Marble leaned against the counter, reading a book with a colorful cartoon of a person masturbating on the cover. Jasmine slammed the bag on the counter.

"Whatcha reading?" Jasmine asked, nearly out of breath.

Marble turned the book to Jasmine. "Nerve Endings: The New Trans Erotic."

"Is it hot?" Jasmine asked.

"Very hot," Marble said, watching Jasmine collect herself and hoist the heavy bag back up to her shoulder.

"You need some help with that?" Marble called out.

"Nope!" Jasmine whistled all the way back to the kitchen.

Marble followed her. Jasmine poured all thirty pounds of flour into the vertical mixer. She spun around in the cloud of flour like a ballerina.

Marble chuckled in the doorway. Jasmine put a hand on her hip. "What?"

"Oh, nothing." Marble walked to the mixer and watched Jasmine work.

She swung the fridge open and pulled a tub of butter from the top shelf. She loved the scale of this place. The weight of three pounds of butter. Three pounds of sugar. The machines were so powerful, you could lose an arm making cookie dough. It made her feel like a badass. As she gathered ingredients, she pointed to the silver bowl of eggs on the counter by Marble's side.

"Could you beat those some more?" Jasmine asked. She tipped the tub of butter into the mixer.

Marble beat the eggs with an oversized whisk.

"Who needs this many croissants?" Marble asked.

"Conference at the hotel. Lesbians who tech or something. We're doing chocolate as well." Jasmine skipped back to the walk-in.

"So was it good? Like real, real, real good?" Marble asked.

"Was what good?" Jasmine kept her eyes on the thick, elastic goop as she poured it into the mixer.

"Wow, that smells good." Marble stood over the mixer and inhaled the scent.

"It's the yeast. I'll teach you this one next week."

"Ooh! Yay!" Marble bounced, excitedly.

Jasmine grinned.

"Wait a minute. Don't try to change the subject." Marble wagged their finger at Jasmine. "Was it GOOD or nah?"

"Was what good?" Jasmine asked absent-mindedly.

"The sex. You're acting like your life is a fucking musical. So I'm assuming it was good?" Marble tilted the bowl for Jasmine's approval. Jasmine nodded and they poured the eggs into the mixer.

Jasmine grinned. Marble set the bowl down and stared at her.

"It was very good," Jasmine said, nodding.

"Oooh!" Marble squealed and the two of them clasped hands and jumped in a circle like children.

"Good sex! Good sex! Good sex!" Marble began chanting and Jasmine joined in. They both giggled as they flew apart. Marble carried the metal bowl to the sink. They tapped rhythmically on the bowl with the whisk. Jasmine danced and undulated her hips proudly. She laughed and looked down at the mixer. The dough was forming beautifully in its rounded metal cocoon.

"So I'm assuming you're too dainty to give me details?" Marble shouted over the sound of the faucet. They snapped a pair of rubber gloves on and drizzled the bowl with soap.

"Not dainty," Jasmine replied. "But. Cautious, maybe," she went on, looking up at Marble for a moment.

"Cautious about what?" Marble shouted.

Jasmine sighed. "I don't know. It feels too good to be true, you know?"

"Yeah. It is," Marble replied. "She's fine and rich and smart and she can fuck? I mean there's gotta be a catch." Marble rinsed the bowl and set it gently on the drying rack.

"Right?" Jasmine bit at her nail.

"Right." Marble walked to Jasmine's side and looked down at the dough. "But for now, why not enjoy it?"

"True," Jasmine said. She leaned against the counter, thinking.

They both watched the mixer arm spin. It was hypnotic. The way the dough danced with the rotating arm. The arm moved the same way like clockwork, around and around. The dough followed. Pulling and squeezing, the shape was slightly different with every rotation.

"Are you thinking about she-who-must-not-be-named?" Marble asked.

"A little." Jasmine frowned. Marble looked up at Jasmine.

"Zora isn't Dia. You know that, right?" Marble said.

"Yeah." Jasmine folded her arms.

"And you're not really you. Anymore. I mean you've grown so much, Jasmine." Marble went on.

Jasmine ducked down and opened a giant drawer. She lifted a scale from the drawer and placed it on the counter.

"So we're measuring out portions of four kilograms. I'll do

the first one, then you."

Marble sighed. "Sure."

When Marble started working at the T Spot, Jasmine's sisters gravely cautioned them about the Dia topic. Ella and Layla explained that her ex had left her a year ago, but Jasmine was still raw and she'd just started AA. Marble would find Jasmine in the cafe working quietly. She'd give them instructions and nothing more. They weren't friends. They didn't tell stories or get to know one another. Her eyes were swollen for weeks. Marble never saw it, but they could tell that Jasmine cried every night. A couple of months in, Jasmine began to change. She laughed. She looked rested. She sang as she baked. She asked Marble about school and their love life. They talked about gender and sex and movies. Marble told Jasmine all about what twenty-somethings were up to these days. They became friends. Marble needed friends.

Marble was in their last year at Howard. Howard was a magical and deeply flawed place. They loved Howard because it gave them the gift of Blackness everywhere. They came into their gender identity there. They made art and they fucked around and had that perfect balance of work and play and being almost grown. But the lows were beginning to outweigh the highs. They were misgendered constantly, they wore gloves to class in the winter because the heat was broken (maintenance didn't seem to prioritize the art buildings), and they had no real friends at school. Their parents were very sweet, but they understood nothing about Marble, and going back to small-town Georgia was too painful. They were constantly renegotiating their boundaries, translating, biting their tongue. They decided they weren't going home again. This choice felt so incredible, so freeing. And it also felt deeply lonely. Free and lost all at once. So when Marble took the job at the T Spot, they needed Jasmine. It seemed like Jasmine needed them too.

"Well, even if there's a catch, I'm excited for you. Can I say that?" Marble offered.

"Thank you, Marble." Jasmine looked at Marble with tenderness.

"And whenever you're done dating her, I get next." Marble spoke with a straight face.

"Oh, I'm sorry. Won't that get in the way of you DATING MY MOTHER?" Jasmine flipped a switch on the mixer and it slowed to a stop.

"Though I would love nothing more, and I would absolutely rock her world, respectfully, I am not dating your mother." Marble pushed up the nose of the mixer, and the arm emerged from the dough. Jasmine threw a handful of flour into the bowl.

"So what are you doing?" Jasmine pulled two pastry scrapers from the shelf. She handed one to Marble.

"I was talking to her about teaching." Marble took the scraper and watched Jasmine for a reaction.

"Teaching?" Jasmine said as she muscled a heavy chunk of dough from the mixer. She cut at it with the scraper edge and handed a piece to Marble.

"Yes." Marble plopped the dough on the scale.

"Um. Teaching . . . children?" Jasmine went on.

"Yes. The school she used to work at needs a sex ed teacher." Marble watched the numbers on the scale. They used the scraper to remove a small portion of dough.

"Ah." Jasmine put her hands on her hips and stood still for a moment.

"It's only part-time, boo. I'll still be your apprentice slash lil sibling." Marble pinched Jasmine's cheek with a doughy hand.

"Are you worried about the kids? Being ignorant? Cuz those rich white kids are ignorant. And dumb. And mean."

"I know. But I'll be okay." Marble smiled, touched to be the victim of Jasmine's overbearing big sister reflex.

"Okay . . ." Jasmine said.

"Sex ed at Beechwood. With a nonbinary teacher. A Black, poly, sex-positive nonbinary teacher. That'll really shake things up." Jasmine shook her head.

"Yeah. I got the impression they're a little conservative over there."

"A little." Jasmine rolled her eyes.

"But now nonbinary people are on TV, and everyone is hopping on the gender-is-a-construct bandwagon, so I might as well get paid for all that white cis guilt, right?"

"Absolutely." Jasmine nodded.

Zora listened to Jasmine and Marble as she walked down the hallway toward the kitchen. She stood in the door, waiting. Zora watched Jasmine pull at a huge chunk of dough. She loved watching Jasmine in the kitchen. Every time she was doing something different. She watched for a moment, drinking it in. Then she knocked lightly on the doorway. Jasmine's cheeks were flushed when she looked up.

"Zora?" Jasmine said.

"Zora!" Marble exclaimed.

"Hi," Zora said as she leaned in the doorway.

"Hi," Jasmine said.

"Hiiiii!" Marble grinned cartoonishly at Zora, then at Jasmine.

"Hi, Marble. Good to see you again." Zora closed her eyes and bowed her head just barely.

Marble's shoulders lifted bashfully. "You too!" Marble chirped.

"Jasmine, I didn't mean to interrupt. But I was wondering if I could take you out on a date."

Jasmine turned to Marble.

"Go," Marble whispered.

Jasmine turned to protest. "But the order has to be ready by—"

"Sis. You better let this fine gentleman take you on a date. Don't be dumb," Marble hissed.

Jasmine looked at Zora, then back to Marble.

"Um. OK, yes I'd love to go out on a date. With you." Jasmine grinned, wiping her hands with a dish towel.

"You know what to do?" Jasmine looked at the remaining dough like a worried mother.

"Yes." Marble nodded eagerly.

"Four kilos ..." Jasmine began.

"Make rectangles, pop them in the fridge. I know what to do. Go." Marble swatted Jasmine away.

"And I like to keep the extra ..."

"Save the scraps, I know what to do. Go away." Marble folded their arms.

Jasmine looked nervously at the clock on the wall.

"Okay." Jasmine looked at Zora. "Let's go." Jasmine left her apron on the counter and Zora took her hand.

26. JASMINE AND ZORA

Black, queer and fine on a hot DC summer day, Jasmine and Zora ascended the steps of The National Gallery of Art. Zora took the steps in long strides. As always, poised and handsome in her crisp slacks and fitted black tee. Jasmine danced at Zora's side, swimming in her oversized ripped jeans and big black boots. The building sat stately and imposing against the summer blue sky. Designed like a Grecian temple, the architecture made Jasmine feel small. Mortal. But the woman at her side looked like Apollo. The way she walked with authority. Her masculinity was a stride away from cocky. Like she owned everything. Jasmine liked it. She felt almost girlish by Zora's side.

They strolled through the gallery. Whispers echoed gently against smooth marble steps. Vibrant oil paintings lit up the pale blue walls like windows. They sauntered apart. Walking soft carpeted strides around the rooms. The art inspired a quiet formality. Like a library or a church, it was all so serious, so sacred that it required hushed tones. Prayer and worship. Jasmine and Zora acted like strangers. Crossing paths quietly. Jasmine's hand grazed Zora's arm as she walked by. A slow-motion duet. Jasmine watched Zora as she studied the exhibition description. Degas at the Opéra.

"Are you the kind of museum person who reads everything?" Jasmine asked.

Zora laughed. "I might be."

"Well, I'm not," Jasmine whispered into Zora's ear.

"I noticed," Zora whispered back.

Jasmine pretended to read at Zora's side.

"What's your favorite museum?" She asked.

"Probably the Blacksonian. I was surprised you didn't want to go there," Zora said.

"Oh, I love it there. But it's always packed," Jasmine said, pausing at a charcoal sketch. "And I didn't like the flow."

"The flow?" Zora asked. She stood behind Jasmine.

"Starting in the basement? With slavery. The slavery basement."

"Well, that's where it starts," Zora said, stepping away.

"I get it. That's where the diaspora story starts. But Black people didn't spring into existence on slave ships. We had family, spirituality, worlds long before those ships came. And every day is trauma. You know?" Jasmine said, as they moved on to another sketch.

"I hear you," Zora replied. She moved to stand too close to Jasmine. Close enough to breathe into her.

"I mean, yes. Yes, we should learn about and talk about slavery. But I don't know if it should be the beginning of our story. You know? They should make white folks go to the basement to learn about slavery. Make them do it. Black folks should be able to visit the basement or just celebrate and feel some joy. Or both. But it's not my museum, so." Jasmine skipped into the next room and sat on the narrow-cushioned bench. Zora followed slowly. She fastidiously read every placard and took in every piece on her way.

"So what would your museum look like?" Zora asked as she sat next to Jasmine.

"Well. It would just be full of art and music and photographs. Black people feeling. Just lots of feelings." Jasmine closed her eyes and tilted her head back, imagining.

"You think you could figure out a better way to represent Black history?" Zora asked.

Jasmine opened her eyes. She closed them again, trying that thing Meditating Leslie had taught her. Her mobile gratitude list. Jasmine was grateful for this moment. For Zora. She inhaled into the darkness, her ears focused on the hushed voices weaving through the gallery. Zora watched Jasmine. She couldn't put her finger on it, but something about her in that moment felt familiar.

"I don't think anyone can represent Black history. Or any history, really. It's about perspective. What you choose to focus on. There are just pieces and glimpses. Feelings. I don't know." Jasmine looked at Zora. Zora was smiling at her.

"So why did you want to come here? Seems like the whitest, most Eurocentric spot we could have picked," Zora said.

Jasmine closed her eyes and smiled again. "My mom used to take me here."

Zora nodded. "Lucky."

"And I thought Degas would remind you of Paris," Jasmine said.

"That's thoughtful. Thank you."

"It's my pleasure," Jasmine said, smiling earnestly.

"Actually, it reminds me of my grandparents," Zora said, her eyes scanning the walls of the gallery.

"Yeah?"

"They renewed their vows here years ago. I was like thirteen."

"Wow. Fancy!" Jasmine replied.

"It was a James Van Der Zee exhibit. Gorgeous prints of Black people with money. Furs and big cars and everything Harlem. Which was very appropriate for them. Grandma had the long gloves and the gown and everything." Jasmine watched Zora light up.

"I mean it was mostly very pretentious. I probably hid in a corner the whole night. But I remember when they did their vows, something really stuck with me."

Jasmine waited. Zora looked up to the ceiling, recalling the memory.

"They were doing vows and my grandfather said all this stuff about maybe we're not perfect, and maybe we're not even perfect for each other. But I wouldn't choose another soul to spend the rest of my life with. You know all that corny wedding stuff. And then my grandaddy actually got on one knee. And I never seen him do anything to humble himself. I mean he was so fucking old school. You know, Black masculinity, proud. But he looks up and he's weeping. Like a baby. I mean he can barely open his eyes there are so many tears. He was a mess. Then he says: Mrs. Augusta Mae Scott, will you be my sweetheart?" Zora shook her head.

Jasmine searched Zora's eyes. "Why did that stand out so much to you?"

"I don't know." Zora sighed. "Maybe seeing my folks separate around that time—I didn't really see anyone in love like that." Zora looked back at Jasmine.

Jasmine touched the smooth skin of Zora's cheek. Zora held her hand there. And because neither of them knew how vulnerable they were allowed to be, their hands fell and their gazes wandered.

"Do you believe you'll have that one day? That humbling, will-you-be-my-sweetheart kind of love?" Jasmine asked. She stared at the holes in her jeans.

"I don't know. You?" Zora said softly.

"I don't know," Jasmine replied.

"I think I want that. I think I always did," Zora said.

Jasmine nodded. They both stared up at "Ballet Scene," a blur of pink tutus and movement.

"But it feels kind of like Santa Claus. Like a thing I really want to exist. But maybe it doesn't."

"Are you saying you don't believe in love?" Jasmine asked.

"I believe in it. I'm just not sure I believe in that kind."

"What kind?" Jasmine asked, tilting her head.

"The will you be my sweetheart kind."

"Do you think your grandfather was just acting like he was in love?"

Zora thought for a moment, then shook her head. "No. I believe they were in love. It's just that I've never been in love before," Zora said. Her gaze drifted.

Jasmine stood suddenly. She picked her favorite painting in the room and meandered to it. She gazed up at the thick strokes of paint. The dancers' arms were pale cream with hints of green. Their tutus thick and gauzy with flecks of blue and yellow. An orange sky in the distance, curling with clouds. When Zora stood behind Jasmine, the painting faded away. The whole room faded away.

Zora took Jasmine's hand and pulled her in. Jasmine exhaled sharply. Zora's hand rested at the small of Jasmine's back. Jasmine's fingertips found Zora's jawline. She melted into Zora. Brave enough to hold her gaze. It would be easier, safer to look away. But Jasmine stared and Zora stared back. Searching for something in each other's eyes, leaning in to look closer. They kissed slowly. Zora's long locs floated up, tangled between Jasmine's fingers. The air in the room changed. Every ghostly Parisian dancer in every hundred-year-old painting turned to watch them. A pair of white women in their eighties averted their eyes and shuffled away. A group of high school kids giggled and cheered from down the hall. They were a vision. Zora held Jasmine's waist and they melted into each other. Somewhere between Degas' "Four Dancers" and "Ballet Scene," two Black women fell in love.

27. JASMINE AND ZORA

Jasmine danced into Zora's room. Tickling the spines of every book on the shelf as she bounced past them. Zora followed her, grinning. Jasmine glittered. Maybe she was just as much of a catch as she imagined Zora to be. She did have magic, after all. Maybe she was a warm shimmer to Zora's cool silver glow. Maybe she was the fairy to Zora's vampire. Maybe she was a powerful being. A dancing, giggling witch. Because today, only two hours ago, she'd kissed Zora in the middle of the National Gallery of Art and that kiss ... that was something. Everything. They wanted each other. It felt like she was stepping up onto the godly pedestal she had placed Zora on from the moment they met.

Jasmine kicked off her boots and dropped her satchel on the floor.

Zora chuckled. "Please. Make yourself comfortable."

"I will," Jasmine replied, her hands on her hips.

Purple and gold beamed through the trees in Zora's windows. The sunset radiated behind them.

"So?" Jasmine said, waiting.

"So..." Zora said. She put her hands on her hips, attempting an impression of Jasmine.

Zora's smile curled up the right side of her face. Jasmine's body clenched. A jolt of power pulsed through her. She crossed to Zora.

"Can I kiss you?" Jasmine whispered.

"Yes," Zora said.

Jasmine's lips pressed hungrily into Zora's. She pulled her shirt off and breathlessly clawed at Zora's clothes. Zora's head tilted back as Jasmine pulled her locs, tracing her tongue to Zora's earlobe. Her lips pulled it into her mouth. Zora's breath caught in her throat. She bit her lip as she exhaled, their breath quickening together.

Jasmine loved giving and receiving the most delicious bits of every gender role she could get her hands on. She had been demure all day and she enjoyed it. Letting Zora open the car door for her and Zora's hand resting on the small of her back. Today, she was blushing, giggling, and arching her back. Switching when she walked. Giving her power away. All of it felt good with Zora. That performance of girlishness. But too much of anything bored her. And now, she felt herself impatiently transforming. Jasmine was starving.

They feverishly pulled each other's clothes off. Asking and giving permission in doubletime. "Can I?" Jasmine whispered.

"Yes. Is this OK?" Zora panted as she pulled at Jasmine's waistband.

"YES!" Jasmine snapped.

They littered the bed with their socks, pants, bras until they were both stripped down to their underwear. Jasmine rolled on top of Zora and opened her legs.

"Can I touch you—"

"Yes," Zora said. She covered her face.

Jasmine slid her fingertips across Zora's clit. Zora moaned. A deep, melodic breath full of air. Jasmine shook under the weight of Zora's pleasure. They both gasped for breath. Zora's legs pinned open, Jasmine's heat grinding hard and slow into her. Again. This was too much. Too good. Zora's hands gripped Jasmine's thighs. She lifted Jasmine up and nearly tossed her. Jasmine giggled as she fell and bounced into a mountain of pillows. Zora rolled on top, pausing for a moment to take Jasmine in. Her skintight with goosebumps, her nipples stiff, boy shorts riding up her ass, her chest rising and falling. The deep purples and blues of dusk glowed on their skin. Zora took a breath.

"Are you OK?" Jasmine asked, panting.

"Yeah. Are you?" Zora asked.

"I'm great," Jasmine said, snuggling her head into the pillow.

"I wanted to see if—" Zora began.

"Yeah?" Jasmine propped herself up.

"I don't know if it's too soon for you . . . but—" Zora tilted her head.

"Yes . . ." Jasmine said, giggling. Zora wasn't one to be at a loss for words. She seemed nervous.

Zora opened her mouth to speak and said nothing. Instead, she turned to her nightstand, and opened a drawer. Zora leaned back to Jasmine with a bundle of black leather straps and a large, chocolate brown dildo in her hands. Jasmine fell back into the bed, roaring with laughter. Zora shook the dildo, and it waved comically between them.

"Well, I don't know if it's too soon but . . ." Jasmine said as she swung her leg over Zora, bounced out of bed and reached into her backpack. She pulled out a sparkly purple dildo in a tangle of green leather straps. Zora's eyebrows nearly reached her hairline.

"Ah!" Zora said. Her voice emerged higher than she expected it to.

Jasmine hopped back into bed with her dildo.

"What?" Jasmine giggled.

"I mean. Wow. You're so prepared," Zora said, nodding anxiously. "And it's so . . . sparkly."

"I would have preferred green with sparkles. This is a bit femme for me," Jasmine replied, studying the purple phallus.

"Right," Zora chuckled.

They sat for a moment, grinning at each other.

"So . . ." Jasmine said. She touched her dildo's head gently to Zora's.

"So . . ." Zora said. She exhaled.

"Would you be . . . into this?" Jasmine asked gently as she grazed Zora's thigh with her disembodied purple cock.

"I don't do this with everyone. And usually not this soon. But. I want to," Zora said.

"Mmmh. Lucky me," Jasmine replied, coyly. She pretended not to be overwhelmed with joy. Jasmine didn't count on Zora being flexible, but she'd hoped for it.

"So then. Who goes first?" Zora asked.

Jasmine looked up at Zora, a mischievous smirk on her face.

"Race for it?" Zora said, grinning.

Zora's eyes shot down to her strap. Jasmine perched up on her hands like a cat.

Suddenly, Zora scrambled out of bed, lifting her collection of black leather straps up to the fading daylight. Jasmine sprinted to her satchel. She pulled a strip of condoms out of her bag, tore one off and threw it at Zora. Zora laughed as she attempted to untangle her black leather straps. Jasmine hopped on one foot. She made fast work, pulling her strap tight and securing the Velcro. Zora struggled. Her strap jingled with silver buckles. Jasmine rolled the condom up her purple shaft, spirited around the bed and slapped the condom from Zora's hands.

"Shit!" Zora cursed, looking Jasmine up and down. Jasmine kissed Zora then looked into her eyes.

"I let you win," Zora said.

"Come on," Jasmine said as she pushed Zora back onto the bed. She looked down at Zora's brown cock, eagerly reaching up for her. She ripped it out of its ring and threw it against the wall. Zora's eyes widened.

"DAMN Jasmine!"

"What?"

"You're kind of studish right now. I mean I know you have a fade, but damn," she said as Jasmine took Zora's nipple gently between her teeth. Zora bit her lip, suddenly pacified with pleasure.

"Do you like it?" Jasmine asked, looking innocently up into Zora's eyes.

"Maybe," Zora said.

"Hmm." Jasmine kissed Zora, her hand guiding the tip of her purple dick up Zora's thigh. She let it slide down until it dragged along Zora's swollen clit. Zora's low, guttural moan made Jasmine's clit harder, pushing against the base of her cock, muscles tightened. She bowed down to taste Zora's mouth. To inhale her. Jasmine arched her back and slid her cock up and down against Zora's clit. How long could she hold herself above Zora? How long could she sustain this almost fucking? She hovered there for what felt like a lifetime, waiting for Zora to lose her patience. Waiting for the wetness to flow over and make her dick glisten. They exchanged breaths.

"Tell me when," Jasmine whispered.

"Now. Fuck me right now." Zora exhaled.

Jasmine eased the head of her cock into Zora. Zora held her breath. Jasmine let it rest there. Zora's hips churned anxiously. Jasmine moved slowly and slid deeper into Zora. They moved together. Jasmine leading with stillness, a forced patience. Zora rushing, breathing, pleading for more. Her hips lifted to meet the stroke. Zora was so wet and impatient she grabbed Jasmine's ass in her hands and pulled her hips in. Jasmine felt her cock pushing deep, a shock of pleasure ripping through her. Her breath quickened suddenly. She collapsed onto Zora, a quiet whine escaping her lips. Zora turned her head, watching Jasmine collect herself.

"Are you? Did you?" Zora began.

"Shhhh. Nothing. Don't worry about it," Jasmine said, rising back up to meet Zora's gaze, a fervent smile tight across her face.

"Wow. I got a one-minute man over here?" Zora teased.

"Okay, okay I'm enjoying myself but I'm not done." Jasmine blushed.

"Show me," Zora said, lifting an eyebrow.

Jasmine's strokes dug deeper, faster into Zora. Their tempo created percussion, the beat of rising energy. Zora closed her eyes and fell back into her pleasure.

"Harder," she whispered.

Jasmine obeyed. Harder and harder. She hit a rhythm, then stopped, grinding to a slow and deep halt. Zora pushed into Jasmine impatiently. Jasmine sped up again, scooping and arching up into Zora with every stroke. Zora moaned, pulling Jasmine's ass into her again. Jasmine propped herself on one hand and pushed her fingers onto Zora's clit.

"Shiiiiit," Zora said, her voice deep and breathy. When Jasmine felt Zora tighten around her cock, she slowed down again.

"I'm gonna come," Zora whispered.

"Not yet," Jasmine whispered back. Her fingers and hips circled slowly.

"Fuck you," Zora said, shaking her head.

Jasmine giggled. "Fuck you."

She pushed deeper. Zora lifted her legs up and felt her body clenching. Zora's back arched sharply up from the bed. Jasmine's stroke pushed faster and harder, meeting Zora's hips as she came, then slowing down as Zora's body shook with convulsions. Their lips met. Zora moaned into Jasmine's mouth. They moved together. Rising and falling slowly.

"Tell me when you want me to stop," Jasmine whispered, catching her breath.

"Not yet," Zora said.

They kissed again. Jasmine slowly pushed into Zora again. Feeling the last wave of their pleasure.

"Okay," Zora whispered.

As Jasmine pulled out, Zora's body wilted. She curled up and Jasmine fell flat on her back. Zora closed her eyes. Her breathing slowed. Jasmine turned her head and watched proudly as Zora drifted off for a moment. She lifted a stray loc from Zora's face. Her chiseled jawline, her angular stoicism softened with pleasure. She was still magical. Still devastatingly beautiful. But instead of metal—now she looked like water. Jasmine could float here. Bathe in the cool liquid of her beauty. Reflections of moonlight on the ocean. Jasmine smiled as Zora opened her eyes slowly. She frowned and nodded affirmingly.

"O-K." She breathed. Jasmine laughed.

"Okay?"

"I mean okay. You got strokes, huh?" Zora continued, nodding sleepily.

"Oh. You thought cuz I wear eyeliner and tight pants, I don't got strokes?" Jasmine teased.

"Well . . ." Zora cocked her head.

"Assumptions, assumptions," Jasmine said playfully, as she kissed Zora.

"It's a pleasant surprise. That's all I'm saying." Zora was nodding again.

"I'm glad." Jasmine kissed Zora's neck, inhaling the scent of her sweat and cologne.

"Did you ever let somebody strap you down before?" Jasmine asked.

"Strap me down?" Zora laughed.

"What do you call it?" Jasmine asked.

"I mean that works I guess. And yeah, a couple of times. But. Those times were different," Zora said, looking Jasmine up and down.

"Oh and the strap race. Wow. That was definitely a first for me," Zora said, laughing.

"HA! Strap race!" Jasmine said, as she laughed into the pillow.

"You're fast." Zora tickled the back of Jasmine's neck with her fingertips.

"I was motivated," Jasmine said.

Zora kissed Jasmine and whispered in her ear. "Is it my turn now?" Zora wrapped her fingers around the sticky purple cock.

"Yes please," Jasmine hissed.

Zora ripped Jasmine's dildo out of its harness. She tossed it behind her back and it hit the lamp on her nightstand.

"Oh shit!" Zora giggled as she turned to check the damage.

Jasmine laughed.

Zora hopped off the bed. She found a fresh condom and handed it to Jasmine. She secured her chocolate dildo back in its place and tightened the straps as Jasmine peeled the condom from the wrapper. Jasmine put the condom in her mouth and Zora's eyes widened. Before Zora could make sense of it in her mind, Jasmine was pursing her lips and leaning down to kiss the tip of Zora's cock. Her hand hovered over the back of Jasmine's head, resisting the urge to push her dick deeper down Jasmine's throat. Slowly, Jasmine took it into her mouth until her lips pursed at the base of Zora's cock. She shook her head aggressively, sucking it in as deep as she could, and let it go. The condom-clad dildo bounced as Jasmine sat back on her heels. Frozen, Zora stared down.

Jasmine giggled. "What? You thought cuz I strapped you down I can't be a switch?" Jasmine asked, grinning.

A line of spit hung from the tip of the latex-clad dick. Zora shook her head. She felt like she was high. Floating. "Jasmine. I—"

"Yeah? You okay?" Jasmine blinked, waiting.

Zora bit her lip. "I want to fuck you so bad right now."

"Come on," Jasmine said. She didn't skip a beat. She turned over and pushed her ass into Zora. Zora snapped back to consciousness at the sight of Jasmine's ass in the air. She traced the curve of it with the tip of her cock as Jasmine arched her back.

Zora's fingertips felt Jasmine's lips swollen and dripping, slick with cum. She didn't want to wait. To tease. To go slow. She wanted it all. She slid her cock in deep. The base of it turning slick. Jasmine bucked against Zora's stroke. Zora pulled Jasmine's ass up into her. Fingertips gripping, thumbs pushing into the flesh of Jasmine's ass. Jasmine moaned into the blankets, reaching down to work her clit.

"Harder," Jasmine whispered softly.

"Say it again. Louder," Zora said, slowing down, watching her cock slide into Jasmine and emerge shining.

"Fuck me hard," Jasmine growled.

Jasmine's hand reached back and cupped her own ass. She spread it open.

And Zora was gone. She locked her hands into the thick curve of Jasmine's hips, lifted and fucked her hard and slow. Jasmine moaned into the sheets again, throwing her ass back onto Zora's cock. Zora's clit pushed back under the pull of her leather straps. The pattern of their rhythm stayed slow and excruciating. Currents of pleasure radiated between them, inside and outside, consumed, filled up, pulling, and pushing. Skin wet with breath, spit and sweat. Somewhere between love and animal hunger, Zora picked up her pace and Jasmine followed her. Faster and harder, the cord of feeling between them thickening. Jasmine could feel Zora's clit throbbing beneath layers of leather. Zora could feel Jasmine. The swell of pleasure connected, and one couldn't tell where the other's body ended and where her pleasure began. Jasmine's breath stopped. Time stopped. Zora continued fucking her up and up and over the edge of the peak. Jasmine's pleasure fell from her lips in cries. That blue green. That underwater weightlessness. Zora held her cock deep inside her as the final waves of Jasmine's orgasm washed over them.

Zora pulled Jasmine up to her and pressed her lips into Jasmine's back. Zora felt her eyes stinging. Their chests still heaving with breath. Zora kissed Jasmine's back and cried. She didn't understand the feeling. Her heart was miles ahead of her. What did this mean? What could it mean? Jasmine tilted her head back and they held each other there. Jasmine turned around and pulled Zora into the bed with her. Zora said nothing. She just closed her eyes and the tears ran down her cheeks.

"I got you," Jasmine whispered softly.

Jasmine remembered bits of the day. Kissing in the museum. Standing by Zora's side, pretending to admire the art. Zora's expression when she talked about her grandfather. Will you be my sweetheart?

And Zora dreamt about tomorrow. The cafe she would take Jasmine to. The one with fancy high tea and the three-tiered platters of tea cakes and sandwiches. Zora wondered if Jasmine would like a place like that. Zora curled up and Jasmine snuggled behind her. The faint thought occurred to Zora: she'd never been the little spoon before. Her thoughts and worries drifted slowly into the air. Warm and exhausted, they both closed their eyes, floating, drifting into a dream.

A thin beam of sunlight pierced through the trees when Zora's phone startled her awake. Her phone never rang. She lifted her head slightly as she tilted the screen up and gazed at its white light. Jasmine peeked an eye open as Zora sat up. She squeezed her eyes closed again, wishing they could stay like this. Cozy and sleeping. Drunk with sex. It was too early to get up now. But Zora stood and walked away from the bed.

"Hello?" She said in a whisper. Zora dressed quietly as she whispered into the phone. Jasmine heard the sound of a man's voice as Zora tiptoed out of the bedroom.

Jasmine opened her eyes. Something didn't feel right. The way Zora left the room. The way she seemed to get up with such urgency. Jasmine sat up in the bed, listening to Zora's voice in the next room. She couldn't make out the words, but she could tell

Zora was worried. She pushed her head into the pillow, waiting.

When Zora appeared in the doorway, her face had fallen.

"Something's wrong. With my dad," she said, staring at the wall.

"Is he okay?" Jasmine asked, sitting up.

"He's fine. It's about work." Zora's eyes wouldn't meet Jasmine's. She stared at the wall.

"... Okay. What do you need—"

"This was a mistake." Zora looked at her phone then back at the wall. "I need you to go. Now."

Zora's voice was cold. Monotone. A stranger's voice. Jasmine felt like she had been punched in the throat.

"What?" Jasmine said. She squinted at Zora.

Zora sighed. She shook her head slowly.

"Zora?" Jasmine moved closer to Zora. She couldn't read Zora's body language. She couldn't feel their connection. That pull was gone. She could feel her heart beating in her throat.

Zora turned away from the bed, her back to Jasmine. Then she turned back. When her eyes met Jasmine's, their color had changed. They were lit up like embers. She was furious.

"So your sister was using my dad. This whole time? Y'all were trying to set him up? What the fuck, Jasmine."

"Zora. What happened?" Jasmine moved to the edge of the bed.

"Did you plan this? To fucking ambush me and my family? Seriously, Jasmine, what is this?" Zora's voice remained low and placid. Her anger simmered below the surface of her skin.

"If you don't tell me what's going on, I can't really respond to your questions, Zora," Jasmine snapped. She moved quickly. Still naked, barely awake. The dream, the intimacy of last night evaporating into nothing. Just gone. She managed to get her shirt on as Zora folded her arms.

"Is your sister Layla protesting my dad's property?"

"Yes. That's her job," Jasmine replied.

Zora scoffed.

"Zora. Was I supposed to tell you everything about my sister's activism? I didn't realize it was—"

"You acted like you liked me. So yeah. Probably that could have come up at some fucking point, Jasmine." Zora's voice grew louder.

Jasmine climbed into her pants. "I did like you. And honestly, it didn't feel like any of my business what Layla does. But if you want to know, I believe in what she does. And your rich daddy having a little resistance from the Black community in DC is probably not the end of the fucking world, Zora." Jasmine spat her words like venom.

"You have no fucking idea, Jasmine. You really don't," Zora said.

"I don't? Okay." Jasmine nodded.

"No, you don't."

"Zora. Your dad's company displaces low-income families and makes money off of the rich people who come to gentrify the city."

"It's more nuanced than that, but I wouldn't expect you to know—" Zora snapped.

"Oh yeah, more nuanced? Did your daddy tell you that?" Jasmine spat.

"You don't know anything about how real estate law works and I'm not having this conversation with you. There's absolutely no way for you to know how this works."

"I know you hate your job," Jasmine scoffed.

Zora shook her head. "Look. Jasmine. I thought I could try to ... be with someone like you. But it's clear to me, you and your family. You're just not on my level."

Jasmine's smile pinched at her face. She nodded. "Right."

Zora unfolded her arms. She studied something on the wall.

They both dressed quickly and quietly. Jasmine's mind raced. Somewhere between numb and heartbroken. Somewhere between devastated and fucking pissed. Jasmine slammed Zora's bedroom door open to leave. Zora followed Jasmine down the stairs. She wasn't sure what to do. When they emerged from the house, Jasmine ran down the front steps and walked swiftly across the driveway.

"I can . . . I can call you a car. If you need," Zora called out.

Jasmine suppressed a scoff. She kicks me out of her house and offers to pay for the Lyft. What a prince, she thought.

"I'm good," Jasmine shouted as she waved a hand in the air. She walked down the road and didn't look back.

28. THE SISTERS

Jasmine ran as fast as she could, beads of sweat forming at her brow. A choir of birds sang wildly in the treetops. The morning sun cut through the leaves. The beech, red oak, and tulip trees seemed to lean in and watch, like elders noticing a lost child. There was too much morning light, too much beauty. Jasmine swallowed hard. She wouldn't allow herself to cry. Not over this. She wished she could have left Zora's house in the blur of night. She could pretend it was all a bad dream. There would have been no color, no music. She would disappear in monochrome and shadow. Maybe then she could have forgotten the whole night. The sex. The hope. And this morning. The look of disgust in Zora's eyes.

A deep percussive sound echoed from the sky. Jasmine stopped running, sharp heat blooming in her lungs. She stood still for a moment, looking up. She followed the sound of a giant drum, echoing through the trees. Her eyes cut across the sky until they caught a blur of red. A pileated woodpecker perched at the top of a tall, rotting tree. Its bright red crest and black-and-white body bounced up the trunk, knocking into the face of the wood. The knocking rang out like a drum in an ancient song. For a moment, Jasmine forgot her grief. She just listened. What was the forest trying to tell her? What kind of metaphor was she supposed to craft from this moment? Was she the woodpecker?

Searching for the grubs in the dead tree stump of life? Or was she the tree?

When Jasmine reached the house, she found Layla sitting on the front step. Layla looked up at Jasmine with an exhausted smile on her face. It melted Jasmine's heart to see her sister looking all grown up. Her baby sister. Even when Layla was a kid, she had the capacity to worry like an adult. She would fret over things kids shouldn't care about. Slavery. Global warming. Racism. Factory farming. While her classmates were hungry for Disney movies and cartoons, she wanted to watch the news. She was so little, and her troubles were so big. The grown-ups all thought it was cute. As a child, Jasmine couldn't understand why. Kids weren't supposed to be so worried. She was the one attempting to rock Layla to sleep when her nightmares kept her up at night. But Jasmine understood now that their mother and her friends saw promise in Layla. She offered a kind of hope. Maybe a five-year-old could one day grow up and change the world. The adults certainly weren't going to do it.

"Hey Jazz," Layla said.

"Hey honey," Jasmine replied. She sighed as she lowered herself next to Layla.

"Walk of shame?" Layla asked, tilting her head toward Jasmine.

Jasmine shook her head. She didn't have the words to describe just how shameful her morning had been. Layla neatly unfolded the newspaper in her lap.

"You should probably see this," Layla said. She handed Jasmine the newspaper, open to the metro section of *The Washington Post*. The lead story's bold lettering scrolled across the face of the paper: "Chocolate Chip City: Four Faces of Change in DC." Above the headline, four circular frames featured a portrait of each face, along with their name and title scrawled in ornate cursive font. Jasmine smiled at the picture of Layla with her dark eyes and big hair. "Layla Jones: The Activist." Jasmine's heart swelled up with pride.

"Oh my God, Layla!"

She found Layla's hand and squeezed it excitedly.

The next picture featured a young Black woman, the cursive below her photo reading: "Brianna Washington: The Native." The next portrait featured the familiar photo of DC's Black woman mayor, Mirabelle Brown. Her title was, of course, "The Politician."

Then Jasmine's mouth fell open.

"Ah," she said aloud, almost by accident.

"Yeah." Layla nodded and looked out at the empty street.

Malcolm Scott looked rich, charming, and happy in his circular frame. His teeth shone too white. "The Developer" curled in cursive below his picture. Jasmine exhaled. So this was it. The reason Zora lost her shit this morning. Layla's true motivation was finally revealed, and Malcolm Scott would be the very public casualty of her crusade. And apparently the Scott family (or at least Zora) was livid about it. Well. It was fun while it lasted, Jasmine thought.

Her eyes danced across the page, racing through the article. It was good. It was different from anything she'd read about the city. The writer didn't attempt to summarize everything. It was exactly what its headline boasted. Four faces and four specific perspectives. First-person experiences and impressions of DC. These personal stories and experiences spoke to the larger crisis, and every story connected and intertwined at one, fine point: the forthcoming Scott property on U Street. The story began with Brianna.

> *The Washingtons were one of many African American families in the neighborhood who'd owned their U Street row house for generations. Brianna Washington recalls her memories of holidays in her family's home. She remembers the smell of turkey in*

the oven and Stevie Wonder on the record player. The house was full of family, food and laughter. But Washington remembers most clearly the day she found out their family home wasn't theirs anymore. She remembers the day she had to pack up her things and find somewhere to go. In May of last year, the Washington family home was demolished to make way for the Scott Development. "Me and my son—we're homeless now. I never said that out loud before. Homeless. I wouldn't say it cuz people judge you. They think you're on drugs or something. I'm not on drugs. But now I think, why not? They can judge me. They can make fun of me. But they can't pretend I never existed. I won't let them."

Jasmine looked up at Layla. "Is this the same Brianna who said she didn't want to talk?"

Layla smiled weakly again. "Yeah. She did a 180. She came to chrch that day we went to the river." Layla looked out to the road.

Jasmine raised an eyebrow. "Oshun," Jasmine said. They both nodded.

Mayor Brown's story was the dullest part of the article. Every quote was scrubbed squeaky clean by her team of PR people. As usual, she leaned into her struggle and triumph as a Black woman in politics. Her success as the youngest mayor in DC's history, her ability to "overcome the odds," and her deep love for the "roots of the city." This self-promotion melted into an explanation.

"Affordable housing is and has always been our top priority. The Scott Development on U Street is one of many new projects designed to stimulate growth for the cultural and economic communities of the district."

The mayor insists that the Scott development will be beneficial for all levels of socioeconomic communities in DC, citing job growth and what she calls "a high ratio of affordable housing units." However, now in her second term, Mayor Brown continues to combat negative criticism. Even her #AFFORDABLEDC media campaign has fallen under fire. The Office of the Mayor defined the term "affordable" as a household that pays no more than 30 percent of their income on housing. In theory, this program is designed to support individuals and families with an income less than 40 percent of the Area Median Income (AMI) according to the household size.

However, both the mayor's office and Department of Housing and Urban Development (HUD) declined to comment on what metrics they're using to calculate and adjust the AMI for inflation, cost of living, and the influx of high-earning young professional populations. There is little transparency around how HUD calculates the AMI for the DC metro area. Former coun-cilmember and affordable housing advocate Omari Walters offered this insight. "The city defines 'affordable housing' based on AMI and the metrics for AMI calculations are outdated to say the least. If a senator's income is vastly different from a line cook's—whose income determines the cost of living? It begs the question—affordable for who?"

Jasmine shook her head as she read the mayor's portion of the article.

"Stimulate growth for the economic communities of the district? So basically, make rich people richer." Jasmine sucked her teeth.

"Yep." Layla nodded solemnly. They shook their heads.

"I hate it here." Jasmine sighed. She folded the paper and continued reading. When she reached the portion of the article dedicated to Layla, she felt her hands turning clammy with sweat. Like she was watching her little sister in a kindergarten recital. She was nervous for her. But of course, Layla's piece was incredible.

> *Activist Layla Jones is working with Rise DC to shine a light on the injustices of gentrification in the city. As a DC native, this issue hits close to home. Jones grew up in a row home on 9th Street, just a few blocks from the new development on U. Jones' dedication to the low-income and Black communities in DC will materialize in what she calls a 'protest party.' "This city has treated Black folks as disposable. It's shameful. And it's sad. But instead of a funeral—we're having a party. We're going to celebrate the golden era of Black culture in DC. We're going to remember the past in an effort to create a new future."*

Layla worked in the histories of Black Broadway, references to the three hundred Black businesses and an invitation to her "protest party." She was brilliant. Jasmine knew this about her sister, but it felt like a surprise every time she had the pleasure to see it up close. And this was exceptional. She was getting smarter. She was an innovator. Layla was shifting the conversation. Pushing the activists' motivation from tragedy to celebration, a movement grounded in joy. She was holding up a mirror up to the Black folks in the city.

"Wow," Jasmine heard herself say aloud. She shook her head. "Layla. I—I am so fucking proud of you, honey." Jasmine covered her mouth as the tears welled up in her eyes.

"Jesus. Am I crying right now? You made me fucking cry I'm so proud!" Jasmine blubbered.

Layla smiled weakly again. She took Jasmine's hand in hers.

"Thanks, Jazz," Layla said, lowering her head. "It means a lot. Coming from you."

"Wow." Jasmine's tears ran down her cheeks as she watched Layla squirm with modesty.

"It says I grew up on Ninth. I didn't mean to imply I was from the neighborhood. I just said I was born there and we moved. I think she really wanted it all to tie in. So it sounded like . . . I don't know—like I lied?"

"Layla, stop, it's a tiny detail. And you were born in that house. I will not let you downplay how amazing this is."

Layla nodded. "Yeah. Well," Layla said, pointing further down at the page. "Keep reading."

"Right," Jasmine replied. She wiped the tears from her face and lifted the paper.

And there it was: Malcolm's profile. Unlike the mayor, Malcolm Scott clearly didn't have a team of publicists at his disposal. Maybe it was his ego, or his excitement at the prospect of being quoted in *The Post*. He saw himself as inspiring. A young Black man from Northeast. He built his own empire, and he was proud of his money.

> *"These are the highest levels of investment and wealth. And for that reason, the development industry is a shamelessly racist world. Most people would look at me and say I don't belong here. And I'm happy to prove them wrong," Scott says. "Developers at this level face the task of building equity and recruiting multimillion-dollar investments. As a Black developer, I have to be ten times more qualified and thorough than my white counterparts." But Scott insists that he's up to the task. Thanks to Mayor Brown's focus on "developer diversity," the new Scott Development is slated to receive government subsidies in the form of capital*

gains and tax deferrals. The Scott Firm will break barriers as the first Black-owned development company contracted to spend over $100 million on one project in DC. However, when the question of affordable housing comes up, Malcolm Scott is as vague as Mayor Brown. "As a DC native, serving the community is important to me," Scott says. "We're offering luxury apartments–high investment risks require high gains." In accordance with the city's Inclusionary Zoning Affordable Housing Program (IZ), new developments are required to offer at least 88.3 percent affordable housing units in all new developments. Scott insists that the development will offer an impressive ratio of affordable units. However, when prompted, Scott wouldn't specify if his new development would offer the 8.3 percent minimum, or more.

Jasmine took a breath. "Damn. He made himself look worse than the mayor," she said, almost feeling sorry for the man.

"Keep reading," Layla repeated. Jasmine read on, wondering how much worse it could get.

The article concluded with a series of statistics. No matter how objective *The Post* pretended to be—the numbers were undeniable. None of it was new to Jasmine. You didn't need a graph to know that the percentage of Black residents in DC had dropped from 70 percent to 40 percent in the past fifty years. And even 40 percent seemed generous. She didn't need reminders of the class disparities or evidence of the homeless population nearing ten thousand. Anyone who grew up in DC already knew. They didn't need to see the numbers. They were the numbers.

The piece closed with a quote from Layla that gave the article its name.

> "The mayor and developers like Malcolm Scott are complacent. [They are] high-tech house slaves and overseers. They get their piece of the capitalist pie, and the rest of Black DC is left to suffer and scatter. But they're not free. Nobody is. And DC isn't Chocolate City anymore. It's Chocolate Chip City now. In a few years, what's left of Black DC will disappear. We all have the choice to sit back and let it happen—or show up and do something about it."

Jasmine pursed her lips as she folded the paper into her lap.

"House slaves, huh?" she repeated as she darted her eyes to Layla.

"Yeah." Layla reached into her backpack. She pulled out a battered box of cigarettes.

"Well, you're not wrong," Jasmine ventured.

"I shouldn't have said it. I honestly thought *The Post* would be too white to print it." Layla shook her head. "Of course, they printed it. I mean that part is for clickbait. An article about gentrification featuring four Black people? Like it's not white people pulling all the fucking strings. Jesus," Layla scoffed.

"It's a really good piece, Layla. And even if they used your quote for clickbait, that'll get it seen, right?"

"Yeah. It's fucking flawed, to say the least. But favorable? I guess," Layla said. She lit a cigarette and watched the smoke rush from her lips and curl up into the air. Jasmine plucked the cigarette from Layla's fingers and took a long drag. The taste reminded her of being thirteen. Smoking cigarettes and weed in Rock Creek. Giggling up at the trees. Blissful and giddy. The sweet, dark flavor of tobacco on her tongue.

"This," Jasmine said, her words thick with smoke, "is gonna inspire people. That's what you wanted." Jasmine took another drag and handed the cigarette back.

"What about Malcolm?" Layla asked.

"I mean, it was brutal. But that was mostly his fault, and so what? You think he won't be rich tomorrow?" Jasmine asked, waving at the air.

"What about you and Zora?" Layla asked, looking out at the street.

Jasmine thought for a moment. "It's over." She shrugged.

Layla handed the cigarette back to Jasmine.

Jasmine swallowed hard. The tobacco tasted bitter now. She blew smoke out and watched it float up into the morning sunlight.

"And what about Ella?" Layla asked.

Jasmine nodded. "That . . . I don't know." They both looked up.

As if summoned by her name, Ella stood at the edge of the yard. Jasmine stomped the cigarette out in the dirt. Ella stopped for a moment, then walked swiftly toward the house. Layla and Jasmine exchanged a look, then looked back at Ella as she approached.

"Hey El . . ." Jasmine said.

Ella said nothing.

"Ella," Layla said, louder.

Ella was a blur. She walked up the porch stairs, past her two sisters and straight to the front door.

"Ella!" Layla said, now standing.

"What?" Ella snapped. She turned away from the door, her eyes were red and swollen.

Layla sighed.

"What, Layla?" Ella folded her arms.

"Can we talk?" Layla asked.

Ella forced a tight smile as she tilted her head. "That depends, Layla. Will this talk include an apology?"

Layla rolled her eyes. "Apologize for what?"

"Yeah, I thought so," Ella said as she opened the door.

"I'm doing my job," Layla called out as Ella stepped into the house.

"No. You're being a spoiled, reckless little brat. And as long as you don't take ownership for your actions, we don't have shit to talk about." Ella raised her voice. She was losing her composure. Layla stepped closer. And Jasmine stood, slowly positioning her body between her two younger sisters.

"I want things to change. I actually give a fuck about the Black and brown people in this city," Layla said.

Ella snickered. "Right. The middle-class Black girl who went to private school her whole life is going to save all the poor Black people in the world. Layla. That's fucking delusional."

"Ella," Jasmine cut in.

Layla stepped closer. Jasmine rested her hand on Layla's shoulder as if to say I love you, and please calm the fuck down.

"I'd rather be delusional than selfish. You wanted your rich boyfriend and his daddy to keep exploiting people in peace? Did you even read the article? Did you meet Brianna? She's unhoused because of him." Layla's words came faster and sharper. Ella stood still. She looked at her sister. It was no secret, Layla could turn into a powerful warrior when challenged. But she'd never turned it on one of her sisters before.

"You're just like Mom," Ella nearly whispered, her voice cracking.

Annoyed, Layla exhaled and said nothing. Jasmine took Ella's hand and squeezed it. She felt something breaking inside her sister's core.

"You can go out and save the whole world and come home and have no idea who your fucking family is," Ella said. Her eyes welled up. Jasmine couldn't remember the last time she saw Ella cry. "You don't know what it's like. You don't know what it's like to really want someone. To choose someone and to feel chosen. You're skinny and spoiled and no one ever told you no. You have no clue what it feels like."

"Said the light-skinned sister," Layla said, rolling her eyes.

"Layla, you never even asked me how I felt! I was really

happy," Ella said.

Layla crossed her arms. She wasn't prepared for this kind of fight. "OK, Ella. Do you want me to stop organizing for our community–because you like a boy?" Layla said, squinting her eyes in disgust.

"Do you even care? About my life? About what I want?" Ella whispered.

"Not more than this. One person's wants can't be more important. Nothing is more important than this, Ella."

"Yeah. That's what I thought."

Ella opened the door. Jasmine reached for her.

"Stop," Ella said.

"Ella, come on. You know it's not that simple for her—" Jasmine began.

"So you're on board with this? You have nothing to lose?" Ella said, staring at Jasmine.

"She's doing something incredible," Jasmine said.

Ella nodded. She straightened her posture and wiped the tears from her chin. Jasmine felt Ella's energy looming. Ella was reading her. Jasmine tried to pull away, but it was too late. Ella was feeling Jasmine's pain. Her heartbreak. Her secret, quiet desire to end everything and disappear.

"Jasmine. When did you give up?" Ella whispered to Jasmine.

Jasmine had no words.

They stared at each other in silence until Ella tipped her head down and released a defeated sigh. She disappeared into the house, closing the door softly behind her.

Jasmine and Layla stood in silence on the porch. The cicadas' high-pitched love song buzzed in the morning air.

"Should I go in?" Layla asked quietly.

"No." Jasmine shook her head. She sat back on the step and rested her head in her hands. Layla looked out at the road.

"Do you think she's right? That . . . I'm like mom?" Layla pulled at the hem of her T-shirt.

"We're all like her."

Jasmine thought about their mother. The woman had changed so many lives. The privileged white kids at Beechwood. The people at chrch. And yes, she had missed a lot at home. She'd missed Ella's struggles with the boys at school. Layla's anxiety. Jasmine's addiction. And out of the three sisters, it was true, Layla was the most like Ro. Saving the world. A hero in her community, and absent when it came to family. But what did it matter? MLK may have been a cheating husband, but that didn't stop him from changing the world. It was all so exhausting. Black women were supposed to be feminist heroes with perfect families, friendships, and dazzling lives. They were supposed to somehow be ambitious and fierce and also still kind to everyone. They were expected to be strong, vulnerable and lovable in a world that hated them all. They were all doing the best they could.

Jasmine took Layla in her arms. As they rocked together, she whispered a prayer.

"She'll come around, I promise."

29. THE SCOTTS

There was something about the DC skyline. Compared to what Zora had seen, it wasn't particularly extraordinary. It was actually quite understated. Nothing like the bustling, glittering lights of Manhattan or Tokyo. There were no skyscrapers. There were a few tall office buildings and hotels downtown. But DC was a relatively short city. There was a widespread myth that DC was stunted due to an old rule that no building was allowed to exceed the height of the Washington Monument (that white phallic obelisk on the National Mall). But Zora had read in one of her architecture books that it was actually the 1910 Height of Buildings Act. Apparently, it was motivated by Thomas Jefferson's vision of a "light and airy" character for the capital city. The act stated that all buildings in DC were only allowed to reach a height proportional to the width of the street they were built on. This meant that at the time—no building in DC exceeded 160 feet, about twelve stories. This arbitrary rule made the city center look small. But DC had something that big cities like Manhattan had lost years ago. DC still had its sky. The grand marble buildings, the White House, the Capitol—they all had to share the frame with a wide swath of blue. And Zora decided she loved the DC skyline for the sky.

The Scott offices sat high at the top of that skyline. On the eleventh floor Zora sat alone in a white room. She gazed out at the big sky. She looked like a fly in the buttermilk. Her rich, brown skin and sleek dark suit clashed against the bright whites in the office. For as long as Zora could remember, Malcolm had favored this modern, Scandinavian-style of design. The office was all bright whites and space, sharp angles, and custom pieces made of honey-colored wood. Elegant and simple. She knew she had inherited his style. She'd evolved it, of course. Her taste was more inspired by architecture and function. Her father's style seemed to be inspired by currency. He became an expert in the subtle aesthetic of wealth. The kind of expensive that didn't boast; it merely whispered its presence. And he was good at it. Surprisingly savvy for a man in his late sixties. He had turned a sharp corner from the dark, chunky, polished cherry wood desks of his father's time.

Zora tapped her fingers on the long wooden table. She closed her eyes. She thought of Jasmine. Jasmine's mouth open, grinning and laughing. Her eyes becoming half-moons. Zora thought of looking down at Jasmine. Watching Jasmine kiss the thin, soft skin on her belly. Her lips pursed and plump on the tip of Zora's dick. Zora shivered back to the present as David hurried through the glass door.

"Did you read it?" David whispered on his way to her.

"Yeah," Zora said. Her brow furrowed. She looked him up and down. His dress shirt hung loose at his waist.

"Did you know?" David asked as he sat next to Zora and leaned toward her. Zora leaned back.

"Jesus. David. Your breath!"

David rolled his eyes.

Zora patted at her breast pocket. She handed him a slim packet of gum.

David exhaled dramatically as he chewed at the gum, sliding the pack to Zora.

"Please keep it," Zora said, pushing it back in his direction. She smiled, waiting for him to get the joke. She was being the big brother. She was poking fun, but David didn't smile. He looked down, deflated.

"Zora. Did you know?" He whispered.

"No," Zora replied.

"So," David began. He looked like a child. "What should we do?" He asked.

Zora's mouth pinched into a frown. "I don't know."

David folded his arms defensively. "Ella didn't know about the article. We read it for the first time together. She—"

"David. Did she tell you who her sister was? Did she warn you?" Zora asked.

David sat back in his chair. He shook his head. "No. But I don't think she knew. Not really."

Zora watched closely. What was the matter with him? David had always been too sensitive for business. Couldn't he just let Ella go? She had let Jasmine go, and everything was going to be fine. Zora opened her mouth to speak when Eric, the white twenty-something administrative assistant sprinted through the glass door with his hands full of to-go coffee cups. Zora rolled her eyes immediately. David sat up. She sneered, quietly scrutinizing his white guy fade and orange plaid suit. He was one of those loud, vaguely fashionable "ally" white kids who seemed like he was a hair away from saying the N-word. He probably had a BA in Black Studies and a Black boyfriend at home, but he was too cool to mention it because he knew that was not PC. Zora hated Eric because he got all his suits tailored. And so did she, but what twenty-three-year-old has a fucking tailor? Zora hated Eric because he was the perfect, book smart, responsible son Malcolm never had. He was Zora. But white. And male. And cheerful. He was basically her nemesis. "Hello, Eric," Zora sighed.

"Hello, Zora. Hi, David." Eric waved nervously.

"Hey, Eric. Nice suit," David said weakly, nodding in Eric's direction.

"Wow, thanks." Eric blushed.

Zora chewed at the inside of her cheek. No matter how much she hated him, Eric was a necessary evil. He was their father's assistant, and without him they were their father's assistants. Eric may have had their father's ear and favor, but he also inherited all the administrative bitchwork and the emotional abuse that came with it.

"Latte no sugar, latte two scoops. Oh, and in case you don't already know, we're fucked," Eric said as he slid the coffee cups to Zora and David.

"Thanks. And yes, Eric, we already know," Zora snapped.

David grabbed his cup and stared out the window.

"It's worse," Eric said, shaking his head. "Two investors just pulled out of the U Street development." He paced behind his chair.

"Shit." Zora rested her head in her hand.

"Can they do that?" David asked.

"They can try. We might have to delay construction. Did you know about the interview?" Eric pointed to Zora.

"No, Eric. That's actually not my job."

"Well, we can all play the blame game but it's done. And I might not have a job after today."

Zora looked up at Eric.

"Is it that bad?" she asked.

"It's that bad. Everything is tied up in this development. It's supposed to have an insane return, but the investment is—" Eric seemed to sense Malcolm's impending arrival. He turned his head in time to watch Malcolm approach the glass door. David buttoned his blazer and sat up straight. Eric sprinted across the room to hold the door open. Malcolm nodded as he walked in. He looked regal. His shoulders were wide and strong. His beard was freshly shaped. His gray suit buttoned, his white shirt crisply ironed. He looked sharper than usual. Zora shifted in her seat. The air tightened as he entered the room. Eric scurried to hand him the remaining coffee cup. Malcolm took a seat.

"Thank you, Eric," Malcolm exhaled. Eric nodded energetically as he sat at Malcolm's side. He pulled an iPad from the bag at his hip. His hands hovered above the tablet.

"I'm not sure what you've heard," Malcolm began, "but let me start by assuring you. The company will be fine."

Eric shot a glance at Zora.

"The investors are under contract. There's not a lot of wiggle room there, but we'll need to work with Zora on our strategy in the case of any . . ." Malcolm's eyes drifted. "breaches." He finished his sentence and sipped his coffee. Eric, Zora and David collectively held their breath, waiting for Malcolm to speak again.

"And I'll need you and David to find an organization to work with in conjunction with the groundbreaking. As our image is . . . suffering. To say the least." Malcolm's eyes darted up to his son.

David stared at the wall. Their father didn't yell. He didn't have to. Disappointing him was punishment enough. Malcolm leaned back in this chair.

"This is my fault," Malcolm said. He stared at the table. "I overestimated the journalist's integrity. You all know what I've been through. What this family has gone through to get here. There were several parts of the interview he decided to omit. And that's his job. It was naive of me to think otherwise."

Malcolm sipped his coffee. "I also overestimated the integrity of Miss Jones. And in doing so, I put this company at risk."

Zora's cheeks grew hot. She attempted to read her father's face. It was worse than she thought. Worse than her father would admit. He doesn't deserve this, she thought.

Malcolm stood and nodded with finality. "I think it goes without saying. But I'll say it for the sake of clarity. David, your relationship with Miss Jones' sister is . . . inconvenient at the moment."

Eric raised an eyebrow.

David didn't move. He didn't look up at his father. Malcolm stood there, unwavering, looking down on his son.

"David," Malcolm said, softly.

David lifted his eyes to meet his father's.

"Layla Jones wants to tear this company down. I see now that she'll do anything to get what she wants. Your connection with this family left us open to exploitation. You should know better. And if you weren't my son, you'd be fired. But please don't mistake my kindness for leniency. From now on, I expect more from you."

Zora noticed David's right hand clenching under the table. She felt her throat tighten. How would her father feel if he knew that both of his children were sleeping with the enemy?

Zora took a breath. She leaned in.

"Dad, I think there's a lot of work we could do with the community relations work. We could offer more affordable units, and there could be more transparency about what that means." Zora heard herself. She was rambling, the eldest child attempting to appease her father.

Malcolm folded his arms. "Zora, this isn't your mess to clean up. And frankly, it's not your job. This is David's mess. And the development on U Street is a luxury building. The implication that we, as Black developers, are somehow obligated to give our product away for free because the city doesn't take care of Black people? Because of poverty and racism? Please."

Malcolm took a breath. His expression softened. He melted from employer mode back into a father.

"You know I love you both."

David was looking at the wall again.

"We'll make it through this together," Malcolm said. He smiled tightly at Zora, then turned to go. Eric rushed to Malcolm's side, opening the door for him, glancing back once more at the shell-shocked siblings.

Zora and David sat in silence for a moment.

Zora stared at her brother.

"David," she said. David said nothing. "There are other girls."

The words tasted stale in her mouth. She wanted so badly to believe them.

"Yeah," David said, staring at the wall.

30. THE SISTERS

Ro

The sisters had ancient magic in their veins. They were the descendants of people who had survived a spiritual genocide. The people who learned to conjure spells. Who learned how to fly and read the stars and the wind. They were descendants of West African farmers, common folk, soldiers and prisoners of war. They came from lines of women who had survived serial rape and sadistic violence. They came from people whose families were torn from them, people who could grow things in the garden and kill with quiet subtlety. They were either born with it or they learned it to survive. The sisters knew they had power because all Black women in the diaspora have power.

But they had no book of instructions to tell them what to do with all this magic. Ella knew she could read and heal with her touch. Layla had the power of a leader—a connection to the community of the living and the dead. Jasmine knew she could heal and nourish with food. But what could a person do with that knowledge? As powerful as she was, their mother wasn't sure how to guide them. She wasn't even sure she'd used her power correctly in her lifetime. But Ro did learn one thing about Black women and their magic. There are women with power and there are women who work their power into a craft. This is what white people would call witches. A witch (or Ajẹ in Yoruba) has a practice. She creates or inherits rituals that allow her to hone her skills. She takes time to shape her power. She connects with herself, with Spirit, and she connects with the community. A woman with power may become an Ajẹ—but she must develop a practice. As her daughters grew up and dabbled with candles, crystals and potions, Ro didn't hesitate to remind them: a powerful woman cannot harness her power alone.

Ella

Ella's hands glowed with heat, hovering above the white man's freckled shoulders. Layla's words and implications burned in her brain. Layla had called her a servant. She was right. Here she was, serving another rich white man. Lifting his burdens and guilt for a few pieces of silver. Why was she here? Ella's focus tightened as her hands worked. Her thumbs pushed soft dimples into thick flesh. She worked heat into the skin. She cradled her client's hand delicately. Her other hand lifted the man's wrinkled elbow. She turned it slowly. Dancing his limbs into circles. The man moaned. Ella rolled her own shoulders back, attempting to shake Layla's voice from her mind. She was doing her best. She was good at her job. The joint, the shoulders, the blood and energy rushing through the body on the table. Ella breathed in and swallowed the knot in her throat.

It had been three days since she last heard from David. She almost believed he never really cared for her. But she knew better. Didn't she? David could only defend his father. Stand by his family. What choice did he have? Ella lifted the man's shoulder with her fingers, working and combing the trapezius muscles slowly. There it was, the source of pain. Ella could feel it. Hiding beneath all the muscle in his shoulders. Most people hid their pain beneath strength. Ella felt her pain there too. Beneath her confidence and laughter. But today, she felt like a stone wall built on fault lines. Ella pulled the man's arm into wide circles. She pushed her thumbs into his back. The heat of her anger swelling. She never needed a boy. She learned that a long time ago. She didn't need anyone else to affirm her beauty or her existence. I don't need him, she thought. But I want him. I want what he made me feel. I deserve that feeling.

"Jesus!" The man's face jerked up from the cradle. "Take it easy!" he barked.

"Oh. I'm so sorry," Ella whispered, her hands rising up in the air. "I think. I think I need a minute." Ella rushed out of the dark room. She stood in the hallway, waiting for her breath to slow down.

Jasmine

The cafe's giant steel dough sheeter was affectionately known as Chuck Brown. When she opened the T Spot, Jasmine knew she needed that dough sheeter. The industrial Estella Floor Reversible Dough Sheeter 700 would multiply her production tenfold. At least. It would take her business to the next level. She could make a thousand croissants in a day! She could take on big business orders. Maybe even supply to a few local markets. With that shining silver machine, she could make cookies, pasta, pastries, and she could make everything faster and more efficiently. She needed that dough sheeter. But by the time she opened the cafe, she couldn't afford it. All the money went toward renovations and supplies. Jasmine burned through her business loans before she even opened the place. Still, she spent all winter scrolling eBay and Craigslist. Praying that the Estella Floor Reversible Dough Sheeter 700 would miraculously appear at a deep, deep discount.

There were moments that felt like fate. Jasmine would ask

Spirit for the thing she needed, and somehow it would suddenly materialize. The following spring Jasmine had been driving uptown when she stopped at Giana's, an old Italian bakery she'd worked at as a teenager. She asked for Giana, but the dark-haired boy at the counter said she'd retired and planned to move down to Florida that year. "Good for her," Jasmine had said. The boy shook his head, informing her that the bakery was closing. Giana was too tired to keep working and too particular to trust her grandkids with the business. Jasmine bought a box of sfogliatelle and left her name and number at the counter, telling the boy that she'd love to hear from Giana. And that's how she inherited the Estella Floor Reversible Dough Sheeter 500. More seasoned and broken in than the 700 she'd wished for, but Giana told Jasmine she could have it as long as she paid the fees to have the machine removed. Jasmine knew the ancestors were affirming her passion. This bakery would succeed.

The day the dough sheeter arrived Jasmine wanted to celebrate. She wanted to make a thousand croissants and hand them out in the streets to passersby. Instead, she sat next to the sheeter with a mug of warm champagne and cried. Ro had called that morning to tell her that Chuck Brown had died of heart failure the night before. The Godfather of Go-go. The musical ambassador for all of DC was gone. Jasmine plopped her hand on the silver machine and declared it her personal monument to the man. She imagined him there by her side, wearing wrap-around sunglasses and a brimmed gambler's hat, surrounded by a haze of smoke. His baritone voice melodically speaking proverbs and OG wisdom back at her. Chuck would know what to say. About a failing business. About women. About life.

"Another one bites the dust, huh Chuck?" Jasmine said to the machine as Chuck's conveyor belt slowly pulled the wide slab of dough through the heavy metal rollers. The dough emerged longer, thinner, smooth as skin. She lifted the slab of dough to the measuring platform. If she couldn't control anything else, she knew how to make a damn good pastry. Nothing would change that. She carefully laid thick pats of butter on the surface of the dough, lining the pieces up to form an airtight puzzle. She folded the cold dough over and molded an envelope. Her fingers pink with the cold, working quickly. She lifted the slab back to the belt. The low hum of the machine vibrated as the dough passed under the rollers. This is where her practice began. In the dough and butter. In folded precision. In the layers of the pastry growing exponentially with each fold. A long, thin slab of dough emerged. Jasmine danced with the dough. Folding and folding and offering it back to the mouth of the sheeter.

Jasmine imagined Chuck's voice through the loud hum of the machine.

"Sweet Jasmine. There are so many fish in the sea."

Jasmine cut off the uneven ends of the dough.

"You're right, Chuck. As always." She laughed as she cut the dough.

A voice startled her. "You okay?" Marble asked, leaning in the kitchen doorway.

"Oh! Yeah." Jasmine laughed nervously. "Just me and Chuck." She nodded to the dough sheeter.

"Right . . ." Marble said. They stood in the doorway, hesitating.

"Why does it feel like people are constantly appearing in the kitchen door like ghosts?" Jasmine asked, cutting and removing another margin of dough.

"Maybe it's a portal." Marble said, folding their arms.

"Maybe. Are you okay?" Jasmine asked, looking up.

"I wanted to ask if I could have this Saturday off. I was gonna go to chrch with Ro. If that's okay with you?" Marble picked at their chipping nail polish.

"Sure," Jasmine said. She continued working, cutting deep lines into the dough with a wheeled pastry cutter. "Are you sure y'all aren't dating?" Jasmine asked, keeping her eyes on the dough.

"We are definitely not dating." Marble said dully. They turned to the sink to wash their hands.

"Okay." Jasmine laid out a doughy triangle, pulling and rolling it into a perfect curled sculpture. Marble watched her make three croissants, then joined in. They worked slowly, taking Jasmine's example. Jasmine nodded approvingly.

"You'll be better than me soon." Jasmine said.

"Yeah right."

"It's true. You're a natural." Jasmine walked to the sink and washed her hands. Marble took over, pulling and rolling each portion of dough.

Jasmine wiped her hands as she walked back to the counter, watching Marble work.

"So. No more prince?" Marble asked. They kept their eyes on the dough.

"No more prince," Jasmine said. She lifted a long baking sheet from the shelf. It sounded like a cymbal as it shook loose.

Marble nodded.

"You gonna try and get her back?" they asked.

Jasmine smiled. She lifted one of the formed, raw croissants from the floured board.

"No."

"Why not?" Marble asked, looking up for a moment. Jasmine kept her eyes on the work.

"I barely know her." She gently laid the soft dough onto the baking sheet. The little croissants felt like baby birds. Jasmine slowly lifted one croissant at a time, placing each gently on the baking sheet with obsessive reverence.

"Right," Marble said.

"And she told me I was a mistake." Jasmine placed the last croissant on the baking sheet. She folded her arms.

"And her family is much more concerned about money than basic moral principles. And they hate Layla. And they're maybe single-handedly wiping out the last seven Black people who live in the city. Do you know that Ella never cries? Like she broke her arm when she was seven and her eyes didn't even water. But the past week? She hasn't stopped crying. I have no idea what David said to her, but if it's anything like what Zora said . . ." Jasmine trailed off.

"Okay I see your point. Maybe don't try to get Zora back." Marble nodded. They turned away to open the refrigerator door, and lifted the sheet of croissants into the cool, smoky vault. They turned back to Jasmine, wiping their hands on a dish towel.

"So. Would you fight for Ella's sake?"

Jasmine folded her arms. "What do you mean?" She asked.

"Well, maybe it's too fucked up for you to salvage anything with Zora. But you could try to fix Ella and David's thing. Maybe you could tell Zora what's going on. Tell her how Ella feels. So she can tell David." Marble hopped onto the cool steel counter.

Jasmine remembered when Zora pushed her up against that same countertop. She shook the memory.

"But she'd think I was really there for her," Jasmine said, pacing.

"Who cares? That's over, right?" Marble asked. They picked at their nail polish.

"Yeah . . ." Jasmine squinted her eyes at Marble. "I don't know." She walked to Marble and hopped up on the counter by their side. Marble pinched a bit of flour between their fingers and sprinkled it into Jasmine's lap.

"You care, don't you?" they asked.

Jasmine sighed. "About what?"

"You care what Zora thinks about you."

Jasmine rolled her eyes and jumped back to the ground.

"Let's go back to talking about your sex life." Jasmine said, waving her hand in the air.

"Maybe it's not over if you still care," Marble said. They sat back, leaning on their hands, swinging their legs.

"Can both be true? I care, and it's over with Zora?" Jasmine asked.

"I don't know, Jaz. What do you think?" Marble asked, shrugging.

Jasmine sighed.

"I think I care and it's over. And everyone is gonna be okay. Eventually. And I think I'll go up front in case we have a customer at some point today," Jasmine called out as she walked to the front of the cafe. She poured a generous scoop of Columbian coffee beans into the grinder and turned it on. She fixed herself a cup of espresso and sipped it slowly.

Layla

Layla's feet burned. Her whole body felt tired and swollen. She squinted as she pulled hard on her spliff, tasting a blend of lavender, tobacco, hash, and mint leaves. Something Sean used to roll for her mother when she was in treatment. He called this particular blend "dance with the ancestors."

She didn't smoke often. A cigarette here and there when she was really stressed. Maybe an edible on a slow day. But she needed this today. A slim, floral spliff. All to herself. She sat back on the bench, crossing her legs and rolling circles with one heavy foot. She'd walked miles across the city in the past few days. Canvasing the few scattered remains of Black neighborhoods all over DC. Some old houses with finely cropped lawns and wrought-iron handrails. Some stout brick buildings with skeptical pit bulls staring at her through screen doors. She stood, humble and ready at one hundred doorsteps. Most people assumed she was a salesman. She learned quickly to tell people what she was not there to do. "My name is Layla. I'm not selling anything, I'm not pushing a politician, and I am not a Jehovah's Witness. I'm here to tell you about our city block party." The word "protest" made folks' eyes glaze over with uninterest. Probably conjuring images of eager white folks and tear gas. And "protest party" didn't seem to make sense to anyone either. So she started calling it a block party. She handed out postcard flyers with an old picture of the Crystal Cavern Dancers. The line of bejeweled women grinned in black and white. Layla had chosen this photo because the women in it looked so familiar to her. Each dancer in that picture looked like somebody's auntie. Somebody's play-cousin's mama. Nobody would have thought twice if they found this photo in an old box in the attic. It could have been any Black folks' old family photo.

Layla flicked the ember from her joint and placed the roach delicately in a tin. She opened the double doors to the dated library building. She walked the worn linoleum floors of the community meeting room. Dozens of volunteers painted poster boards with black and gold lettering. A little girl giggled as she poured heaps of gold glitter onto pools of dripping glue. Layla walked with authority, a general observing her army in training. Ellington's orchestra rang out a triumphant rendition of "Waltz of the Flowers." Her energy lifted with the wild curling melodies. Horns sang low and the high hat buzzed like scores of bees in the air. Layla felt the haze of the weed slowing her limbs.

She turned to see a graying Black man two-stepping with a woman in a headwrap. Layla smiled, then giggled. They both looked well past seventy, but their flirtation was so young. So playful. He pulled her toward the center of the floor and she shook her head coyly. She covered her face and laughed as his shoulders rose and fell to the rhythm. When he started moving his hips, she snapped into the beat, moving fast then slow then fast with her partner. The room lit up with shouts and affirmations. Then, they danced. What dance is this? The jitterbug? Layla thought to herself. Their dance was hopping, skipping and playful. Then it was smooth and curving. The man led this woman with such finesse. Layla cursed her generation for letting partner dancing go. Who didn't want to be led like that? Or to lead like that. Just to move with a stranger or a lover with such grace. Layla closed her eyes. The music held her body as she rocked and let her eyes close and open slowly.

A couple in their fifties took the floor and danced a high-speed hand dance. Spinning, feet sliding, hips twisting, a soft kick, a pair of hands clasped lightly, letting go and meeting again. The room was full of whoops and clapping. A trio of too-cool teenage boys covered their mouths. Their curiosity and awe safely disguised with laughter. A white couple in their forties stood and took to the dance floor to show off a few swing moves. The room was full of dancing and laughter. Layla blinked slowly. Almost wondering if it was real. Wondering if maybe Sean had blessed the weed and lavender with something else. Or maybe she was just tired. Everything happened so fast. But she saw it in slow motion. Like the air was made of warm, clear broth and everyone was under water, leaving an echo of liquid with each spin and step. Ellington's orchestra melted into "Satin Doll," a slower, deeper swing of a song.

A graying man in plaid highwaters held his hand out for Layla. She felt herself shaking her head like she'd seen the woman in the headwrap do, but she meant it. She didn't know any of these dances. Her heart beat faster at the prospect. The man wearing highwaters just smiled and waited. His hand held out like an offering. When her hand fell into his, she was suddenly spinning. Her limbs loose in one moment, then tight when he pulled her in. A laugh leaped from her belly. She couldn't believe how free she felt. How her body moved like she knew the steps. The man smiled and spun her around. She closed her eyes and felt herself floating.

When she opened her eyes, she was airborne. A seed with feathery bristles floating high above the trees. A vein of water running dark and fast beneath her. Not the Potomac. But a river. One she'd seen before. She rose and fell softly. Up and up as she inhaled. Swooping down and down with each exhale. She felt drawn to the river. Pulling herself down to hear it rushing beneath her. She turned to lean on the wind. Her back arched into the air's current, her palms facing up to the sky. Ellington's orchestra was a whisper in the distance now. The river and the sound of old drums and chanting carried on the wind. She dipped lower, wanting, craving the cold touch of the river. Instead, her body was cradled by a barrier. Something like a clear boat. She floated down the river, touching the water with her fingertips. Bobbing slightly up and down. She heard words in the chanting now. A choir of voices calling out names from either side of the river. Their melodies and rhythm harmonizing, melting together with the drone of the river. Anaquashtank. Igbo. Igbo. Yoruba. Anaquashtank. Layla closed her eyes. Felt the wind on her face, the cool water of the river on her fingertips.

When she opened her eyes, she emerged from a spin. Her body suddenly felt weighted. She felt the linoleum tiles under her feet and heard the crowd cheering. The jitterbug and hand-dancing couples basked in the applause. The men bowed and spun their partners in one final flourish. Layla smiled at her partner as he bowed his head in gratitude.

"Satin Doll" crooned through the PA and the volunteers danced back to their posters. The room shimmered now. The babies watched the elders wide-eyed. The teenagers craned their heads over their phones, looking for words to describe what they saw. To find more of it. To learn it. Hand dance. Old black folk dances. Old black partner dances. Jazz dance. They would dabble into research on the Nicholas brothers and Josephine Baker and lindy hops and cake walks. Layla breathed in and out. The vision was gone, but she could still feel the cold water of the river on her fingertips. Anaquashtank. Igbo. Igbo. Yoruba. Igbo. Layla whispered to herself.

31. ELLA

The trees around Ella blurred into streaks of light. Green, gold, and dark columns of bark whirred by as she ran faster and faster. Panting in and out, her muscles contracting as her feet hit the concrete. The music in her ears thumped too loudly, etching rhythm into her brain. If she ran this fast and played her music this loud, she found seconds, sometimes whole minutes of peace. She could focus on the shin splints, or her lungs burning, or the stupid lyrics of this god-awful pop song. She could solve these problems. Ice it. Skip to the next song. Keep running. Run harder.

Ella looked up at the last hill. A long, gradual incline. This hill always looked harmless. It looked pleasant, even. But it was always the most painful leg of her run. She didn't mind steep hills. A steep hill made itself known. It was hard and fast and then it was over. She could sprint a steep hill. But this was something else. Ella hated this last hill. The way it slowly chipped away her last shreds of motivation. Give up, give up. The hill seemed to whisper to her as she breathed harder and harder. Most days she listened. She'd stop in the middle of the hill and let the walk home function as a cooldown. Not today. Her thighs tore through the air. Her feet pummeled the ground. She took the hill too fast, but she didn't stop. Sharp pain tore at her lungs. She kept running. The balls of her feet grew numb. She ran and ran, streaks of light and green flashing, and when she tripped onto the grassy front lawn of her mother's house, she had nothing left. She fell to her knees. She leaned down into the dirt and wept. Her forehead against the earth. She wept and heaved with every burning muscle in her body.

The front door slammed open. Ro flew down the steps, leapt and fell to the ground at Ella's side.

"Ella? Are you OKAY? What happened?" Ro's heart raced. Her hands shook as she held her daughter's head up from the dirt. Ella smiled weakly. She shook her head.

"No, Mama. I'm okay. I just. I got winded. That's all." Ro sat back on her heels and watched Ella closely.

"Really. I just took the run too fast." Ella stood and reached out for Ro's hand. She pulled Ro up.

"Did you eat enough today?" Ro felt Ella's forehead.

"Yes, Ma. Full breakfast. Same as always. I'm fine."

Ro sighed. Her daughters lied to her these days. "Let's get you inside." Ro said. She squeezed Ella's hand as they walked up the porch steps.

"Mom?" Jasmine called out from the road.

Ro and Ella paused at the front door.

Jasmine ran up the steps.

"Ella? What's wrong?" Jasmine said, lifting her sister's chin up to the light.

"I'm okay. I just need to lie down," Ella said, squeezing Jasmine's hand.

"Okay," Jasmine whispered. Ella disappeared into the house. Jasmine sighed.

"She won't talk to me," Ro said quietly.

Jasmine nodded.

"Neither will you apparently." Ro said. Jasmine looked up.

"I know you're heartbroken too. But if you won't talk to me, promise me you'll talk to her about it. Or Layla," Ro said, folding her arms.

"I promise," Jasmine said, nodding.

Jasmine knocked on Ella's door. Ella was still and quiet on her bed. She was curled up, her breath slowing. Jasmine sat on the bed next to Ella. She ran her fingers through Ella's hair.

"What did he say to you, Ella?" Jasmine whispered. "Did he say something to you?"

"No," Ella said. Her voice was mostly air. "He. He was kind. But. He said he had to choose his family or—" Ella trailed off. "He's just gone, Jasmine."

"I'm so sorry, El." Jasmine said, softening.

Ella lifted her head to study Jasmine's expression.

"Are you okay?" Ella asked.

Jasmine thought for a moment. "Well, I'm sober. I didn't run my car into a ditch. I have a cafe. And I have you," Jasmine said, affectionately smoothing the hair around Ella's face. "I think I've seen worse."

Ella shook her head. "That doesn't mean you're okay, Jaz."

"Yeah. You're right."

"Do you love her?" Ella asked.

Jasmine exhaled. "No. It's not love. But, being with Zora. Maybe in spite of my pessimism, I let myself believe in something. The hope of something. I think the last few years I forgot how to hope. You know?"

Ella smiled weakly, nodding.

"Do you love him?" Jasmine asked.

Ella's gaze fell. Jasmine pulled her into an embrace.

"I know. I'm here," Jasmine whispered.

Ella didn't weep. She didn't make a sound. She just stared out the window. Tears collecting at the corners of her eyes and falling fast down her cheeks. Jasmine sat with Ella and watched her blink away the tears. Jasmine pulled the covers over them, lying by her sister's side, resting her head in the warmth between Ella's shoulders. They breathed together. Slower and slower until they both drifted into sleep.

32. JASMINE

Jasmine raced up the stairs, pulling furiously at the handrail. She felt too pissed off, too feral to stand politely in an elevator. She thought the stairs would calm her. Maybe the exertion would even out the anger. Eleven stories was a long way to climb. But when she burst through the glass doors of the Scott Group Offices, she was not calm. She was breathless, sweaty and just as angry as she was when she'd left Ella's side. She looked around the space. White walls, large plants, windows everywhere, expensive looking, just like Malcolm's house, and Zora's house. Just looking around made her angrier. She stomped to the white boy at the standing reception desk. He blinked up from his tablet.

"Hello, I'm Eric; how are you feeling today?" Eric chirped, looking up at Jasmine with a sincere smile.

"Hi. I'm Jasmine. I'm . . . I'm fine." She replied, still panting. Her hands on her hips, panting. It suddenly dawned on her that she had no plan. She was angry. So she decided to come here and she was going to fix everything. She was going to yell at somebody. She was here to fight for her sister, for fuck's sake! But she hadn't really thought past the point of sprinting up eleven flights.

"I'd like to . . ." Jasmine breathed.

"I'd like to see David Scott." She folded her arms.

"David won't be in today," Eric replied. He smiled, waiting. Jasmine unfolded her arms. She swallowed.

"Oh. Then. I'd like to see Zora Scott."

"Do you have an appointment?"

"No. But we're . . . friends." Jasmine lied.

"Ah, okay. May I have your name?" Eric asked.

Jasmine paused. She considered giving the white boy an alias. She sighed.

"Jasmine." Her eyes wandered down the hall behind the desk. Zora was back there. She knew it. She felt the heat of her anger now peppered with a numbing prickle of nerves. The thoughts raced and bounced around in her mind. Why was she so nervous? What was she angry about? Who was she angry at? Zora might be back there. How could she fix this? How could she change David's mind? How could she catch her breath? ZORA MIGHT BE BACK THERE!

". . . And your last name?" Eric asked.

"J-Jones?" Jasmine spoke her last name, praying it didn't sound familiar to him.

Eric's polite smile fell.

"Jones . . ." He repeated.

"Yes." Jasmine replied.

"As in . . . Layla Jones's sister?" Now Eric wore a sincere, if not mischievous smile on his face.

"Yes." Jasmine said. She folded her arms again. Eric pointed at Jasmine, his head tilting.

"I would not have picked you out for David."

Jasmine sighed.

"I'm not that sister. There are three of us. You're thinking of my sister Ella."

"Oh! I didn't know there were three of you!"

"It's fine," Jasmine said.

"Well, it doesn't really matter which sister you are—if my boss catches you here, I'm probably fired. So—"

"What?"

"I can't let you stay here. I'm sorry, Miss Jones."

Jasmine sighed. She looked at Eric's pinched face, then down the open hallway, then back at Eric.

"I understand. Thanks anyways." Jasmine said. She turned and walked toward the elevator.

"Have a good day?" Eric called out as Jasmine slowly walked away. She pushed the elevator button, then turned back to look at Eric. Again, her eyes wandered down the hall. If she could just get past the reception desk ... her thoughts wandered. Her heartbeat was still racing from climbing all those stares. All that anger.

Jasmine didn't make the decision. Her heart started beating faster all on its own. Her feet seemed to have made the choice for her. She was walking into the elevator one moment and then she was running down the hall. Running and then sprinting. Past the reception desk, not knowing where to go, just sprinting. Eric called and ran after her. When she ran past the reception area and its wide partition, the rest of the office walls were made of clouded glass. Only shapes and shadows behind frosted panes. She ran to the end of the hall, Eric hot on her heels. When she spotted a door, slightly ajar, she snatched at the handle, scrambled into the room, slammed the door and pushed the lock behind her.

"FUCK." Jasmine hissed. What the fuck was she doing? The doorknob wiggled. The silhouette of Eric's hand banged against the glass from outside. Jasmine panted as Eric shouted and cursed at her from the hallway.

"Jasmine?" Zora stood behind a thin wooden desk in a perfectly tailored gray green suit. Her body framed in the backlit glow of blue sky. An illegible expression on her face. Eric pounded at the door before Jasmine could think of something to say.

Zora walked across the room, approaching Jasmine with

urgency. Her heart pounded. Zora reached out her hand. Jasmine breathed sharply in.

Zora grew closer and closer and slid behind Jasmine. Zora opened the door and whispered as Eric protested frantically from the hallway.

"Eric. It's fine. I know, I know. I'll handle it."

Jasmine quickly stepped away from Zora and waited.

Zora closed the door and leaned against it. Jasmine stared at the wall.

"I'm actually not here to see you, but since David isn't here, I'll tell you and you can let him know."

Zora raised an eyebrow.

"Ella and David have something. I don't know, maybe it's just a fling, maybe it's infatuation—but I have a feeling it's more and it's not for you or your father to decide what they should do." Jasmine's words poured out of her. Less articulate than she would have liked, but she was getting the point across. Her face was hot.

"I know Layla crossed the line. She should have been more professional; she should have been honest from the start. But she's doing what she thinks is right. She's twenty-two. And honestly, she's trying to save the world and that has nothing to do with me or Ella, AND she's the only one here thinking about other people. Compared to the rest of us, I think Layla's a fucking saint."

Zora shifted her weight, sliding her hands into her pockets. Jasmine's eyes wandered down Zora's body. She was losing her train of thought. She paced to the window and crossed her arms.

Zora took a step forward. Her expression was blank. She spoke slowly.

"So. You broke into my office to tell me that?"

Jasmine rolled her eyes.

"I didn't break in. I mean. I didn't intend to break in. But your secretary was being bitchy, and I didn't really have a choice."

Zora's face broke into a smile. She covered it as fast as she could. Jasmine furrowed her brow. She was angry. Ready to fight. She wasn't ready for Zora to smile. She put her hands on her hips and waited for Zora to collect herself. Zora leaned against the desk.

"I'm sorry." Zora said. Her voice a low whisper.

Zora watched Jasmine think. Her anger softened. She let her hands fall to her sides.

She walked to the other end of the desk and leaned against it. A soft silence fell in the room like a blanket of snow, everything muted. Zora watched Jasmine staring at the door.

And for a moment, Jasmine wanted to stay here. She would fight with Zora in circles if it meant she could share this moment with her just a little longer. But that's not what she came here to do. Jasmine exhaled.

"Ella never cries. I mean, she's honestly the strongest person I know. I envy her for that. She's got armor, you know? All three of us do, really." Jasmine looked up at Zora. Zora stared back at her.

"But. I think she's also maybe never let anyone in. Not really. Or nobody could really get through before."

Jasmine swallowed a tightness in her throat.

"But David got through."

Zora nodded. "I know. I wish there was something I could do."

Jasmine stood. She looked past Zora at the clouds in the window.

"Maybe it's nothing." Jasmine said, shrugging. "Or maybe it's everything. Don't you think they deserve a chance?"

Zora stood. "Your heart is in the right place, Jasmine. I admire that. But it's out of my hands."

"How? Can't you talk to him?" Jasmine snapped.

"Nothing I could say would make a difference. He's afraid of our father. Which is completely reasonable. This article might have cost our company millions of dollars."

Jasmine shook her head. Zora went on.

"I know it sounds fucked up. But this is David's job. And my dad's legacy." Jasmine felt like throwing something. It was all so archaic. Are whole entire families still suffering over one man's money and pride? Do people still do that?

"Does David love Ella?" Jasmine asked. Zora stared at her. That silence again. She looked down, like she couldn't calculate the equation.

"I don't know." Zora said. She held Jasmine's gaze for a moment.

"You should ask him," Jasmine said.

Zora nodded. "I wish things were different, Jasmine. I really do."

Jasmine shook her head. This was a waste of time. Maybe it was for the best. Maybe Ella deserved someone who would risk everything for her. Or someone who didn't have to.

"Well. I had to give it a shot. We fight for our sister." Zora smiled at this. Jasmine opened the door and stepped into the hallway. Eric watched her nervously at the end of the hall.

"Jasmine?" Zora called out.

Jasmine turned. Zora walked to the door.

"I'm sorry. About us. And what I said."

Jasmine took a breath.

"And I'm sorry I said you weren't—" Zora went on.

Jasmine turned. The light was suddenly too bright. Zora closed her eyes. She stood there in the darkness as she spoke.

"I'm sorry I said you weren't on my level. I know how that must have sounded. I really do . . . respect the way you and your sisters care. About people. And each other. I wish I could be more like that. I'm just. I'm sorry." When Zora opened her eyes, Jasmine was staring at her.

Jasmine didn't take a second to think. She stepped into the doorway and pulled Zora's jawline to her lips. One last time,

Jasmine breathed Zora in. One soft inhale. She pushed her lips into Zora's neck. Kissing her skin slowly. Zora's shoulders fell as she exhaled. Jasmine could feel the pressure of Zora's hands on her hips. Zora was there with her. It came right back to them. The electric current of the nights they spent together. Jasmine's lips grazed Zora's earlobe.

"Me too," she whispered warmly into Zora's ear. She paused there, then released Zora and turned to go. She was energized. Something had shifted in her mind. It wasn't over for Ella and David. She knew it. And maybe it wasn't over with Zora, maybe it was. But she would move on either way. She wasn't a mistake. She wasn't disposable. Zora was a fool for letting her go and she knew it. She always knew it. She grinned as she walked past Eric. She was skipping. She was wild! Her boots stomped hard into the floors. Zora stood frozen watching her walk away. Eric's head shot back and forth, wide-eyed staring at Zora, then Jasmine as she disappeared behind the elevator doors.

33. RO

Bonfire tonight. COME HOME.

Ro texted each of her daughters separately.

As the last moments of daylight melted into the horizon, she sat on her knees in the yard and stretched. She rolled her shoulders, breathing in the thick summer air. There were new knots in her neck—pinching her shoulders up to her ears. Sweat gathered at her brow and under her arms as she moved from one stretch to the next. She stood up and rooted the soles of her feet on the ground. Mountain pose. She visualized her connection to the dirt. The cool energy flowing between earth and the body. Her palms turned out to face the altar. Blackberry, the altar goddess, stared back at her, surrounded by offerings. Ro's assorted deities looked out with serene smiles. The clay mermaid with a blue glazed tail. A wooden fertility doll with her round head and carved half-moon eyes. The small brass Buddha. What were they trying to tell her? What more did they want? She had done everything right. She ate well. She prayed. She meditated. She worked and gave and gave. She did everything she was supposed to. And here she was again.

Ro laughed back at the figurines on her altar. This is life. Everyone dies. Sometimes cruel, hateful people live long, soft lives. Good people get sick. I know. Ro thought. But what is all this God for? All this spirit and prayer? All these attempts at calm. What was she supposed to do when all the mindful breathing, faith, and offerings didn't work? She would get sicker, she would die, and maybe she was ready. She could be ready. But her daughters weren't. Ro exhaled. She shook hands and flicked her fingers out. Well then. This is it. Fuck it. Fuck the spirits of the river and the wind. Fuck closing your eyes and listening to the universe and whole grains, and herbs and crystals and blah blah blah. Ro reached down to touch the metal face of Blackberry, the altar goddess.

"I love you, spirit. I trust you, spirit. But also. FUCK YOU, spirit." Ro laughed, cackling at the altar. She felt faithless. But she also felt godly, somehow. This time, she could feel the war inside her blood. The cells fighting and killing one another inside her body. She was a battlefield. It felt powerful and infuriating all at once. The first time she got sick, she was quiet and pensive. A martyr. She planted seeds and listened to trees. She cut all her hair off and walked around the house like a monk. Well. This time would be different. She turned away from the altar. She walked into her house and let the door slam behind her.

First, she made herself a very strong gin and tonic, with half a lime squeezed into the clear sparkling glass. Juice and pulp smeared along the rim. The drink was sour. It made her chest glow with heat. She kicked the back door open and howled a high note into the night. She danced her way across the yard. She stood before the altar. No more plants and water. She could feel it. Spirit wanted fire this time.

She held the glass with one hand and with the other she built a pointed house of sticks and logs. Beneath the logs, she made a wild nest of dried leaves, sticks and shredded newspaper. She lit a match and watched flames lick at the kindling. The fire quickly consumed the twigs and took its time with the logs. When she tossed hands full of dried sage and rosemary into the fire—they sizzled and burned into puffs of fragrant smoke. The fire was hungry. Popping sparks and sizzling. The altar turned gold in the firelight. The reflection of flames danced on the surface of the crystals, the curved green copper arch, and all the figurines of laughing gods. Ro sipped her too-strong drink and stared at the fire.

Jasmine arrived first. She followed the rich scent of burning wood and herbs. She smiled and kissed Ro on the cheek. The floral aroma of juniper laced the air around her mother's head. To Jasmine, this veil of sweetness smelled like an ex's cologne, both intoxicating and nauseating. She was only two years sober. She still had romantic cravings and dreams about the taste and feelings alcohol could inspire. She looked at her mother, wondering how drunk she already was.

"Hey, Mom. Isn't it . . . a little warm for a fire?" Jasmine asked.

"It's not for us." Ro said.

"Riiight." Jasmine replied.

"Don't roll your eyes at my offerings. You make coffee and cupcakes and call it a business. But I know what it really is." Ro said, wagging her finger and squinting at Jasmine.

"Okay, what is it?" Jasmine asked.

"That's just your kind of offering." Ro said, smiling. She sipped her drink.

Jasmine slid a small guitar case from her back.

"I was hoping you'd bring the guitar!" Ro sang and nodded her head. Her short locs bounced around her eyes as she danced.

"Any requests?" Jasmine asked as she sat on the ground next to her mother. She unzipped the case and carefully pulled the guitar into her lap.

"Play some nice chords. I just wanna hum something." Ro said, staring up at the hazy glow around the moon.

"I got you."

Ro sat back and admired her eldest daughter. Her short hair, her boyish clothing. She grinned.

"You were such a stubborn baby." Ro said, shaking her head. "You only wanted me. You hated sitters, you hated not being in my arms. You'd just scream and scream."

"And now I'm perfect." Jasmine said, grinning.

"Well, I think you are. Perfectly well adjusted. And healthy. Even if you're still very, very stubborn." Ro giggled into her cup, watching her daughter's eyes drift. Jasmine stared at the flames.

"It's not forever, honey." Ro said.

"What's not?" Jasmine asked.

"The bad stuff comes in waves. This is just a bunch of really big waves." Ro said grinning. She reached out her hand, affectionately brushing the fuzz on the back of Jasmine's head.

"I know." Jasmine said, nodding. She thought for a moment.

"Did you give up on finding somebody?" Jasmine asked, still staring at the flames.

"Is somebody missing?" Ro replied, looking around.

"I mean. Did you ever think that maybe you were better off without . . . a partner?" Jasmine asked.

The guitar's thin weaving melody hung in the air. Floating up like the bits of ash around them.

"I don't know if I'd call it giving up." Ro shrugged.

"Yeah." Jasmine nodded.

"But honey. I'm old. And Black. And smart."

"OKAY, are those bad things?" Jasmine asked.

Ro sighed. "You'd be surprised how disappointing straight men can be. I don't think I ever had anything like what you had."

"What I had . . ." Jasmine repeated. She rested her hand on the guitar strings. In the absence of melody, the sounds of crackling firewood and cicadas seemed to grow louder.

"What you had with Dia. That closeness. You both always had such a deep capacity for love."

"Yeah."

"Did you give up?" Ro asked.

Jasmine didn't answer. Her gaze drifted back into the fire.

Jasmine shook her head. "I don't know. Maybe."

"So your sisters hate each other and you've given up on love."

"That's a bit dramatic, Mom." Jasmine said. She began to play a new melody. Something faster, as if she could change the subject with a song.

"I don't think it is. I think the three of you are losing your pretty little minds." Ro said. She found a long twig on the ground and threw it into the fire.

The back door slammed open as Layla emerged from the house.

"Hey," Layla called out.

Ro waved as she finished her drink.

"Who else is coming?" Jasmine asked.

Layla skipped across the yard.

"Isn't it a little hot for a fire?" Layla asked.

"It's not for us," Jasmine said, side-eyeing the altar.

"Aaaah. Indeed." Layla nodded as she hugged Jasmine.

"How's your protest party coming?" Ro asked. She petted Layla's long, thick braids affectionately.

"It's going well." Layla grinned as she sat by her mother's side. She leaned into the warmth of the fire and whispered. "Actually, I think I had a vision."

"A vision?" Jasmine whispered back.

Ro brushed her hand in the air. "Are you surprised? You know we all see things in this family." Ro said.

Layla nodded enthusiastically. "I know! I've always felt things. Ideas, little suggestions here and there, but I never saw something this clear before."

"Cool!" Jasmine said, nodding.

"Did it come to you in a dream?" Ro asked.

"No. I was awake ... I may or may not have been a little bit high ..."

"Layla! You were high?" Jasmine asked, laughing.

"High on what?" Ro asked, concerned. Layla rolled her eyes.

"Just weed, mom."

"What kind of weed?" Jasmine asked. Layla shook her head.

"That's not relevant. It wasn't the weed. I swear. It was a vision! I was flying over a river. And floating down. It was so clear. Like I could feel the cold water on my fingertips."

"That was some good weed . . ." Jasmine muttered.

"And there was this chanting. Have you ever heard the word ah-nekah-chank?" Layla asked.

"Did you google it?" Jasmine offered.

"I tried but I don't know how to spell it. At the end of my vision, I kept hearing voices chanting the names of West African tribes like Yoruba, Igbo and then they were saying another phrase. Ah-nekah-chank. I think that's what it was . . ."

"Anaquashtank." Ro interrupted her. Layla and Jasmine turned to look at their mother.

Ro returned their gaze.

"The indigenous tribe. You've never heard of the Anaquashtank tribe?" Ro asked, waiting for a glimmer of recognition to flash across her daughter's faces.

"No . . ." Layla began.

"The Anacostans?" Ro went on.

"No . . ." Layla and Jasmine said together.

"Well, if you took any of my art classes, you would have gotten the full history lesson."

Jasmine and Layla sighed. Ro never forgave her daughter's efforts to avoid her classes at Beechwood. Everyone in the school gushed over how amazing Miss J was, how she changed their lives, how she challenged them. But being Miss J's daughters, life was always a classroom and they felt that they'd already been challenged enough.

"The Anaquashtank are the indigenous people of DC, before DC was DC. They lived here for thousands of years before white folks set foot on this earth. They were also known as the Anacostans. They were trades people. That's how the Anacostia

River got its name," Ro said, snapping into her lecture voice. She sat up in her chair, lit up with knowledge.

"The river," Layla whispered, remembering her vision.

"I thought that was the Piscataway Tribe?" Jasmine ventured.

"The Piscataway Tribe is mostly Southern Maryland. But I believe Piscataway was their shared language," Ro said.

"Wow." Layla sat back, considering this.

"What do you think it means?" Jasmine asked, turning to her sister.

"I don't know." Layla said.

The sound of laughter poured out from the back door as Marble and Ella emerged from the house. When Ella spotted Layla, her face fell. She paused at the door. Layla rolled her eyes and stared at the fire.

"Come on, El," Jasmine called out, waving her arm in the air. Marble squeezed Ella's hand as they headed toward the fire. Marble pulled two chairs from the picnic table toward the fire pit. Ella sat down in the chair and said nothing. Layla rolled her eyes.

Ro threw another handful of dried sage into the flames. She watched the pale green leaves turn to dust. They all sat and stared at the fire for a moment. Ro pressed her hands together, and rolled her shoulders back.

"I don't have much to say." She began. "I want you two to make up and stop being children." Ro shot a glance at Layla, who shifted in her seat.

"I don't have a problem with her." Layla interrupted, raising an eyebrow.

"Except you refuse to apologize. You lied to the Scotts, put their business at risk, and you basically told me my career was a waste of time," Ella said.

Her voice was melodic and cold.

"If you think your work is a waste of time, that's one thing. I never said—" Layla barked.

"Oh, and what about your work? Lying to people? Ruining one of the last thriving Black-owned businesses left in this city because you're convinced you'll save the world. If that's the kind of work that fulfills you, do your thing." Ella looked at her nails as she spoke, her voice remained calm and steady.

"Thriving Black-owned business? Ella. You're kidding right? So if Black folks opened up a gun store and lined the walls with AKs and Klan robes, would you support them too?"

"Baby sister. That's a bit of a reach." Ella lingered over the word baby when she said it.

"It's not, actually. But you wouldn't know because you're too busy playing servant to your rich white clients—"

"Layla!"

Jasmine held her hands up to keep her two sisters from further insulting each other.

"You're both hurt. That's all it is. Maybe if we just listen to each other? Talk without pointing fingers?" Both Ella and Layla rolled their eyes at Jasmine's tone.

"I'm not pointing fingers." Layla muttered.

"That's because no one did anything to you. You're the one who won't own your shitty choices. And Jasmine, please stay out of it. If you want to act like you're not hurt—that's fine. You let Layla walk all over people and do anything she wants cuz she's the baby, but you know what? She's fucking GROWN. But somehow no matter what dumb shit she pulls—you stay on Layla's side." Ella said. Layla's eyes widened. Ella never came for Jasmine.

Jasmine stood. "Ella, you have no clue, do you? Everyone is on your side. You know I fucking broke into the Scott offices, trying to talk some sense into your boyfriend? Despite the fucking disappearing act the two of them pulled and despite the fact that I don't think he really deserves you, I was over there breaking and entering on your heterosexual behalf!" Jasmine was yelling.

All three sisters were standing now, growing louder and angrier as each sister talked over the next. Marble stared wide-eyed at Ro. Ro sighed. She stood.

"Enough."

The sisters shrunk into a tense silence. Layla folded her arms. Ella put her hands on her hips. Jasmine massaged her left temple. Ro took a deep breath and closed her eyes. Why did she suddenly feel the urge to start laughing? Was her drink too strong? Why did all of this feel deeply hilarious? She attempted to remain serious. Dying was serious. Talking to your kids about dying was really, really serious. But it all felt silly to her at this point. She pressed her lips together, attempting to suppress her laughter. She grinned, chuckling as she spoke.

"You need to make up because I'm going to die." Her daughters turned their heads. They stared at her, waiting for a punchline that wouldn't come. Ro shrugged. Marble watched each sister's face twist into realization.

"Here goes! I'm playing the cancer card. I'm playing the I'm-going-to-die-so-do-what-I-say card." Ro said, laughing now.

"What—" Jasmine stared at her mother.

"Mom. Are you serious?" Ella whispered.

"Serious as a heart attack. Or I guess—as serious as breast cancer? In this case," Ro said.

She leaned into Marble, giggling uncontrollably. Marble looked up at Jasmine.

"Did you know?" Jasmine asked, staring at Marble.

"She told me she needed an advocate. So, I took her in for some tests last month," Marble said, looking in Ro's direction, waiting. Ro nodded. Marble spoke in a hushed tone. "They found some irregular tissue growth and I took her in for another biopsy."

Ro cleared her throat. "They're not optimistic," she said. She felt a bout of giggles on the tip of her tongue, but she coughed it back. The heat in her chest grew. She sat down. Marble pulled their chair next to Ro's. Ro tilted her head up and watched her daughters think.

"We can go on and on about how unfair it all is," Ro said, smiling at Marble. She looked up and noticed Layla's face was wet with tears. She made her baby cry. She felt the desperate impulse to hold Layla in her arms like she was five again. Ella stared at the ground, lost. And Jasmine stared at her. She watched her daughters fall apart, again. And she didn't have the energy to save them. She sighed.

"Just stop," she said. She closed her eyes for a long time. No one moved. No one said a thing. Ro opened her eyes and looked at each of her daughters.

"Maybe I have a little less time than we thought. So what? You're taking your magic for granted. You're sisters. Do you know how much I wish I grew up with sisters? Do you know how LUCKY you are?" Ro was yelling now, gesturing wildly with her hands.

"You'll find love and you'll change the world and you'll have the things you need, and you'll have more. But none of it means anything without this. You have nothing without this." Ro lifted her hand. Above the warmth of the fire, she drew an invisible circle with her hand from Jasmine to Ella to Layla to Marble, and a dancing swirl of small sparks followed as her hand moved. The embers stirred between them, and in the blink of an eye they turned to white ash and floated up into the night.

"Marble is going to take me to my appointments this month. Until I get an understanding of the timeline."

"What can we do?" Ella whispered.

"All I want is for you three to make up. And don't talk to me or try to wait on me until you do," Ro snapped.

Jasmine, Ella, and Layla watched their mother stand and turn to go. She walked quickly. Still warm and giddy. The sisters didn't move. They watched their mother walk to the house. The sound of the door slamming behind her cut every tendon holding them together.

Layla sobbed into her hands. Her tears shone slick in the fire light.

Jasmine reached over to find Layla's hand. Marble stood and looked at Jasmine.

"I wanted to tell you. I'm so sorry," they whispered. Jasmine nodded her head gently. She pulled Marble into an embrace. Her head rested on Marble's shoulders.

"I'm glad she felt comfortable," Jasmine began. "I mean I'm glad she has you. Thank you."

Marble smiled. They squeezed Jasmine's hand.

"I'm gonna make sure—" Marble began, pointing at the house.

"Yes, go. Thank you." Jasmine watched as they walked out of the firelight and disappeared into the house.

Inside, the house was dark. Marble found Ro sitting by the window. Ro and Marble sat together in the quiet darkness of the living room, watching the sisters' silhouettes against the fire. Jasmine slowly sank to the ground. Layla slid to the ground by her side. Jasmine looked up and held her hand out to Ella. Ella's knees touched the earth, then her hands, then she was in Jasmine's lap. Marble held Ro's hand as she watched her daughters cry in each other's arms.

34. ELLA AND LAYLA

The sisters hadn't had a blanket bath in years. Before their father left for good, when they were all kids and there were shouting matches in the kitchen, Jasmine had read stories in the bathtub to Ella and a squiggling baby Layla.

When Jasmine left the house, Ella and Layla turned into children. They filled the clawfoot bathtub with pillows, blankets and assorted stuffed animals and soft things. They changed into footie pajamas. Ella's were pink with green polka dots. Layla's were black with dancing peacock feathers. Ella put her hair in a cartoonishly high bun on the top of her head. Layla braided her clouds of black hair into pigtails.

Ella slid into the heap of blankets. Layla followed her with a bottle of wine in each hand.

"Red or white?" Layla asked, holding the two bottles up.

"White," Ella replied, holding out her hand.

Layla slid into the tub opposite Ella and took a swig of the cabernet.

The sisters stared blankly at each other. Both puffy-eyed and dazed after a night of weeping.

"So. Do you forgive me . . . or something?" Layla asked, half smiling.

". . . Or something." Ella replied, sucking her teeth.

"You're my big sister. You're supposed to be the bigger man."

"You're my little sister. You're supposed to be cute." Ella replied. She leaned forward to pinch Layla's cheek. Layla swatted her hand away and laughed. Ella found a tattered one-legged stuffed bear in the soup of blankets and pillows.

"Doctor bear!" Ella cooed.

"Oh?" Layla replied, laughing.

"Doctor bear was our favorite! He always lost his leg and mom taught us to sew it back on. That's how I learned to sew. But I was terrible at sewing. So his leg always fell off again." Ella said. She rubbed clouds from the bear's black marble eyes.

"Why was he the doctor?" Layla asked.

"That's a good question," Ella said, thinking. "I'm not sure!"

"Maybe it's like how therapists are always kinda crazy? The broken toy fixes the other broken toys?" Layla pondered.

"Healers need healers too," Ella said, hugging the bear close to her check.

"Damn right," Layla replied. She tipped her head back and stared at the curtain rod. She wished she had something to say. More stories. More distractions. But their mother's sickness was there in the silence. Like a ghost. Cancer grew in the silence now. They both took a long drag from their respective bottles of wine.

"She doesn't deserve this." Layla spoke at the ceiling.

"Nobody deserves this," Ella replied, pulling the blankets around her. She discovered another stuffed animal. She lifted the pink cat up for Layla to see.

"Do you remember Mitten?" Ella asked excitedly.

Layla tipped her head back up.

"Mitten . . ." Layla took the cat in her hands.

"Mitten the kitten?!" Ella said, grinning.

". . . Not really," Layla replied.

Ella sighed and snatched Mitten back. She placed the cat next to Doctor Bear.

"You don't remember anything!" Ella pouted.

"I was never really into stuffed animals," Layla said.

Ella petted the stuffed creatures gently.

"I was too busy trying to act grown-up like you and Jas," Layla said.

Ella smiled.

"And we were both wishing mom would coddle us like babies again. Like you. Greener grass and what not," Ella mused as she swigged at her bottle of white.

"I worshiped you when I was little. Do you know that?" Layla felt the warmth of the red wine and the blankets cradling her. Ella watched her sister daydreaming into a memory.

"All the clothes you wore, your music, the sports and the boys. I used to steal your T-shirts," Layla said.

"No FUCKING WAY. I always blamed Jasmine!" Ella replied, laughing.

Layla picked at the label on her wine bottle.

"I wanted to be you." She said it quietly.

Ella softened. She sat still for a moment. "Why would you say that?"

Layla felt her heart tighten. "Because it's true. I always felt like I had to try. Like I was never really me. You were the only real person I knew."

"I was the fat black girl. I've always been real and cool and genuine or whatever. But I had to try really really hard."

Layla shook her head. "I didn't mean that you didn't have to—"

"Pretty girls like you don't need personalities. They don't need character, you know? You have both, which is very heroic of you. But I didn't have a choice. I wanted to be ordinary and vapid like all the wispy hipster white girls. I wanted to be a wallflower! I didn't want to be COOL and REAL. I wanted to fit in, Layla." Ella's words were thorned, guarding the tenderness beneath them. Layla looked an inch shorter.

"I didn't fit in either," Layla whispered.

Ella sighed. "I know. I'm sorry, I know. It was hard for you too. But Layla, you're pretty and skinny. And instantly adored. You don't want to be me. Not really."

"What does being skinny have to do with who I am?" Layla snapped.

"You're right," Ella replied calmly. "But honey. You got skinny privilege. You'll have more chances. More open doors. Maybe for the wrong reasons. But that's life. I'm just saying. You got it good too, bitch." Ella shrugged. She swigged at her bottle. Layla nodded.

"And another thing: I don't want to work for white people my whole life. You know that, right?" Ella said, pointing her finger at Layla.

"I know." Layla nodded.

"No, listen. We all know you went to WESLEYAN and you are A BLACK INTELLECTUAL and the rest of us are cavemen. But don't be a fucking snob. Okay? If you want to be a leader for the people, you need to start here. People work, Layla. Our grandmother was a domestic. Most Black folks work for white folks, okay? We can't all be Black intellectual heroes like you." Ella smiled as she spoke.

"I never should have said that shit about your job. I respect the hell out of you, El. I was just pissed off. For real. I'm sorry."

"Just don't say it," Ella said, shrugging. Layla took a breath.

"So, which one of us suffers more? Is that what we're really fighting about? Me, the fat, light-skinned body worker, energy healer-slash-goddess. Or you—the chocolate runway mod-el-slash-activist-slash-messiah?" Ella said laughing.

"Wow, this was all so stupid. I'm sorry, Ella," Layla said.

"It's okay, baby sister," Ella teased.

"And. I'm sorry. About David," Layla whispered.

Ella shrugged again. "He's just a boy."

Layla searched Ella's eyes.

"You don't really think that." Layla nodded.

Ella tipped her head back and looked at the ceiling.

"I'm not desperate," Ella said.

"Of course you're not," Layla whispered back.

"I'm beautiful and smart and funny, and I know I deserve the perfect man." Ella sniffled and laughed as she spoke.

"You do! Of course you do!" Layla brushed a soft swoop of hair from Ella's eyes.

"Layla, he was kind of perfect. For me. I wish I didn't care. I usually don't care." Ella smiled.

"I know," Layla said, squeezing Ella's hand.

"I just—I don't know if I'll have any more chances." Ella's smile faded.

Layla said nothing. Of course Ella would have more chances. That wasn't the problem. The problem was that she didn't want any more chances. Ella wanted one boy.

Ella stared at her half-empty bottle of white wine.

"What are we gonna do?" she asked dully.

"We're gonna finish this wine," Layla began.

"Uh huh," Ella replied.

"And snuggle."

"Okay," Ella said.

"And tomorrow we're going to tell Mom we made up and she has to let us make her tea."

Layla counted the items on her fingers as she listed them.

"And you're going to call the boy you love and become secret lovers. For now."

Ella laughed.

"And I'm going to keep being naive and try to save all the Black people in the world. And you're going to keep being a healer of rich white people and saving the world in your own way. And you and me and Jasmine and Ma, we're all going to live like we'll die tomorrow because some of us might."

Layla exhaled.

"Okay?"

"Okay."

Ella laughed and nodded as they clinked their wine bottles together.

35. JASMINE

Jasmine watched the steam rising from her cup. She took a sip and winced. The unsweetened green tea tasted like paper. A fluorescent light flickered above her. The murmur of chatter and laughter blurred into the back of her consciousness. Since her mother's confession—it seemed like everything blurred into the background. Like she couldn't cling to one thought or action. So her feet brought her here. Going to a meeting was her cure for everything. Depression, restlessness, resentment. The dark church basement with the bad coffee, the flavorless tea, and a gaggle of jovial yet surly alcoholics in their fifties. She stared at her cup. Her mother was dying. Again. Her two sisters were at home crying in each other's arms. And Jasmine was in a church basement thinking about all the things she wanted. She wanted to be at home with them. She wanted to drink wine until they all forgot what they were so sad about. She wanted to shake her mom. Why didn't you tell us? Why are you laughing? Why aren't you fighting this? She wanted David to go back to Ella. She wanted Layla to change the world. And she wanted to be with Zora. She wanted to feel Zora's arms around her. Jasmine looked down at her paper cup full of sad green tea. She wanted this tea to not taste like dust. How could she go back to just being grateful? To wake up and listen to wind move through the trees? How could she go back to feeling like small things were more than enough. How could she stop wanting so much?

Jasmine flinched at the hand on her shoulder.

"Jasmine?"

She looked up. Leslie's serene smile felt like a beam of sunlight.

"Leslie!"

Leslie held her arms out, and as they embraced Jasmine felt herself suddenly falling apart, sobbing in Leslie's arms.

"I'm so sorry." She choked and laughed.

"It's okay, Jasmine. It's okay!" Leslie was laughing too.

"I had a bad day," Jasmine said, shrugging.

"I get it, honey," Leslie said. Jasmine closed her eyes, wincing.

"Did you tell your sponsor?" Leslie asked.

"I sent her a message. We meet every Wednesday, so I'll see her soon." Jasmine said, looking down at her phone.

"Okay." Leslie nodded.

"It's okay. I'm okay. I'm great," Jasmine said.

"Well, I'm your cool new AA friend, remember?"

"I remember." Jasmine sniffled.

"Seems like it's time for that coffee?" Leslie's smile grew as she spoke.

"Oh. No. You don't have to—"

"Yes I do. Come on. Let's go," Leslie said. She took Jasmine's hand and pulled her down the aisle of folding chairs.

"But . . . the meeting?"

"We're gonna go have our own meeting." Leslie said as she marched Jasmine down the basement corridor.

"Okay," she said, laughing. She waved goodbye to the room full of alcoholics.

"So where can we get coffee this late?" Leslie asked.

"I know the perfect place," Jasmine replied, smiling.

Jasmine and Leslie sat in the window seat, bathing in the

buttery yellows of The T Spot.

Jasmine whipped up two steaming Americanos. Almond creamer for Leslie. She turned off the overhead lights and left all the art fixtures on. The ink blots glowed from wide squares of canvas. Leslie closed her eyes. Jasmine knew she was making a gratitude list. She smiled. Breathing slow and calmly. Watching Leslie felt like time was slowing down. When Leslie opened her eyes again, Jasmine couldn't tell how much time had passed. Leslie leaned in.

"Since we only just met, I think we should start from the beginning. Tell me your story," Leslie said, taking a sip of her coffee.

"You want me to do a lead? Experience, strength, and hope? The whole thing?" Jasmine asked.

"The whole thing," Leslie repeated, smiling.

Jasmine took a breath. She'd spoken at a few meetings before. Whenever she was asked to do a lead, she said yes. But it never felt easy to unveil all your shame and darkness to strangers.

"Okay. Okay." Jasmine closed her eyes. She breathed in. Ground in prayer.

"God. Spirits. Ancestors. Relieve me of the bondage of self that I may better do your will. Let my words be honest, from the heart, guided by you. And not my ego. Not my need to be impressive and likable."

Leslie nodded firmly at this. Jasmine opened her eyes.

"My mom always told us we were beautiful. And brilliant. And worthy. Really, I had everything I could have asked for—growing up. But racism is a bitch. And going to school with white kids is traumatic because no matter how sweet and liberal and well-intentioned they all are—being marginalized and Black—that will make you question everything. Your intelligence, your beauty, your power. So. I questioned everything. I wanted to be like everyone else. But I was so weird. Always different. I was Black and so very very gay. I felt uncomfortable all the time. I wanted to figure out how to be good enough. There was this desire to understand what people wanted. Friends, parents, teachers. I needed to know what they wanted from me so I could be that. And to be better. But no matter what I did, I wouldn't fit in. I couldn't. I was anxious. Constantly trying to be something I could never be. When I was twelve, I drank my first screwdriver. And all that anxiety and worry and shame just disappeared. Alcohol fixed it. I was beautiful now, and confident. It was like the whole world softened for me. That was it. If I needed to drink to like myself, or to go somewhere, or to get through something—I mean what's so wrong about that, right?"

Jasmine chuckled here. Leslie smiled. She nodded, but didn't speak. Jasmine went on.

"High School taught me how to drink hard. By senior year, it was every day. I thought I was such a rebel. I wasn't going to college like all the snobby kids around me. I wasn't getting into all that debt. I knew what I wanted to do. I'm gonna go to culinary school. I was gonna make money. I was going out to gay clubs and finding my people! And shit. When I found out where the Black queers hung out, it was over. I was beautiful for the first time in my fucking life. Like maybe I was actually hot? People wanted me. And I desired the people around me. Of course, none of these gorgeous community spaces came without a bar. Without a tab I couldn't afford, and daily hangovers. That deep affirmation was inextricably connected to being drunk and high. So. Basically, I learned to be my whole Black, queer, gorgeous self in the middle of a blackout. I fucked everyone. I fucked people I didn't want to fuck. I had a lot of sex I didn't want to have."

Jasmine paused here. She felt her throat tighten. This part always hurt. That younger version of her deserved so much more.

"But. When I met Dia, I was finishing culinary school. And she was everything. Like get married and have kids, I want you forever in every way . . . kind-of-thing. I was myself with her. I was really happy. I thought I was anyway. Still drinking every day. Sometimes sneaking drinks before we would get in bed. And long term—the drinking made me more anxious. More paranoid. Insecure. I just knew Dia was flirting with other women. Lying. Not telling me everything. And I didn't trust her because I didn't trust myself. I was the one fucking other women. I was the one lying. The whole time I was justifying it. I was telling myself she wouldn't understand if I told her, and I love her the most and I'm a really good partner and that's what matters."

Jasmine took a breath.

"It sounds so dumb now. But I believed it. Anyway. She found out. About all of it. And she tried to trust me again. We tried for a few years after that. But I just kept lying and cheating and not trusting her and being jealous, possessive, insecure. Oh, and manipulative. Can't forget that one. That one's sneaky. It doesn't make sense to me now. Because I really wanted to be with her. But that younger me didn't believe I was worth any of it. I didn't believe I could just be in love with her and happy. Or be in love with her and honest about my feelings for other people. I was completely self-centered. I needed to drink and fuck women and be wanted constantly to feel worthy. Anyway. After trying, then trying again—eventually, she left me. Right when I opened this place."

Jasmine looked up and around at the yellow walls.

"It was strange. Like one big dream coming true, and another just gone. So I stayed sober enough in the mornings. Came to work at 4:00 a.m. Did everything I had to do to get by. Closed at six and drank from six until I passed out. And every day I woke up in pain. My brain feeling like it was too big for my skull. That sharp, sharp headache. My stomach would be in knots. And I did it again the next day. Honestly, I wanted to die. I was living off of self-pity and anger. How could she give up on us? How could she leave me when I'm at my worst? That was my take.

I did that for a couple years. I didn't want to kill myself. But I didn't want to live. My mom told us she had cancer. And I had no energy to feel what I felt about losing her. I couldn't even sit in a room with her unless I had a couple drinks in me. Isn't that fucked up? My mom is maybe dying and I need to take the edge off to show up for her. I moved back in with her; my two sisters moved back too. And I managed to keep them out of it. Drank alone. Drank here at the cafe. That night I was here. I don't remember getting in the car. I don't remember running off the road. I just remember waking up in the hospital. And seeing my sister's faces. They fell apart when they saw me. In my whole life, nothing felt worse than that. So. Then it was rehab. I did everything they told me to do. Everything. I was desperate. I didn't want to leave. But after I got to my mom's house, I asked her to drive me straight to a meeting.

It was a depressing room that day. A lot of newcomers in rough shape. Toothless crackheads, soccer moms who drove blackout drunk with their toddlers in the car, people whose hands shook from withdrawals. I heard the most wretched stories. I just sat quietly in my chair and sobbed and sobbed. I didn't feel like I was better than anyone there. I wasn't. I'd just spent years hurting the person I loved most in the world and justifying it. What's more fucking crazy than that? I just cried and cried. And I looked around and I realized—I was sitting in a room full of people trying to quit. Just like me. There were rooms all over the world like this. I wasn't special. I wasn't alone. I was part of this weird group and we were all going to be there for each other. It felt like god. That connection. That sad room. So. I didn't pick up a drink after that day.

I got a sponsor who has a sponsor. I didn't want to do the

steps. I felt like being dry and taking my ass to meetings every other day was enough work-but that fucking slogan got me. How free do you wanna be? Those stupid fucking slogans. So corny. And so obnoxiously true.

So I did the steps. Heels dug into the ground, but still. I did it. And fuck me if that shit didn't work. It felt like every step taught me to be better at life. How to be present. Honest. It's been two years, and I've gone through the steps, the traditions, and we're doing the steps again now. I pray and I meditate. My higher power changes all the time. Sometimes HP is nature, or music, or good food. Sometimes it's the meeting, the people in the room. Today, she's a many-armed Black woman who is also a tree. She has brown skin and she's thick. She kinda looks like Sarah Vaughan. And she sings like her too."

Leslie shook her head, grinning wide and snapping.

Jasmine began to smile and laugh as she spoke. She was glowing.

"The Black woman-slash-tree with many arms is called Azul. Her arms are my friends, my sisters, my work, my sponsor, the meetings, prayers. And when I fall, if one arm can't catch me, another one will. That's what I believe in. And my life is really not perfect. My cafe is failing. I'll probably have to close once my lease runs out this year. I can't seem to maintain any kind of romantic relationship or even date for very long. So I gave up on finding love. Or even like. I think I'm just going to settle for mediocre sex at this point. And it's fine. Oh, and by the way, my mom is dying of breast cancer. For real this time. So I'm very fucking sad. And also . . . I don't know. My life is a little bit great. I don't hate myself. That's big. And I don't feel dependent on alcohol to make it through the day. I'm not afraid of everything. I don't question my power or my brilliance. I don't wake up ashamed, or afraid. I wake up so fucking hungry for life."

Jasmine paused, shaking her head. Sometimes she couldn't

believe how much had changed in her recovery. It felt so good to take a moment and let it all soak in.

"My sponsor and I did all the steps and we're on step one again. Two years later, I'm figuring out how to admit I'm powerless over alcohol. Again. And I'm thinking. The world treats us like we're so amazing for being strong. So resilient. Matriarchs and single moms and athletes and pillars of strength and Black girl magic blah, blah, blah, blah, blah. It's just the superwoman myth with a new twist. It's bullshit. We think we can do anything and everything because everyone expects us to do EVERYTHING and ANYTHING. Even two years in, the idea of saying I am powerless still makes me feel like I'm a failure. I think I AM magical! I CAN do anything! But I fucking can't. I can't control the weather. Or how many Starbucks pop up in a two-block radius. Or how many people buy their stale, depressing pastries. Or white supremacy. Or racism. Or the patriarchy. I can't carry everything. I can't control my mom's health. It's just—out of my hands. It's so weird but it feels radically empowering. Letting go."

Jasmine exhaled aggressively, then rested her hands in her lap and smiled.

"Wow. Okay, I think if I don't stop here, I'll never stop. Thank you for letting me share."

"Jasmine. Thank you." Leslie said, squeezing Jasmine's hands.

"You want a pastry?" she asked, suddenly jumping up to her feet. Leslie laughed.

"Sure."

Jasmine jogged to the pastry display and brought Leslie a croissant on a small plate.

Leslie's eyes lit up at the sight of the offering.

"I want to hear your story!" Jasmine said.

"Oh, you will. I'll tell it next time we meet."

Jasmine's mind snapped back to Zora for a moment. She

shook the thought away. She tried instead to think about her gratitude list. How grateful she was to meet Leslie.

They each took a bite of croissant and savored the quiet between them. Leslie daintily covered her mouth as she spoke.

"I needed to hear that. It's been a long time since I've had a hangover. But your story took me right back to my drinking days. I wouldn't trade that misery for the whole world," Leslie said, shaking her head.

"Oh yeah. Daily hangovers. I don't know how I did it. It was actually torture," Jasmine replied.

"Thank you, Jasmine. Truly. You inspire me. And I'm so sorry about your mom."

Jasmine nodded. "Thanks for suggesting this. I probably wouldn't have shared in the meeting tonight. I'm really good at hiding when I need to ask for help," she admitted.

"So what happened with the girl you shared about the other day? The one you kissed?" Leslie asked, leaning forward.

"Right." Jasmine said, her eyes falling. She stalled, taking a long sip of her coffee.

"It's not really important. I don't have a shot with her anymore. It's a long story." Jasmine said, shifting in her seat.

"Not important? How many times did you think about her today?" Leslie asked, folding her arms.

Jasmine frowned.

"What are you? Psychic?" Jasmine asked.

Leslie laughed.

"No. I'm just old. And you just said you're good at hiding," Leslie said as she took a bite of her croissant. She stared at the pastry as she chewed.

"Okay. Honestly, I think about her—" Jasmine began. She closed her eyes. "All the time." She sucked in a breath.

Leslie nodded.

"And I know I'm supposed to be sad about my mom dying. I am. But I'm also really sad that I can't kiss her right now. It makes no sense. I don't even really know her." Jasmine laughed.

"It doesn't have to make sense. But I noticed something in your share. When you said you were settling for . . . casual encounters, I wondered. Do you believe you deserve romantic love?" Leslie asked.

Jasmine wagged her finger cartoonishly. "Aaah! That!"

"Well. Do you?" Leslie waited. Jasmine sighed.

"Of course. Everyone deserves romantic love. But I don't know if it's meant really for me, you know?"

"I don't." Leslie replied.

"I've never been good at it. All I did was hurt people." Jasmine shrugged.

"So you don't deserve another chance?" Leslie asked, her brows furrowed.

Jasmine stared out at the empty street.

"Maybe I do," she said, nodding.

"But I probably need time. To really believe that. You know?"

Leslie nodded.

"I do."

Jasmine shook her head and smiled at Leslie.

"Thank you, Leslie."

"Of course." Leslie leaned in. "And not to change the subject, but I have to say—this croissant. Is perfection."

"Music to my ears!" Jasmine sang and danced in her seat.

"Your cafe cannot close. Even if I have to come in here and spend my life savings." Leslie said, her mouth full of croissant.

"You're sweet." Jasmine watched with delight as Leslie slowly finished her pastry.

"This has been the best part of my day. Seriously. I can't thank you enough." Jasmine said.

"Well, thank you." Leslie pointed at her cup. "This also might be the best Americano I've ever had."

Jasmine batted her lashes, beaming.

"Oh, you stop."

"Don't be modest," Leslie said. She stood and embraced Jasmine.

"Let's do this again?" Jasmine asked.

"Please," Leslie replied. Jasmine walked Leslie to the door and turned the lock.

"So why can't you kiss her? The unimportant girl you can't stop thinking about?"

Jasmine laughed.

"Well. Long story short: her father is sort of building the luxury property and my sister is protesting it. And they're basically mortal enemies now. Two households, star-crossed lovers and what not. Also she's kind of a rich snob so—" Jasmine waved her hands in the air.

Leslie stared at Jasmine for a moment.

"A luxury building?"

Jasmine nodded. "Yeah. On U Street. If it wasn't completely gentrified already, it will be now."

"Right," Leslie replied, looking distractedly down the dark street.

"So she's a prince and I'm a peasant and all that."

Leslie's smile fell for the first time.

"Jasmine—"

"It's fine. Powerlessness, remember? I can't control the fact that her father has banished my family from their lives. I'm surprised she even gave me a—"

"Jasmine." Leslie's stern voice sucked the air from Jasmine's lungs.

She recoiled, feeling the sting of a mother's scolding.

"You probably shouldn't. You shouldn't tell me any more. About this."

Jasmine blinked.

"Why?"

"Because I know Zora." Leslie said sternly.

Jasmine's heart raced. Hearing that name in this context. It was strange. And confusing. She hadn't mentioned Zora's name, had she? And then she thought about it. The expression that reminded her of something. Zora's presence. It couldn't be, Jasmine thought. Leslie looked down the street as if searching for a word. She turned back to Jasmine with an apologetic expression.

"Zora is my daughter."

36. ZORA

David dribbled the basketball as he walked. Pivoting, shooting the ball into the air. Spinning past invisible defenders. If they didn't look so much alike, Zora would have wondered if they were related. He was the golden retriever puppy to her old, jaded cat. Her stoicism clashed with his chipper. She was all shadow and logic. And he was a goddamn patch of sunlight everywhere he went. His hot pink sneakers and green Day-Glo tracksuit in stark contrast to Zora's black-on-black-on-black basketball fit. Zora wondered if she could learn to be lighter. Softer. She wondered if she could pull off a pair of hot pink LeBrons.

"How far is it?" Zora asked.

"Two more blocks on Ninth."

"I'm starving."

"Me too."

"Those guys were cut-throat." David said, checking the ball to Zora.

"They weren't cut-throat, boo. They were young," Zora replied, checking the ball back.

"Young? You tryin' to call me old?" David scoffed.

"You can be whatever you want. I feel old. Old enough to know I shouldn't play ball with guys in their twenties," Zora muttered.

"I think we held our own," David replied.

The sound of the ball against the concrete punctuated David's words.

"We were great," Zora said.

"I think we still got it!"

"Mhmm. I might need to ice my knees tonight. But sure, baby brother. We still got it."

"I know that's right!" David spun the ball on his fingertips. He slapped the ball with a congratulatory nod. Zora watched the sun melt into the horizon. The brick buildings turned dusty pink. Her gaze drifted to a wide swath of pink sky between the faces of buildings. An open city block full of sunset sky.

"Shit. Is that—is that the U Street lot?" Zora whispered, staring across the street.

David held the basketball at his hip.

"Oh shit. Yeah. That's it." David exhaled.

David and Zora stared at the demolished block.

"Come on." David took Zora's hand and pulled her across the street. Zora walked slowly, taking it all in. She threaded her fingers through the chain link fence. Nothing but mountains of dirt, and a hole so deep it looked like it went on for miles.

"I haven't seen it since before the demolition." Zora said, staring.

David sighed.

"I know." David replied. Zora turned to her brother. She looked up, calculating.

"David. Did you—did you take me here on purpose?" Zora asked.

David looked through the chain link.

Zora stepped closer.

"David?"

"Maybe. I mean. Yes. I brought you here on purpose," David said.

"Why?"

"I don't know, Zora. Just felt like you needed to see it."

David stepped back.

Zora sighed.

"You're fucking kidding me, right?"

"I'm not," David said, attempting a stern tone, folding his arms.

Zora laughed.

"You trying to teach me something, baby brother? Is this what's happening here?"

David shook his head. He looked six years old again. That sweet, artsy kid. He was so used to disappointing their dad, he didn't have to try so hard anymore. And she never stopped trying. He didn't know how lucky he was.

"I'm not trying to teach you anything, Zora. I just thought you would want to see it again. Before it becomes The Scott. DC's brand-new destination for luxury lifestyle U Street." David turned his voice into a commercial for a moment, opening his arms out to the demolished block.

"And now you've seen it. So. We can go get our food and go home. Nothing has to mean anything. That's all." David said, shrugging.

Zora sighed. The whole sky was gray, pink purple now. In a year, this pile of dirt would be a work of art. Function and art meeting in the middle in black glass and concrete. A wide-open lobby full of lush plants and hammered black steel. All the changes and design choices she'd added herself. She was proud of this one. In a way she hadn't been before. So why did it feel like something was off? Zora shook her head.

"Go," Zora whispered.

"Huh?"

"Go get our food, David. You want me to have a deep-ass spiritual revelation or whatever so, go get the food. I can be spiritual but don't make me do it hungry. Please."

A smile spread across David's face. He nodded giddily.

"Okay!" David handed Zora the basketball and took off

running, staring back at Zora and grinning so wide she could see his goofy smile a block away.

She threaded her fingers into the fence.

Her father was right. He was. Wealthy Black people shouldn't have to save the world.

The metal shook and undulated in waves. Down the block, a young boy climbed the fence. He looked like he couldn't be older than nine.

"Hey!" Zora yelled as she ran down the block. She reached him just as he landed on the other side of the fence.

"Hey. You can't ... play in there. It's really dangerous." Zora stared at the child. He stared back defiantly.

"I know."

"Come on, I'll help you climb back over. Let me help you." Zora smiled as she spoke.

"I don't need help." The boy shrugged. He began to walk the length of the fence. Zora followed him, walking along the other side of the chain link.

"How old are you?" Zora asked.

"I'm ten." The boy replied.

"Wow. Cool."

The boy squinted at Zora.

"You don't think that's cool."

"Yeah I do." Zora said, nodding.

"How old are you?"

"Thirty-nine."

"No way."

"Yeah."

"That's old." The boy said. He kicked a lump of dirt.

"Well. Compared to you, yeah. But it's all relative, you know?"

"Whatever." The boy looked distracted.

Zora looked up and down the street.

"Where's your ... adult?" Zora asked.

The boy stopped walking. He sat in the dirt and leaned his back into the fence.

"I ran away."

"Okay..."

Zora sat on the ground by his side. She winced, brushing off the dust on her shoes.

The boy turned his head, staring at Zora.

"Are you a boy or a girl?" The boy asked.

"What do you think?"

"I think you're a boy," he said.

Zora shrugged.

"Yeah, I'm a boy."

"But you're not really, are you?" the boy said, grinning.

"Why did you run away?"

"I always go back. I just come here sometimes. To think."

Zora nodded. "Okay."

The boy found a stone in the dirt. He threw it into the darkness.

"What's your name?" Zora asked.

"Jayden. What's yours?"

"Zora."

"Hey Jayden, you play ball?"

"Yeah."

"You any good?"

"I'm really good. I'm better than most of the boys in my grade!"

Zora sucked her teeth.

"Probably not as good as me."

"Whatever. You're old."

"Right. So. Jayden. If you let me walk you home, I'll give you this basketball. Would you want that?"

Jayden cut his eyes to the basketball.

"I don't want that old raggedy ball."

"Damn." Zora shook her head.

"I was gonna leave soon anyway." Jayden jumped up and climbed the fence. Zora braced herself nervously as he jumped down on her side. Jayden and Zora walked down the road together in silence.

"So, if you walk me back to my mom . . . you gonna give me the ball or what?"

"Oh, you mean this raggedy ball?" Zora chuckled.

"I mean it would be good for practice. Probably. Even if it's not that nice." Jayden shrugged.

"Okay but you have to let me walk you home."

"It's just around the corner," Jayden mumbled.

"You want the ball, you gotta let me take you home."

"Okay. There's a place on the way there. They have chips and stuff."

"Chips! Now you're pushing it, my g." Zora said, grinning.

"I'm just sayin'." Jayden sighed.

"If it's on the way, I'll get us some chips," Zora said, shaking her head.

Jayden took Zora's hand in his. Zora held her breath.

"It's this way," he said, pulling her down the block.

"Okay!" Zora pulled her phone from her basketball shorts.
CALL ME.

She texted David. Jayden swung Zora's hand wildly as they walked down the street together.

"Jayden, why do you come here to think? Wouldn't you rather go to a playground or something?"

"I come here cuz we used to live here."

37. LAYLA

Layla danced down the bike trail in her best attempt at activewear: electric blue Air Jordans, leopard print leggings, and an oversized T-shirt. She never felt the need to "exercise" the way her sisters did. But she loved to dance. So she body-rolled, skipped, and twirled down the path as runners and bikers swerved around her. She rolled her eyes at the training-for-a-marathon types as they bounced by. White people running in Anacostia. Hell has officially frozen over. She scoffed. When she was growing up, everyone at Beechwood gasped at the mere mention of Southeast DC. Back when *that's so ghetto* was a casual, white insult. When you couldn't go an hour without hearing a playful reference to crack. *Are you on crack?* The white kids' parents cautioned their children to stay away from places like Anacostia. *There are dead bodies in the river. Gang violence. Shootings. Crackheads. Trash on the streets.*

Layla remembered feeling some residual shame about Southeast. Didn't people live there? Families? Children? What about them? She couldn't dismiss an entire quadrant the way her classmates did. She couldn't dismiss any Black people. She felt something tight in her chest when she saw the homeless Black man on her middle-school field trip to the monuments. The white kids and the teachers pretended he wasn't there. She pretended, too. But she felt a line between them. Like they were connected by an invisible thread. All she had was her dark brown skin. But the more she learned, the more she became infuriated. Black people lived east of the river and the city had essentially abandoned them. Decades without federal or city-level environmental protections. For years, city planners and developers ran sewage lines right to the water. The Anacostia was called "the forgotten river."

But now! Now there are fucking white people jogging along the river with overfed rescue pit bulls and cheerful labradoodles. On every block a demolished housing project making way for gray square rows of townhouses. The Nats stadium. Whole Foods. Blocks of shining new apartment buildings and restaurants around the Wharf in Southwest. Layla watched a family walk slowly along the trail. A Black couple in their thirties holding hands with a wobbling baby boy. The little boy could have been three. She wasn't sure. The father lifted the child up to his shoulders and the baby squealed with joy. Layla smiled. Of course there was some good, too. Seeing the city finally clean up the river was a triumph. But she knew it wasn't for Black folks. So how long would it be before all the Black families from DC were gone? How old would that little boy be?

Layla walked to a steel bridge perched above the water. She looked out at the river. The water was dark and green. She leaned over the steel railing and watched the water rushing downstream. What was she supposed to get from the dream? What was she supposed to do now? Her mother was probably going to die. She had to change something. For the Anaquashtank. The original people of this land. The Anacostan people. For the Yoruba, and Igbo tribes—the enslaved African people who arrived in chains. And her ancestors. They were all connected. Stolen land and stolen people. What were they telling her? She closed her eyes. She'd forgotten how to pray. But for now she decided to fake it. Meditate. Think. Or don't think. She whispered the names to herself over and over. Anaquashtank. Anacostia. Igbo. Yoruba.

Breathe in. Out. In for four. Out five. In Four. Out five. Out six. Layla heard the sound of someone talking in the distance. She squeezed her eyes shut. In four, out four. Breathe. Igbo. Yoruba. Anaquashtank. Anacostia. She imagined the river back then. The people. The songs. Breathe. The sound of laughter pierced the rhythm of Layla's breath. She opened her eyes and stared at a woman laughing at the air. A Black woman in her fifties power-walked her way toward Layla. The woman wore a pale purple track suit, a white visor over a short, relaxed bob. As she punched at the air, her speech lilted up and down in exaggerated extremes. The other side of the conversation buzzed through her baby blue headphones. Layla chewed at her lip as the woman ran in place by her side. She checked her watch and stretched. She spoke in fragments. Waiting patiently, nodding aggressively until she had a chance to speak again.

"Oh no, no—it's my pleasure, Maria.

Haha! I'm more than happy to accommodate—

Well, only if you make your famous pork chops for us again. Hahah!

Well, I'm not vegan just yet. You save the lentils for Booker!

Oh no, absolutely. I would never!"

The woman threw her head back when she laughed. Her smile pinched hard at her face. Layla turned her head and watched. She wondered how long it would take the woman to realize she was being rude.

Layla walked a few paces down the path. She rolled her shoulders. The sounds of the dark green water hushed her back into her breath. In three. Out four. In four, out five. Breathe. Listen to spirit. Breathe. In four, out five. Listen to spirit. Listen.

The woman spoke louder now, her voice audible even from a distance. "Exactly. Haha.

"So what do you think—a city-wide curfew to keep your teenagers in the house? Absolutely reasonable, exactly!

"Oh, right away! Squad cars at both ends of the block.

"Right, right.

"Oh, she's doing great. Almost ten, can you imagine? And she loves to read. I couldn't believe it. I hated books as a kid.

"Hahaha! Exactly!"

Layla took one deep breath in. An apology to Spirit for what she was about to do. She walked to the woman. She stopped a few feet away and cut into the conversation mid-sentence. Layla clapped twice as she yell-talked at the woman. "HELLO." Her smile was wide and strained. The woman looked back at Layla, suddenly worried. "Um. Hold on, Maria. There's someone here—"

"Would you mind keeping it down? Or maybe, going somewhere else for your phone call?" Layla asked with a tight smile.

The woman held her index finger up in the air. "Maria, let me call you back this week. I'm—yes that would be perfect."

The woman clicked a button on her earbud, then crossed her arms. "This is a public space. And I don't appreciate you interrupting my private conversation with—"

"That's kind of my point. I didn't come to the park—a public space, like you said—to listen to your private conversation. Because it's, um, you know—private?"

Layla smiled again. The woman smiled coyly back at her.

"So what are you proposing? No cell phones in DC parks? No talking? No noise at all?"

Layla felt heat growing in her chest.

"If you want me and every stranger out here to know that Maria is going to make you pork chops and you're not vegan and you didn't like books as a kid—then go on. Keep talking. I don't want to know."

The woman held an open hand up.

"People talk on their phones. If you're having a bad day, that's one thing, but that's not my fault."

"Yeah. I was having a bad day. I just found out my mom

is dying, and I'm over here trying to pray and listen to nature. But it was hard with your business conversation just out in the air—and. It's. I know people talk everywhere on their phones, but that doesn't make it okay. We're in a park. And . . . it's rude."

Layla's voice broke. She lost the direction of her argument as her anger melted into sadness.

The woman shifted her weight impatiently, then conceded with a weak smile.

"Well. I. I'm sorry. I didn't know you were praying. Um. Are you alright?" The woman asked.

Layla softened. She sighed and looked out at the river.

"Yeah. It's fine. You were just doing your thing. Whatever." She heard herself say.

The woman unfolded her arms as Layla went on.

"I came here to, like, connect with the ancestors, I guess? But I don't feel connected. I'm trying to pray and listen to god and I can't hear anything. And I don't know what to say. And my mom is dying."

Layla leaned against the railing.

"Cancer?" The woman asked, taking a small step toward Layla.

Layla nodded.

"Mine too." The woman said. She leaned against the railing and looked out at the water. "Six years ago. But the grief is still there. It changes. But it's always there."

Layla watched the woman and waited for her to say more. But the woman said nothing. They stood there in the quiet hush of the river. A pair of white men jogged by. Layla remembered her call. Nacochtank. Igbo. Yoruba. Anacostia. Layla closed her eyes. She could almost hear the chanting from her dream. The drumming. Slow and deep, with syncopated high notes between. The sound of the river. Floating on the water.

"I know you . . ."

Layla opened her eyes and turned to find the woman by her

side, pointing a finger at her.

"No. I don't think we've ever—"

"Are you Layla Jones?"

"Yes . . ." Layla blinked, suddenly puzzled.

The woman laughed. This time a hearty belly laugh.

"The activist," the woman said.

Layla tilted her head and took the woman in.

"You read the article," Layla said dully.

"Oh yes. And I heard you've been calling my office every day for the past two months. No one told me until the article came out. And your little article put a little dent in my approval ratings. So. Now my team thinks we should find a way to work with you. They think it'll help. Even if we're playing for opposing teams. So to speak." The woman said this with a sour smile on her face.

"I'm sorry?" Layla frowned.

"Mira," The woman said, holding her hand out for a shake.

Layla's eyes widened, darting from the woman's outstretched hand to her face, attempting to put the pieces together. She looked completely different without her full face of TV makeup. But Layla could see it now.

"Like, Mira as in Mirabelle? As in Mirabelle Brown, the mayor?"

The woman flashed a pearly politician grin.

"That's the one."

38. ZORA

Zora opened her eyes slowly, wincing into the morning light. Everything hurt. The glimpses of last night burned her brain in hot sparks of recollection. She remembered being in a Lyft. Walking with David into the purple neon glow of LORDE. The bar was packed. There was dancing. Drinking. More dancing, more drinking. Someone kept ordering rounds of DC Tap Water—the disturbingly green cocktail, which seemed to consist of simple syrup, lime, pineapple juice, something blue? And LOTS of bottom-shelf vodka. David was pretending to be very gay so the lesbians wouldn't hate him for being there. Zora remembered rolling her eyes because David's interpretation of very gay appeared to be limited to an endless loop of mediocre voguing and failed death drops. It would have been offensive to anyone who knew how straight he was. But no one knew how straight he was—and the lesbians actually seemed charmed by his display. Zora remembered twerking. And ironically dancing the electric slide to more than one trap song? And then. She remembered craving Jasmine. Her eyes scanning every dark corner of the club. She wanted so badly for Jasmine to appear on the dance floor. Zora wanted to dance with her. And eat croissants with her. Zora wanted to be near her. To kiss her. And the drinking didn't help. It only made the cravings worse. The more she drank, the more she needed to kiss Jasmine. She really fucking needed to kiss Jasmine!

But then she had a brilliantly drunken idea. Maybe she could just kiss someone? Maybe she could kiss anyone. And then Zora remembered curls. Laughter. More dancing. More drinking. A round of Tap Water, swirling green and ice and curls and dancing and . . . Aubrey? Fuck. SHE WENT HOME WITH AUBREY.

Zora held her breath, turned and pulled slowly at her blankets, revealing a nest of curls on her pillow. Aubrey was asleep in her bed. Shit. Shit. Fucking SHIT. Zora closed her eyes. What happened last night? Stupid. Stupid! Sleeping with your ex is SO FUCKED UP. Being into someone else and then sleeping with your high-strung ex from high school (who still has a crush on you) is just stone dumb, rock bottom, fuckboy type shit. Zora sat still on the bed when her train of thought was suddenly interrupted by the sound of windchimes.

The doorbell? No. It couldn't be the doorbell. What time is it? Zora felt around the covers for her phone. Her head pounded. When Aubrey stirred in the bed, Zora froze. Carefully, she slunk from beneath the covers, tiptoed out of the bedroom, through the corridor and leaped down to the foot of the stairs, where she collided into David.

"Fuck!" David shouted.

"Shhhh! God dammit, David!" Zora whispered aggressively.

They stood by the front door and stared at one another—both in a daze, both wearing crumpled pairs of boxers and undershirts. David rubbed his eyes.

"The doorbell?" He croaked.

"NOW?" Zora whispered. David shrugged.

They both lunged down the stairs to the front door. David swung the door open to find their grinning mother holding two tote bags overflowing with produce.

"Mom!" David jumped up and down like a toddler.

"Hello, munchkins!" Leslie pulled David into her arms.

"Mom?" Zora exhaled.

"What are you doing here?"

"Snooping," Leslie said in a matter-of-fact tone as she walked past her children to the kitchen island.

"And I stopped by the farmer's market. I thought y'all could use some fresh fruit."

"Ooh!" David cooed as he rummaged through the grocery bags.

"Help me wash these." Leslie rolled up her sleeves and handed David a basket of blueberries.

"Coffee," Zora murmured as she shuffled to the espresso machine.

David nodded, his mouth already full of berries.

"None for me," Leslie said, smiling.

Zora leaned over the counter, closed her eyes, and pushed the button on the coffee grinder. Both Zora and David cowered at the sound.

"Did you two ... overindulge a bit last night?" Leslie asked sweetly as she handed David a bag of green apples.

"Maybe ...?" David said innocently.

"Mom. Don't judge us. Please," Zoran moaned.

"I don't miss those days," Leslie said, shaking her head.

"Zora took me to the gay bar and plied me with alcohol," David said.

Zora packed the coffee grounds into the metal filter.

"The drinks were his idea. But. Whatever."

"DC Tap Water." David groaned.

"Lord. They're still making that shit?" Leslie gasped in horror.

"Yes," David and Zora said in unison, nodding.

"What's even in that shit? Gin, Kool-Aid and Alizé?"

"What have we done?" Zora whispered into her hands.

"Mmh. I didn't think you two were big drinkers ..." Leslie said as she busied herself with the fridge, filling the shelves with yellow squash and bundles of kale.

Zora locked the metal piece into the espresso machine with an aggressive pull at the handle.

"Mom. Yes. We're hung over. Please. Skip the lecture."

"No lecture. I'm just wondering what inspired all this."

David and Zora stared at each other and said nothing.

"Is this about Jasmine?" Leslie asked.

David's eyes opened wide. Zora folded her arms.

"How do you know about Jasmine?"

"Well..." Leslie hesitated. "I went to a meeting yesterday."

Zora looked up, a flash of recognition blooming on her face. "Right. Y'all met in AA. Of course you did."

Leslie's face colored with surprise. "So you know she's—"

"Yes. I know she's in recovery. She tells everyone." Zora froze for a moment. "Oh God. You're not her sponsor or something, are you?"

"No, honey. Just a friend in the rooms. And when we met, neither of us knew about this...connection," Leslie tilted her head.

Zora turned back to the machine. She fiddled with the dials until it hummed. She turned and sat at the island, waiting for her mother to speak. Leslie stared back at her, waiting.

Zora sighed. "Yes, Mom. I got too drunk because I like a girl—a girl you've apparently already met and shared intimate secrets with. What else?" Zora's voice was flat.

David raised an eyebrow. Of course he knew this. They were both heartbroken. But they were brothers. They didn't ordinarily say these things aloud.

Leslie took a seat at the island. "I just wanted to check in. Of course I support everyone you...show an interest in. I just wanted to ask." Leslie's voice became more hesitant as she went on.

"Ask what?"

"How do you feel about dating someone in recovery?" Leslie asked.

"I feel fine. What does that have to do with anything?"

"Well, you didn't speak to me for my first few years." Leslie's tone remained steady.

David jumped as his phone buzzed on the island counter. He stood and stepped away, tapping at the screen.

"My relationship with you is a bit different. For obvious reasons. And I actually have a lot of respect for people in recovery. Even if it took me a while with you." Zora said. "Anyway. It's irrelevant. I can't date Jasmine. And David can't date Ella. Dad basically told us he would fire and disown us. So. It's irrelevant." Zora's words trailed off as she rummaged through the fridge. She emerged with the carton of milk.

David lifted his head, his eyes still fixed on the screen. "Hey Zo. You wanna go back to Lorde tonight? I heard it's karaoke."

Zora squinted. "You heard? Who are you texting?"

"That lesbian I was dancing with at the end of the night? Xena?"

"Xena. Of course." Zora rolled her eyes.

Leslie stood. "Who is Ella? And what does your father have to do with anything?"

Zora sighed. "It's a very, very long story."

"Can you give me the bullet points?" Leslie asked, folding her arms.

David held his hands up. "I got this. Okay So. Zora likes Jasmine Jones, and I really like her sister Ella Jones, and the third sister—Layla is basically plotting the downfall of dad's company. Well not dad's company specifically. She's . . . you know fighting for affordable housing and what not. But dad's new project is like the thing she's focused on right now? And last week—a very big, kind of embarrassing article ran in *The Post*. And in this article, Layla Jones maybe a little bit called dad an Uncle Tom or Black colonizer or something—"

"A high-tech house slave. I read the article," Leslie interrupted.

"You read it?" David asked, still looking down at his phone.

"I got twenty-eight missed calls about that article; of course I read it. Everyone read it," Leslie replied.

"Well, because of Layla and that article, BIG, BIG investors are pulling out of the development and so basically the whole Jones family is off-limits." David said, catching his breath.

Leslie did the math in her head. She spoke slowly

"So the activist in the gentrification article is the sister . . . of . . . the two sisters you two are both in love with?" Leslie asked.

"Yes," David said. He pointed affirmingly at Leslie.

"No. No. He's in love. I don't know what I am," Zora said.

"And your father forbade you from dating them?" Leslie asked, still working on the calculation.

"Yes," David and Zora replied and nodded in unison.

Zora turned back to the counter and focused on steaming the milk.

Leslie sighed. She closed her eyes, searching for calm.

"Well, I enjoyed the article. I think it said a lot of things that needed to be said. And I like Jasmine. If that counts for anything."

"Mom, we can't date them." Zora said, shaking her head. Zora poured the espresso and handed a steaming cup to David. Zora looked down at her cup as she spoke. "Dad gave us everything. Don't you think we kind of owe him?"

Leslie sighed. "I know your father gave you everything. He is an incredible man. He would fight the whole entire world to keep you two safe. And you should feel deeply loyal toward him. I would never argue that point." Leslie shook her head. "And I know I haven't been nearly as present as your father. But I'm still your mother. And I have to tell you he has no say over who you date. And you don't owe him your happiness."

Zora considered this. "Mom. David and I are fine. We'll be fine! We have a beautiful home, great jobs. We're going to be fine. OKAY? Everything is FINE." Zora said. She took a satisfied sip of her steaming coffee.

"Maybe I could speak with your father," Leslie began.

David shook his head. "He's pissed. I think that might make everything worse."

Zora flinched at the sound of footsteps down the hall. Aubrey beamed as she walked cheerily into the kitchen. "Mrs. Scott? David!"

Zora coughed.

Leslie and David both raised their eyebrows.

"You guys remember Aubrey. From Sidwell?" Zora said as she sprinted to the doorway.

"Hello, Aubrey. Please call me Leslie," Leslie said tenderly.

"Hey Bree," David added.

"It's so good to see you both! Wow, Mrs. Scott . . . I mean Leslie, you look incredible! You betta get it, girl!"

Leslie smiled and nodded.

"Aubrey, would you like some coffee or something to eat?" Zora asked hurriedly.

"No, I only drink water in the mornings actually, and I have to run," Aubrey began.

"Oh no. Sorry to see you go." David frowned, cutting a glance at Zora.

Aubrey waved enthusiastically as Zora hurriedly ushered her into the foyer.

"I'm so sorry, Aubrey, it's kind of an impromptu family meeting in there. Can I get you a Lyft? Do you have everything you need? Phone, keys, wallet?" Zora asked.

"I do." Aubrey nodded and her curls bounced cheerfully.

Zora took a breath. Aubrey stared back, her eyes growing wider.

"What?" Aubrey snapped.

"I'm so, so sorry Aubrey. I shouldn't have. I shouldn't have taken you home last night. I shouldn't have led you on. It's not fair to you. I can't start anything with you. Or anyone right now.

And I wouldn't normally act this way, but I'm in a really strange place, and my mom is here and I'm just not sure I can—"

Aubrey shook her head.

"Aw sweetie. Let me stop you there." Aubrey held her hand up in the air. Zora blinked.

"We did not have sex last night. I came home with you because you and David were wasted. I wanted to make sure you got home safely. And you literally could NOT stop talking about Jasmine. And at some point in the night you said we should kiss and I told you that was very stupid and very presumptuous of you." Aubrey opened the door with sharp precision.

"Ah," Zora said with a nod. Aubrey turned. She looked back with an expression of benevolent pity.

"Zora. You are fine, or whatever. But let me tell you something. There's way more to being fine than a pretty face and nice clothes. Okay? Good looks and money are lovely. And maybe they got you by in your twenties, but, Zora, we are grown. Mmmkay? Girls like me have standards. I don't settle for crumbs. And, Zora, what you got going on right now?" Aubrey's hand scanned Zora up and down like a metal detector. "You are looking very crumby this morning. And I say that with love." Aubrey cocked her head to the side and smiled.

Zora nodded slowly.

"I. Yes. I receive that." Aubrey gently patted Zora on the chest.

"Good. Do your best. I wish you all the luck." Aubrey turned on her heel and switched down the driveway to her car.

"Th-thank you Aubrey." Zora stuttered. She stood in the door for a moment and watched Aubrey's car speed down the road.

When Zora slunk back into the kitchen doorway, David and Leslie stared at her blankly.

David sipped at his coffee with his pinky in the air.

Zora sighed. She walked to the sofa and slowly slid down

onto the cushions. She lay on her back and stared up at the ceiling.

David and Leslie frowned at each other, watching from the kitchen.

Leslie shifted in her seat.

"Honey. It's completely natural for you to go out and drink and spend time with young women. As long as you're communicating and it's consensual."

"I know, Mom. And we didn't sleep together. Apparently." Zora said. She covered her face with a cushion.

"And you want to make sure you're not using alcohol, or relationships, to fill a god-sized hole..." Leslie said, gently.

"Or a Jasmine-sized hole..." David added, snickering.

Zora groaned into the cushion.

David's phone buzzed again. He looked down and tapped at the screen.

"So Zora. In the interest of spending some consensual time with young women, how about karaoke at Lorde tonight?"

Zora sat up.

"David, are you fucking kidding me?"

David shrugged. "How about this time, no DC Tap Water?"

Zora sighed. "Shit. Why not?"

39. JASMINE

Jasmine stared down at the text from Marble. She sighed.

> Marble: Tonight's fit shld be fashion/editorial/weird but make it sexy. LOL
> Jasmine: ???? What.

Jasmine slid down the side of her bed, already exhausted. She looked up at her closet.

Then back down at the phone.

> Marble: Editorial. Like. Magazine. Fancy. WEIRD. And Scary to straight people. But also cute/sexy. Storytelling.
> Jasmine: …….. WHAT.

Jasmine stood and tentatively approached the closet. She didn't have much in the way of fancy clothing. She lifted a black leather vest from its hanger, wondering if it would still fit.

> Marble: No 2010's butch realness.
> Jasmine: . . .
> Marble: No button dwns no vests.
> Jasmine: That's kind of all I have.

Marble: Find something else. This is not an indigo girls concert.

Jasmine laughed. Am I that guy now? The old lesbian who only wears button-down shirts and vests and hates going out after 8:00 p.m.? Shit. Jasmine sighed. Maybe I am that guy. She looked down at her phone. It was already ten. Way past a baker's bedtime. And Marble probably wouldn't pick her up until eleven. Jasmine imagined how her night would feel if she stayed in. Maybe she'd watch some bad TV. Eat chips. Curl up in bed. Maybe it would be fun! Get to sleep early. Feel rested in the morning. That would be nice, wouldn't it? Jasmine groaned. Who was she kidding? That's not how the night would go. She would stay up. She would try as hard as she possibly could to NOT THINK about Zora. Distract herself with snacks and movies, and inevitably her mind would wander back.

She stood up suddenly. I'm going. That's it. I'm just going. I'm gonna dress up and have fun and maybe I won't have fun but I'm gonna fucking try and that's that. This is what recovery taught her to do. Tonight—it's time for OPPOSITE ACTION! The most counterintuitive yet weirdly effective strategy she had. When you're depressed and all you want to do is collapse into your bed and close the blinds on everything and everyone—THAT'S when you do the opposite thing. Jasmine channeled her higher power. AZUL. Tell me what to do.

Take a fucking shower. Put on a fucking ridiculous costume. Dance to one whole terrible song the whole way through without stopping. When you want to drink, or disappear or drink–do something extraordinarily beautiful. Gorgeous. Joyful. Make bad art! Help someone who needs it more than you. Call someone in pain. Run a mile. And if you can't do anything else—baby, put on some fucking eyeliner.

Jasmine sighed. She slid the 2010's butch leather vest back onto its hanger and wrestled her way to the back of the closet. Pushing past a variety of patterned button-downs, slacks, lukewarm androgynous looks, and responsible grown-up sweaters. At the back of the closet, she found the young and dumb section of her wardrobe. Her clubkid slutty phase looks. Leotards. A dress made entirely of lace. A Where's Waldo cropped sweater vest. A sea of sequins. And there it was. The lime-green twink boy scout romper. Cuffed shorts, cuffed sleeves, and the patch of some fictional boy scout troop sewn on the back with red thread. Jasmine smiled. She used to swim in it, but it probably wouldn't fit anymore. Her late thirties metabolism plus the years of flaky pastries and butter had softened and expanded her shape. She pulled the romper from its hanger and held it up in the mirror. She stepped into the short shorts. It . . . sort of fit. She pulled her arms into the sleeves and turned in the mirror. Well. Her ass was certainly fatter. One small gift of growing older and constantly eating croissants. It was tight. But it fit. Jasmine zipped the romper to her neck and slid her hands into the pockets. Boyish. Camp. Gay. Not a vest. She slid into her black boots and tightened the laces. She turned in the mirror. Marble would be okay with the fit, but not quite satisfied. It was too simple.

Jasmine walked down the hall. She heard music blaring from the tinny speaker. She walked into the bathroom, finding Ella done up and dancing in a floor-length red dress. She pursed her lips and drew a line up and down and up at Jasmine's outfit.

"Okay. That's cute. But we're doing editorial." Ella whispered magic into the word.

"Jesus, can't you tell me what that means please???" Jasmine frowned.

"Oh darling. It's fashion. It's witchy! It's storytelling!" Ella twirled her fingers in the air, flashing long plum purple nails.

"So Marble texted you too?" Jasmine replied, rolling her eyes.

"Yes they did." Ella turned back to the mirror. She applied a thick coat of red mascara, and her lashes became the antennae of some poisonous tropical insect. She turned back and pointed to Jasmine's face.

"Editorial."

"Yeah, yeah I get it. You want me to put on something that looks kind of bad."

"Bitch. It's ... fashion. Not your everyday," Ella said as she focused her attention back on the mirror.

Jasmine watched her.

"Ella, I know you like to become a drag queen when you get dressed up. But don't call me bitch, bitch."

"What about cunt?" Ella asked, tapping her fingernails on the mirror. Jasmine folded her arms.

"You seem different. Like. Happy." Jasmine's tone turned slightly accusatory.

Ella shrugged. "Yeah. Well. I'm going out. That helps."

Jasmine nodded. "Yeah." Ella scattered a collection of brushes and palettes into the bowl of the sink.

"Come on. Look at this delicious spread of cosmetics. Tell me a story."

Jasmine stood next to Ella, and they painted their faces side by side. Jasmine smudged her fingertips into a pigmented green circle of eyeshadow.

Ella cut her eyes to Jasmine, watching her paint.

"More," Ella said, grinning.

Jasmine sighed. She smeared her fingers across her face, a bar of neon green melting from her eyelids to her ears.

Ella tipped head.

"Okay, I like this for you. It's giving Bowie. But I want more. Let's go all the way to Grace Jones, baby. Into the hair."

"Huh?" Jasmine stared.

Ella smudged her finger into the green dust and pushed

the color farther, past the prickling line of Jasmine's faded hair. The color glowed through the shadow of her short hair. A green mask, a thin sparkling veil disappearing into her scalp.

"Wow." Jasmine raised an eyebrow in the mirror.

Ella nodded.

"Very editorial." Ella whispered.

"Whatever you say." Jasmine whispered back. But she caught her reflection in the mirror and felt something lifting. For a second there, she looked like she wasn't someone trying to do a thing. She looked like a creature from another world. Strange and confident.

Layla padded in, wearing an oversized pair of pajamas and slippers. She stared at her sisters in the mirror. "Woaaah."

Ella gave Layla a spin.

Jasmine shook her head. She pulled Layla into the bathroom. "Layla, please come with us. It's more fun when you come. You're young and cool and you make us look cooler."

"I would love to join you. But I have to keep working on the action."

Ella pulled Layla into an embrace. Jasmine grinned.

Layla stared at Ella. "Wow. You look like a couple of gorgeous gay clowns."

Jasmine laughed. "Thanks?"

Marble arrived wearing what could only be described as a leopard-print stocking. Some long, see-through turquoise nylon thing with a clear plastic-pink raincoat over it, a pair of platform sneakers, and oversized pink glasses. Ella finished her look off with a whimsical feather fascinator that constantly tickled at the air. Ella and Marble decided to go sober in solidarity with Jasmine, despite her protests.

By the time Jasmine, Marble and Ella walked into LORDE, they were high on confidence. They'd matched their silly gay editorial outfits with fabulously inflated alter egos. They danced in, feeling all Soul Train and glittery, but they were not greeted with applause and confetti. Instead, the room full of polite queers stared back at them blankly. Jasmine glanced around the dark room. Everyone looked sensible. Slow moving hordes of folks donned button-down shirts, plain tees, slacks and vests. Jasmine pulled self-consciously at the cuffs of her too short shorts.

"Did we come on the wrong night or something?" She hissed into Marble's ear.

"Nope. Karaoke night. See?" Marble pointed at the stage bathed in purple light where a pair of studly folks were singing a drunken rendition of "If I Ever" by Shai.

"What kind of Karaoke night? Is it Karaoke fashion night? Karaoke Studio 54? Karaoke editorial night??" Jasmine hissed.

"Nope. Just plain Karaoke. Tonight might be '90s-themed? Think." Marble shrugged.

"Marble. Why are we dressed like this? Why did you insist that we dress like this??" Jasmine shouted in the empty space of a music break. A gaggle of stylish femmes shot an icy glance at them.

"Because it's fun." Marble giggled. They skipped onto the empty dance floor. Jasmine turned her head. Where the fuck did Ella go? She squinted at the shrill voices crackling through the speakers.

Marble was two-stepping their way back to Jasmine.

"You wanna sing something together?"

"Absolutely not," Jasmine said, nodding exaggeratedly.

"Okay." Marble lifted a thumbs up and switched their way to the DJ booth.

"Marble what—" Jasmine called out as they disappeared through the crowd.

Jasmine put her hands in her pocket and prayed she didn't run into an ex. This looked bad. Dressed up at the bar on a Wednesday. Alone. She pretended to be interested in the singers on stage. She nodded her head absent-mindedly. Yep. I'm very confident. Yep. I'm wearing a tulle bow tie. This is normal.

Marble bounced back across the dance floor.

"Why and how are you this cheerful?" Jasmine stared at Marble. The room erupted in applause.

"Okay Boy baaaaand!" The DJ, an old-school woman who looked like Ice-T's twin sister, sang into her muffled mic.

"All right, next up we got Marble and Jasmine with the ultimate '90s slow jam classic by the one and only Janet, haha! MISS JACKSON if ya nasty. What time? Any time and where? Any place, y'all. Now I see some of y'all younguns in here. Some of y'all asses probably got conceived to this song. Let's give it up for Marble and Jasmine!"

Jasmine squinted her eyes closed. No. No. No. The applause melted into a muffled white noise. Marble snatched Jasmine's hand and pulled her to the stage. Jasmine felt her feet moving without her. Opposite action. Do the thing. Even if it's the most embarrassing, horrific thing, corny thing . . .

The gentle push of a guitar, the beat, the snaps laced the air. The song cast a spell of remembering. A few heads nodded with recognition. The room turned into a slow undulating wave of nostalgia. A dance floor full of grown black and brown folks closing their eyes, giving shape and rhythm to desire. Jasmine felt suddenly high on the cinematic lull of the moment. Like none of it was real. The warm glow of the purple stage light and the melodies from her adolescence. Being too young to know what love or sex was but wanting it so badly. Falling in love with every girl who looked her in the eye. Jasmine remembered watching the music video. Janet's glowing golden skin. Her jeans opening. The pretty love interest kissing her belly.

Jasmine tipped her head back. Bathed in white and purple light.

Marble beamed, handing Jasmine the microphone.

"In the thundering rain stare into my eyes." Jasmine heard herself singing low. Not Janet's high tone. Instead, she sang in a soft, deep whisper. The lights in the club slowed to the pace of the song. Marble wasn't singing. They just two-stepped and whispered affirmations like a slow jam hype person.

"Yeah. Yeah. My eyes. Riiiiight," Marble whispered.

Jasmine reached out to squeeze Marble's hand aggressively.

Marble nodded and beamed at Jasmine's side.

The room swayed to the rhythm of the beat.

Marble stepped to the mic and sang with her.

"I can feel your hands moving up my thighs. Skirt around my waist. Wall against my face. I can feel your lips."

Jasmine winced. Marble's voice was crude, almost talky. But their enthusiasm and their scandalous see-through dress made up for any lack of skills.

"I don't wanna stop just because people walking by are watching us. I don't give a damn what they think. I want you now."

A half-dozen queers and lesbians sang along at the foot of the stage. Marble and Jasmine turned to each other and back to the room.

"I don't wanna stop just because—"

Jasmine noticed the silhouette of a tall woman with long locs on the dance floor. The woman's shape reminded her of Zora. The grace in her movement. The burning ember of her. Jasmine thought of Leslie. She should have known they were related. But what were the odds? Jasmine felt small. She pictured the naive kid she used to be. Wishing for love. Wishing, nearly begging to be heartbroken. Because that heartbreak meant she was alive. She was human. She had a wide ocean of heart, and she wanted it all. She wished to be wrapped up in an embrace. She wished the woman on the dance floor really was Zora.

Jasmine and Marble danced on the stage together. Jasmine sang the harmonies, her voice soaring just below Marble's. Marble stepped away from their mic and watched Jasmine sing on her own.

"Anytime. Anyplace. I don't care who's around."

Jasmine stared at the woman on the dance floor as she walked toward the stage. No. It can't be. It can't. Jasmine's voice caught on the lyric. Only air escaped her lips. It was her. Zora's brown skin glowed in the purple neon light. She looked up at Jasmine. Jasmine lost her words. She lost her place in the song. She stared down at Zora. Something about being in the middle of a '90s slow jam. It made things possible. In the light of the '90s R&B yearning—even the corniest sincerity looked beautiful. Jasmine wasn't stupid. She knew someone like Zora might never admit to wanting her. Zora's pride couldn't allow that kind of vulnerability. But in that moment, in the middle of a Janet song, Jasmine could see pleading in Zora's eyes. A question she wouldn't ask. Zora's eyes told Jasmine everything. I want you. I need you. I'm sorry. Jasmine knew she'd regret this, but she had no choice. Marble grinned sheepishly as they finished the song alone. The room full of queers watched as Jasmine stepped off the stage, took Zora's hand, and pulled her across the room.
    Jasmine and Zora ducked into the darkness of the hallway. They dodged a pair of giggling gay boys and slipped into the bathroom. Jasmine pushed Zora against the black tile of the bathroom wall. Their lips pressed together, their breath hot and quick. Zora drew her fingertips against Jasmine's scalp. Jasmine felt her clit rising against the seam of her romper. Zora pushed Jasmine against her thigh, cupping her ass high. Jasmine felt her whole-body relaxing, melting beneath the warm pressure of Zora's tongue. She pushed her body harder into Zora. Zora's arms tensing against the cold tile. Their hands moved with familiar urgency. But there was something different between them now. Surrender. Jasmine gave in to Zora's pleading eyes looking up at her. Zora was giving in to Jasmine's power. And the thickness of judgment in the air. Everyone telling them no. You're not allowed. You're not supposed to. But it only drew them closer. Zora pulled her thigh up between Jasmine's legs, lifting her for a moment. Jasmine gasped. Her head tilted back.

A group of loudly chatting bois burst into the bathroom. Their laughter struck silent by the sight of Jasmine and Zora scrambling to detangle and pretend they were both casually leaning against the wall. Just hanging out in the bathroom. Zora looked studiously down at her wristwatch. Jasmine studied her nails. One boi paused before them, her thick eyebrow raised high. She bowed politely.

"Well good evening, lovers. Please don't stop on our account!" Her friends giggled as they leaned toward the mirror to examine their reflections.

Zora turned to Jasmine.

"Come over?"

Jasmine smiled, thinking about the last time she slept over. Then she winced, remembering how that night ended.

"Ella's still here. I shouldn't leave her."

"You know this was a setup, right?" Zora said.

"What do you mean?" Jasmine asked.

"Ella and David." Zora said, nodding.

"Oh. Wow." Jasmine replied.

"Yeah. I figured it out when I saw you."

"Yep. That makes sense." Jasmine said.

Zora stepped closer to Jasmine. She grazed Jasmine's hair with her fingertips, admiring the wild green makeup in her hair.

Jasmine ignored the nosy stares of the other queers in the bathroom.

"Want to take a walk? There's a Black-owned bookshop down the street. We could go get tea and come back?"

"Perfect," Zora said, nodding.

The boi at the mirror called out to them as they scurried out of the bathroom.

"You kids have fun now!"

40. ZORA

Zora and Jasmine stepped from neon purple into the traces of a summer storm. The air was wet and heavy. Thick droplets of rain fell around them. Shimmering puddles lined the street, reflecting the warm orange of the streetlights. The air smelled of hot concrete, rain, earth. Jasmine skipped out onto the sidewalk. Opening her palms up to the sky. Zora laughed, squinting slightly up at the rain. They walked in silence, both looking ahead. The quiet felt right, like a rest in the music.

"I'm sorry about your mom," Zora whispered, watching Jasmine for a reaction.

Jasmine paused slightly, then nodded and went on dance-walking. She twirled her hands and fingers into the air.

"It's okay. We knew it might come back. I think she knew it would."

Zora looked up the street at the red and white car lights pulling into the Golden Skillet lot.

"Are you okay?" Zora asked softly.

Jasmine took a moment to consider the question.

"I think so," she said, nodding.

Zora smiled.

"How did you know? About my mom..." Jasmine asked suddenly.

"David. I have a feeling he's been reaching out to Ella..."

Jasmine stood up straighter. "Well, the setup tonight made that pretty clear. And that explains why she's so happy lately."

"Yeah," Zora said, giggling.

"Aren't our families at war? Or something?" Jasmine asked through her smile.

"Or something." Zora replied, pulling Jasmine into her. They kissed tenderly. This time the kiss was not just a prelude to sex. It was its own moment, a different kind of intimacy. Zora searched for something in Jasmine's eyes. Jasmine pretended not to notice Zora staring. She turned and walked on.

"So, did you come and kiss me because my mom is dying? Or because you really wanted to come and kiss me?" Jasmine asked with a skip in her step. Zora frowned.

"Wow. You really figured me out, Jasmine. Nothing turns me on more than a girl with a dying mom. But no, that's not why I'm here."

"Why are you here?" Jasmine asked.

Zora peered down the street.

"So what bookstore is open this late on a weekend?"

"It's sort of a cafe too. Actually, this is the spot that inspired me to open my place."

"Cool!"

"I'm surprised you don't know it. It's called Tea Cake." Jasmine stared at Zora expectantly.

Zora stared back, confused.

"You know, from Their Eyes Were Watching God? The book??"

Zora squinted into space. "Was he the hot young boyfriend?"

Jasmine laughed. Her laughter made Zora glow with pride. Nothing felt better than making Jasmine laugh.

"I assumed you were named after Zora Neale Hurston?" Jasmine asked, clutching at Zora's jacket.

Zora sighed. "I was. And I probably read the book four times. But I didn't really get it, you know? I think my mom was more into that stuff than I ever was." Zora shrugged.

Jasmine shook her head. "Oh you sweet, sweet, poor child." Jasmine sucked her teeth and took Zora's head in her hands. "Raised with all the money and riches in the world but no poetry to speak of." She pinched Zora's cheek as she attempted to squirm away.

"I have plenty of poetry, thank you. I just don't like metaphors."

"Ha!" Jasmine nearly shouted. "I'll bet you five dollars, if you read that book with me, you'll fall in love with that metaphor. It's like copper siding on a building. Or a silver accent wall. It doesn't have a specific scientific function. It's this beautiful, open thing. You make it yours." Jasmine's hands danced in the air to embellish the phrase.

"Fine!" Zora teased.

Jasmine laughed and took Zora's hand in hers. They walked and swung arms and laughed to the end of the block when Jasmine's laughter suddenly faded into silence. She stood frozen, looking up at the dark storefront window.

Just below Tea Cake written in cursive lettering on the window, a large FOR LEASE sign stared out at them. Jasmine raced to the window, peering in, her eyes darting around, searching for something familiar. She looked down at her phone and typed something.

Zora moved closer to her. Jasmine's hands fell to her sides as her eyes glazed over.

"Maybe they moved?" Zora asked.

Jasmine peered into the dark window. Zora stepped closer.

"A lot of independent bookstores are closing. It's a tough business to keep going these days."

Jasmine didn't move.

"Most brick-and-mortar retail folds these days."

"Well, you would know." Jasmine replied dully.

"What does that mean?"

"This wasn't just an independent bookstore. This was a BLACK-OWNED bookstore. In what used to be a fucking BLACK city." Jasmine's voice grew louder.

"This was beautiful. It was full of community and it's FUCKING GONE." Jasmine turned and walked to the edge of the sidewalk. She sank to the ground and sat on the curb.

Zora slowly followed her. She looked down at the wet ground.

"I'm sorry, Jasmine."

Jasmine looked wearily up at Zora. "What do you believe in, Zora?"

"What do you mean?"

"I mean your dad is a great businessman. And capitalism is not his fault, and gentrification is not his fault, and he can get rich off the places where Black folks lived for generations. Fine. That's fine. You worked for him your whole life because he's your father and family and you are all about loyalty. That's fine. But what do you believe in? Is this what you want to do your whole life?"

Jasmine looked up, waiting for Zora to answer. Zora looked out at the empty street. She sighed, looked down at Jasmine, and said nothing. Jasmine nodded slowly. She stood and folded her arms.

"I think we got it right the first time." Jasmine said. She looked at Zora, but Zora could tell she wasn't really looking. Like her eyes were fixed on something in the distance. Jasmine's eyes wouldn't meet Zora's. Jasmine studied a puddle on the sidewalk.

"I know it's not fair. I want to do more to change what my dad is doing. I'm trying to do more—" Zora began.

"Will you come to Layla's protest?" Jasmine asked.

Zora sighed. "I don't think I can, Jasmine." She waited for Jasmine's gaze to meet hers.

"Well, I'll be there." Jasmine said. "Goodnight, Zora."

Jasmine walked back down the street toward the glowing purple light. Zora watched her walk away.

41. JASMINE

Jasmine followed signs to Rehoboth. She stared out at the stretch of highway, the lush green trees and partitions racing by. Ro turned to smile at her; then she tilted her head back up to the sunlight in the window. In the back seat, Marble and Ella leaned to the left. Both falling lazily in and out of sleep. Layla stared at her phone. Scanning her inbox for last-minute loose ends. This last beach trip was mostly for Layla. Her laser focus had become obsessive. She was secretive about meetings she took. She'd disappear into her computer for hours. Ro decided she needed the ocean. They all did. Ro and Ella teamed up to DJ, and they decided to play only musicians from the DMV the entire trip. Meshell Ndegeocello, Chuck Brown, Gaye, Ellington, Ginuwine, Rare Essence and Eva Cassidy for three hours.

Jasmine exhaled dramatically. She yelled over the music.
"Can we skip this song please?"
"Why?" Ella asked, her eyes stuck on the phone.
"Ella. Just skip it." Jasmine sighed.
Ella stared at Jasmine in the rearview mirror for a moment, then skipped to Meshell Ndegeocello's "May This Be Love. "
The whole car felt suddenly like underwater with a shimmering splash of cymbals. A cushion-muffled bass drum and Rhodes floated up like bubbles. Strings seared through the

blue tones like ribbons of sunlight. Jasmine's head tilted back. She smiled. Dia's song. It occurred to Jasmine that she could imagine Dia differently now. She still felt the love, but there was a new kind of tenderness there. Like she stepped back and the photograph of Dia's face had context. A landscape, or a source of light she hadn't noticed before. How strange the way new love could make the others look farther away. Not gone. Just distant. The woman she thought she would marry smiles at the lens. She's always smiling. She's always perfect. She's not cruel. From this distance, Jasmine wasn't sure how many details were true. Was she ever really happy with Dia? When she was so unhappy in her own skin, could she have been? She knew she was some kind of happy now. A quiet, grounded version of herself. Closer to God. Smiling in meditation. Falling for a prince with all the wrong values. Driving her family to the beach. Still grateful and offering herself grace for wanting. Jasmine's mind floated and spun in the murky blue water of the song. Zora. Living, breathing, her eyes glimmering in the purple stage lights. Looking up at Jasmine.

Jasmine watched Layla's head fall onto Marble's shoulder, her eyes closing slowly. Marble watched Layla fall asleep. Ella stared out the window.

Marble and the Jones women walked over the dune. Their walk was slow and reverent. They took their time, as if they'd never seen the ocean before. Layla let out a guttural moan. She walked determinedly to the waves and into the water with all her clothes on.

"Wow," Marble said as they stood still, watching Layla dive into a wave.

The beach was nearly empty. One sprinkle of young, beautiful gay men in stylish short trunks. And farther down the beach sat two families; they looked like aging versions of the young men. Older, fatter, happier men with pair of awkward tween kids.

Ella pushed the umbrella into the sand. Ro opened up the

beach chairs. Marble just stood and watched Layla. Jasmine sighed. Marble was constantly falling in love with pretty girls. It was probably inevitable that they would fall in love with Layla. Ro's paperback creaked as she cracked it open. Her glossy book cover reflected with sunlight.

"Whatchareading?" Marble asked, settling onto their beach towel.

"*Black Sun Signs: An African American Guide to the Zodiac*," Ro said, waving her book in the air.

"Very cool." Marble smiled. They slid on a pair of oversized emerald green glasses.

Jasmine lay back on her towel. She looked up and watched white clouds drifting in a baby blue sky.

Jasmine walked to the water and stared out at the waves. She inhaled sharply as her feet reached the cold foaming water. The sand and surf fizzed with salty effervescence. The spray sounded like a million tiny stones dancing into one another and whispering with each wave. Ro appeared by Jasmine's side, smiling at Layla as she played and laughed in the waves.

"You used to stay in the water for hours. All three of you," Ro said.

"I know."

"No matter how big the waves were, you'd be in there," Ro said, grinning.

Jasmine nodded and glanced over at her mother.

"And now?" Jasmine asked. Ro thought for a moment.

"Well. You're careful now. It's very grown up," Ro said. She squeezed Jasmine's hand.

"Mom."

Ro exhaled. "Jasmine. I'm sorry I wasn't there more. Dia left—"

Jasmine watched the ocean churning.

"I didn't know how hard it was for you," Ro said.

"Mom. It's okay."

Layla let out a howl, her arms in the air.

"It was the riptide," Jasmine said, folding her arms. "When I was sixteen, I got pulled out. I looked back and the beach was so far away."

Ro furrowed her brow, searching for the memory.

"Was I there?"

"No. I think I was with friends. It was fine. I just swam with it. I knew it would get worse if I struggled. So I didn't struggle. I mean I was fucking scared to death. My heart was beating out of my chest. But eventually I just . . . floated back."

"You knew what to do."

"You taught me." Jasmine watched her mother try to hide her prideful smile.

Jasmine sighed. "But since then, I've been a bit scared of the ocean."

"Cautious. That's smart. Be scared." Ro nodded.

They watched as Ella and Marble walked into the waves.

"Be scared and get in anyway." Ro walked back to join Layla, Ella and Ro.

Jasmine walked into the ocean. She jumped up into the foaming crash of the surf. Her body seized up with the cold. Beads of salt water gleamed like jewels on her cheeks. She stumbled and tripped into the crash of the wave. Jasmine felt the water rise up her body. Her toes floated up from the sandy floor. She exhaled. The cold salt water and the waves lifted and held her. She felt the moon and the earth and the pull between them. She was breathless. It felt just like that blue green. That crashing and foaming into falling in love. Like fucking and coming and dying and giving birth and being born at one time. There, in the peak of a wave on the coast of the country, Jasmine knew exactly what to do.

42. ZORA

Zora woke up at 4 a.m. from a dream. She was being chased by a winged dinosaur. Or some kind of giant bird. Maybe it was an emu. It was something large and fast and it was going to eat her. That's all she could remember when she woke up in a sweat. She tossed and turned for an hour. Maybe a quick orgasm would help her sleep. She tried masturbating. Some backshot POV hetero porn. The orgasm was quick and cheap. Just about as pleasurable as a good sneeze. And she still couldn't sleep. So, she sat up in bed, opened her laptop, and scrolled through her notes again and again and again. This made sense. This was right. This was a good idea. She walked the length of her room in the dark. She ironed her shirt until each crease looked sharp enough to cut glass. She sat in the dark kitchen, fully dressed in fitted slacks and crisp button-down, sipping espresso and staring at the glossy concrete floor. David slid his way into the kitchen wearing loose pajama pants and one sock. He jumped at the sight of Zora's rigid figure.

"Jesus," David gasped, clutching his pearls.

"Hey," Zora replied coolly.

David watched his sister carefully as he opened the fridge.

"You okay?"

"I'm good."

"Good . . ." David nodded slowly.

Zora stood suddenly, folded her arms. "I'm nervous." She furrowed her brows as she spoke.

"You?"

"Yeah."

"Wow. I don't even know what to say. Being scared of dad was always my job." David was getting too much pleasure out of this.

"Yeah well." Zora paced around the island. David chased her down and placed his hands on her shoulders.

"OKAY. Breathe. I'm on your side. This is a really, really good proposal. And the worst-case scenario is that he'll say no. Right?" David said, shrugging.

Zora nodded. It wasn't as simple as that. If their dad said no, she'd have to leave the company. Everything she had, she got from working for her father. The car, the shining espresso machine, the glossy concrete floor she stood on.

"Do you want me to be there today?" David asked, suddenly solemn.

Zora shook her head.

"I'll be okay."

The Scott Group Office was eerily quiet. Zora sat in the empty boardroom. The air was too cold. The office was always too cold in the summertime. Zora ran her palm along the smooth surface of the blond wooden table. She wondered what kind of wood it was. Cedar? Or cypress? What kind of tree lived and died to become a boardroom table in this glass box? She stood and gazed out the window at nothing. She paced; then she sat back down. She felt like a child. She couldn't remember the last time she was nervous to see her father.

Zora heard Malcolm before she saw him. His laughter bounded down the hallway. Zora straightened in her chair. Suddenly feeling all the sleep she didn't get last night.

"Hi, honey." Malcolm's smile beamed as he entered the boardroom. Eric followed in Malcolm's shadow—his arms full of folders and to-go cups.

"Hey, Zora." Eric smiled up at her as he arranged the folders on the table. Zora clocked Eric's orange-and-tan plaid suit and managed a smile.

"Cool suit, Eric," she said as he handed her a coffee. He nearly froze in his tracks.

"Wow. Um. Thank you, Zora. You know. I always really admired your style." Eric stammered nervously.

Zora sighed. She was nervous. Pacing. She was complimenting white men. Something was clearly very wrong with her.

"That's kind, Eric. Thank you." Zora said.

"I'll have you know she gets her style from me." Malcolm grinned and plucked at Zora's collar.

He sat by her side. Zora sat down slowly and held her breath as Malcolm opened his folder.

"Where's Leo?" Malcolm asked. Zora swallowed.

"He's not coming." She exhaled.

Eric turned the pages in his folder, pretending to look for something.

"We're finalizing the plans. This was supposed to be his lead—" Eric said.

"Leo isn't coming," Zora said flatly.

Malcolm stared down at the documents.

"This is sort of," Zora took a breath.

"This is an architecture meeting, but I'd like to propose some changes to our plans."

Silence.

Eric and Malcolm studied the pages.

"I consulted with Leo on a new proposal. We split the three-bedroom two-bath units in half, added kitchens—that doubles the units on the top four floors."

Eric stared up at Zora, then back at Malcolm. When Malcolm looked up from the page, his smile faded.

"Zora, I'm confused. What is this?" Malcolm asked. His voice was calm and steady.

"If we use these new plans, we could offer affordable units for half the property. It would shift the overall plans, but I believe we can make—"

Malcolm interrupted Zora with a sigh. "Zora, is this about David's girlfriend?"

Zora ignored the question. She went on, pretending she didn't have this speech rehearsed and memorized cold.

"If we want the company to have long-term growth, the optics need to align with the roots of the city. We could be the example of change and—"

"How sustainable would we be if we lost our investors? You're talking about eliminating the high-est grossing units in the property for the sake of optics?"

Eric's eyes bounced from Zora to Malcolm and back.

"It's actually not just for the—"

"Zora, please. You know enough about business to know we can't give the building away."

"And I also know enough about business to make money and do the right thing at the same time. Did you ever consider that?"

Malcolm stood. His fingertips pressed into the tabletop. He sighed.

"I'd love to have your ideas on the next project. But this one—it's just too high risk and it's too late to change plans now. If we could match the profit, I'd consider, but it's just not possible without—"

"What if we could?" Zora asked, looking up at Malcolm. He looked exhausted.

"What?"

"What if we could match the profit? What if my plan could do better?"

"Zora."

Zora's phone buzzed in her vest pocket. She looked down at it.

"Eric, I have a guest at the front desk. Would you mind letting her in?" Zora smiled at Eric as she spoke.

"Sure . . ." Eric said hesitantly. He scrambled out of the room, no doubt relieved to avoid the rising tension in the room.

She felt the cool confidence rushing back into her bloodstream. She had said it. Her plan was better.

Malcolm walked to the window. Zora stood and watched her father think. His voice reflected against the window.

"I admire your intentions, Zora. But I hope you know the world won't bend over backwards to do the right thing for you. Not rich people or poor people—not even Black folks. You have to know that."

"I know."

Malcolm turned his head. The morning light burned at the edges of his silhouette. His long, slim form: the strong square shoulders, his perfectly tailored suit—even his shape reminded Zora so much of herself. She was just like her father in so many ways. Zora couldn't tell if he was angry or sad. Or both.

"It's not our job to change this. And we couldn't if we tried," Malcolm said. His voice was so even it betrayed no feeling.

"So you'd rather do nothing." Zora said. She hated walking the precarious line between child and subordinate.

"I didn't raise you to be this naive," Malcolm said, shaking his head.

"And you didn't raise me to be you. You raised me to be smarter than you."

Malcolm turned.

Just as Malcolm opened his mouth to speak, Eric appeared, opening the glass door.

"Dad—" Zora began, a knowing smile spreading across her face.

"I believe you've already met Layla Jones."

Malcolm smiled reflexively. His charm was the oldest tool in his box and a great way to disguise confusion. Layla nodded. She paced to the table. She wore a long black turtleneck dress, silver bangles, and necklaces glimmering against her skin. She looked elegant and professional. Zora smiled, thinking of Ella and Jasmine. These sisters truly were their own little coven.

Layla reached her hand out to Malcolm. "It's a pleasure to see you again, Mr. Scott."

Malcolm didn't move an inch.

"I'm sorry I can't say the same to you, Miss Jones." Malcolm replied.

Zora stood, offering Layla a seat at the table with an open palm. Eric stood and fidgeted with the top button of his oxford shirt. Layla nodded toward Zora.

Zora took a breath and began.

"Layla and I actually created this proposal together. I took on the investment and architectural details, and she covered construction costs and community impact. Our overall goal was to make the development more accessible to low-income tenants."

Malcolm exhaled impatiently. Zora knew what he was thinking. This is a business, not a charity. Eric kept his head down, pretending to take minutes on his tablet.

Layla leaned forward and spoke firmly in Malcolm's direction.

"There is a promising new mayoral candidate currently campaigning for next year's election. The mayor's office is highly motivated to generate good press and the *Post* article was a big part of that. She's willing to offer the maximum allotment under the Revitalization Tax Credit and the High Need Credit programs. She's also prepared to offer a number of subsidies under the Affordable Housing Program."

Zora opened Malcolm's packet to the middle and pointed at a long list of numbers. Malcolm tilted his head down, taking it all in. He sat back in his chair.

"Ms. Jones, from my understanding—these incentives aren't usually offered in Ward 1."

"Absolutely. U street doesn't exactly qualify as a high-need neighborhood. But for better or worse, the legislation is a little vague in its definition of need. So it's ultimately at the discretion of the mayor's office. Obviously, there's not much of a high need for wards with wealthy, predominately white populations. But you could argue that makes this kind of development even more valuable. Don't you think?" Layla smiled innocently at Malcolm. Zora shifted in her seat. She had the feeling that Malcolm was slowly losing his patience. She leaned in and pointed to the number at the bottom of the page.

"Once you account for the changes in costs of construction, with the city's support our investors could actually end up spending less than we originally projected."

Malcolm set the packet down on the table and looked up at Layla.

"So is this your strategy, Miss. Jones?"

Layla tilted her head.

"Is what my strategy?"

"You smear my development company and my character in the press and then come in and force us to change our entire development?" Malcolm said, a grin on his face. He almost looked amused, tickled by this moment.

"No. This wasn't my strategy. I don't exactly make it a habit to collaborate with any luxury developers. But I'm willing to work with you. Of course, I can't force you to do anything." Layla returned his smile with one of her own. Eric's eyebrows were so high they nearly touched his hairline.

Malcolm pointed at the sheet of paper. "I don't know how you convinced the mayor to pull these strings, but it's completely unethical."

Layla spat out a belly full of laughter. She sipped in a sharp breath of air and collected herself. Zora sat in silence. She'd imagined worst-case scenarios, but she hadn't imagined this.

"I would argue that a developer in bed with the city council is unethical. Or. You know, displacing Black families from their homes. Or rampant homelessness. Or maybe—I don't know—you making more money in a minute than I make in a year. That seems unethical to me." Layla shrugged. Malcolm nodded once, then stood.

"Thank you for your time, Miss Jones. I'll consider these proposals, have my team take a look, and you'll hear back."

Layla nodded and stood. Layla and Malcolm shook hands with painful civility. Eric escorted Layla to the glass door. He held it open and when Layla reached the threshold, she turned. "I just wanted to do the right thing for this city. That's my job. I never wanted to mislead you or to hurt you or your family. I didn't want any of it to be personal. I'm sorry for that."

Malcolm nodded.

Layla smiled at Zora, then back at Malcolm.

"Thank you for your time, Mr. Scott," she said and turned to leave. Eric scurried down the hall in Layla's wake.

Malcolm returned to his seat. He exhaled.

"I'm at the mercy of a Goddamn twenty-year-old. Unbelievable." He huffed under his breath.

Zora slowly collected the piles of papers and open folders on the table.

"She's brilliant, Dad. I wish you'd give this a chance. A real chance."

"Do I have a choice?" Malcolm snapped.

Zora sighed. She sank into her chair. Malcolm looked down at the papers on the desk.

"We could move mountains with that woman on our team," he said, shaking his head.

Zora looked up.

"She is on our team, Dad."

Malcolm leaned back in his chair and closed his eyes.

"Get the mayor's deal in writing. And get me an individual confirmation from every last investor."

Zora dropped her handful of papers.

"So. We're doing this?" She was so excited she sounded like a child.

"If it's not too good to be true, we're doing this." A smile curled at the end of his mouth.

"Dad!" Zora leaned in and wrapped her arms around her father. He chuckled heartily.

"If we go bankrupt over this, I'm holding you responsible," he said, pretending to be serious.

Zora leaned her head on his shoulder.

"I'm okay with that."

43. JASMINE

U Street sat quiet in the moments before dawn. The brightly colored bricks and storefront signs looked muted in the blue darkness. Then there were flutterings. Jasmine sat on the empty stoop and watched the sun rise. She hadn't been on U Street in months. There were some parts of the city that didn't feel right anymore. A gray pit bull appeared out of nowhere, pushing its nose into Jasmine's crotch. She stood suddenly; her hands shot up into the air. A small white woman with a blonde pixie cut struggled at the end of the dog's leash. Jasmine looked up at the woman, waiting for her to do something.

"Jesus," Jasmine snapped as the dog jumped up and snapped at the air.

"She's still only five months, so she's really playful." The woman leaned with all her weight against the pull of the leash.

Jasmine looked down at the mud on her shorts.

"Oh! Sorry..." The apology sounded like an afterthought.

"Do you think everyone is a dog person? Because I like dogs, but I don't know your dog, and yet I have its nose in my crotch. Does that make sense to you?"

Jasmine's voice grew louder. The woman stepped back.

"Does it look like I want to play with your fucking dog?" Jasmine yelled.

The dog and the small blonde woman both suddenly looked

like kicked puppies.

"He's a puppy. I said I was sorry. Okay?" Shocked, somewhere between apology and explanation. The woman looked like she might cry.

"So what is the dog for? Does it make you feel safe? Does the dog protect you from all the scary Black people that you're displacing with your fucking wealth and privilege?"

Jasmine stepped down from the stoop.

The woman pulled the dog to her side. "I'm sorry!" The woman cried out as Jasmine walked away.

"Fucking unbelievable," Jasmine said, shaking her head.

She would be the monster. The crazy Black woman who made the white woman cry at 6 a.m. The goddamned villainous, trigger-tempered angry Black dyke. Cursing the gods. Scaring white women with pit bulls. Fuck, fuck, fuck. Jasmine walked down the street huffing and cursing under her breath. If I see one more obnoxiously cheerful white person on U Street I might crack. Jasmine looked up when she heard their voices. The sight of Layla and Ella melted her. Jasmine laughed at how ri-diculous and gorgeous they looked. They wore long black dresses dusted with golden glitter. They each wore gold-and-black cleopatra makeup and headbands with golden peacock feathers dancing a foot above their heads. Jasmine felt her eyes well up. Her sisters. Her whole heart lived in these women. Layla and Ella would be her loves. And her reason to keep going. And keep yelling at sorry white women.

Layla held Jasmine at arm's length and studied her expression.

"Are you okay?" Ella placed her hand gently on Jasmine's back.

"Not really. Just got molested by a white woman's pit bull. Then I yelled at her. Probably made her cry. But I'll be fine." Jasmine swatted her hand in the air.

"Is that a euphemism for something?" Layla asked, giggling.

"I wish," Jasmine said.

Ella pulled Jasmine back into a locked embrace, her thumb pressing into the base of Jasmine's neck.

"Breathe," Ella whispered. Jasmine inhaled. Something tender and swollen dissolved under Ella's thumb.

"Wow." Jasmine exhaled. Ella smiled. Jasmine felt the urge to cry, but she swallowed it back. Instead, she scooped each of her sisters into her arms and pulled them to her. She just held them close.

"I'm so proud of you. Both of you. Your magic is growing, and I can feel it everywhere," Jasmine whispered. They each smiled proudly.

"Thanks, Dad," Ella teased.

"What about your magic?" Layla asked, her hands on her hips.

"I have about a thousand croissants in the car. Will that be enough magic for you?" Jasmine asked, grinning.

"Perfect," Layla replied.

"And you're sure you don't want to just burn it all to the ground?" Jasmine asked with a straight face.

"I'm sure," Layla said, looking down, tapping at her phone.

"Are you going to finally tell us what all the texting and secret meetings were about?" Jasmine asked, leaning over to peek at Layla's phone.

"I still think she's taken a lover." Ella said as she adjusted her headpiece.

"I really, really want to tell you about it. But. You'll know by the end of the day. Okay?" Layla said, smiling mischievously.

"I'll take it." Jasmine shrugged.

"So what's the plan for today?" Ella asked.

Layla took a breath and switched into organizer mode. She slid a small black backpack from her shoulder and fished a notebook from it. She flipped to a page with a dozen neatly scrolled bullet points.

"Okay, so the volunteers will be here in twenty. I scheduled three hours for setup."

"Naturally," Ella said sarcastically. Layla rolled her eyes.

"Well, we have to get the stage and the band and the sound set up at Ninth, and we're getting things ready at the beginning of the march. So it's a lot. It's like ten events all in one day."

Jasmine nodded supportively.

"The volunteer homebase is going to be Lady Clippers Barber Shop at U and Fifteenth."

"Homebase?" Jasmine ventured.

"Like headquarters. If you need supplies, first aid, stuff like that. You might just need to sit in some air conditioning for a minute. It's going to be a long day. That reminds me—don't forget to drink water." Layla went on.

"You're doing so great, Layla," Jasmine said, nodding.

Layla sighed.

"Okay, so the participants arrive at ten. That's school groups, floats, marching bands, drum troupes—"

"Marching bands, plural?" Ella asked.

"Yes. Plural. We called everyone. The parade people. The march people. Carnival people. High Schools, middle schools. It's gonna be wild." Layla said. She sounded somewhere between excited and overwhelmed.

Jasmine squeezed Layla's hand. "It's a party-slash-protest-slash parade-slash march. You're creating something completely new. Don't question it."

Jasmine shot Ella a sharp glare.

"Then we'll have a go-go/R&B chill music set from noon to one. Then speeches and talks for thirty minutes. And a closing go-go dance party from 1:30 to three."

Ella and Jasmine nodded quietly, staring at their superhero of a baby sister.

"I know. It's a lot. Okay, so ask me about the secret sister homebase," Layla whispered.

"Tell us about the secret sister homebase," Ella whispered back.

"Okay. Someone on the board donated their apartment for the organizers to take breaks. It's on Ninth. It's very fancy, there are snacks, and there's roof access. So, you're both welcome to literally do nothing and watch from the good seats."

Ella and Jasmine both looked relieved.

"We're not doing that, Layla," Jasmine said flatly.

"Well, we don't want to do nothing . . ." Ella purred.

Layla laughed.

"We want to do a lot and then get tired . . . and then do nothing," Jasmine added.

"That's completely reasonable," Layla replied with a subtle bow.

"So what can we do now?" Jasmine asked.

"Jazz, can you make sure the volunteers are fed and coffeed?"

"I only brought food . . ." Jasmine said.

"Already taken care of. This spot here is donating the coffee. Just delegate a couple of volunteers to bring it over in trips."

"Okay, delegating!" Ella said, throwing up an enthusiastic thumbs up.

"Ella, you can go to the stage and make sure the tech crew stays on schedule with the sound checks. Mostly it's about tracking down the musicians. Here's a checklist." Layla handed Ella a sheet of paper.

"Got it," Ella said, nodding.

Layla paused then. She looked at Jasmine, then Ella. The weight of the moment slowly descended between the three of them.

"I guess, this is it." Layla smiled nervously. Jasmine could have cried. The way Layla sometimes could look like a kid. That lanky baby deer she used to scoop up and toss into the air. But she wasn't a kid. She was grown. She was brilliant and crazy enough to think she could change the world. Brave enough to try.

Jasmine took Layla's hand in hers. The three sisters formed

a circle. They closed their eyes. The chatter and music faded away. Three sisters stood in the middle of U street. Jasmine drifted up from her body and watched them in their sacred ring. Three sisters all dressed up like witches. A healer, a leader and—Jasmine wasn't sure what kind of witch she was. She made good food. She loved hard. She protected her family. She stayed sober so she could do all these things better. She had always been organized. Responsible. Driven. The eldest. But what was her magic for?

When the sisters lifted their heads and opened their eyes, Jasmine felt tears running down her cheeks. Layla and Ella's faces tensed with concern.

"Jazz?" Ella whispered.

Jasmine smiled.

"It's okay!" Jasmine said. Covering her mouth, she chuckled. She shook her head and pulled Layla into an embrace.

"I'm so proud of you, Layla." Jasmine grinned.

As the sun rose on U Street, Layla's army of joy spilled onto the hot concrete. The Hand Dancer's Society of the DMV spun and stepped their way down the sidewalks. A couple dozen Black and Latinx elders showed out with the most formal attire. Black and gray hair coiffed and combed up into pinned buns and cascading curls. Black chiffon skirts with gold charmeuse accents. Sensible black shining shoes. Men with slim-fitting slacks, gold-threaded pinstripes and gold belt buckles. Next came the babies. Black, brown, and white potbellied angels in stubby tulle tutus waddled down the street. Some running, spinning guardians hunched and chasing behind them. Some clutched at grandmother's thighs. Cautiously observing. There was a group of basketball players from a few local high schools. They were all decked out in the most fashionable, young men's summer attire. Jordans with hot white soles. Reflective shades and small shorts. Do teenage boys wear small shorts these days? Jasmine wondered, feeling like an old man. The Asians for Black Lives group carried signs decorated with black and gold balloons. The signs Filipinos for Black Lives, Koreans for black DC, POC DC. Their faces painted with gold lines curling and bending like cursive on eyelids and cheeks.

Then there came Batala, the Afro-Brazilian-style women's drum troupe. Women in red, black and white patterns, walking wide-stanced with giant bass drums bouncing heavy at their knees. White hipsters in straw hats, old jeans, and new shoes. They huddled together, tilting their faces toward the action—wondering how to show up without taking up space, wondering how close was too close. Everyone was there. People without tribes or causes. Just curious. Drawn in by the collective joy. The women of Batala began to beat gently on their drums. A low thump held a slow and steady beat be-neath the excited chatter. The sun rose sharp and hot in the sky.

Jasmine was lost in the majesty and chaos of the moment when she noticed something in her periphery. A flutter of something familiar. A shape. Her heart dropped. She felt her throat seizing. Her circulation slowed, fingertips turned cold. Jasmine felt Dia there. The way you can feel eyes on you before you see them. Dia. The big life-ending ex. She wore a yellow fitted hat and gold slacks. She had a spray of twists fluttering from the top of her head. Her smile was wide. It was always wide. Opening with sunbeams of laughter. Dia. Everyone's favorite. Kind. Sincere. The one Jasmine built a world of dreams around. Dia. Jasmine felt hot with anger. Cold with jealousy. A jumble of uncom-fortable temperatures and feelings that made her sweaty and clammy and confused. She'd only seen Dia a handful of times since their breakup, and she tried to keep her distance for this very reason. Dia was Jasmine's rock bottom. No matter how much she'd learned, how far she seemed to have grown in the past two years, Dia had the power to remind Jasmine of her old self. Jealous, insecure, and ugly. A woman stood by Dia's side. Jasmine's chest burned with a wave of possessive jealousy, followed by a damp, foaming layer of shame. She is not yours. She never was yours.

The girlfriend stood tall in a flowing black dress. Her hair tied up and wrapped high in a gold scarf. Even from this distance, Jasmine could tell Dia's girlfriend was beautiful. Good, Jasmine thought. Dia deserved a beautiful girlfriend. Still, she felt a pinch of jealousy that made her face tighten into a fake smile. Dia didn't see her. She could run. She could slip away and pretend she never saw them. Jasmine turned and looked for an alley to sprint into when she heard Dia's voice.

"Jasmine?"

Dia's face brightened when she saw Jasmine.

Jasmine waved with her nearly empty coffee cup in her hand and felt the two remaining gulps of latte pouring down her shirt.

"Fuck," Jasmine said, looking down at her wet shirt.

"Oh!" Dia scrambled at the snacks table for a handful of napkins.

"Here—" The beautiful new girlfriend said as she poured water into the pile of napkins.

Dia held the wet napkins out tentatively. Jasmine took them and dabbed at the stain, leaving a trail of white residue down the front of her shirt.

"Very cool!" Jasmine said, laughing, nodding and shrugging. Trying much too hard to look casual.

"How are you?" Dia asked.

"Still a hot mess I guess!" Jasmine said, still dabbing at her shirt. When she looked up and saw Dia's look of pity, she realized it wasn't a funny joke.

"I'm good." Jasmine replied, nodding solemnly.

"Good." Dia nodded.

"I'm Jasmine—" Jasmine held her hand out to her ex's beautiful new girlfriend.

"Nina." Nina shook Jasmine's hand softly. How very adult of them.

"Nice to meet you, Nina." Jasmine smiled.

"Layla is so old I can't believe how grown she looks. And she did all this?" Dia said beaming.

"Yeah. It's kind of unreal," Jasmine said. She looked around at the gathering crowd.

"How's the bakery?" Dia asked.

"It's okay. A bit slow, honestly. But, it's good."

"I'd love to come one day. If you're cool with it," Dia said.

"That would be great." Jasmine said.

Jasmine's vision glazed over.

One thousand memories flooded into Jasmine's mind. Her breathing slowed. She felt time dissolving into shapelessness. Jasmine smiled and disappeared into it. She breathed in deeper. My sisters. Breath. Layla's tenacity. Breath. Ella's heart. Mom. The time we have with her. Marble. Their joy. Their love. The bakery. Sobriety. Pastries. Good coffee. Sex. Kissing. Zora. The moment they had. Love. Maybe she could love someone again. Eventually.

It could have been a second. It could have been an hour. But when Jasmine opened her eyes, Dia and Nina stared at her, waiting for an answer to a question she hadn't heard.

"I'm sorry. What?" Jasmine asked.

"Dia!" Layla's sing-song voice cut through the air as she skipped over and hopped into Dia's embrace.

"Layla, I'm so freaking proud of you," Dia said, beaming.

"I am so glad you made it." Layla pinched Dia's cheek.

"We must, must catch up AS SOON AS YOU'RE FREE, my love." Layla grinned as she spoke. She could be so charmingly dismissive.

"But I have an organizing emergency and I have to steal my sister. Love you, sweetness!" Layla was pulling Jasmine away before Dia had a moment to respond. Layla power-walked Jasmine down the block and turned to look at her sister. They were both sweating and panting. Layla looked back as if they'd escaped an ax murderer.

"Are you okay?" Layla asked, leaning over.

"I'm fine." Jasmine surprised herself with a laugh.

"For real?" Layla cocked her head.

"I think so?" Jasmine giggled. Layla stared at her sister for what felt like three minutes.

"The last time you saw Dia you slept with a twenty-two-year-old stud who insisted on being called daddy. Like it was her last name or some shit?"

"Aw, but Lex Daddy was really sweet," Jasmine said, laughing.

Layla's eyes widened.

"Right, right. Didn't she work at the strip club? The one who picks up ones for the strippers?"

"Well, that was just a summer job," Jasmine said giggling.

"I'm glad you reminded me of her. I should call her." Jasmine looked down at her phone as Layla snatched it away.

Layla watched Jasmine laugh into the sky. She searched for cracks in Jasmine's armor.

"For real, Jazz. Are you okay?" Layla's face looked stone serious. Jasmine wanted to laugh. Her little sister was so wise.

"I am."

"OKAY." Layla nodded.

"But I'm glad you stole me away. Can I maybe not hang out with my ex and her new girlfriend? I'm not really at that level of maturity. Not yet."

"Um. No. That's just bullshit. If you were okay with that you'd be dead inside."

"Okay, cool." Jasmine nodded eagerly.

Layla looked down the block.

"The apartment is at the end of Ninth. Wanna hide out there for a while? Or at least until the march starts?" Layla said, looking at Jasmine like she was the big sister.

"Okay I'll go. But just for a minute. The pit bull, and then my ex. I feel like today has already been—interesting." Jasmine sighed.

"Okay, I texted you the key code." Layla pulled Jasmine into a tight embrace. "There's a rooftop garden that's supposed to be really gorgeous. You should go up and see it. And text me or Ella if you need anything."

"I will not. I'm fine, Lay. Really."

Layla squeezed Jasmine's shoulders, then turned and disappeared into a crowd of black clowns on four-foot stilts. Ex or no ex, this was already the best protest she'd ever been to.

44. JASMINE AND ZORA

Jasmine

When the elevator doors opened, Jasmine found herself at the center of a rooftop greenhouse. She was transported to a tropical Eden. Orchids and wide-leafed plants towered ten feet up to the glass ceil-ing and leaned over the wooden walkway. She smelled the sweet soil in the air. She walked down the glass-sided corridor and grazed her fingers through oversized potted ferns and fig leaf trees. Shining green heart-shaped leaves poured from baskets lining the ceiling like chandeliers. Jasmine looked up, breathing deeply, savoring the life in the air. She walked along the wooden path to the glass door at the end of the greenhouse and opened it to a Japanese garden. Black and white coy swimming slowly beneath lily pads. Swaths of deep red Japanese maples in oversized pots lined the wooden walkway. A long line of outdoor lounging couches surrounded by flowers perched up from white rectangular pots. Lavender and hydrangeas and flowers Jasmine couldn't recognize. The water, the breeze rushing by, the green tendrils and leaves all around her stole her breath for a moment. Jasmine's heart felt all swelled up, a cup spilling over with joy. It didn't feel real. She kneeled down to smell a bunch of lavender. She lay down on the smoothly sanded wooden walkway.

"Jasmine." She barely heard the milky deep voice it sounded so far away. As if it came from an-other dimension.

"Jasmine?"

She slowly opened her eyes. Zora stood over her. Her face bore traces of amusement and concern. Jasmine sat up.

"What are you doing here?" Jasmine crossed her legs and hunched like a child.

"I lent Layla the apartment. We own it."

Jasmine scoffed. "Of course you do."

Zora watched as Jasmine fiddled with a sprig of lavender.

"I don't have much of a green thumb. But I designed it. The garden." Zora's eyes traced the tops of the trees. Jasmine pretended to be completely unimpressed.

"Wait. So you're talking to Layla now? Why would you help her with this protest? Isn't that a con-flict of interest or something?"

Zora smiled.

"She didn't tell you."

Jasmine felt her cheeks growing hot.

"Tell me what?"

Zora knelt down by Jasmine's side. Picked a stem of lavender. She held it to her nose and inhaled.

Jasmine felt her body tighten. Zora handed Jasmine the stem.

"There's a jasmine vine in bloom on the south end of the garden. Would you like to see it?"

Zora's voice was softer than Jasmine remembered. A crushed velvet warmth she wanted to curl up into. Jasmine rolled her eyes. Zora was changing the subject. And flirting.

"What's going on with you and Layla?" Jasmine regretted her tone immediately. Transparent. Like her bruised ego was showing.

"Jasmine," Zora said, staring. Jasmine turned away.

As the wind picked up, Zora looked out across the city. She

looked pensive the way vampires looked pensive. Like she was remembering great loves from centuries ago.

Jasmine turned her head at the faint sound of an elevator ding. The elevator doors slid open. The sound of voices.

Jasmine and Zora flinched as the glass door creaked open and Ella and David danced out of the greenhouse into the sunlight. Jasmine looked to Zora. Zora looked to Jasmine. They reflexively hit the ground and crouched together behind a lush wall of blue wisteria.

Zora stood behind Jasmine, her breath warm and sweet on Jasmine's neck.

"Why are we hiding?" Zora whispered.

"I don't know! I was matching your energy!" Jasmine hissed back.

They both tipped their heads out to see David and Ella making out against the greenhouse wall. They looked like the stuff of Black romance novels. Beautiful, young, and stupid in love with each other.

"Wow," Jasmine said.

"Yeah," Zora whispered.

"So I guess that's happening again," Jasmine said as she turned to find Zora grinning.

"I'm pretty sure they only stopped dating for like two weeks."

"Oop! Scandalous!" Jasmine gasped as she turned back to watch Ella skipping and giggling to the edge of the roof. His hand followed the line of her waist, and he pulled her into him. The two lovers began to dance a slow waltz.

"I'm proud of him," Zora said.

Jasmine watched as David released Ella into a slow spin.

"Why?"

"He never questioned it, you know?" Zora said.

Jasmine watched Zora for a moment, then gazed back at David and Ella.

"Yeah. They're either fearless ... or dumb. Or both." Jasmine laughed to herself.

Jasmine watched the two lovers leaning into each other. She felt Zora behind her. Not touching her, but close enough to feel her warmth.

The sounds of snare and bass drums echoed up from the street below. The go-go band. Or the drum troupe. David and Ella kissed, then scurried back into the greenhouse, disappearing behind the elevator doors.

Jasmine sighed.

"I should go back down," Jasmine said. She didn't turn to look at Zora's face.

"I like you, Jasmine," Zora blurted.

Jasmine looked up to find Zora's eyes on her.

Jasmine stood.

"Zora. You know I like you. But you made me feel—"

Jasmine exhaled, wringing her hands out. Zora stood.

"You made me feel disposable. And you treated my sisters like they were disposable. And—" Jasmine took a step back, remembering the feeling of Zora's hand on her hip that morning. She wanted to forget how good that felt. Zora just stood there. Hands in her pockets, waiting for Jasmine to say it.

"And you don't get it. You're a rich girl and you and everyone you know has never lost anything like this. You know? What it's like to see this city disappear? It's just business to you. You don't get it, Zora. And that's OKAY. I mean there are a thousand girls in this city who would sell their souls to date you. So, you'll be just fine."

Jasmine took a breath. A new drum beat echoed up from the street.

"I should go back down—" Jasmine stepped away. She felt Zora's fingertips on her forearm. Jasmine turned.

Zora took Jasmine's hand.

"Let me prove you wrong," Zora said.

Jasmine found that look in Zora's eye again. The pleading.

The desire to be forgiven, to be under-stood. Jasmine wanted that too. She stared at Zora for a moment. I don't want to want you. I don't want to need you. I'm afraid. All the things Jasmine wouldn't say rushed through her mind.

Zora

Jasmine had all the answers to questions Zora couldn't ask. Zora wondered if Jasmine felt like a sell-out. Like Zora represented everything wrong with Black people, with the world. Zora wondered how she managed to wound Jasmine so deeply. What was she thinking that day? Jasmine's eyes glowed a burning dark brown. As the sun set below the rooftop, it turned everything gold at the edges.

"You're right. I'm nothing but a rich, snobby Black girl. This was all business to me. And I don't know what gentrification feels like. Not really."

Jasmine hesitated. She still seemed on guard, unprepared for Zora's surrender.

"I'm going to learn. I never wanted to before." Zora's eyes fell. She didn't have the capacity for regret. But she knew now; her father's pride had blinded her.

"It's not for you. It's because of you," Zora said, shaking and lowering her head. She was never tongue-tied. She hated that she suddenly couldn't speak when it really mattered. Jasmine gently lifted Zora's chin with her fingertips.

"Say more," Jasmine whispered. Her face had softened.

"You and your family—they inspired me. I want to do more with my life and my privilege. I want to figure out what I love." Zora spoke at the ground. Jasmine lifted her chin again. Zora's eyes found Jasmine's again.

Zora closed her eyes. Said more.

"Jasmine. Remember when I told you about my grandfather?

That old man with that classic old-school proud Black man masculinity? This man with all that pride got on his knees and wept for my grandmother. He humbled himself for that love. I want to do that for you. For us." Zora's voice broke.

Jasmine drew in a breath.

"I want you to be my sweetheart," Zora said, her eyes squeezed. When she opened them, Jasmine was grinning and shaking her head.

"You know what? Fuck it." Jasmine said, throwing up her hands.

"Well fuck it is not really the response I was going for but," Zora began.

Jasmine leaned in, wagging her finger in Zora's face.

"I can't fucking stop dreaming of you. And wishing you're everywhere I go. I feel insane," Jasmine said, her voice buttery with laughter.

"And this terrifies me. But I would love to be your sweetheart." Jasmine took Zora's face in her hands. She pulled Zora close. Their lips met. They touched slowly. Zora lifted her hands and let them float just above Jasmine's chin. They fell into each other. Weightless. Their tongues moved slowly. Pushing deeper. Holding each second with reverence. They kissed for the first time without fear.

They were both beaming as their lips parted.

"Jasmine," Zora whispered.

"Yes, Zora?" Jasmine whispered back.

"Can I show you something?" Zora asked.

Jasmine sighed.

"Now?"

"I'm not good at keeping secrets and I've already kept it for so long—" Zora began, bouncing like a small child.

"Okay! Okay!" Jasmine relented. Still dizzy from their kiss.

Zora pulled Jasmine to the edge of the building. She pointed down at the demolished block of land surrounded by caution tape and chain-link fencing.

"I know you think I'm just a rich girl. And I am. But. The cool thing about being rich is you can buy very cool things. Right?" Zora's smile looked mischievous.

Jasmine rolled her eyes. "Uh huh. Like custom Teslas and fancy houses. You know that doesn't make me like you more, right?"

"I know that." Zora nodded. "And I love that about you. But I think you'll like this one."

Jasmine planted her hands on her hips.

"What is it?" She sighed.

"I kind of bought a Black-owned bookstore," Zora said flatly. The same way someone would tell you they got you a coffee. Or a pack of gum.

"What?" Jasmine giggled.

Zora pointed down to the patch of land.

"Tea Cake will reopen on the ground floor of the development. And they're looking for bakeries to collaborate with for their cafe." Zora looked up at Jasmine, whose hand floated above her mouth.

"No," Jasmine whispered.

"Yeah." Zora laughed.

45. LAYLA

Layla smiled so wide her cheeks hurt. She watched the street pulsing with movement. Her eyes caught the moments she'd dreamt of the nights before. The food, the music, the people. Layla spotted Sean cradling his bass low against his thighs and nodding his head at her. His locs swayed against the thick strings as he plucked them. The man with a green-and-gold fedora spinning like a ballet dancer. The woman with the black-and-white headwrap and matching summer dress lifting a smoking bundle of sage into the air. A glittering scatter of feathers and beads atop head pieces on carnival dancers. Queer boys in short shorts twerking and grinding up on each other. Hand dancing and feet beating and fried shrimp in red baskets with clear-white parchment paper. Ice cream cones melting down babies' plump hands. The go-go drum beats, conga slapping against the faces of the row houses and brand-new walls of condo buildings. The crash and cymbals swelled and fizzed up above the crowd like ocean foam after a wave curled into the shore. Brianna lifted Jayden up to watch the drummer. Layla made a mental note. Make sure to ask Jayden if he wants bass lessons with Sean. He's watching the band like his little heart has music in it.

    Layla stepped to the podium. She whispered a thank you to Sean. She knew it was dead wrong of her to cut into the go-go set. But the song probably would have been twenty-some minutes long on any other day. At the lead singer's request the band played a James Brown-style five hits and at five there was silence. The crowd exploded.

"Give it up for Big DISTRICT Energy Band, yall!" Layla smiled into the mic. She loved their music and hated their name. The crowd chuckled and settled back into quiet. Layla waited for a moment. She looked down at her speech. A jumble of printed letters on damp sheets of paper.

"My name is Layla Jones. I'm here representing Rise DC, and I am so grateful that y'all joined us today. I was born and raised in DC. And this city is my home."

Murmurs and affirmations swelled throughout the crowd.

Layla looked up from the page as the faces of ancestors appeared throughout the crowd. She could tell them apart because their pupils glittered like deep black ocean water. West African faces, Black, Brown Indigenous, ancient-faced ancestors. Their skin had traces of glowing pink like the blushing sunset in the sky behind them.

"I'd like to begin by acknowledging the land we stand on today. This land was originally the home of indigenous people. The Anaquashtank and Piscataway Tribes. I say the names of these tribes with as much reverence and care as I say the names of Black lives stolen. And though these histories may have been erased, there was life here. And I want to acknowledge the enslaved and freed Black people who built this city. Who built this country and its wealth. I want to acknowledge the immigrant communities of DC. Salvadorian, Ethiopian, Guatemalan, Jamaican, and all the people who found a kind of home here on this land. And now, I want to call the ancestors in. If you want to bring your people in, anyone you've lost. Anyone who has crossed over, please say their names now." Layla watched as heads bowed down and a hush fell over the crowd. For a moment, silence hung in the air. Layla's eyes scanned the crowd. She waited.

Amari!

Someone yelled into the air.
Layla closed her eyes.

Cypress.

Another name called out.

Brazil.
Jimmie!
Bernice!
Eddie. Harrison.
Oscar. Leo. Alexa.
Gretchen. Louis. Michelle. Tamir.

And then the names overlapped. A chorus of prayer.
The ancestors all remained still. Watching. Layla inhaled.
"This city, this country is built on stolen land by stolen people. The emotional devastation is immeasurable. That is the context of where we are. But I don't want to focus on devastation today. Today is about OUR JOY. The space Black DC communities have carved out to thrive here. Today is a celebration of the hidden joyful histories of this city. From 1900 to the 1960s, this neighborhood right here was known as Black Broadway."

Layla lifted her arms and motioned to the buildings around her. As she spoke, Carmen, Marble, Ro, and a dozen volunteers lifted oversized black-and-white photographs above the crowd. A wide shot of Lincoln theater. The Crystal Caverns dancers in their glittering costumes. Shining, curvy black cars. Howard Theater. A Black couple dressed to the nines dancing the waltz. The photographs floated above the crowd as Layla went on.

"The U Street corridor was home to hundreds of Black-owned businesses, churches, Black families, and the flourishing of Black artistic and political communities."

A few people in the crowd clapped enthusiastically.

"When I first learned about Black Broadway—I didn't believe it. I didn't have the imagination for it. This street? Hundreds of Black businesses? How did we have so much and lose it all? What happened?"

The sun disappeared beyond the horizon, and now all the pinks dissolved into purples and blues.

"What happened? This is American history. The crack epidemic, white flight, the metro construction, integration, and the rising cost of living—all of these events contributed to the evisceration of Black communities and businesses in this neighborhood. The root of all of these events is racism. Politicians, developers and transplants have treated Black people like we are expendable and disposable. This is the history of our diaspora. This is the history of Oakland and Brooklyn and New Orleans." Layla's voice was getting louder. The fire was growing in her. The crowd was right there with her. Clapping and shouting out in fierce affirmation. She took a breath.

"Today is the day we honor our ancestors, the people who built this city. Today we end that cycle. Today we make space to celebrate the success and culture that people of color enjoyed here. And today we demand to take it back."

Layla's eyes scanned the crowd. She found Ella and David. His arms wrapped around her. Now her eyes glittered like the dark ocean too. Everyone's eyes glittered. The god glowed so strong in everyone's eyes—now she couldn't tell the ancestors and the living apart.

"And with that celebration in mind I have a very, very exciting announcement to make." Layla found Zora's face in the crowd. She stood by Jasmine's side, nodding at Layla. Jasmine looked to Zora.

"The surprise? You know about the big surprise?" Jasmine whispered into Zora's ear.

Zora turned to Jasmine and smiled.

"I do." Zora said.

Layla nodded and looked back out at the crowd.

"Take a minute to look at this giant block of dirt behind me."

Layla gestured toward the chain link fence behind her.

"It took a lot of hard work. A lot of generosity and leaps of faith. But. With the help of Rise DC, the Office of the Mayor, and the Scott Group Development Company—we've come together to create the plans for Rock Creek Village. This is the first ever DC development that—" Layla paused. She hadn't lost her place. She just had to pause because she could barely believe what she was about to say.

The crowd collectively held its breath.

"Y'all. This property will offer 100 percent units for affordable and low-income housing."

In the distance Jasmine turned to stare at Zora. The crowd erupted with joy. The drummer and percussionist made the block sparkly with improvised beats. Layla went on, attempting to shout over the cheers.

"The ground floor will offer retail and restaurant spaces for Black and/or Indigenous-owned businesses."

Someone in the crowd screamed out "YES!" The rest of the crowd followed, cheering, throwing their hands up. The drummer played a long wild riff, rising and rising in volume and energy. The cymbals crashed and the whole crowd of faces was glowing with spirit.

"This is what we deserve. This is our city. All of ours."

Ella and David moved through the crowd and stared up at Layla. Ella reached her hand out. Ella's eyes looked so beautiful with the ocean in them. Layla turned to find Sean. He nodded.

"And tomorrow, we WILL demand more. Humanity. Care. A beautiful place to live. To thrive. Investment in our communities. But today. We will celebrate. Let's go." Layla pointed to Sean, who shook his head in time. The drummer rolled the band back into a go-go groove. And everyone danced. And somewhere at the far edge of the crowd, Malcolm Scott watched the crowd celebrate. He watched Layla lift her fist in the air. He felt some kind of pride watching her. We could move mountains with her on our team, he thought.

Layla felt her legs giving out. All the energy she had dissolved away in an instant. Ella rushed up onto the stage. Layla held Ella's hand as they inched away from center stage. The people in the street were all wrapped up in drum beats and joy. Layla's eyes flickered sleepily, slowly as she disappeared into a cool shadow at the edge of the stage. Ella sat on the stage and pulled her sister down into her lap. Layla felt the warm, deep pressure of Ella's hands on her neck and shoulders. David leaned down to offer her a bottle of water.

"Just give her a minute," Ella whispered as she pressed her thumbs into the knots between Layla's shoulder blades.

Marble and Ro pushed through the movement of the crowd. Jasmine and Zora followed from the opposite side of the street. Their worried faces all pulled into focus as Layla smiled up at them.

"I'm good. I'm just happy. And really fucking tired," Layla whispered.

Ro nodded. "Layla, I am so proud of you. We all are," she said.

She reached her arms up to hold Layla's hands. Then quietly, one by one: Jasmine, Marble and Ro rested their hands on Layla's back.

Layla felt the swell of energy from their hands. She lay back in Ella's arms, closed her eyes, and received it.

She couldn't tell how long it had been. The drumbeat turned into a school of fish, echoing notes under water. Her blood was saturated with spirit. She was high. Taking in more future and history than her body could handle. Layla fluttered her eyes open with a smile. Between her big sister and her mother, Layla saw the purple blue pink of the city sunset. She saw the sparkling eyes of the ancestors with ancient faces. They danced and laughed, beat their feet, and threw their heads back.

"Thank you," she whispered.

46. EPILOGUE

The pool glittered. Sunlight cut through the treetops and a breeze whispered at smooth slabs of concrete. Lush spheres of hydrangeas lined the walls of a mansion. Their laughter peppered the air. Their toes drew lazy circles. At the far edge of this secluded estate the Jones sisters sat in the grassy lap of the garden. It was two years ago to the day. David Scott had stumbled in on the Jones sisters' naked dance party in the pool. Since then, they established a weekly sisters-only pool party. Jasmine lovingly kicked David and Zora out of their own house. And the sisters made it theirs. Naked and magic where no one else could see. Ella giggled as she slipped into the pool. Stretching her limbs up and out to the sky. Layla did a cannonball. And Jasmine dove in. They danced in the sunlight. Their skin glittering with water and melanin. Black mermaids. They splashed at the water, sang, danced and laughed. As they sang louder and louder, and all their anxious thoughts about the loss of their mother, and birth of their babies, blooming loves, cities and communities, about being strong and broken—all the fears and ties that held them back from joy evaporated into the air. They rose above the water. Each inhale lifted them up and up. Their shadows danced on the waves. Three shades of brown and gold dripping with cold beads of light. Their breasts, calves, arms, the curves of fat that jiggled, Ella's stretch marks like bolts of lightning, Jasmine's wide boyish back, Layla's hands dancing in the water. It was like remembering. For one blissful moment they remembered that god made them and everything was exactly where it should be. They were fairies. Holding each other's beauty up to the light, holding their own beauty until everything glowed, warm in the sun.

> *Once upon a time*
> *somewhere far, far uptown*
> *tucked behind a veil of white oak leaves in the thick DC summer heat*
> *three Black women were at peace.*

ACKNOWLEDGMENTS

My heartfelt gratitude goes to Malik, Meka, Nikki, Brenda, Steffane, Salem, Kit, Bywater Books, and all those who so generously gave their time to read the roughest drafts of this novel. To my Patreon community—thank you for showing up. Your unwavering support makes it possible for me to continue writing queer love stories. Love to DC for being my hometown and to Baltimore for being my home. Thank you to Kate for holding my hand through all of it. Thank you to my parents for supporting their gay, line cook??, musician??, playwright??, author???, filmmaker????, nonbinary????, kid through all the plot twists of my selfhood. And to my partner, Sahim—thank you for helping to shape this book into something better. The most profound dreams of love I imagined couldn't compare to the reality of being with you.

    Twitter | @BeSteadwell
    Instagram | @BeSteadwell
    Facebook | /be.steadwell/
    Website | //besteadwell.com/
    Patreon | //patreon.com/besteadwell/

ABOUT THE AUTHOR

Be Steadwell (They, She, He, Be) is a queer pop composer and storyteller from Washington, DC.

Be composes songs on stage using looping, vocal layering, and beatboxing. Be's original music features earnest lyricism and affirming queer content. Be's goal as a musician is to make other black girlies, introverts, and weirdos feel seen and loved.

Be earned a BA in Black Studies from Oberlin College and an MFA in film from Howard University. Be's thesis film *Vow of Silence* screened in film festivals worldwide, including Black Star, HBO's OutFest, The Schomburg Center, and Inside Out Toronto—and it received Best Experimental Short at the Black Star Film Festival.

In 2019, Be composed the music for The Alvin Ailey Dance Company's production of *The Gone*. Later that year, Be wrote and directed *A Letter to My Ex*, the musical. *A Letter to My Ex* imagines a queer black woman's experience of healing after a breakup. In 2021 Be released their latest album, *Succulent*.

In 2023, Be joined the cast of Octavia E. Butler's *Parable of The Sower* the Opera by Toshi Reagon and Dr Bernice Johnson Reagon. In May 2024, they released their album, *Dear Ex The Musical*. Be currently performs their music internationally.

Bywater Books believes that all people have the right to read or not read what they want—and that we are all entitled to make those choices ourselves. But to ensure these freedoms, books and information must remain accessible. Any effort to eliminate or restrict these rights stands in opposition to freedom of choice.

Please join with us by opposing book bans and censorship of the LGBTQ+ and BIPOC communities.

At Bywater Books, we are all stories.

For more information about Bywater Books, our authors, and our titles, please visit our website.

https://www.bywaterbooks.com